TEEN
PIC
Jackson

SEP

THE
WEIGHT
OF
BLOOD

THE WEIGHT OF BLOOD

TIFFANY D. JACKSON

KATHERINE TEGEN BOOKS
An Imprint of HarperCollins Publishers

Katherine Tegen Books is an imprint of HarperCollins Publishers.

The Weight of Blood

Library of Congress Control Number: 2022931781
ISBN 978-0-06-302914-9

Typography by Erin Fitzsimmons
22 23 24 25 26   PC/LSCH   10 9 8 7 6 5 4 3 2 1

First Edition

This one is for me!

For the little girl in pigtails who went running for the TV whenever her favorite horror movie came on, doing the absolute unimaginable when so many doubted her dreams, including herself.

Look at you now, Tiff-Tot! Look at you now.

PART

ONE

ONE

MADDY DID IT

EPISODE 1

"It all started with the rain"

THE SPRINGVILLE MASSACRE COMMISSION

From the Sworn Testimony of Mrs. Amy Lecter

We heard the crash first. Right before the lights went out. We don't live too far from the country club. Our son, Cole, even worked there during the summers as a caddy. Made good money too. Anyway, next we smelled the smoke and ran out onto the porch. I could just make out them flames over the treetops. That club must've been brined in gasoline—it lit up the sky purple. My husband, George, jumped in his truck to head on over there while I sat on the porch and waited. And waited. And waited. Two whole hours, I waited to hear something. Had no idea what was going on. Phones weren't working.

Just as I was finna to head over there myself, I see Cole walking out the dark, limping down our driveway, eyes wide like he saw the face of God. I was so relieved that he was alright that I ran up and gave him a great big hug. But . . . he was soaking wet. Like he done grabbed his tux right out the wash and threw it on. It wasn't until I stepped away that I noticed red all over my robe and started screaming.

We took him down to the hospital. Not a scratch on him but they transferred him to the mental ward on account that he wouldn't talk. Still won't talk much. And my Cole, he was a talker. From day one, we couldn't get him to shut up if we tried. He was the tattle-tale of the family, always ripping and running. Now, he barely moves. Barely blinks, just stares off at nothing.

Only two kids survived Prom Night at that country club. Cole was one of them. They say when you go through something like that, your instincts kick in. So his mind must've told him to come on home. He walked over two miles through the mud with one shoe, covered in the blood of other children.

When I asked him what happened . . . he just kept mumbling, "Maddy did it."

May 1, 2014
FIRST PERIOD. Gym.

Maddy Washington tugged at the bottom of her green gym shorts, eyeing the dark gray clouds circling above Springville High School's racetrack. Her nose twitched.

It was going to rain.

"Jules Marshall?" Coach Bates bellowed.

"Here," Jules yawned.

"Wendy Quinn?"

"Here!"

"Ali Kruger?"

"Here!"

The girls gathered by the far fence, using it to help them balance as they stretched their calves and hamstrings. Maddy nibbled her thumbnail down to a bloody stump, simultaneously touching the roots of her bone-straight hair, feeling for its silky smoothness.

"Coach, are you really gonna make us do this?" Charlotte McHale whined, stomping in place like a toddler.

Coach Bates checked off her attendance list without looking up. "You ladies need a run. Do those muscles some good."

The girls grumbled in response. Coach stuffed the clipboard in her armpit, her long gray hair tucked under a Springville Pirates softball hat.

"Don't you want to stay nice and thin for your prom dresses?" Coach teased.

"I don't have to worry about that," Jules quipped, bumping Wendy with her butt. "Don't know about the rest of these fat asses."

Wendy laughed, pinching Jules's exposed thigh. "Speak for yourself!"

They giggled, playfully evading each other's grasps. Maddy

wasn't paying attention. She could only hear a pulse beating against her eardrum, nose picking up the scent of her greatest nightmare.

It wasn't supposed to rain. She'd checked. She always checked. Every day, she turned the radio on while cooking breakfast and called the weather hotline twice before walking out the front door. Even with a 20 percent chance of rain, she would've stayed home. The forecast called for cloudless skies, seventy-five degrees, low humidity. So why did the sky look like it was about to change its mind?

"Earth to MADDY! Come in, MADDY!"

Maddy whipped around, pushing her crooked brown frames up her nose. "Huh?"

The entire class stared at her, scowling.

"Well, thanks for joining us," Coach Bates snapped. "I only called your name about five times."

Maddy quickly eyed the ground, combing through her long ponytail with shaky fingers.

Coach Bates shook her head and pulled out a stopwatch. "Alright, ladies! Line up. Time to head out. You'll run down by lower field and back. Two loops. On my count!"

Maddy glanced at the sky once more. Something sour dripped down the back of her throat, forcing her to do the unthinkable.

"B-b-b-but . . . it's gonna rain," she blurted out in a shrill voice.

The entire class turned, dumbfounded. Maddy hadn't said

more than three words all year. Now, mid-May, she had strung together an entire sentence.

Coach Bates, shocked at first by the sound of her least favorite student's voice, rolled her eyes.

"Well, guess that means you ladies will be running faster. Now move it! You'll be back long before it starts. Let's go, ladies. Chop-chop!"

Maddy's lungs turned to stone, leaking out quick, shallow bits of air. One drop. That's all it would take to end things. Her eyes darted to the school doors, biting a trembling lip as her father's voice raged inside her head.

"No one can know. No one can ever know!"

She could not, under any circumstance, get her hair wet.

But if she tried to escape, Coach Bates would catch her, and who knew what that would lead to. The principal's office? Detention? Suspension? Maddy had never been in trouble a day in her life.

So she tucked her low ponytail inside her shirt and followed the line down field.

The girls ran in pairs, except for Maddy, who huffed alone in the back, trying to keep up, trying to outrun the threat of rain looming above them. She wasn't as athletic as the other girls. Had never played any sports or taken a single dance lesson. Papa wouldn't allow it. The sweat would've only ruined her hair.

"No one can know. No one can ever know!"

"Well yeah, the dress came, but it's nothing like the picture,"

Jules said to Wendy, winded. "I was gonna have Cindy's momma take it in, but she said she's backed up as it is, and I said I don't want to wait . . ."

Maddy watched their long red and blond hair bounce in sync with their strides. They weren't worried about the rain. They lived a carefree life. Maddy swallowed her envy and tried wrapping her ponytail into a bun, but didn't have a pin to hold it in place. Not watching her footing, she tripped on a stick, nearly tumbling to the ground with a loud "Oof."

Jules shot her a look, shaking her head.

"Jesus, could she be more pathetic?" she grumbled to Wendy, who only laughed.

The wind kicked up, blowing Maddy's hair to the side. The buttery grits, bacon, orange juice, and daily vitamins she'd had for breakfast splashed around inside her belly.

"Anyway, what d'you think I should do? I can go on down to Atlanta, but all the good dresses are probably gone by now and I can't be caught dead twinning with any of these bitches."

"We can go together," Wendy rasped, her face sweaty. "I'll help you pick something."

Maddy's heart hammered. She tried to run faster, wheezing with each stride, and yet still fell far behind her classmates.

"Please. Please," she begged the sky. "Please."

The girls made a right turn down by the old soccer field, running near the edge of the woods. The stench of damp mulch permeated the air. Maddy could spot the high school in the distance. They had one more loop to complete their two miles. Maybe the rain would hold off, she thought. *Maybe it'll be okay.*

That's when the first drop hit Maddy's glasses. Then another. She flinched with each drop, trying to cover her roots with her hands, but the shower came down like an avalanche. The girls screeched and giggled, running faster, wet mud splashing up their legs, thin white T-shirts sticking to their skins.

Maddy's hair, now drenched, wrapped around her shoulders like a cape, the rain masking her sobs all the way back to school.

Maddy studied herself in the mirror, the last in the locker room that smelled of bodywash, hair spray, and wet sneakers. Any other day, she would've changed and rushed to class before the humidity could catch her. She never took showers with the other girls. Couldn't risk her hair coming in contact with water.

But all that had ended in a rainstorm.

Moist lashes rimmed her hazel-green eyes, skin blanched white. Without a towel, she had nothing to help sop up the water from her saturated locks, which had already begun coming to life. Her hair always dried quick, then rose like sourdough. If her scalp could withstand a perm, it might not have been so bad. But instead, it frizzed, growing larger by the second, a massive lion's mane, a sleeping monster no regular brush could tame.

She needed a hot comb.

Her hands trembled, desperately attempting to pull the thickening strands through another rubber band. It snapped, slapping her wrist and falling on the floor, just like the others. A pile of dead worms lay at her feet. *"You look like you have a painted Brillo pad on your head."* That was what Papa would've said if he were standing over her. The words echoed through the chambers of her memories.

Everyone is going to know now, she thought, tears spilling over.

But . . . if she stayed hidden, she could possibly sneak out of school, run home without being seen. Or she could go to the nurse's office and call Papa to come rescue her. He wouldn't be too mad. How could she have known the sky was going to change its mind?

"Maddy?"

Coach Bates stormed out of her office, eyes falling on Maddy's hair, rendering her speechless. For an insane moment, she thought maybe Coach would clearly see her dilemma and take pity. Maybe even send her home without explanation.

Hopeful, she faced the woman, smiling through the tears.

It took Coach a moment to collect herself before barking, "What are you still doing back here?"

Maddy blinked, her smile fading. "I—I . . . I just . . ."

"Get to class! You've missed enough of my classes, now you're trying to miss your other ones too? Why even bother coming to school? You might as well drop out. And you can forget about me giving you a late pass."

Maddy took one last long look in the mirror and resigned herself to her impending fate with a small prayer. Even if she didn't understand, God does not make mistakes. She drifted out of the locker room to sunlight beaming through the hallway windows. The sky was a cloudless brilliant blue. No signs it had ever rained. With the hallway empty and the doors a few strides away, she considered making a run for it.

But behind her, Coach Bates stood by the locker room exit, her arms crossed. Watching.

Maddy had no choice but to go to class.

SECOND PERIOD. US History.

Jules Marshall sat in the back of Mrs. Morgan's classroom next to Wendy, twirling a strand of red hair around her index finger. She was scrolling through her nudes, trying to decide which one to send her boyfriend, when she happened to glance up at the door.

"Holy shit," Jules whispered, gawking.

Wendy, taking furious notes, followed her best friend's gaze. "Oh. My. God."

Charlotte covered her mouth with both hands to keep from screaming, but the sound slipped through like a cough.

Maddy's hair arrived in the classroom before she did. The dark frizzy strands swelled around her tiny frame. She looked more hair than human. Mouths dropped at the sight.

"Holy shit," Jason Conway said, falling on his neighbor and teammate Chris Lively, howling with laughter.

Mrs. Morgan, standing at the whiteboard, held her marker

midair, blue eyes bulging.

"Maddy?" she gasped.

Maddy didn't respond. Head down, she clutched her books to her chest in one hand, using the other to grip the strap of the heavy book bag hanging off her shoulder. She shuffled to her third-row seat while her classmates failed to stifle their collective giggles.

Mrs. Morgan quickly scolded herself for being no better than the brats she was tasked to educate. After all, it was just hair. She didn't dare ask for a late pass, drawing more attention to Maddy. It was clear why she was late. Instead, she turned back to the room and put on her poker face.

"Settle down, everyone," she ordered. "Take out your homework and turn to chapter fifteen in your text."

Maddy slid down into her chair, trying to squeeze herself to the size of a snow pea as Mrs. Morgan quizzed students.

"Now, can anyone tell me . . ."

Jules's face and neck turned beet red as she shook with silent laughter to the point of tears. Wendy laid her head on her notebook, trying to hold it together.

"Hey! Jules? Wendy," Mrs. Morgan snapped. "What's so funny?

"What's so funny?" Jason said incredulously. "Bro, do you see that Afro?"

The classroom erupted with snickers.

Maddy breathed through her nose, tears puddling. She

folded her hands, praying harder than she ever had before for rescue. After class, she needed to run. Didn't matter how much trouble might fall on her. She had to get out of there.

"Jason," Mrs. Morgan said, seething. "Do you want to go to the office and explain why you're disrupting my class? Do any of you? If not, then I suggest you knock it off."

The class simmered down, but not completely. No one was paying attention to Mrs. Morgan. All eyes were on Maddy.

A wicked smirk spread across Jules's face. "Watch this," she whispered, plunging a hand into her book bag. She retrieved a sharpened number-two pencil, twirling it around her fingers. Wendy and Charlotte held their breath. Closing one eye, Jules aimed, then softly launched the pencil across the room. It made an arc in the air before landing in Maddy's hair. Maddy didn't feel it at all.

The girls convulsed with laughter. Jules grabbed another pencil.

The pencil planted in her hair stuck straight up, as if placed there on purpose. Snickers grew into loud cackles. Maddy didn't bother turning left or right to see what was happening. She knew they were laughing at her. They were always laughing at her. Skin burning, her pulse beat harder.

Mrs. Morgan had turned around just in time to see the second pencil sail and disappear into a forest of tight black coils and curls.

The class all but rolled in the aisles, laughter echoing down the hallways.

"Hey! Who threw that! Wendy? Charlotte? Jules?"

"It wasn't me!" Jules said, all innocent, her hands raised. "My pen is right here."

Wendy could barely contain herself, her freckled face turning into a cherry.

Maddy squeezed her eyes shut tight to keep them from twitching. "Please stop it," she mumbled in a small voice, then felt a soft tug of her hair.

"Yo, it even feels like a Black chick's hair!" someone shouted behind her.

"I said, knock it off!" Mrs. Morgan shouted.

At that moment, Debbie Locke's hearing aid squealed like a mic dangerously close to a speaker. She hissed through her teeth and shook the device free from her ear.

"What the fuck?" she mumbled, palming it. But no one heard her. They were all too busy cackling at Maddy Washington's hair, a giant sculpture sitting in the middle of US history.

"Stop it," Maddy begged, tears streaming, as the voices descended.

"Do you see the size of that shit? It's huge!"

"Hey, Maddy, where'd you get that 'fro?"

"Mad Mad Maddy with the Mad Mad Hair!"

"Stop it, please, stop," Maddy begged, trembling.

The only two Black students in the class eyed the room in

disgust. Mrs. Morgan noticed. Her creamy skin flushed red.

"I said, that's enough!" she shouted.

A crack in the window next to Wendy began to snake its way up, splintering out like a family tree. Wheezing for air, Maddy gripped the desk, and the room spun. Something prickled and hummed across her skin.

"How could she have an Afro like that?"

"Wait, is she Black?"

Mrs. Morgan, trying to regain control of the rowdy class, noticed the lukewarm coffee in her mug on the table ripple, as if a strong breeze had blown by.

Suddenly, Wendy cussed under her breath with a wince, covering her ears with both hands.

"What the hell?" she gasped, exchanging a frantic look with Charlotte, sitting wide-eyed. She felt it too. Their ears were on fire.

Something pinched behind Maddy's eyes, her muscles clenching as she muttered, "Stop it. Stop it. Stop it."

"Bro, is she?"

"Yo! Maddy is a . . ."

"STOP IT!"

In an instant, every desk and chair lifted four feet in the air as if snatched up by rope. Wendy gasped at the sensation, similar to that of a carnival ride moments before it plummets back to earth. Then, the desks slammed onto the floor, metal legs shrieking. Windows cracked and overhead lights burst, raining shards of glass down on the screaming students. The ground bucked beneath Mrs. Morgan, bringing her to her knees. Her head popped up in time to see students grabbing their belongings, running for the door.

All except for Maddy, who somehow, was in the back corner of the room, curled into a ball.

TWO

MADDY DID IT
EPISODE 1, CONT.

Michael Stewart: "'It all started with the rain.' That's what the
people of Springville say whenever asked about the fatal
Prom Night that occurred over a decade ago, leaving a
town in complete ruins."

This is the opening line of author David Portman's book
Springville Massacre: The Legend of Maddy Washington.
It examines the events leading up to what he refers to as
"the Bloody Prom," when a girl named Madison Abigail
Washington nearly burned down her entire town, killing
two hundred people, including the majority of her senior
class, at their first racially integrated prom. The opening
line, along with the testimony we played at the beginning
of this program, has haunted me with more questions than
answers. But if you ask anyone from Springville, or at least
anyone still alive, what happened that fateful night, they

all say the same as Cole Lecter—"Maddy did it." How? Well, that's still up for debate. The survivors of that night witnessed the horror unfold firsthand, so why doesn't anyone believe them?

Hello. My name is Michael Stewart. I'm a producer here at NPR radio, and before we go any further, I want to introduce my lovely, albeit unconventional, cohost for this series, Ms. Tanya King.

Tanya King: Hello, hello!

Michael: How about you tell us a little about yourself, Tanya?

Tanya: Sure. I'm an anthropologist and professor at the University of Sydney.

Michael: Okay, so full disclosure: Tanya and I met at a bar a little over six months ago.

Tanya: Translation, he was hitting on me.

Michael: *laughs* Okay, fair enough. Well, I was striking up a convo about what I do for a living.

Tanya: Which is?

Michael: I investigate true crimes. And I had just gotten a break in a case that I'd been obsessed with since my freshman year in college. So I was kinda excited and told her about it.

Tanya: To which I replied that I had never heard of the Springville Massacre.

Michael: Then I promptly said, "What rock have you been living under? Were you too busy fighting off giant spiders and kangaroos down under?"

Tanya: The date ended quickly after that. But he did hold my attention for a bit with his passionate babble about some girl who could move furniture with her mind.

Michael: Honestly, I thought the entire world had heard of the massacre. Especially given all the conspiracy theories surrounding it.

Tanya: And that's probably why I hadn't. Because it just *sounds* crazy. I pride myself on being a realist.

Michael: So, I thought this would make a great social experiment. I mean, what better way to approach this case with a fresh pair of eyes than by presenting it to an extreme skeptic who has absolutely no tainted knowledge of the massacre? For the next few weeks, we're going to retrace the events leading up to Prom Night, turning over old leads, maybe even dig up new evidence, and let you and our listeners be the judge.

Tanya: I mean really, it all sounds like a fantastic urban legend. But I am curious about these conspiracy theories you mentioned. Can I hear some?

Michael: Well, for starters, consider the way the entire town went up in flames. It just couldn't have been the work of one teen girl with quote "magical powers." That's what people have a hard time processing. Hence the state investigation, the interrogation, the burying of facts. The high school was already under a lot of heat as it was, which we'll dive into later, so in the general public's eyes, Maddy had to have had some help destroying the place.

Tanya: Did they consider it a domestic terrorist attack of sorts?

Michael: Something like that. You also have the conservative swamp believing Black Lives Black Pride, or BLBP, had something to do with it, given all the protests that took place in the weeks prior to Prom Night. Then there are people who believe that it never happened at all. That it was all Hollywood effects and crisis actors, which is just disgusting.

Tanya: I believe kids died. I believe they existed. I just don't believe the cause of their death.

Michael: Yeah, neither did the state of Georgia. Neither did most of America, which is why Portman's book went virtually unnoticed. But I do have one theory to add to the mix.

Tanya: Okay, let's hear it!

Michael: I believe Maddy Washington is still alive.

Tanya: Oh God, Mike. You're not serious?

Michael: Remember the lead I mentioned earlier? I spoke to someone who may have proof Maddy didn't die in those fires. And that she had help escaping.

May 1, 2014

Maddy sat on a bench outside the principal's office, clutching a notebook, her heavy book bag by her feet. She rocked softly back and forth, nibbling on her thumb. Her hair, now three times its normal size, draped around her shoulders like a frizzy blanket. Above the bench hung a painted green-and-white banner: *SPRINGVILLE HIGH! Home of the Pirates! 4× State Champions!* surrounded by framed photos of students both current and past. Maddy kept her eyes focused on her lap, ignoring the gawking stares from the administrative staff, mostly women in their midsixties, dressed in mom jeans, grandma sweater vests, shift dresses, and clunky loafers. On the school secretary's red oak desk sat a small white block with a scripture: *For I know the plans I have for you, declares the Lord, plans to prosper you and not to harm you, plans to give you a hope and a future.*

Maddy prayed that was true.

Mrs. Morgan watched Maddy through Mr. O'Donnell's office window, arms crossed around her stomach. She replayed that morning several times, frustrated by all the witty responses she had finally come up with that eluded her while the students had been mocking Maddy's hair. Why hadn't she put those punks in their place? She wouldn't have thought twice about it at her previous school. Her old kids respected the way she could dish it right back to them. But at this new school, it felt as if the kids knew they were untouchable, that they were the ones really in charge, and that unemployment was just one complaining parent phone call away.

"You'll have to move rooms," Mr. O'Donnell said behind her. "Probably for the rest of the school year until we can have those windows replaced."

The incident with Maddy had left her so rattled that she'd

almost forgotten about the broken glass carpeting her classroom floor. That could wait. Her priority was the frightened, mousy student sitting outside Mr. O'Donnell's office. She couldn't fail her again.

"I don't care about the stupid room, Steve," she huffed.

"Okay. So . . . what happened?"

Mrs. Morgan turned in time to catch Mr. O'Donnell reorganizing his desk for the second time and rolled her eyes. She had always made him nervous, jittery. Which wasn't what one would expect from a school's top official. It annoyed her that students were left in the hands of such a spineless slug who bowed at ignorant parents' feet.

"Kids were throwing pencils at her right before the earthquake," she said. "They were making fun of her hair."

He stopped fidgeting long enough to give her a measured glance.

"This all over a bad hair day?" he asked incredulously. "Laurie, your classroom was destroyed. Don't you think we—"

"Steve," she said through gritted teeth, leaning over his desk. "You're not paying attention! Take a look at her hair. Take a *real* good look."

Mr. O'Donnell reeled back in his chair, distancing himself with a gulp. He then tilted sideways, peering out his window. Five long seconds passed before he blanched.

"Oh. Oh! Is she . . . I . . . she couldn't be."

She crossed her arms. "I think so."

He stole another glance and rubbed a hand over his pasty face, stunned. If not in her features, her hair left little to no room for doubt.

On the bench, Maddy squirmed, her foot tapping against the green carpet.

Mrs. Morgan tried hard not to pity her. Maddy didn't need pity. It would only add insult to injuries she might not even be aware of. But Mrs. Morgan failed at her attempt with every passing thought.

That poor girl. That poor, sweet girl. She's been living a lie all this time . . .

Mr. O'Donnell dabbed his forehead. "This is not good. Students picking on a . . . girl? We'll never hear the end of it."

"A Black girl, you mean to say," she corrected him, her tone clipped. "And shouldn't you be more worried about Maddy?"

"Right, of course," he stuttered, rising to his feet. Mrs. Morgan yanked open the door and waved her arm as if to say, *After you.*

He bravely nodded and marched out into the main office, her following.

"Madison," he shouted.

Maddy flinched, scooting down the bench, pulling her knees up to her chest, her bottom lip trembling.

"Jesus, Steve," Mrs. Morgan muttered, rushing to sit beside her.

"It's okay, Maddy, you're not in any trouble," she assured

her, placing a gentle hand on her shoulder. Maddy whimpered, squeezing herself into the armrest.

Mrs. Morgan gave Mr. O'Donnell a nod, urging him to say something. Anything. But Mr. O'Donnell had the paternal instinct of a paper clip. He reset himself and tried again, not for Maddy's sake, she knew, of course. More for his pride.

"Madison," he started, adding some bass to his voice. "Do you know who threw those pencils at you?"

Maddy kept her eyes down and shook her head. She rubbed a palm against her thigh over and over again, as if trying to polish herself right down to the bone.

"You sure you didn't see anyone?" he pushed. "And don't worry, we won't tell a soul what you say in here."

Maddy peered up through her frizzy strands, scanning the office. Everyone was staring, from the assistant principal to the secretary, not even pretending to work. She blinked down at her lap and shook her head.

Mrs. Morgan narrowed her eyes at the gawkers, then glared at him. "Nice work," she muttered.

Mr. O'Donnell straightened his tie and cleared his throat. "Madison, why don't you go home for the rest of the day?" he offered. "I'm sure this was all very . . . traumatizing. We'll call your father and let him know you've been excused."

Maddy's eyes flared at the mention of her father, her jittery hand coming to a stop. "No," she gasped. "You . . . you don't . . ."

"It's school policy to inform parents or guardians of an

incident that requires a student to go home for the day."

Maddy's mouth hung open but nothing came out. The bench beneath her began to shake, sending a jolt through Mrs. Morgan.

Hm? Aftershocks? she wondered, glancing around the room. But no one else seemed to notice.

"Do you need, um, a ride or someone to pick you up?" Mr. O'Donnell asked. "We can have your father come and—"

At that very moment, the office printer in the corner roared to life, spitting out dozens of ink-blot pages, every tray click-clacking.

"Would someone handle that?" Mr. O'Donnell yelled, turning back to Maddy.

Maddy stared at the machine for a moment before shaking her head, hair shifting.

Mr. O'Donnell wouldn't know compassion if it bit him in the ass, Mrs. Morgan thought bitterly, and placed a hand on Maddy's shoulder again.

"Maddy, I'm so sorry this happened. What those kids did was cruel, and you didn't deserve it. I know this must have been very upsetting, so I want you to know you can talk to me about . . . anything. I'm here. Okay?"

Maddy pulled her sweater closed, silence her only reply.

"Okay, Maddy, you can go."

Maddy grabbed her bag, leaping to her feet. She tripped twice, fumbling through the office door. They watched her walk, triple-time, down the hall, her hair a disastrous heap.

She couldn't possibly be white with hair like that, Mrs. Morgan thought, and immediately chastised herself.

Mr. O'Donnell sighed, rubbing his forehead.

"Come with me," he said. "Henrietta, pull Madison Washington's file, will you? Also call the nurse's office, tell them to bring their file here too."

"Right away," the secretary said.

"What are you thinking?" Mrs. Morgan asked, following him back into his office.

He pulled his emergency chocolate Twizzlers stash out of a bottom drawer, offering her one. "I'm thinking we missed something."

She grabbed a string, flopping into the adjacent chair. "Could she be adopted?"

"No. She has her father's eyes."

She raised an inquisitive eyebrow.

"He was in the same class as my older sister," he admitted sheepishly. "The Washingtons were . . . sorta known around here."

Henrietta appeared with the file. She must have already looked it up herself, which made Mrs. Morgan furious at the idea of one of her students' privacy being invaded. First by the kids, then by the adults. She slammed the door at Henrietta's back as Mr. O'Donnell scanned the file.

"Says here she's white," he mumbled.

"Which is technically true," Mrs. Morgan countered. "If you say he's her father."

Mr. O'Donnell's lips wiggled, words heavy on his tongue.

"Whatever thought you're having, you should think better of it," she warned.

He sighed, completely spent, and it wasn't even third period. "There were rumors," he began. "Rumors of him being with a Black woman. Long time ago. But no one took them seriously, especially with a mother like his. Thorny old woman up until the day she died. Or so I heard. Used to spit at kids over at Sal's."

"Last time I checked, children weren't delivered via stork anymore. Where's her mother?"

"Died in childbirth. Or so he says."

"So no one ever saw her?"

"The details were . . . murky."

"Who else knows?"

He scoffed. "By now, the whole town."

Mrs. Morgan winced, glancing back into the waiting room, the framed photos on the walls now all hanging crooked.

"What about the students? The ones who bullied her. How do you suggest we deal with them?"

"Did you see who threw the pencils?"

She flushed. "Well, no."

He shook his head.

"Unless you saw someone specifically, we can't punish the

whole class for one student's mistake."

"It wasn't a mistake," she snapped. "And the whole class was laughing. At the very least, they could benefit from some racial sensitivity programming."

"Fine. But I think we should dismiss her from the class for the rest of the year. Given the . . . hostile environment. We can move her to study hall."

She gave a curt nod. "Agreed."

"Anything else?"

She nodded toward the door.

"We'll need some sensitivity training for the entire staff as well."

"What does the staff have to do with this?" he balked.

"Steve, you just found out one of your students has been pretending to be white. Do you have any idea the shitstorm that's about to go down around here?"

He sighed. "Which reminds me. I have to call Mr. Washington."

Maddy didn't want to run out of the school. Running would attract too much attention. And she couldn't use the front doors, where most of the windows faced and others could see her enormous hair and heckle her further. So she power-walked back toward the gym, down to the lower level, to the side exit, hiccupping breaths to keep from exploding. The earthquake had cracked her glasses, and she could barely see without them.

But something told her that it wasn't an earthquake at all. It felt too targeted, like it had happened under her feet and nowhere else. The thought made her want to run home faster, as if something ugly, inky black was chasing her down the hall. But as she veered around the corner, she slammed into a chest made of marble.

"Oof!" she cried, wobbling back.

"Damn, my bad!" a deep voice said with a chuckle, but he stopped as she glanced up at him.

Kendrick Scott.

He was a giant blur, but she'd recognize him anywhere with his dark complexion, towering height, and blinding smile. Breath caught in her throat; her legs froze stiff. She couldn't remember a single time they had spent more than two seconds alone with each other. And of all days, he had to witness her like this.

What is he going to do?

He took in her appearance, stuck on her hair, his smile fading. "Uh, you okay?"

There was no recognition in his voice. Her heart quickened. Maybe he would forget all about the run-in, mix her up with some other girl, if she would only move her feet.

But as if a light had turned on, he gasped. "Maddy?"

Her name sounded strange on his tongue. A name she'd never heard him utter before. It was the wake-up call she needed.

She ran around him and out the door.

• • •

The hallways of Springville High were abuzz with gossip. Sure, some had heard about the natural disaster that had hit Mrs. Morgan's classroom. But news about Maddy took precedence.

Wendy flew down the hall, protein shake in one hand, books in another, hoping to catch her boyfriend before he left for third period. He always stopped by his locker to switch books and clocked his timing just right so they could walk the halls together. She spotted his head hovering above the other students, standing a solid six foot two, all muscle. She stopped short of his locker, taking a quick breath to collect herself. But the news couldn't wait, and the words burst from her lips. "Did you hear?"

Kendrick "Kenny" Scott jumped at her squeal but held in a sigh of annoyance. She bit her lips, remembering he hated the way she snuck up on him. No announcement, no greeting, just straight to whatever was top of her mind.

"Good morning to you too." He leaned down and kissed her cheek. "Hear what?"

"Maddy Washington is Black!"

He raised an eyebrow. "Who?"

"Maddy," she said, and handed him his morning strawberry shake. "Mad Mad Maddy! She's Black. I mean . . . African American."

Her face flushed, hoping he didn't notice the blunder.

Rolling his eyes, he slammed his locker shut and took a sip of the smoothie, wincing at the chalky vanilla whey powder that Wendy insisted would help with muscle gain—and for the most part, it did.

"That's a really bad joke, babe."

"It's true! I've been trying to text you, but my phone is all messed up."

He measured her face, waiting for the punch line. "Who told you that?"

As they walked down the hallway hand in hand, Wendy breathlessly recounted the hair incident.

"Y'all threw shit in her hair?"

She grimaced. The egregiousness of the act had flown right over her head.

"Well . . . I didn't. Jules kinda did. But . . . it was funny how it all sort of stayed there. She didn't even notice. Crazy, right? Maddy has a real Afro!"

"Yeah, I guess," Kenny mumbled.

"Kara Klaine's aunt works in the office and heard Principal O'Donnell talking about it. I mean, who would've known?"

Kenny stared at the floor, mumbling. "Think I saw her on the way to the bathroom. Didn't even recognize her. She looked . . . scared." He eyed Wendy. "What did y'all do to her?"

Wendy jumped quick to defend herself. "Nothing! Nothing that bad. If you ask me, she was kind of being dramatic," she said with a laugh, redirecting the conversation. "But like, all these years we all thought she was white. So freaking crazy! Do you think anyone in your family knew?"

Kenny scoffed. "Why would we know?"

"I just, I don't . . . well, I thought maybe . . ." Her words trailed off as she rubbed her temples.

"Hey, you okay?" he asked, stopping to cup her cheek. "What's wrong?"

She pushed back her white-blond hair to look up at him. Wendy had pretty strawberry freckles over ghostly pale skin. When she wasn't babbling, he could swim in her ocean-blue eyes all day.

"I just got this killer headache."

He placed the cold shake to her forehead, and she leaned into his touch.

"I can take you down to the nurse," he offered, concern in his voice.

"No, I'm fine. But thanks," she said, kissing him. "Anyway, did any windows break in your classroom?

"Why?"

"Because of the earthquake."

"What earthquake?"

"The earthquake that just happened!"

Kenny frowned. "Really? I didn't feel anything."

"Are you joking?" How had he missed all the chaos? But he did have Spanish second period, up on the second floor. So low to the ground, maybe her class felt it more.

"You sure you doing alright?" Kenny questioned Wendy as they rounded the hall corner. Wendy never got sick. Even when she had her period, she barely complained about cramps and now she was talking of earthquakes.

"I'm fine. I'm . . ."

At that moment, Kayleigh Ray burst through a crowd of kids and rushed over to them, gaping in shock. "OMG! You're never going to believe what I just heard. Mad Mad Maddy is Black!"

Wendy laughed. "Yeah, I was just telling—"

"Yoooo, bro!" Jason stopped to join the crew, tapping his team cocaptain with the back of his hand. "What's up? Yo, did you hear Mad Mad Maddy is fucking BLACK?"

"Yeah, I heard." Kenny chuckled, his back muscles taut.

"Who do you think knew?" Wendy asked in a hushed voice, grinning. "Who do you think was her mama?"

"And what woman would sleep with shit?" Kayleigh shuddered.

"Well, clearly a Black one," Jason quipped. "Gotta be from the East Side."

"Gross." Kayleigh blinked quick at Kenny. "Well, not her being Black, but anyone sleeping with that loon. He smells awful!"

Struggling to rein in his annoyance, Kenny took one last sip of air before pasting on the standard generic smile he would maintain for the rest of the day. Just about everyone would want to talk to him about Maddy, but he had to remain unfazed, the same composure he kept whenever anything happened to Black people and they wanted unsaid permission from him to speak about it freely. Because if Kenny was okay with it, then it must be okay.

He chuckled. "Yeah, he does."

As Jason, Kayleigh, and Wendy speculated, Kenny caught sight of Rashad, Jackie, and Regina talking in hushed whispers by their lockers, debating something. They were easy to spot. All the Black kids were. They only made up 30 percent of the school and hung in tight, secretive circles. Or at least that's how it seemed to Kenny. He wasn't close with any of them.

"I knew it! Just knew it. You could tell in her face," he overheard Jackie insist. But did he know? He wondered. It would be a question that most Black people in Springville were going to ask of themselves: How did we not recognize one of our own?

Rashad looked up and noticed Kenny staring, his face going stoic.

"Kenny?"

Kenny quickly turned to Wendy's cheery voice. "Huh?"

She smiled at him, squeezing his hand. "I said, what do you think? Can Black girls really look that . . . white?"

Kenny froze, meeting each of their eager gazes, reminding him of game-day huddles. The way his team looked to him for direction, guidance, wins. But off the field, they looked to him to be their Black-people whisperer.

He forced out a laugh. "Man, I don't know, but she had y'all fooled."

The group laughed along with him, eating up his words. As the bell rang, he stole another glimpse of the Black kids rushing to class. Other than color, he didn't really have anything in common with them, or have problems like they did. They were always making a big deal out of anything, blaming everything on racism, arguing with teachers over nothing. Kenny breezed through school, didn't cause trouble, and had led his team to the state championship, twice. He didn't belong in those secretive circles.

Besides, he had real friends. When he'd picked the University of Alabama, they'd thrown him a surprise party. When he was nominated for homecoming king, they rallied votes. Whenever they were in the car, they always turned to a hip-hop playlist. They were the most popular kids in school, tight since sophomore year, and that brought a set of perks he'd never see otherwise. Who cares if he was the only Black guy in their crew? They never treated him different. They didn't see color.

So why couldn't he ever shake the nagging longing to know what the Black kids were thinking?

MADDY DID IT
EPISODE 1, CONT.

Michael: So the incident that took place second period was the first incident on record of Maddy using her abilities.

Tanya: Alleged abilities. This is just a verbal account, since the camera so conveniently stopped working the moment we needed it to.

Michael: I'd say the same thing. But look at this girl in the far corner of the video. Can you tell everyone what you see?

Tanya: Okay, so there's a young woman, sitting at her desk by the window. She has a behind-the-ear type of hearing aid. She seems to flinch, or ducks, and takes one of the devices out of her ear.

Michael: Flinching as if she heard a loud sound. Something that maybe would interfere with her device, right?

Tanya: Potentially, yes.

Michael: I want to point out something that wasn't mentioned in the commission report, or in any part of the investigation. Something you'd only notice if you were really looking. When reviewing school records and reports from that day, I found that the nurse's office had an influx of students with near-identical symptoms. Headaches, nausea, extreme earaches, vertigo. I compared the nurse's sign-in book to attendance records and schedules and found that almost all the students with those symptoms were from that second-period history class.

Tanya: So what does this have to do with Maddy?

Michael: Well, I'm not a hundred percent sure, but my theory is that Maddy's abilities or powers had some sort of delayed side effect that only affected kids, and no one put two and two together.

Tanya: Oh, come off it! What about the teacher? She was in the room as well.

Michael: No symptoms reported, and she's not alive to give her own account.

Tanya: Fine. Let's say that is the case. A question for you, then: Why hadn't anyone complained about it before?

Michael: What do you mean?

Tanya: These so-called "powers," they had to come from somewhere, right? They didn't suddenly appear out of the blue. This incident, while traumatic, couldn't have been the inciting source. What was the change agent? Did she have these powers all her life and decide that moment was the right time to reveal her talents? I find it improbable that in seventeen years, no other students experienced these side effects until Maddy's senior year of high school.

May 1, 2014

The air was humid and sticky as Maddy made the long walk home through the winding neighboring streets, hoping to use the tall white oaks as protection against the brutal sun. The rising heat erased all traces of the downpour that had ruined her carefully crafted facade. Mid-May in Georgia could reach hellishly hot temperatures, and ten minutes into her journey she realized that she should have accepted Mr. O'Donnell's offer for a ride. With her hair swelled beyond recognition, the entire town could see her from a mile away. They would know her darkest secret, not that it mattered. They would all find out eventually. But in a last-ditch effort, she ripped a plastic string off a nearby garbage bag and tied her hair into a pony-tail. She stuffed the thick poof under her sweater, refusing to take it off, no matter how much sweat pooled in her collarbone. The rain must have washed clean the three layers of sunblock she applied every morning. Bad enough her hair was in disarray; she didn't dare come home with a tan on top of it.

How many people can see me? she thought. How many people were staring out their windows, saying, *There goes Thomas's daughter. Did you see her hair?*

Her stomach lurched. What was she going to tell Papa? How would she begin to explain that their biggest fear had materialized? How would he punish her? She walked faster, concentrating on the Betty Crocker cookbook sitting by the stove at home, considering potential meals she could prepare to soften Papa's rage.

Two blocks from home, a bee zipped in front of her face, rounding about. Maddy dodged out of its way. She wasn't used to being out in the sun for more than minutes at a time and didn't know if she could be allergic to bee stings. She tried to outrun it, whimpering and swerving, but the bee seemed determined.

Go away, she thought. *Leave me alone!*

The bee buzzed closer to her ear, and she jerked wildly, her ponytail coming loose. She yelped, and her vision pulsed. Once, twice, three times . . .

"Stop it!"

The bee went silent, shooting up like a rocket into the clouds just as a squirrel plummeted from a tree, landing on its stomach with a loud smack to the concrete road beside her. She shrieked, hands covering her face. The squirrel flipped back on its legs, shook its head, and sniffed the air. Its pitch-black eyes looked directly at her and froze. Stunned, Maddy glanced around, wondering if anyone had seen or heard the animal fall.

Are you okay? she thought desperately. *Please be okay.*

The squirrel shook its head once more. Maddy stood paralyzed in its gaze. Finally, it scurried off, up a nearby tree, disappearing among the leaves.

Maddy took a deep breath, her shoulders easing. She stuffed her ponytail back inside her sweaty sweater and continued heading home.

Maddy. Maddy. Maddy.

The name that ran through Wendy's head all day, speeding and throbbing through every artery, rang loudest in the hectic cafeteria. The headache she'd complained about earlier had not relented, even after two aspirins. Her phone buzzed. An email, another scholarship secured, but still short the three thousand she needed for first semester housing. All her friends had already turned in their security deposits, some parents paying both semesters in full. Her parents probably used their checkbook as a drink coaster.

Wendy massaged her temple, only catching snippets of the

conversation Jules and the girls were having across from her.

"Ha! There's no way Maddy's momma was all dark like Kenny and she come out looking like that." Jules laughed. "She had to have been, like, really light-skinned or something."

An arm wrapped around Wendy's waist.

"Why do you got that look on your face?" Kenny whispered, gnawing on a plastic straw.

She stabbed at her salad, too queasy to eat. "I keep thinking about Maddy."

"Feeling guilty?"

"No, nothing like that. I just . . . can't get her face out of my head." She laughed, waving her hand. "It's nothing."

"Maybe. But Kenny doesn't talk all Black either," Jules said. "He talks regular."

Kenny looked up at the mention of his name, his face unreadable. Wendy tensed as she always did at the small comparisons people made about her boyfriend. But he only gave a smile and returned his gaze to her. She exhaled, happy he remained unbothered, and was leaning over to steal a kiss when Jason elbowed in.

"Hey, bro!" Jason tossed a football up. "Me and the guys are getting in a game of touch after school. You in? I know you're about to be big time, but you down to slum it with us?"

Wendy's lips tightened, feeling Kenny's energy shift. She knew he hated Jason's relentless egging—although he'd never admit it. Wendy patted his thigh with a sympathetic smirk, reminding him to ignore Jason's passive-aggressive digs. Really, he should take pity on him. After all, Jason hadn't made it into either his first- or second-choice schools. They heard his dad had to pull some strings for him to play for USC. Meanwhile, Kenny'd had colleges kicking down his door since their first state championship.

Kenny brushed the hair out of her face. "Is it cool if I go?" he asked in a voice just above a whisper. In the past she'd often complained about them not spending enough time together, and there were only a few weeks left before Kenny would be gone, off to training camp.

But Wendy smiled. "Yeah. Of course. I'll just . . . catch a ride with Jules."

"Sweet," Jules said, grinning. "You owe me some Dairy Queen anyways."

Wendy gulped. Did she have enough to cover that? Her parents had already maxed out her emergency credit card.

Kenny raised an eyebrow at her. "You sure?"

Wendy straightened with a sugary-sweet smile. "Totally," she said, kissing his nose, then pulled away to nibble on a carrot stick.

She was completely fine with him spending time with the boys. Because what Kenny didn't know was that Wendy wasn't going to Brown in the fall. She was going to the University of Alabama. With him. After all the investment she put in— helping him get ready for games, extra hours practicing in the weight room, protein smoothies every day, making sure he turned his assignments in on time . . . he would need her. She planned to tell him around the Fourth of July, right before they had to start packing for school. They wouldn't need two cars since they'd be everywhere together, unless he was at an away game, which of course she'd drive to. They'd live on campus their first year, but the next year they'd have to find something off campus, walking distance. Maybe a condo? She wanted to major in psychology but thought business admin would be better. Accounting classes would help her learn how to manage their books. He'd most likely propose right before the draft, maybe at graduation. The wedding colors would be baby blue and sage. They'd have a summer wedding at the country club, two hundred people minimum. And whatever team they ended up with, she'd want a house in Springville to raise the kids. They'd have at least three, all boys. Well, maybe two boys and a girl.

She had it all planned out. Like always.

Maddy had just taken the casserole out of the oven when she heard Papa's keys in the door. She waited by the stove, listening close. Depending on his steps, she could tell if he'd had a good day or bad. Good, he would enter whistling *The Andy Griffith Show* theme song, his step light and easy. Bad, he would throw his store keys on the console and stomp upstairs, barking about his dinner.

She held her breath and waited. No movement. But she could feel his presence in her bones through the walls.

"Madison," he said, his voice firm.

She flinched at the sound of her own name, heart sinking to the bottom of her stomach. Shaking, she glanced at the cookbook on the counter, the one she always imagined had belonged to her mother, and found herself longing for someone she had never even met to save her.

Don't keep him waiting.

She wiped her hands on her ruffled white apron and touched her freshly washed and blow-dried hair, still a puffy cloud, the roots crinkled like packing paper. Not as before, but he noticed when one strand sat out of place.

She took a deep breath to steady herself and stepped into the kitchen doorway.

Papa stood in the narrow foyer, the light above him muted by dust. He just . . . stood there in his white short-sleeved button-down and brown tweed pants that sat high, cutting into his protruding belly. His pale face was the texture of a waxy wrinkled prune, thin lips in a sharp line as he took in her appearance.

"How?" he spat. "How could you be so careless? So stupid? How?"

Maddy twisted her fingers together. "I'm sorry, Papa."

He prowled toward her. "What is the one thing I ask of you? Every day, what do I ask?"

"To check the weather," she mumbled to the floor, tears welling.

"How many times are you supposed to check?"

"Three times." She sniffed, paralyzed with fear. "I did, Papa! I checked! It didn't say anything about rain—"

He closed the distance between them in three swift steps and backhanded her into the wall.

"Don't you lie to me!" he roared, standing over her. "You didn't check. You couldn't possibly have checked!"

He yanked her up by the hair, dragging her to the hallway mirror.

"Look! Look at yourself! You're a mess! A disgusting mess."

Maddy stifled a scream, falling to her knees.

"Please, Papa," she begged. "I'm sorry."

"Aren't you ashamed of yourself, going out in public? Letting people see you like this? Do you want to be a Negro? Is that what you want? You want to bring shame upon this family?"

"No, Papa!"

"How could you do this to me?"

"Papa, I'm sorry!"

He straightened and calmly began taking off his belt. Maddy gulped, scooting backward.

"But Papa," she cried. "They made fun of my hair, they threw things at me, and they—"

"Go to your closet," he hissed, gripping the belt in one hand.

"But it wasn't my fault!"

He pulled his arm back and swung it down, the belt slapping her arm. She yowled. "I said to your prayer closet, now!"

Maddy stumbled back, tripping over a half-empty bottle of sunblock. "Please, no!"

He brought the belt down again and again. Words pushing out with each blow through clenched teeth. "Get. In. Your. Closet. Now."

Maddy scrambled to her feet, prepared to run, but Papa grabbed her by the back of her collar. He yanked her up the creaking stairs, splintering wood ripping her stockings, her cries falling on deaf ears. Papa dragged her into her room, toward the closet door. Maddy desperately reached for anything to hold on to.

"Papa, No. No, Papa, please!"

Papa swung the closet door open, threw her inside, and locked it shut. Maddy slapped her hands against the wall and yanked on the doorknob. "No, Papa, pleeeeeeease!"

The old radio in the living room screeched to life, an ear-piercing sound, lights flickering, then stopped.

Papa paused but said nothing before stomping downstairs.

Maddy slid to the floor, sobbing. She didn't want to turn on the light. She didn't want to see. But Papa would know she was sitting in the dark and would leave her there for hours. He had done it before. So she reached up, swatting the air, grabbed the hanging chain, and pulled. A dull cobweb-covered lightbulb illuminated the cramped closet with a slanted ceiling. Every inch of the walls in her tight quarters was covered with cut-out pictures of women. White women, in various shades of blond, brunette, and red. In tea-length dresses at cocktail parties. In aprons serving roasted chicken to their husbands. In old Hollywood movie posters. Papa had even gone so far as to paste eyes in the collage. Blue eyes, all staring down at Maddy and her frizzy mane. Real beauties, their hair styled perfectly, milky skin immaculate . . . everything she could never be.

Maddy felt sick. The silent judgment from thin pieces of magazine paper seemed to hurt more than anything that had happened that day.

But she sat on her knees and prayed to be like those women. Just like Papa had taught her.

From David Portman's Springville Massacre: The Legend of Maddy Washington (pg. 12)

Ask anyone from Springville about Prom Night: jaws go slack, eyes hollow with regret before muttering the same excuses—they never saw it coming; they were blindsided. It's what they tell themselves at night. Searching for the comfort of self-soothing lies when all along it was right in front of them—a sleeping volcano, waiting to erupt.

Weeks after that fateful night, people started putting the story together. Looking back, Maddy had the worst attendance record of any student in her class, her absences all aligning with huge thunderstorms or high sun days. Never went to camp or swimming in the lake like the rest of the kids in town. She wore long sleeves, even in the dead of summer, with wide-brimmed hats and stockings. When questioned about Maddy's absences, Mr. Washington reported that she had lupus and the weather gave her severe migraines. No one questioned it. No one questioned a thing.

A little over an hour outside of Atlanta, at the butt of the Chattahoochee National Forest, sits Springville, population during its glory days upward of 1,100. You pass miles of farmland, truck stops, and fast-food chains before reaching its center, a quaint Main Street of mom-and-pop-owned businesses. Storefronts, family practices, and a popular pizza parlor. Springville was once a thriving industrial hub, true to its Bible Belt roots. Friday night lights during football season. Thanksgiving Day parades, Christmas carolers, Easter egg hunts, and debutante balls. The all-American dream. But hidden away from progressive cities, Springville was also the type of town where racism was passed down like family jewels. The kind with value. The kind auctioned on TV shows.

The CDX freight line runs diagonally through the town, splitting it in two—East and West: the East Side, the predominately Black and Hispanic population; the West side, mostly white (with the exception of a few Black families), along with a division for the upper crust and old southern money. When the power plant was still operational, trains made frequent stops. Now the arm at the railroad crossings only comes down twice a day. Train operators call it a dead zone.

No one stops in Springville except ghosts.

May 1, 2014

Maddy had fallen asleep on the floor, overpowered by exhaustion. The jarring cuckoo clock rang six, waking her. Papa's heavy strides approached the door, and she shot up, scooting into a corner. The lock clicked, and his footsteps slowly retreated. Maddy waited, then emerged from the closet, her clothes disheveled, face puffy and red from tears. She slumped downstairs and stepped into the kitchen to find a familiar scene.

Papa had set a chair next to the stove. On the vintage red Formica kitchen table sat a jar of blue grease, a smock, clamps, and a metal hot comb with a chipped black wooden handle.

Papa tied on his workman apron. Maddy gulped, wrapped the smock around her neck, and sat in the matching red leather chair, heat from the gas burner warming her.

Over the years, Thomas Washington had tried many things to keep his daughter's hair bone straight. Various chemical relaxers, texturizers, and money-back-guaranteed products.

But Maddy's sensitive scalp rejected them all, leaving painful blisters too large to hide or explain. So he settled for the old-fashioned way, what he read about in Negro magazines: a classic hot comb. He picked up one at a Goodwill store far from town. Grease, hair spray, and other hair supplies he ordered over the phone.

Papa split her hair into four sections. He placed the comb directly on the fire, the iron blackened from use. The clock ticked as it sizzled. Maddy watched the comb from the corner of her eye, keeping her head straight, her mouth dry.

Moments later, Papa grabbed the comb's handle, and her stomach tensed.

"Hold still."

Maddy bent her head forward and tightened her neck muscles. At the nape of her neck, Papa parted her hair, applying a dollop of grease, then gently glided the hot comb from her scalp to her ends. The grease sizzled like butter in a hot skillet. She swallowed hard, trying not to flinch. If she flinched, the comb would burn her, and she already had enough scars on her neck and ears as it was.

Papa worked his way through her hair, section by section. It had taken years and many burns to master his daughter's unruly texture. But every Sunday night, they went through the same routine.

Maddy bit her lip, the heat dangerously close to her skin. Her thoughts drifted back to school. How the kids laughed and threw things. How the room shook beneath her, the way Kendrick looked at her.

"Papa, what do I tell them?"

Her darkest secret had been exposed. Rumors once lingered, the Black kids giving her the occasional inquisitive looks, but since she was twelve, no one questioned her about potentially being one of them. After all this time, how would they ever explain it?

But Papa said nothing. He parted another square of hair, slicked it down with grease, and picked the comb off the stove.

"Tell me about the Battle of Midway," he said.

Maddy's hair sizzled close to her ear. She closed her eyes.

"The Battle of Midway occurred in 1942," she answered. "During the Second World War. The US defeated a Japanese attacking fleet."

"Ah yes. Defeated, right?"

"Yes, Papa. Consequences after the attack on Pearl Harbor."

Papa slid through another section, meticulous and precise.

"Who was our thirty-fourth president?"

"Dwight Eisenhower."

Papa continued testing Maddy's knowledge. Any mistake, and Papa would casually let a finger slip, burning her. She knew the drill well.

When Papa finished, he brushed down her hair, marveling at his artistry. He nodded in approval, then turned off the burner.

"Go to bed."

THREE

MADDY DID IT
EPISODE 2
"White Prom vs. Black Prom"

Tanya: Mike, you'll be pleased to know that I've been doing my
own research.

Michael: Okay! Let's hear it.

Tanya: It was bothering me, you know? All that talk about some
mysterious sound that made kids dizzy. Their symptoms
sounded familiar, so I did a little digging and found the
perfect explanation. I'm going to play something for you,
and I want to know what you hear. Ready? Listen.

Michael: Uh . . . don't hear anything.

Tanya: Right. Because you are over the age limit that it would
affect. I just played a high-pitched noise that neither you
nor I would notice because we do not fall between the
ages of thirteen and twenty-one.

Michael: I'm not following.

Tanya: It's an acoustic deterrent device, a technology originally invented to keep animals away from a designated area—until they realized it worked on humans. And not just any humans, kids. It targets that specific age group whose hearing hasn't deteriorated due to age. And guess who usually uses it?

Michael: I don't know. Who?

Tanya: Military and/or law enforcement. It's been reportedly used at protests to drive kids away. It's also used at playgrounds to keep kids from fraternizing late at night. Some have reported that it sounds like a high-pitched dog whistle. Others say it's like nails on a chalkboard. It's a sonic weapon!

Michael: So you're saying the high-pitched noise was made on purpose? Why? And why pick Springville, of all places?

Tanya: Naturally, due to the rising racial tensions in the surrounding areas, I believe law enforcement was trying to control kids before the town lost control. If there were protests around prom, they probably used it there too. And given the proximity to the power plant, it makes sense they'd want to secure it.

Michael [narration]: The Springville Power Plant is a nuclear power station that sits just west of the town's center, on the bank of the Chattahoochee Reservoir. Built in 1954, it powered the majority of upper Georgia, providing hundreds of jobs. But two weeks after Prom Night, the plant abruptly shut down, and all employees were let go with three months' severance. The official reason was cited as "increasingly frequent issues with the aging reactors and ongoing environmental concerns."

However, after the commission report revealed what happened that night, the people of Springville believed the real reason had everything to do with Maddy.

May 2, 2014

The end-of-the-year cheer banquet always took place at the country club, the evening donated by sponsors and Springville Cheer alumni. Girls, parents, and eager prospects gathered to celebrate the past season and say farewell to the departing seniors.

In the bathroom, Jules sat on the sink counter, angling her phone to find the best light for a selfie.

"Brady said my boobs have gotten bigger," she said, fluffing her hair, giving the camera a juicy pout. "And he sure would know."

Next to her, Wendy leaned closer to the mirror, reapplied some pink lip gloss, her shimmering eyeshadow making her bright blue eyes sparkle.

"Oh yeah. They totally have! I was going to tell you that before!"

"You're so full of shit." Jules laughed and hopped off the counter, her black slingback heels clicking on the tile.

Jules had called it right; Wendy didn't notice a difference. And she'd probably seen Jules's boobs just as much as Brady had. Jules wasn't exactly modest.

"I swear!" Wendy insisted. "And you look hot tonight."

Jules wore a tight strapless red crepe dress that stopped just at her shins. Overdressed for the occasion, but that was Jules. She relished being a bloody spot you couldn't look away from. Her seductive, provocative wit shrouded a nefarious nature. Jules procured two nips of Jameson from her clutch, offering one to Wendy.

"Bottoms up!"

They clinked bottles and threw them back, eyeing each other, racing to see who would finish first. There was always a looming unsaid competition between them that silently boiled, like a tea kettle with a broken whistle. Wendy didn't want Jules to win, to be the butt of another joke. But the liquor stung her tonsils, and she couldn't fight it any longer. She coughed up a gasp, the alcohol burning down her throat. Jules giggled.

A toilet flushed behind them. Jules quickly snatched the bottles and stuffed them in the trash. Wendy scrambled to find a pack of mints as the stall door opened. It was just a girl. A Black eighth grader Wendy had clocked earlier that evening, dressed in a floral smocked dress and white cardigan, an outfit more suitable for Sunday service. The girl's eyes widened at the sight of Springville's two most popular seniors but she tipped her chin up, marched over to the sink, and washed her hands.

Jules grinned at Wendy in the mirror, bumping her hip with a wink.

"I . . . I like your dress," the girl said, her voice quivering, mouth full of braces. Pretty, in a quiet sort of way. "I'm Pamala. I'mma be trying out for cheer next year."

Jules turned, giving her a slow, lingering once-over, eyes stopping on her hair, box braids that sat on her shoulders.

"Well, good luck to you, babe," Jules said, the words almost taunting.

The girl didn't blink, her face tight and discerning, resolve unwavering. She nodded at Wendy, her chin still tipped to the ceiling.

"Nice meeting y'all. Good luck at college," she said, letting the door slam behind her.

Jules scoffed, rolling her eyes. "Hope they make her straighten her hair or something before they let her try out for the team."

Wendy didn't see anything wrong with her hair. Sure, it wouldn't be uniform with the rest of the girls' high spiral ponytails tied with large ribbons, but at least it was neat and clean. Wendy chalked up her pity partly to commiserating. She remembered what it was like being a prospect back in middle school, pleading for her parents to take her to the cheer banquet, and spending an exorbitant amount on a white dress that made her look demure, wholesome even. Cheerleading resembled pledging a sorority. You had to balance a certain number of appearances with the right amount of sucking up if you wanted in.

Wendy checked her phone. Another scholarship for five hundred dollars. She beamed, the gap between her and her goal was shrinking.

"That better be Kenny making you grin like that," Jules quipped.

Wendy shoved her phone away. "Ye-yeah. Of course."

Jules stared into the mirror, playing with her hair again. "Wow. I can't believe this is our last cheer dinner. Remember last year, when Mia James was puking in the bathroom, and it turned out Ashton Carey had knocked her up?"

"Her parents were pissed," Wendy said. "But at least he did right by her, giving up going to play for Florida."

"Ha! I'd throw myself down the stairs before I ever let some baby keep me from Texas A&M."

Wendy didn't doubt it, especially with the amount of Plan B she'd picked up for Jules in the past.

"Have you seen that baby? She's real cute!" Wendy twirled a lock of hair around her finger, heat rising to her cheeks. "I hope I have a girl. Someday."

Jules shook her head with a snort. "And I hope you and Kenny's baby turns out to look just like Maddy."

Wendy stiffened. "What?"

Jules measured Wendy's shock and rolled her eyes.

"Oh, come on. You don't want your kid coming out looking

all . . . dark, right? Or with funny hair you can't do nothing with. You'd want them coming out looking more like you. Otherwise, your family portraits are gonna look a hot mess!"

Wendy winced a smile, as if agreeing, her neck growing red and splotchy. She never thought about what Kenny's and her potential children would look like. But using Maddy as a measuring stick made her feel sick with something close to guilt. Because Jules had called it right again—she would want her daughter to be like Maddy, to pass for something she was not completely, if only to make her life easier. Wendy's life . . . not the kid's.

"Thanks again for the dress," Wendy said, eager to change the subject. The silver belt wrapped around the teal V-neck halter dress perfectly matched her sandals.

Jules leaned into the mirror, her eye bulging as she applied another coat of mascara.

"It's cool. Fits you better anyways. Can't stuff these tits in there."

That wasn't necessarily true; Wendy had double Ds, while Jules was a plain C cup. But it was the standard excuse she provided. She said the same thing about the tank tops she gifted, sweaters, jeans, shorts, even underwear. In the past four years, Wendy had done more shopping in Jules's closet than in any department store. Not that she could afford to step one foot in a mall.

Jules puckered her lips, giving the mirror a kiss, then grabbed

Wendy's hand. "Come on! I don't want to miss the slideshow!"

During the dinner, senior cheerleaders were given certificates as pictures of them were displayed on a projection screen. Wendy and Jules quickly sat in their seats at a table toward the front.

"Took you long enough," Mrs. Marshall quipped. An equally stunning redhead, she hugged a glass of white wine to her designer dress. Her wedding ring, nearly the size of a quarter, twinkled in the light as she stretched an arm over the back of her daughter's chair.

"We were being entertained by a prospect," Jules said with a smirk, nodding across the room at Pamala, sitting bolt straight next to her mother.

"Ohhhh, I see," Mrs. Marshall said, as if holding in a chuckle. "That's the Kendall family. Just moved over from the East. Lucked up on an inheritance. Let's see them try to keep up with their property taxes." She turned to Wendy. "Where are your parents, pumpkin? I was hoping to get to see them tonight."

Wendy took a nervous sip of water. "Oh. Uh, I think they had to work late."

Jules narrowed her eyes. "But it's our senior dinner."

Wendy winced a smile. "It's fine. Really."

Jules pursed her lips, arms crossing. It wasn't fine.

"Well, it's better they didn't," Mrs. Marshall said, scanning the room. "They're letting any old body in here. I thought this was supposed to be a banquet. Feels more like a soup kitchen."

Jules and her mom giggled while Wendy shifted toward the screen, watching the montage of photos and videos taken over the years at various games, practices, and competitions, set to music. Wendy couldn't help being in awe of how she and Jules had grown. Always up front in their green-and-white uniforms, the fearsome duo—the redhead and the blonde, fire and ice—inseparable fraternal twins.

Her stomach clenched around nervous jitters. The day would eventually come when they would have to separate, and Wendy found herself torn between wanting to know who she was without Jules and terrified of finding out. Would anyone consider her interesting, smart, pretty, or funny? Or would the world soon learn of her commonness? Was she just basking in the shared spotlight that seemed to follow Jules wherever they went? The truth was, Jules could live just fine without Wendy, but could Wendy live without Jules?

But next to Kenny, Wendy wouldn't have to worry about that. She would have her own glamorous home full of expensive clothes and a guaranteed spotlight. Her own rich family. Her own daughter to take to the cheer banquet.

Jules, gazing at the screen in childlike wonder, looped arms with Wendy, snuggling in the crook of her neck as they watched the memories pass by.

"Madison! What are you doing?"

In a daze, Maddy blinked up at Papa. "Huh?"

He stood at the stairs, ripping off his glasses. "What. Are. You. Doing?"

Maddy frowned and took a step back, realizing she had been daydreaming at the threshold of Papa's office again. The one room in the house she'd never been in, only catching glimpses of his crowded desk and overstuffed bookshelf. The room seemed so unlike him.

"You know you're not allowed in here," he barked, brushing by her to slam the door shut.

"Yes, Papa," she mumbled, following him down to the living room.

On Fridays, Papa liked to eat TV dinners in front of the television while watching his favorite black-and-white programs. He'd recorded hours of old movies and shows on hundreds of video cassettes. A bookcase with rows and rows of tapes sat on the far left of the room, meticulously labeled and organized alphabetically. If he hadn't been cursed with a daughter, he would have maybe been a film historian. They didn't have cable, internet, or even cell phones. Papa had all the entertainment he and Maddy could ever need.

They set up two peeling brown TV trays with rusted golden legs in front of a wooden TV set. Nestled in his plaid recliner, Papa chuckled in between bites of turkey with gravy, enjoying another episode of *Leave It to Beaver*.

Maddy mixed her watery mashed potatoes with a fork, holding in a sigh. She had seen the episode so many times she could practically recite it word for word.

"Gee, Mom, do I have to . . ."

They had all the classics: *The Dick Van Dyke Show*, *The Andy Griffith Show*, *The Beverly Hillbillies*, and *Father Knows Best*, to name a few. But Papa loved *Beaver* the most. It represented his values: a wholesome family with a father who comes home from work in time for dinner, wholesome kids with milk mustaches, and a mother who cleaned the house, staying in the kitchen where she belonged.

"See? That's how women are supposed to dress," Papa said, pointing to the woman's tea-length skirt. "Modest. Decent."

"Yes, Papa," she answered for what felt like the millionth time.

As the episode finished, Maddy cleared their plates while Papa loaded another cassette into the VHS. Maddy returned just in time to see the opening credits for *To Have and Have Not*.

Maddy smiled at Papa. It was one of her favorites, starring Lauren Bacall and Humphrey Bogart, who were madly in love in real life as well as on-screen. She loved the way Humphrey wrapped Lauren in his arms, their kiss full of passion. She wondered if such a moment would happen in her own life.

"You know how to whistle, don't you, Steve? You just put your lips together and blow."

It must have been amazing, being on a Hollywood set with such famous superstars. Maddy often dreamed of being part of a movie crew someday, working in the design department, sewing elaborate costumes, or maybe in the kitchen, cooking gourmet meals. Everyone would know her name. She'd cut her hair in a bob, wear cat-eye sunglasses, skinny jeans, and drive off the studio lot with the top down each day.

But one look at Papa, and she remembered that would never be possible.

Twenty minutes into the movie, Papa was snoring in his recliner. Maddy tiptoed to the VCR and fast-forwarded the tape. When Papa had first recorded the film, he must not have been paying attention, because the movie that came on right after it was one he would have never wanted Maddy to watch . . . *Imitation of Life*.

Maddy had discovered it on one of the countless nights he'd fallen asleep. It starred Lana Turner as Lora, a single mother rising to stardom. But that's not what interested Maddy. Lana's housekeeper was a Black woman . . . with a fair-skinned daughter named Sarah Jane.

No matter how many times she'd seen the movie, Maddy watched with bated breath as Sarah Jane passed for a white girl, even dating a white boy who eventually finds out and beats her bloody. Sarah Jane resented who she was, resented the mother who loved her fiercely, and ran away to live a normal life as a white girl. Maddy could do that. Run far from Springville, create a new identity, pass as white. No one would ever know her darkest secret.

But Maddy didn't want Sarah Jane's life. She wanted Sarah Jane's mother. She wanted someone to love her with every cell in their body.

May 3, 2014

"Come on! You can do it," Wendy cheered from the end of the bench, holding a pair of sneakered feet. "Another ten, let's go."

Kenny sat up, winded. "Damn, girl. I thought you were done cheering."

Wendy insisted they put in another twenty minutes in the weight room before heading home. She counted out every pull-up, sit-up, and suicide drill for him. She always pushed him, always supported him. And he loved her for it, even if it might kill him. Once done, he roped her into his sweaty arms.

"I'm starving. Let's get some pizza."

The cowbell rang as they entered Sal's Pizzeria, with its homey Italian decor and green-checked tablecloth.

"Hey, superstar! What's up?" Sal said from behind the counter, sweat above his graying brows.

"Hey, Sal!" Kenny said. "Got my order ready?"

"Yes, sir, one large pepperoni coming up soon!" he said, popping the raw dough into the oven.

Damn, we ordered that thirty minutes ago, Kenny thought. *It should've been done by now.*

Reading his mind, Wendy leaned into him and whispered, "You know he'd use any excuse to talk to you."

Kenny's lips pursed. Ever since colleges came knocking during his sophomore year, and he became a top recruit, he had begrudgingly accepted that everyone would know his name. A Black, dual-threat quarterback with potential to go pro living in their small town? They worshipped at his feet, leaving pizza at his saintly altar. The stares, the whispers . . . they made him itch. But Wendy seemed to revel in it, talking to everyone on his behalf.

"Wendy, what are you going to do when this guy gets all big time on ya?" Sal asked, dusting flour off his hands.

"I don't know." She laughed sheepishly. "Probably cry. But I won't be too far away."

Kenny held his breath for three seconds and released it before Wendy could notice. Brown University was far. Rhode Island wasn't up the road or even the next state over. She might as well be going to school in Japan. He'd agreed to try long distance since she acted like the 1,200 miles between them was no big deal. But his plate would be full by the time the season started. How much room would that leave for her? How could he keep his head in the game and not hurt her in the process?

Sal boxed up the pizza and taped the top before sliding it across the counter. Kenny took out his wallet, but Sal waved him away.

"Nope, it's on the house."

"Naw, Sal. I can't."

Sal nodded his head, smiling. "Just don't forget about your buddy this fall. I already have my tickets."

Kenny held back a grimace. "Yeah, thanks."

"Thanks, Sal!" Wendy cheered, grabbing two bottles of Coke from the fridge.

Kenny parked his truck in front of the house, balancing the pizza, while Wendy shouldered their book bags. The Scotts lived in a modest four-bedroom modular home on the West Side, only a few blocks from Wendy, but they almost always hung out at his place. At some point, he stopped asking why, refusing to listen to the tiny voice inside him telling him her parents had a problem with him being Black.

They walked in to find his little sister at the antique dining room table under a glittering chandelier.

"What's up, punk," he said.

Kali looked up from her algebra homework, spotted Wendy, and rolled her eyes before returning to $x + y$.

"Hey," she said dryly.

"Hi, Kali!" Wendy cheered, skipping up the steps. "We got pizza, and I got you a soda."

"Oh. Goodie," Kali deadpanned.

Kenny scowled. Wendy loved Coke, her absolute favorite drink. But she only smiled at him.

"I'm just gonna, uh, grab some water from the fridge. Be right back," she said, disappearing to the back of the house.

"She's real . . . thirsty," Kali said, smirking.

"You said you'd be nicer," Kenny whispered.

Kali played coy. "I am being nice."

He chuckled, swatting her hair puff, noting her BLBP T-shirt.

"Aye, why you gotta be so loud about it?"

"Huh?"

"The hair, the T-shirt . . . everybody knows you're Black, you don't gotta remind folks all the time. It makes people uncomfortable."

Kali rolled her eyes. "They know that *I'm* Black. I don't know about you."

Kenny tensed, that unease creeping in. "Where's Mom?" he asked, setting his bag on the table just as a worn copy of James Baldwin's *The Fire Next Time* slid out and onto the floor. He scooped it up and quickly stuffed it back in, checking to see if Kali had noticed.

Kali smirked, focusing on the next problem. "Was wondering where that was," she breathed.

"Where what was?" Wendy said, returning with paper plates, napkins, and a bottle of water.

Kenny held his breath, eyes flaring at Kali.

"My other textbook," Kali said, her smirk widening as she packed up her books. "Thanks for the Coke. Gonna go finish in my room."

"Oh, okay. Sure, no problem. And, um, I know you have Mrs. Putman this year, so if you ever have problems with the homework, I can—"

"Who said I was having problems?" Kali snapped.

"I didn't . . . I mean . . . I wasn't . . ."

"She was just trying to help, Kali," Kenny snarled, shooting her a warning glare.

Kali raised an eyebrow and swung her book bag over her shoulder, heading down the hall. "Yeah. Thanks, but I'm good."

Wendy flopped into her seat with a pout. "Your sister hates me."

Kenny chuckled and grabbed a slice of pizza.

"She hates everybody," he said, shrugging it off. "Come on, ain't you got some homework?"

The word *homework* always distracted her, a trick he'd learned early on and he watched her pore over an English assignment like a stressed-out freshman while he pretended to read. Almost everyone considered the last few weeks of school a complete farce. But despite being an AP senior, placed in her first-choice school with only a few weeks left to go, Wendy insisted on finishing with honors. Ever the perfectionist, she turned in each assignment like her life depended on it. He found it hilarious. Whenever he thought of their relationship, he considered them more best friends with benefits than girlfriend, boyfriend. And he liked it that way, feelings never overly complicated or perfunctory. But as graduation neared, he wondered what would happen when distance made them take stock of their similarities. Or really, their differences.

"Did you watch that media-training video I sent?" Wendy asked without glancing up from her notebook. "You know you're going to be talking to a lot more reporters in the fall. Maybe even on ESPN."

He sighed, wishing for at least one football-free conversation between them, and let his hand slide up her thigh. She froze, face turning scarlet.

"Stop," she squeaked, her mouth forming a half smirk.

"Stop what?"

"Stop trying to distract me."

He grinned and kissed her neck. "Oh, so you can be distracted?"

She giggled, trying to push him away but with very little effort.

The front door clicked open, and they straightened back into their seats. Kenny glanced up from his textbook, expecting his mother but instead swallowed his disappointment.

"Hi, Mr. Scott," Wendy said like an eager puppy. Kenny hated the way she sucked up to him.

"Hello, Wendy. Nice to see you." Mr. Scott took his time up the steps, dropping his briefcase by the bench. "Kenny."

"Hey, Dad."

Their mutually icy greeting frosted the room.

"We got some pizza if you're hungry," Wendy offered.

Kenny tensed as Mr. Scott sauntered over. He lifted the lid with a raised eyebrow.

"Hm. Pizza. Pepperoni. With a soda, no less." He looked at Kenny, waiting for an explanation.

"I just had two slices."

"Remember what the dietitian said. Less carbs, more

protein. You should be focusing on building five pounds of muscle before heading to camp."

"I just had two slices," Kenny said again. Harder.

Wendy glanced between them and sprang into action. "It's my fault. We worked out after school, and I was just starving. I begged him to take me."

"It's not about just two slices," Mr. Scott continued as if Wendy had said nothing. "It's about making sure your head's in the game!"

Kenny held his breath to keep from screaming. He had heard the phrase all his life. All he did was think of the game.

"I'm carb-loading," Kenny grumbled, eyes still down, slapping his book closed. It was a bullshit lie, and they both knew it.

"Well," Mr. Scott said, taking off his glasses to clean them. "You better add another mile to your run this evening."

Kenny opened his mouth to protest but Kali's scream filled the air first.

"Yooooo!"

"Kali? What's wrong?"

Kali stormed into the dining room, phone in hand. "Did you know about this?"

She shoved the phone in Kenny's face, Wendy jumping up to look over his shoulder. Five seconds in, she gasped in horror.

Kenny peered down at a shaky video of a familiar classroom. The camera shifted, the frame filling with nothing but hair and voices . . . Mrs. Morgan going over the day's lesson, then hysterical laughter. He didn't understand the big deal until he saw the first pencil fly, landing in Maddy Washington's hair.

"Where did you find this?" Wendy asked in a shrieking plea.

Kali sucked her teeth. "Everywhere!"

FOX 5 GEORGIA
School under Fire after Video Showing Students Throwing Pencils in Black Girl's Hair

Cell phone footage depicts a white student throwing pencils into a Black girl's hair as other classmates laugh. It happened in the Springville School District this past Thursday. The video was first posted on Twitter, then on Facebook. Since then, there have been more than a million views. Parents were sent a note to reassure them that the incident was under investigation but weren't given any more details on the matter.

FOX 5 reached out to district administrators, who declined to comment but sent a statement: "The privacy of students is of the utmost importance. We will not discuss those involved or how the school will handle the situation."

But parents in neighboring communities believe that no disciplinary actions will take place and that the issue will be swept under the rug. One parent, Rhonda Richburg, had some choice words.

"In a town that still holds segregated proms, I'm not surprised one bit they bullied that girl."

FOUR

MADDY DID IT
EPISODE 2, CONT.

Tanya: So explain this whole prom situation to me. Because I just can't fathom it.

Michael: Okay, so it's like this. Up until that year, seniors at Springville High hosted segregated proms, known as the "white prom" and the "Black prom." The Black prom was really for all POC and LGBTQIA+ students.

Tanya: I thought segregation in America ended in the sixties.

Michael: Technically, yes.

Tanya: Then how was this even legal?

Michael: Well, since their prom wasn't a school-sanctioned event, and was held privately off campus within the respective communities, it technically didn't fall under federal or state purview.

Tanya: Ahhhh, Americans and their loopholes.

Michael: Springville High hadn't hosted a prom since 1964, one year before the school integrated. Over the years, parents and students chose to uphold the tradition. The white prom was held at the Springville Country Club, which used to be an old train station made of all this French marble and stained-glass windows. The Black prom was held at the Barn, a renovated old farmhouse typically used for community plays or church concerts. And you're never going to believe this. The proms were within walking distance of one another, about the length of a football field. There were times when some of the white students, after they were done with their prom, would sneak over to the Black prom because they quote "had the better music."

Tanya: Could Black kids go to the white prom?

Michael: Of course not. They wouldn't even be allowed through the gates.

Tanya: And they weren't the least bit . . . mortified that people would see them doing something so blatantly racist in the twenty-first century?

Michael: They were a small southern town. Until that video surfaced and put a spotlight on their school, no one would've known. Sad part is, they weren't the only town hosting segregated proms, and the tradition still goes on to this very day.

May 7, 2014
FIFTH PERIOD. Lunch.

Wendy took several sips of ginger ale to ease her stomach. Nerves, she told herself. Just nerves. But it felt more like guilt as the day went on. She chipped at the skin of an orange, the only food she found appealing as gossip swarmed around her.

The video was all over the news and all anyone could talk about. It didn't show faces, not even Maddy's, but everyone knew who'd thrown the pencils just from the audio alone. The sound of her and her friends heckling and humiliating a sobbing girl made Wendy feel like a monster. Strange that the video seemed to cut right before the earthquake hit.

Wendy glanced around the cafeteria of Springville High, catching eyes flicking to their table, where she and her heckling friends ate, the mood somber.

Were we really that bad? she thought, eyes on her orange.

Kenny rubbed her back. "You okay?"

She plastered on a fake smile. "Yeah."

He nodded, unconvinced. "Wanna watch a movie later?"

She slouched. "Ugh. Can't. Got prom committee tonight. Less than a month to go, and we still haven't decided on the menu."

He stilled. "Oh. Uh, okay. I . . . um, forgot something in my locker. Meet after school?"

Wendy nodded and watched him try to smoothly run out of the caf with a sigh.

Wendy and Kenny tried not to talk about prom. It meant discussing their differences, and they'd long ago perfected avoiding such heavy topics. They'd decided since they couldn't go to each other's proms that they wouldn't go at all. Instead, they would dress up, eat a fancy dinner, and meet their friends at the after-prom party in Greenville. But Wendy had still volunteered for prom committee. She liked the planning, organizing, and decorating. She was good at it. It made her the ideal class president, cheer cocaptain, as well as homecoming committee chair. And she always volunteered to throw Jules the best surprise birthday parties.

"Well, I love the club's strawberry cheesecake," Jules said from across the table. "Daddy always brings me back a slice after a golf game. They even made me—"

"Ugh! No," Charlotte moaned, head down in her phone.

"What?" Jules snapped.

"Another article. This time on CNN. Ugh, this is, like, so embarrassing."

"Must be a slow news week," Jules said, rolling her eyes. "They're totally milking this. What I really want to know is who's the asshole who filmed us? That's so not cool."

Charlotte moaned again. "I don't want to be known for being *that* girl who went to *that* school and bullied *that* Black girl!"

"No one bullied her!" Jules barked. "Yeah, we threw some shit at her, but so what? Happens every day in the caf and nobody else goes crying over it. No one shoved her into a locker, made her drink piss, posted naked pics of her on Insta, or anything like that."

Wendy cocked her head to the side with a raised eyebrow.

"What, Wen?" Jules barked.

Wendy remained silent. It wasn't worth the fight.

"Oh no! Now they're talking about our proms," Charlotte whined.

Wendy's back straightened. "Why?"

Jules threw her a sharp "Don't play dumb. You know why."

Charlotte pouted. "But we're not the only school that has separate proms. Other schools do it too."

"Yeah, but it looks bad that we do after . . . well, you know," Kayleigh said, nervously glancing at Jules.

"Great! Now our school is totally going to be known for being racist! It's gonna follow us wherever we go!"

"Don't be so dramatic!" Jules snapped. "And who gives a shit what they think? We already got into college."

"But what if they rescind?" Charlotte cried, her voice peaking. "It happens, you know."

Wendy's stomach turned. Charlotte had a point. This black mark could stay with them through their collegiate careers. What if scholarship committees noticed? What if people brought it up when Kenny went pro?

"Oh God, what if cameras show up to prom and start filming us?" Charlotte cried. "We'll be all over social media, and everyone is gonna know. Is this about to ruin our lives? What'd we do? I can't go to prom now!"

Wendy's mouth dropped. Charlotte had been talking about prom since they were in middle school. She'd practically fainted during Chris Lively's promposal. So, if she of all people was reconsidering . . . then it must be really bad.

Were other kids going to bail out on prom? The very prom she was in the middle of planning?

"Would you relax?" Jules chuckled, wrapping her hair into a messy bun. "I'm telling you, they'll forget about this in two weeks."

"Not with all the attention those Black Lives Black Pride protests are getting over in Greenville," Wendy countered, her brow furrowed. "Those protests have been popping up all over the country."

"Why?" Charlotte asked.

Jules waved it off. "Something about some kid getting killed for doing something he wasn't supposed to be doing in the first place."

"So what do we do?" Kayleigh asked.

Wendy felt the familiar pressure calling her to action. She was good in a crisis, good at fixing things. Wasn't she the one who got Jules out of that whole beer-in-the-locker-room fiasco? And when Jason banged up his dad's new truck, hadn't she found the perfect mechanic to fix it before he came home? Wendy had to do something. She couldn't let the end of their senior year be marred by scandal.

I could fix this, she thought, tapping her chin, then snapped her fingers. "A distraction! We just need to give them something else to focus on."

"We can upload that video of Jason and Kayleigh hooking

up on V-day," Jules said with a chuckle. Kayleigh threw a fry at her.

"No. That's the total opposite of what we need," Wendy said. "We need something that'll bring out our best! To show that we're good people and that we all get along just fine around here."

"Like volunteering at a soup kitchen?" Kayleigh offered.

"She means get along with Black people," Charlotte said. "Not get along with the homeless."

Wendy glanced across the room at the table where most of the Black kids sat. *They must think we're a bunch of assholes. Wonder if Kenny ever wanted to hang out with them. Does he talk to them when I'm not around? They probably sit at parties trashing us . . .*

That's when the idea hit her. "What about . . . instead of two proms, we combine them?"

The group stared at her in silence.

"Combine proms?" Charlotte uttered in disbelief.

Adrenaline rushed through Wendy's veins. "Yes! Like have one big giant prom that everyone could go to, all at the same place."

"OMG! That would be amazing!" Kayleigh squeaked, clapping her hands.

Jules scoffed. "You're joking, right? Tell me you're joking."

"No, don't you get it? It'll show that we're all really friends here. That we're not racist or anything like that."

"Of course we're not racist," Jules snapped. "We have Black

friends. You have a Black boyfriend. We don't need to have one prom to prove that!"

"But we could invite the press to cover it." Wendy beamed. "To really show the world that everything is fine here!"

"Are you insane? There's no way anybody would go for that!"

"Actually, I think that's a good idea."

They all turned to the unfamiliar voice. Regina Ray stood behind them, her braids in a tight bun, with a near-empty tray, clearly on her way to the trash.

"Excuse me," Jules sassed. "Uh, I don't think we were talking to you."

Regina rolled her eyes. "You weren't. But you were talking about combining proms. And since I'm chair of *our* prom, I'm in the position to bring this proposal to the table."

"What's in it for you?" Charlotte asked, skeptical.

She laughed. "A chance for our school to not look ridiculous and maybe shame some of your white-trash kinfolk along the way. Besides, more people at prom means more ticket money for prom means a better prom."

"Money," Jules scoffed. "Of course."

Regina cocked her head to the side, eyes narrowing, and Wendy quickly stood up to face her. "Do you think everyone will go for it?"

Regina shrugged. "Don't see why not. None of us are down with looking like we stuck in the 1950s."

Wendy squealed with delight, the plan was perfect. It would

clean up the school's image, paint her a saint for thinking of the idea (which would look great on a résumé), and they'd have so much good press that people would forget all about the whole Maddy business.

And the best part of all . . . she'd be able to go to the prom with Kenny. A dream come true.

Kayleigh joined, gushing over the possibilities. Charlotte sat baffled by the prospect as Jules jumped to her feet.

"Hold on!" she shouted, bringing the cafeteria to a standstill. "Y'all can't just make these types of decisions by y'all's selves. It's everyone's prom, not just yours!"

"Okay, fine, then," Regina countered. "Let's vote on it. Graduating seniors only. We either have an all-together prom or do the usual."

All together, Wendy mused. She liked the sound of that.

Jules grabbed Wendy's arm, pulling her away. "This is crazy! No one is gonna go for it."

Wendy looked at the Black kids' table, Regina already there, spreading the word, and held her best friend's hand.

"We gotta try, Jules."

Kenny stuffed his face full of potato salad while he listened to his mother recount her run-in with a guy who broke his collarbone driving a four-wheeler. Kenny could eat an entire tray of his mother's baked ziti, barbecue chicken, and greens and would still ask for seconds. The moment he walked through the door and smelled her cornbread, his mouth watered.

"Slow down, baby," Mrs. Scott said with a chuckle.

"Bruh, no one's gonna steal your plate," Kali laughed.

He looked up, appreciating the familiar scene: his parents at the heads of the table, Kali sitting across from him, cups full of ice water, and platters of delicious food in the center. There would only be a few more nights like this, with just the four of them, before he left for training camp midsummer. Everything in his life was about to change at warp speed, and as much as they had prepared for the moment, he found himself wanting time to slow down, to sit longer in his seat.

The Scotts had moved from the East Side to their West Side home right before he'd entered middle school. Their new neighbors weren't excited to see them. But once Kenny started showing real promise, Christmas party invitations began flooding in, his father welcomed to the country club for eighteen holes, and his mother a beloved member of the women's book club. Mrs. Scott often bragged that her baby was going to buy her a new house once he went pro. Kenny couldn't imagine a Thanksgiving anywhere but in the home he'd grown to love.

"Didn't you eat lunch today?" Mr. Scott asked, regarding his son's plate with a low level of disgust.

"Yes, sir," he mumbled. But that was hours ago, before his father added on a practice session with a personal trainer who'd made him run suicide drills on the field. He had worked up a mighty appetite since.

"Better schedule another visit with that nutritionist," Mr. Scott chided. "Now's not the time to start slacking off. And after dinner, I have some new tapes for us to review. Auburn. A scout friend of mine sent them over."

Kenny held in a groan. Despite being a five-star recruit and committing to Alabama, his father tried to hold some sense of control over Kenny's athletic career. Yes, his relentless determination to the game had brought them far, even Kenny had to admit that. But it felt as if they were still preparing for a finish line that they'd already crossed, and for once he would have liked a break.

Across from him, Kali's eyes ping-ponged between them. "Well, Daddy, are you going to ask me about my day?"

Mr. Scott frowned at her, momentarily confused, as if he'd forgotten she was there. "Oh. Uh, yes. How was your day?"

"Great," she said, a bit too cheery. "The school approved the Black Student Union's Poetry Night. We're going to hold it in the library, and some parents are donating refreshments."

Mr. Scott's mouth formed a tight line. "Well. Sorry I won't be able to make it."

She scoffed. "I didn't even tell you what day it is."

A heavy silence filled the room, and Kenny's bottomless stomach quickly shut closed. He glanced at his mother's crestfallen face, torn about how to intervene. Kali knew their father hated the Black Student Union, furious she'd started it to begin with. But she seemed to enjoy recklessly pushing his limits. As long as she proved her point—no matter how well intentioned or politically correct—she didn't care who was hurt in the line of fire. It made Kenny both annoyed and envious of her defiance.

"So, um, Mama, you think we can have barbecue for graduation? Maybe invite family from the East?" Kenny asked, breaking off a piece of cornbread.

"That sounds like a great idea," Mrs. Scott said.

"Now, we gotta be careful who we invite. Especially around here," Mr. Scott warned. "Folks don't know how to act. And everyone's gonna want a piece of you."

Kali pursed her lips with an eye roll then grinned. "So. Kenny," she started, practically singing. "How are you gonna vote?"

Mr. Scott lowered his fork, his eyebrows pinched. "Vote for what?"

"Prom," Kali said, still staring at Kenny.

Mr. Scott turned to him. "You're not getting mixed up in all that mess, are you?"

Kenny shot Kali a stony stare, pissed that she would bring up what the entire town was gossiping over. As if their father needed another reason to give him a lecture about keeping his head in the game.

"Well, I don't think it's such a bad idea," Mrs. Scott said. "Prom been like that since we were kids. About time they switch it up."

Mr. Scott shook his head. "Makes no sense, coming with all these changes late in the year like this."

Mrs. Scott raised an eyebrow at him. "It ain't never too late to do the right thing."

Kenny tensed, smashing a slice of cornbread with his fork.

"Don't see why I gotta vote," Kenny mumbled. "Ain't like I'm going to prom."

Kali snickered. "You tell Wendy that?"

He hesitated, his eyes flickering down to his near-empty plate, hands rolling into fists under the table. Wendy hadn't said one word to him about prom, hadn't even brought up the insane idea that had thrown everyone into the fryer. Per usual, she just went forward full-throttle without running anything by him. If he voted, no matter how anonymous they insisted the vote would be, someone would find out, and it would be a blatant choice of sides. Voting for a combined prom would be a betrayal to his friends—friends who could really do some screwed-up shit, but still his friends. Voting to keep it the same would be a betrayal to his kind—a kind he barely acknowledged but couldn't deny. Damned if you do, damned if you don't.

And in the middle of it all was Maddy Washington. He wondered what she thought of the aftermath of her hair video, how it had divided the entire town. He'd watched her once in AP Chemistry. Not checking her out, just curious about Jules's daily punching bag. The way she picked at her nails, clawed at her hair, fidgeted in her musty sweater. If he had known she was Black . . . would he have done anything different?

"You're right, son," Mr. Scott said with an approving nod. "What they do with prom has nothing to do with you. What'd I always tell you?"

Kenny sighed. "Be silent but deadly."

"That's right. You lay low, keep quiet, mind your own business, and be so good they can't ignore you. That's how you win the game."

MADDY DID IT
EPISODE 3
"The Good Old Days"

Michael: Alright. Take a look at this clip one of our associate producers found. It's a segment from the local news channel, featuring none other than Thomas Washington.

Tanya: Well, there's definitely a resemblance! Those eyes . . .

Michael: Get this—he had the first-ever issue of *The Incredible Hulk* comic from 1962, in mint condition, that sold for almost two hundred thousand dollars at auction.

Tanya: Wow, quite a bit of money, isn't it?

Michael: Indeed! That's how he was able to buy his antique shop on Main Street and named it—wait for it—the Good Old Days. And it actually was quite a hit. People from all over the south came to trade memorabilia. Western-themed tin lunch boxes, retro furniture, vintage radios, old

Coca-Cola posters . . . you name it, he had it. According to locals, Maddy worked there every Wednesday, and some weekends, starting in middle school, when the state no longer allowed her to homeschool. But until that point, no one had ever seen her. Here, read what Portman wrote about Mr. Washington in his book.

Tanya: *clears throat* "Thomas Ralph Washington was the youngest son of Reverend John and Reba Washington. Reverend Washington was from a long line of godly servants. He ran a tight ship with an iron fist. A woman's place was in the kitchen, and his three boys were responsible for maintaining the home. He founded First Evangelical, a protestant church with a small congregation of no more than fifty on their best day. But he always believed the Lord would provide.

"Thomas was a late baby for the Washingtons, leaving him eighteen years younger than his siblings. Once his brothers left the nest, they were never heard from again.

"In school, Thomas had an affinity for world history and, like his baby-boomer mother, he was obsessed with the golden age of America. That 1950s post-war era when girls wore poodle skirts, boys had James Dean haircuts, records played Elvis, and everyone gathered to watch *The Dick Van Dyke Show*. He wanted to live in an idyllic Norman Rockwell painting. With his pocket protectors, high-waist pants, and thick glasses, he was an easy target for bullies. While most teens his age wanted a Mustang, he drove around in a 1960s Oldsmobile. By his senior year, he began tracking down collector's items, traveling as far as Texas for yard sales and antique shows. He transformed the family's bomb shelter into his own museum, where he could hide away from his abusive father, drinking Coke out of glass bottles and flipping through old *Archie* comics.

"When Reverend Washington died of alcohol poisoning, Thomas tried to take over the family business, but tithes and congregation membership were nearly nonexistent. They were forced to move their worship to the living room and became a church of two. His mother, completely dependent on her son, left no space for him to find a wife of his own.

"According to medical records, Reba was diagnosed with stage 4 lung cancer at eighty-one and had less than six months to live. Since she refused to be put in a home, Thomas hired a live-in nurse while he worked at the local grocery to pay the rising medical costs. After her sparsely attended funeral, the town assumed that Thomas, so distraught by his mother's death, became a recluse in his family's crumbling home on the West Side border.

"Ten months later, Thomas walked into Dr. Paul Foreman's pediatric office with a six-week-old baby girl named Madison Abigail, and little explanation. Dr. Foreman wouldn't examine the girl again for another twelve years. The mother's name was left blank on most records, and after the town burned, no one could locate a single copy of Maddy's original birth certificate.

"There is no available information on Reba's family history, but many believed she was from the New England area and met her southern husband at seminary school."

May 8, 2014

The Good Old Days had a smell that Maddy could never find the right word for. A combination of dank musk and decay, mixed with the lingering presence of lives that each item in the store had once touched. Filled to the ceiling with relics and coveted collectibles, the shop had little room for anyone to walk through, leaving the space dark and looming, like the inside of a wasp hive. Dust peppered the air at the slightest movement, and Maddy sneezed often. Papa worked in a tiny back office, returning phone calls from interested buyers and posting items on eBay, a necessary evil that just kept them afloat since no one from Springville ever shopped in their store. The previous week, he had made $1,500 selling a 1956 Coke wall clock.

The Good Old Days sat diagonal from Sal's Pizzeria, and on the days Maddy worked the register, she watched kids pour in and out of the restaurant for hours on end. Kids from school. Hanging out, laughing, joking, kissing . . .

Being normal.

Papa condemned the place. "A cesspool. And those girls,

refusing to protect their modesty. Have they no decency?"

One of Maddy's favorite movies, *Roman Holiday*, starred Audrey Hepburn as a princess who sneaks away from her security detail just to have one day off in Rome, where she meets a reporter who offers to show her around. She goes where she wants, eats what she wants, dances, drives a Vespa, even cuts her hair short. And she does it all without her father breathing down her neck. Maddy would give anything to escape, anything to have one normal day.

Watching her classmates live the life she wished for through a foggy glass door—so close she could hear the laughter and smell the baking dough—felt torturous. Just once, she'd like to put on blue jeans and sneakers, walk across the street into Sal's, and order a slice with a large Coke. She'd imagined the exact scenario so many times that she'd often felt a heated rush surging, pushing her aching hand forward to grab the doorknob and pull. But she always stopped herself. The kids would never accept her, especially now that they knew the truth. She was doomed to live in purgatory behind the counter until she was old and gray. She had taken the SATs (in secret, of course) but college wasn't in her future. Papa would never let her go, even if he did have the money.

Maybe now . . . I can apply for minority scholarships.

The thought made her tense. Was she really a minority? She'd never considered it. Never thought of anything other than being white. What would her mother have called her, if she was still alive? Would she have made her hide like Papa had? Would she have agreed with his tactics? She probably wouldn't have had a choice, just like her, but at least they would've had each other in the fray.

Maddy looked into the gold oval mirror that hung by the register, selling for thirty-five dollars, her reflection dulled by speckles of rust.

I am Black, she thought, trying out the unnatural words, seeing how they fit, testing their durability against doubt. Would anyone believe her? Didn't matter. She would never need to say it. Papa acted like the incident at school hadn't happened, and so would she.

I'm white, she thought, but the lie sat crooked on her skin.

Maddy shook the thought away and tried to busy herself with work. She had just finished writing a shipping label for the 1950s classic pay phone being sent to Philadelphia when she noticed that the address Papa had given her differed from what was in the email. It was missing an apartment number.

He'll blame me, she thought, feeling the rising panic, and scrambled to find something to correct it with. She stretched across the counter for a pen just out of her reach . . .

And the pen wiggled and rolled toward her fingertips.

Maddy gasped, reeling back into her stool, clutching her extended hand as if it had been burned. The pen sat in the middle of the red countertop, unmoving. There were no open windows, no drafts. Yet it had moved. She'd seen it with her own eyes.

She spun around, expecting to find Papa. But he was still on the phone, not to be disturbed.

Maddy tried steadying her breathing, her heart beating too fast for her small frame, the pen still where she'd left it. Or where it had left itself.

The pen had moved on its own. No strings. No magic tricks. It had moved toward her at the very moment she wanted it.

She wanted it. Had she moved the pen? Was it possible?

Quickly, she placed the pen back and straightened in her stool. If it happened again, she would know she had something to do with it. If not, then the shop had a ghost. Hand up, fingers splayed, she focused on the pen and took a deep breath.

"Move," she whispered.

The pen sat motionless. Maddy licked her lips, wringing out her jittery fingers.

"Move," she whispered again, brows pinched.

"Madison," Papa called. "Did you finish that order yet?"

Maddy hesitated. She didn't want to end her experiment; she needed to know.

Come on! her thoughts shouted at the pen.

The pen gave a slight jiggle. Maddy brightened at the sight, an invigorating, delicious wave of adrenaline coming over her. She, Maddy, the girl who everyone swore was nothing, was doing the unthinkable, the unimaginable . . . until she heard a door open down the hall.

"Madison?"

Come here!

The pen shook, but the mahogany dining table with the $150 price tag lurched across the room, its feet dragging. It kicked up dust, knocking over chairs and a baseball card display before stopping just shy of the counter. Maddy yelped, covering her mouth with both hands.

"Madison!" Papa shouted.

He can't know.

She leaped out of her seat, picked up the two chairs and stood near the table.

Papa rushed into the showroom, frantic eyes scanning the floor.

"What happened? What was that noise?"

"Nothing, Papa," she squeaked, hands behind her back. "I . . . bumped into the desk."

He scanned the room once more, landing on the spot the table typically lived, then shifted to where it now sat.

Papa shot her a sharp glare. He knew she was lying. She could feel his doubt swimming around them. But he didn't know about what or why.

"Clean up this mess," he hissed, storming back into his office.

Maddy touched the table and grinned.

May 9, 2014

It was the day of the prom vote. Early that morning, Wendy had set up two large boxes in the senior hallway, and during homeroom announcements, urged her classmates to fill out their ballots.

Kenny listened to his girlfriend's voice over the loudspeaker, swallowing a silent, bitter pill. He had no interest in going to prom. Couldn't care less. He wanted to cruise-control through the last few weeks of school. Instead, the prom vote disturbed the very ecosystem of Springville High, the one they all were accustomed to, poking at unwritten rules and unsaid understandings between the Black and white students. Heated debates in the caf replaced chatter about hookups, parties, and social media posts.

And his damn girlfriend was leading the charge.

Why did she feel the need to say or do anything at all? Was she doing it on his account? Didn't she know it was the last thing he'd want? The vote was about to cast a bright spotlight on him, and the thought made that bitter pill slogging down his throat unbearable.

Kenny had perfected the art of remaining impartial, though some would call it acute obliviousness. In history class, he ignored the nervous glances during the slavery unit. When a Black kid was murdered for wearing a hoodie, he stopped wearing one. When BLBP protests broke out all over the country, he pretended the news coverage didn't exist, convincing Jason to have a party at his place instead. He ignored every ignorant comment and causal drop of the N-word. After all, it was in all the songs they loved. He almost managed to make his friends completely forget he was Black. Now, there had never been a bigger elephant in the room.

And as Mrs. Morgan finished attendance, with the pot ready to boil over, Jason stewed at his desk, taking it upon himself to address his homeroom class.

"Look, no offense," Jason started, angling himself away from Kenny. "But I don't see a reason to combine proms. Springville has been doing this for years. Why change it now?"

Students murmured agreement with one another, Jason saying what everyone was already thinking. Kenny scribbled nonsense in his notebook as if he hadn't heard him at all.

Mrs. Morgan tapped her pencil, watching the class's reaction. "Well, I think combining proms is a start toward restorative justice, community healing, and unity against an archaic practice," she offered.

Jason shook his head. "Prom's not supposed to be about all that. Prom is about tradition! Our parents, even our grandparents, they all had separate proms. You just don't get it because you're not from here."

"Well, your 'tradition' is rooted in segregation, the very foundation of the systemic racism that has oppressed people of color in this country for centuries."

Jason shook his head. "You're making this about race, and it ain't about that!"

"You call your proms 'the Black prom' and 'the white prom,'" Mrs. Morgan shot back. "That sounds a lot like race to me."

"You're just trying to push some liberal agenda on us. Crying foul whenever something doesn't go your way."

She smirked. "I'm merely stating historical facts."

Jason's face turned into a beet as he glanced around for support. "Well, just because I don't want to combine proms doesn't make me a racist."

"I didn't say you were," she said. "I said the traditions that you're trying to uphold are rooted in racism."

"So wait a minute," Ali Kruger started. "If we combine proms, does that mean we have to have it at a barn?"

"It's not a barn," groaned Jada Lewis, one of the Black prom committee members. "It was renovated years ago. It even has a chandelier!"

"Well, why don't we just have prom at the country club instead?" Ali offered.

"Because the country club said they can't handle a prom with the entire senior class," Jason said.

Ali frowned. "But Laura Todd's sister had a wedding with over two hundred people there."

Jada pinched the bridge of her nose as if frustrated with having to state the obvious.

"They *can* handle it. They don't want to because they don't want Black people in their bougie-ass club."

Kenny glanced at the clock. One minute before the bell would ring, but he was ready to bolt through the door, anxious to be anywhere in the world except in his seat.

"They said they can't handle the numbers," Jason snapped.

Jada pursed her lips. "Cannot and *will* not are two separate things!"

"But we have dances together all the time," Jason carried on. "Spring Fling, homecoming, Sadie Hawkins . . . Why can't we leave this one tradition alone?"

"'Cause it's a stupid tradition!" Jada popped. "You know how ass-backwards we look?"

Ali crossed her arms. "If you want to have your prom in the farmhouse, fine, but the rest of us shouldn't be forced to."

"And I don't even see color," Jason shouted, still wounded by the earlier implication. "You don't think I wanna party with my brother Kenny? Of course I do! But it's about tradition! He understands. Why can't the rest of you people get it?"

Kenny stilled as the bus rolled over him. The words *you people* had a bite that broke through the dam. Because after all those years, he didn't understand why his best friend wanted to hold on to a tradition that meant they couldn't party together, that separated them, when they were supposed to be, like he said, brothers. Which made him question, for the first time, whether they were ever brothers at all.

Kenny eyed Jason, his tone deadly. "What do you *think* I get?"

Stunned, Jason opened his mouth, but Jada's laugh distracted him.

"Why you asking him?" she snorted. "He don't give a shit about us, no way."

Kenny gripped his seat, avoiding Jada's sharp gaze. Mrs. Morgan cocked her head to the side as if something had clicked to her.

"You guys, this is silly," Debbie Locke said, trying to keep the peace. "Jada's right. This whole separate but equal thing is making us look like some backward-ass hicks. When we're in the real world, it won't be like this! So shouldn't we all just . . . get along?"

At that, Jason detonated, sealing everyone's fate in a final blow. "Look, it doesn't matter what that stupid vote says! My dad already talked to the country club. He put a down payment for those of us who still want to have prom the regular way. The rest of you can do what you want! You want to party on a farm like some animals, then good fucking luck!"

Maddy dunked the licked-clean dishes in a sink full of soapy water.

"Did you like supper, Papa?"

"It was fine," he grunted, stomping off to the living room.

That night, she had made a rack of lamb with glazed carrots and steamed cabbage, a recipe out of her favorite 1969 Betty Crocker cookbook. Over the years, she had tried different dishes and desserts from the book, never straying far from the instructions yet still adding her own personal touches. She needed something complicated to take her mind off what had happened at the store until she was ready to face it. Fear mixed with curiosity sat ready to devour her whole. But the kitchen made her happy, and her father loved her cooking—the only thing about her that he did love. She glanced at the minuscule leftovers on the stove, after he'd gone back for thirds.

"It was fine," she mimicked under her breath.

No matter what she did, she could never escape being her father's greatest mistake. A mistake carved in her features, painted on her skin, knitted in her hair. She would never be good enough or white enough. For him. For the kids at school. For the women in the photos plastered on her closet walls. She hated them. All of them. Why couldn't she be like them? Why, why, why?

Her elbow slipped, knocking a glass over, and in her panic, she reached for it.

The glass stopped inches from the vinyl floor and shot back into her hand.

Maddy froze, her mouth gaping, soapsuds dripping off her arms. The checkered floor twirled like a kaleidoscope. She glanced at the kitchen door, expecting Papa to be standing there, catching her in the act. But Papa was still in the living room, watching *Father Knows Best*.

She swallowed hard, turned off the water, and hung up her apron.

Papa's magnifying glass sat on the tip of his nose as he tinkered with the cuckoo clock, eyes bouncing to the TV screen.

It took all she could muster to remain calm. "I'm . . . gonna go to bed early."

Papa sipped his milk without glancing up. "Don't forget to say your prayers."

"Yes, Papa," she squeaked, and raced up the stairs.

Her attic bedroom had dark wooden floors, a steepled ceiling that creaked whenever the wind picked up, and peeling beige wallpaper with tiny red rosebuds. The one narrow window let in just enough light to make it not feel like a coffin.

Alone with her thoughts, her heart hammered. She sat at her vanity, trying to put the pieces together. Or at least the pieces she could wrap her mind around. In the deepest parts of her, she had always known that something dark lay inside her, feral and dangerous. Something feverish and desperate to show itself.

She could move things with her mind. But . . . how?

Maddy couldn't tell Papa. She knew how he would react—throw her out of the house for being in bed with the devil, for being a witch. Her gut told her she wasn't any of those things, but it would take a miracle to convince him of that. Besides, she liked having something just to herself, something life changing, her own little secret. A gift from God, maybe. He had seen her struggle—with Papa and the kids at school—and decided to bestow upon her a great mercy, a gift to help protect herself. If only she really knew how to use it.

But God makes no mistakes.

Maddy picked up her silver paddle brush. Forty strokes every night kept the naps away, Papa always said. She counted, pretending not to notice the eyes boring down at her, watching. Plastered around the oval mirror were pictures of Audrey Hepburn, Marilyn Monroe, Grace Kelly, Jane Fonda, the girls from *The Brady Bunch*, Shirley Temple, Jacqueline Kennedy . . . image after image of all the women she would never be. They all gawked, laughing and taunting in their silence, judgment sewn into their polished smiles. Papa liked to add new photos to his work of art. He often stepped back, admiring the women as if they were cut from the sun. But not her, never ever her!

Maddy's eye twitched, and the brush slipped out of her hand. Frustrated, she bent to grab it.

The vanity jerked and skated across the floor, crashing into the far wall.

For a silent minute, she couldn't move.

"Madison?" Papa called from downstairs. "What was that noise?"

Maddy wobbled back against the bed, gripping the aging quilt.

"Uh . . . nothing, Papa."

She knew better than to lie, and it wouldn't be long before Papa would come up to check. She had to put it back.

You could move it, she thought, *just like the table in the store*.

Maddy bit her lip, the idea terrifying but no more terrifying than her father finding her room out of order. He liked everything to be in its place, neat and tidy. Even a chair not pushed under the table would land her in the closet. She rolled her shoulders back with a deep breath. Wiggling her fingers, she focused on the vanity.

Move, she thought. Nothing.

Bearing down, she pushed her brain to concentrate. Her muscles hummed. She could feel every single item in the attic. From the bed to the hangers in her closet, invisible threads tugged softly at her skin. She focused on the vanity, and it felt no heavier than a paperweight. Her eyes narrowed.

Move.

The vanity shook, then lifted off the floor.

A thrill coursed through her veins. She flicked her fingers, and it glided through the air, landing back in its original spot. She gasped, her smile giddy.

Maddy spun around, gleeful. What else could she move? The lamp, her books, the nightstand? She glanced down at her bed.

Could she really?

She climbed in the middle of the bed and felt for the threads that had tugged at her before.

Move.

The bed lifted off the floor with a creak, slowly rising. The bed was heavier than the vanity, forcing her to concentrate harder. Hands trembling, she wasn't sure how high she'd risen until the top of her head hit the ceiling. Something dropped, slapping the floor, and she peered down. An unfamiliar leather journal wrapped in cord lay under the bed.

What's that?

"Madison?" Papa's footsteps hit the stairs.

Maddy blinked hard, losing focus. The bed dropped like a stack of bricks back down to the floor.

"Madison!" he shouted, his step moving faster.

Maddy hopped off the bed and grabbed the journal. She stuffed it under her pillow just as he opened the door.

"What's going on?" he barked, scanning the room.

Maddy, kneeling by her bed, hands clasped in prayer, glanced up. "Nothing, Papa."

"What was that noise?"

"I dropped my Bible . . . and it knocked over a glass of water. I cleaned it up."

Papa stood in the doorway, eyes narrowed, inspecting the room for five long silent seconds. He gripped the frame and shut off the light, leaving only the bedside lamp on.

"Go to sleep. I don't want to hear another sound."

"Yes, Papa. Just finishing my prayers."

He nodded and slammed the door. Maddy grabbed the notebook. The cord seemed shriveled and stiff. It must have been tied to the slats under the bed, she thought. She unraveled it and flipped the book open. The pages were weatherworn, crinkled as if they'd been wet, then dried on a radiator. She turned a page and read the first line:

You, my child, were created in a hurricane, leaving destruction in your wake. You, as they say, are a storm with skin. Death and rebirth will follow you everywhere. How can one man who knows nothing of the weight of blood tame you? For wherever you go, there you are.

Maddy stared at the elegant cursive handwriting, overwhelmed as the letters blended, and said a word she had never uttered until that very moment.

"Mama?"

PART

TWO

FIVE

MADDY DID IT
EPISODE 4
"Halloween in May"

Michael: Hey, man, why don't you introduce yourself to our
 listeners?

Rashad Young: Hey, what's up. My name is Rashad Young.

Michael: And you are?

Rashad: I'm the guy who recorded the pencils being thrown in
 Maddy's hair.

Tanya: Ah! The mystery man comes forward.

Rashad: Living around all them racist assholes, it wasn't safe
 for me to tell anybody. Especially after everything that
 happened. They would've pointed the finger at me and
 strung me up.

Michael: So what made you press record?

Rashad: Two weeks before everything went down, there was
 a shooting of an unarmed Black kid caught on video in

Greenville. BLBP organized a huge protest down to the mayor's office. The marshals came and tried to break it up, but it got ugly, and businesses started burning. Yeah, the cops got fired, but if they hadn't caught it on video, they would've got away with it. I guess I thought that I should start recording things that happened in Springville too. It's like, unless we had proof, people wouldn't believe the fucked-up shit we went through. I just didn't think I would catch something happening so soon.

Michael: Walk us through a little of the race relations in Springville.

Rashad: Man, we lived parallel lives, never intersecting unless it's school or sports. White kids hung out with white kids, Black kids with Black kids, except for the few who were stuck in the sunken place. Both of my sisters have natural hair, and they were always being made fun of a lot. So, when I saw it happening to Maddy . . . it was just . . . fucked up, you know? Jules and them, they were always a bunch of assholes. I know you ain't supposed to talk bad about the dead, but it's true.

Tanya: What I really want to know is what happened when you turned off the camera before the earthquake? And why did you turn it off?

Rashad: I didn't turn it off. Maddy did it.

Michael: Did what exactly?

Rashad: I was recording, and my phone just started spazzing out.

The screen went black right as the lights blew. And that shit was no earthquake. The ground didn't move at all. But just like prom, she, I guess . . . did it with her mind or something.

Michael: Do you remember what you did the rest of that day?

Rashad: I went home early. Man, I was crazy sick. Later, when I went to get a new phone, I saw the video had uploaded to my cloud. I had kinda forgot about it.

Michael: Were you also the one who posted the photos from Halloween in May?

Rashad: Nah. No one knows who did that. Most of us weren't even there.

May 16, 2014

Senior week at Springville High always landed three weeks before prom and was considered a going-away party for the outgoing class.

Monday—Pajama Day, in which Jules came in a satin nighty.

Tuesday—Switch Day, where the girls dressed in football jerseys and the boys wore field hockey skirts.

Wednesday—Pizza Day, during which Sal personally delivered dozens of pizzas to the caf.

Thursday—Karaoke Day. Jason rapped a Drake song.

Friday was the infamous Halloween in May pep rally, the only event the entire student body was allowed to attend, where seniors came in dressed in old costumes and competed for silly prizes like a coupon for water, or a kiss from a football captain.

Wendy wanted to be salt and pepper shakers for the couples category. Kenny had convinced her that eggs and bacon were a better fit. They lined up with the rest of the couples in the hall outside the gym, waiting to be called.

It wasn't an official pep rally for any specific sport, more of a rally to cheer seniors on toward the next phase in their lives. The moment felt bittersweet to Kenny. This would be the last time his school would root for him as a fellow student. Would he ever step into this gym again? Was there a reason to?

"Hey, have you guys seen Jules?" Charlotte asked, dressed as Little Red Riding Hood, Chris her Big Bad Wolf.

Wendy straightened her bacon tip, searching with a frown. "She said Brady was dropping off her costume. But she should be here by now."

"Do you know what she's going as?"

"No clue. But you know Jules. Probably trying to make an entrance." Wendy turned to Kenny, beaming. "How do I look?"

Kenny grinned, kissing the tip of her nose. "You're a cute piece of pork."

Wendy's smile took up half of her face. "And you look EGGceptional!"

After the junior varsity cheerleaders performed a farewell routine, each couple was called to the center of the gym and scored by applause from the audience in the bleachers. Kenny scanned the crowd for Kali, wishing she'd at least try to be more outgoing, for his sake. Looked like most of the Black students had cut the assembly. But at the far corner sat a fidgeting Maddy. A rare sighting, as she skipped almost anything that didn't have to do with class. Keeping her distance from the other students, she gripped her sweater, eyes darting to Coach Bates standing by the door, as if on guard. Kenny couldn't help noticing how desperate Maddy seemed to escape.

As the rally wrapped up, there was still no sign of Jules. Wendy kept searching behind them, growing concerned.

"Okay, everybody." Kayleigh, their emcee for the event, read off a folded scrap of paper passed to her. "Next up, and our last couple is . . . uh, Maddy Washington and her . . . daddy?"

"What?" Kenny uttered.

The gym spiraled into collective confusion before Maddy strutted through the double doors. An astonished audience gasped.

Except it wasn't Maddy. Instead, Jules strutted in with Brady, his arm wrapped around her thin waist. You wouldn't know it was Jules right away. Only because her face was covered in black paint.

Wendy spun around. "Oh my God!"

Jules wore a giant Afro wig, a yellow button-up shirt, and a pink poodle skirt. The sign hanging around her neck read, *Hello, my name is Maddy.* Brady wore tweed pants, a white button-up, and thick glasses with his blond hair parted to the side. They waved to the crowd, who responded with uneasy cackles and weak applause.

Kenny blinked slow as if he was seeing things, then instinctively searched for Maddy's face. He'd never thought of her much before, but Jules had crossed such a line that anyone with half of a heart would take pity. Or so he thought until the gym began to fill with laughter. Maddy shrank with a quivering lip, fumbling with her books before tripping down the bleachers and hightailing it out of the gym. Not a single teacher followed her. Most of them were too busy staring at Jules, dumbfounded by her audacity, some even holding in a snicker. Kenny's hands rolled into fists.

Not everyone was laughing. The Black kids scowled, their mouths in straight lines before they looked pointedly at Kenny, as if daring him to ignore what was right in front of him. Again.

Mrs. Morgan shook her head as she crossed the court to Mr. O'Donnell, spitting heated words no one could hear over the growing laughter.

As Jules and Brady strutted in their direction, Wendy released Kenny's hand, rushing to cut her off.

"Jules," Wendy whispered. "What are you doing?"

"What do you mean?" She giggled, feigning innocence. "This is my costume!"

Kenny felt Wendy eyeing him, as his jaw clenched in restraint, turning from the crowd to regain his composure.

Make her leave, he thought. *Please, make her leave before I have to.*

"This isn't funny," Wendy mumbled, gripping Jules's arm.

"You need to go. Now."

"Excuse you. I don't have to go anywhere! This is my rally."

Kenny had had enough. An observant Chris jumped over, trying to stop him. "Wait, hey bro, don't!"

Heart pounding, Kenny railroaded through him, storming up to Jules. "You think this shit is cool?"

The audience's laughter died quick.

Jules coughed out a nervous laugh, glancing at the crowd. "Dude, it's just a joke. Lighten up."

Smoke streamed out of Kenny's ears. Wendy clutched his costume, trying her best to calm him.

"I'm sorry," she whispered, her eyes desperate. "I had *no* idea. I swear."

"Hey, man," Brady began with a haughty smile, pushing an index finger into Kenny's chest. "I think you need to back up. You're getting a little close to my girl."

Jules gave him a smug smirk, puffing her chest.

Kenny's eyes narrowed as he leaned into Brady's finger, ready to snap it off his weak hand.

"Or what?" Kenny said, his tone deadly.

The smile fell off Brady's face.

"Kenny," Wendy begged, grabbing his arm. "Please. Let's just go."

Then there were more hands. Half the defensive line, trying to pull him back.

"Yo, bro, cool it," Jason mumbled in his ear.

Kenny gave him a once-over. "The fuck you just say to me?"

For a change, Jason appeared speechless. He swiveled around, confirming he still had backup. "Come on, man. It's just Jules. You know she's just being . . . Jules."

Jason didn't see anything wrong with it. None of them did.

"Hey, let's just walk this off, man," Chris added, always trying to be a voice of reason. But reason wasn't going to put a leash on the rage blazing in Kenny.

The gym remained eerily quiet, watching the group like sharks in a fishbowl.

The group parted as Mr. O'Donnell made his way to the center with school security, probably to kick out Brady for trespassing.

Words strangled by fury, Kenny shoved a trembling finger in Jules's face. "You fucked up this time."

Jules merely rolled her eyes as Brady placed a protective arm around her shoulders.

"Miss Marshall, a word in the hallway," Mr. O'Donnell said. "Now. You too, Mr. Scott."

Kenny's head snapped in his direction. "What for?"

Mr. O'Donnell swallowed, eyebrows hitting his nonexistent hairline. "Let's just . . . take this somewhere private, son."

"But I didn't do anything," he barked, waving his hand at Jules. "She's the one in fucking blackface! Why aren't you focused on her?"

"Kenny, please," Wendy begged. "Just do what he says."

He gaped at her in disbelief. "Why?"

Wendy cringed, the bacon tip falling forward as her eyes welled with tears. "So you can just . . . explain."

"Explain what? I didn't do shit!"

"Don't yell at her!" Kayleigh shouted, standing beside Wendy for support.

"It's okay, son," Mr. O'Donnell insisted. "We just want to talk. Clear the air. No harm, no foul."

No harm? Jules stood there in blackface, and he had the audacity to say "no harm"? What about the disrespect, not just to Maddy but to him and all the Black kids in school? Why didn't anyone see that? Why did he have to be the one to point it out?

Kenny eyed every person circling him as if he was something to be captured, as if he was the one out of control, and not Jules. The group exchanged nervous glances, avoiding his glare. His "friends" were avoiding him when they should have been on his side.

"Man, whatever." Kenny sucked his teeth, shoving through the circle.

Wendy rushed after him. "Kenny? Kenny, please, wait . . ."

Kenny shook her away, ripping off his ridiculous costume as he stormed out the gym doors, leaving everyone in stunned silence.

SIX

MADDY DID IT
EPISODE 4, CONT.

Michael: So when did you retire and close your medical
practice?

Dr. Paul Foreman: 'Bout few months after it happened, give or
take. I had my fill of blood after that day.

Michael [narration]: This is Dr. Paul Foreman, Maddy's
physician. It took a while to find any mention of him in the
investigation report. But I think it's crucial that we learn as
much as we can about Maddy's overall health before the
prom.

Dr. Foreman: First time I met Maddy, the state had actually
mandated her to come to me. At that point, she had only
been taken to the emergency room after a fit of hysteria.
Something about some bird attack. Anyway, when she
was brought into the ER, doctors learned she had no clue
what a menstrual cycle was. Poor girl thought she was

dying. They had a nurse explain it to her, which got child protective services involved, and the state sent her my way. She hadn't had the proper immunizations to attend middle school.

Michael: Do you remember anything about that first meeting?

Dr. Foreman: She was quiet. Shy. Every question I asked her, she'd looked to her daddy for permission to talk. I thought it was strange, but there were no signs of abuse.

Michael: So maybe you can help put this rumor to rest. Did Maddy have lupus?

Dr. Foreman: No, not at all. Not sure where that idea came from. Probably her daddy.

Michael: And when's the last time you saw Maddy?

Dr. Foreman: Exactly three months before Prom Night. She came in, I'm assuming without her daddy's knowledge, concerned about period pain. She had an extremely heavy menstrual cycle that left her exhausted. Her extremities were often cold, and she constantly craved ice chips. All signs of iron deficiency or anemia. I prescribed her an iron supplement and told her to see a gynecologist within the month. That's the last time I saw her.

Michael: Anything else unusual?

Dr. Foreman: You know, that's what the state asked me too. Over and over. Was I aware of any unnatural "abilities"? The best answer I could give them was I don't think anyone knew what she was capable of. Including her.

Michael: Do you think she could still be alive?

Dr. Foreman: With no body, it's hard to confirm. But ultimately,
I find it almost impossible for her to have walked away
unscathed, and no one notice.

From CNN.com article, May 19, 2014: "High School Investigating Reports of Students Dressed in Blackface"

A photo of a girl posing in blackface, dressed as a fellow student, has come to the Springville school district's attention after being widely circulated on social media.

District administrators issued the following statement: "We hope, as a community, that we can work together to ensure that the racial insensitivity and inappropriateness of the students' actions can serve as a teachable moment."

The school declined to release the name of the student, but fellow students identified her before her social media accounts were deleted.

This is the second incident in recent weeks at the town's high school, drawing questions about district protocols.

May 19, 2014

Wendy hadn't seen Kenny all morning. His car was parked in the lot, but he wasn't in his usual spot, and for some reason, she couldn't shake the feeling that he was avoiding her. She drank the smoothie she had prepared for him, guzzling the chalky liquid, trying to drown her nerves. He couldn't still be mad about Jules, right? Wendy had managed to smooth things over, and they'd made up over the weekend.

But Kenny still felt distant. She clung to the hope that once they were away from Springville, they would be *them* again, Wendy and Kenny. She checked her email with anxious fingers. Still no word from that last scholarship. All she needed was another thousand dollars, and once they were on Alabama's campus, she'd be taken care of. Being the girlfriend of Kenny Scott just had to come with some privileges.

When the bell rang, she nearly sprinted down to the caf, hoping Kenny would be there, waiting for her. Missing her. But as she skipped down the staircase, she ran right into a traffic jam that blocked the hallway leading to the lunchroom. Chanting voices boomed over the crowd.

"Hey, hey! Ho, ho! Racist students have got to go!"

"What's going on?" she said aloud.

"The Black Student Union is protesting," a kid beside her grumbled.

Wendy sucked in a breath. Could Kenny be there too? He had never once showed interest in that type of stuff before.

She bulldozed her way through the crowd, coming upon the clearing in front of the caf doors.

The Black Student Union consisted of half the Black kids at Springville High. Wendy found them somewhat militant in their approach. Not all white people were racist, but BSU sure had a way of making everyone feel like it. *What if Kenny started acting like them?* she thought. What would people think? And what would people say about her? Other than Jules's crude comments about Kenny's potential dick size, no one really made a big deal about her dating a Black guy. Most commended her for landing the town's celebrity. But all that praise could easily switch to hate, something she couldn't afford.

The BSU were dressed head to toe in black, holding blown-up posters of Jules at the pep rally. And standing in front was none other than Kali Scott, shouting at her audience.

"We are sick and tired of the lack of action taken by our school's administration! There have been no consequences for the student who arrived at a school function in blackface, a disgusting racist spectacle. It is a demeaning and hurtful, stereotypical misrepresentation of who we are. Yet this school district feels this blatant disrespect doesn't deserve punishment.

"We've brought up issues like this to teachers and administrators before. But our complaints have gone nowhere. The lack of repercussions for these hurtful actions have forced students of color into a hostile learning environment. We demand action! If the student isn't removed, we'll alert the press of every racist act that has happened in this school. And we have receipts."

Students mumbled among themselves. Wendy locked eyes with Kali, the corner of her mouth curving into a smirk.

"And while you were all so desperate to have a joint prom,

it wasn't lost on us that the country club refused to host it because that would mean they would have to open their doors to people of color. So we will have weekly protests outside the country club until it admits to its racist practices."

Wendy's heart slammed into her chest. No, Kali couldn't bring any negative attention to prom. She had worked too hard for it to not go as planned.

The hall monitors finally managed to disperse the crowd, pushing the Black Student Union aside to permit everyone into the caf for lunch. Wendy seized her chance and grabbed Kali's arm.

"Kali," she said through clenched teeth, "what are you doing?"

Kali looked down at the hand on her elbow, narrowing her eyes. Wendy yanked back her hand and straightened.

"I'm doing what needs to be done."

"But Jules didn't mean to hurt anyone," Wendy insisted. "It was stupid, but there's no need to drag prom into—"

"She knew exactly what she was doing," Kali snapped. "And it wasn't just her in blackface. It was her pretending to be a Black student. Openly mocking Black people. Is that what you think we all look like?"

"No! Not at all!"

"You're her best friend. You condone that bullshit, yet you're dating my brother. What does that say about you?"

"I don't condone it! I told her it was messed up!" Wendy felt herself losing her footing.

"Whatever. You don't give a damn."

Wendy balked. "What do you mean? Don't you see me trying to plan this prom for everyone to go to? So what, some of them are still gonna have prom at the country club, but we're still gonna have ours, and a lot more people are gonna be at that one."

Kali leaned back with a smirk. "You really don't think we see right through you and this little show you're putting on, do you?"

Wendy blinked, her lungs hardening. "What?" she squeaked.

"You're pushing this prom shit so you get to go with Kenny because otherwise, you wouldn't go to prom at all, and I know that was eating you alive."

Kenny's morning smoothie curdled in Wendy's stomach, threatening to bubble up.

"You're also pushing this so you can look like the perfect little 'white ally,' thinking that's gonna make my brother stay with you as he rises to the top. You trying to look like you were always down, the woke bae we invite to the barbecue. This whole charade is all about *you!*"

Wendy's throat constricted. "That's not true. I'm trying to . . . I'm trying to help . . ."

"Yeah, sure you are." Kali chuckled, picking up her book bag. "You wanna help Black people? How about you start by actually helping them instead of just helping yourself?"

Kali stormed off, leaving Wendy speechless.

At that moment, Kenny strolled around the corner, book bag hanging off his shoulder; the timing so impeccable it felt comedic.

"Hey! What's up?" he said, kissing her forehead. "What are you standing out here for?"

Wendy gave him a tight smile. She had no doubt that he knew all about the protest and didn't tell her. *What else is he keeping from me?*

Jules wrapped a long curl around her pinky, swinging her crossed leg, a smug grin on her face. She didn't typically relish being in the principal's office. Most days, Jules didn't pay the sad, balding little man any mind. But today, she couldn't wait to see her daddy eat him for lunch.

"So what's this all about, Steve? Jules seems to think she's in some kind of trouble, and I know you all know better than to waste my time."

Keith Marshall, CEO of Marshall's Hardware, sat across from Mr. O'Donnell. Everything from his hair to his shoes screamed corporate life, corner offices, and meetings on the golf course. A life Mr. O'Donnell would never know about. He was a pathetic little man on a power trip.

And now, he has to deal with my daddy, Jules thought, her grin widening as she glared at Mrs. Morgan, sitting in the corner. Her teacher might have had the principal on puppet strings, but she was no match for Jules's power of persuasion.

Mr. O'Donnell rearranged his desk for the third time, sweat covering his forehead. "Well, it's . . . it's . . ."

"It's about your daughter's behavior these past few weeks," Mrs. Morgan chimed in. "Maybe even years, considering what others have told me."

Mr. Marshall swiveled in the chair as if noticing her for the first time. "I'm sorry, and you are?"

She gave him a sly smile. "Her history teacher. Sorry we weren't properly introduced at the parent-teacher conference you missed."

He eyed her up and down, measured her worth, then refocused on Mr. O'Donnell. "Look, Steve, I have a flight to catch out of Greenville, so you mind hurrying this along? Now, Jules came home very upset the other night, claiming that you threatened her."

This seemed to steady Mr. O'Donnell's shaky hands. "I did no such thing! As I told your wife, I sent her home so we could do a thorough investigation before deciding the best course of action."

"Investigation about what? A stupid costume? Don't you people have better things to do?"

Mrs. Morgan scoffed. "Mr. Marshall, I don't think your daughter understands the severity of her actions. She came to a school function in blackface."

"And the school has a no-tolerance policy for bullying," Mr. O'Donnell added.

"But I didn't bully anyone!" Jules turned to her father. "You can ask Wendy or Jason. They were there too!" Jules knew the combination of both those names would win him over, with Jason's family being the richest one in town next to theirs and Wendy being too sweet to lie.

Mr. Marshall sighed as if the whole meeting was utter nonsense. "Do you have proof of this 'bullying'?"

Mr. O'Donnell folded his hands on the desk and enunciated every word to be clearly felt. "Mr. Marshall, there is a picture. Of your daughter. At a school function. Dressed in blackface. With the name of a Black student written on her shirt. All over the internet. And CNN."

Mr. Marshall sat stone-faced and shrugged. "It was just some paint. I've seen kids at games dunked head to toe in white and no one cries about it."

Mrs. Morgan's eyes flared. "It wasn't a football game or white paint. It was black and purposefully inciting. Aside from it being grossly inappropriate, crude, and racist, it was hurtful and insulting, not only to a fragile young woman of color but to all of the Black students at Springville High."

Jules's seat burned beneath her. "Excuse me, but why is she even here?" she snapped.

"She's here as a witness of the previous incident," Mr. O'Donnell explained, nodding at Mrs. Morgan.

Mr. Marshall scowled. "What incident?"

"Your daughter threw pencils into a student's hair. The

same student she pretended to be for the pep rally."

Mr. Marshall turned to Jules with a frown. A frown of disapproval—she didn't see it often. It made her fidget.

"It wasn't me, Daddy, I swear," Jules insisted, gripping the arms of her chair. "It was the other girls. I told you how kids are always trying to blame stuff on me! I'm not even in the video!"

Mr. Marshall nodded and turned back to the principal. "She said it wasn't her. And without proof—"

"I saw her throw it," Mrs. Morgan announced, a touch of haughtiness in her voice. Jules wanted to rip her tongue out with pliers.

Just then, Jules's phone pinged loudly, startling Mr. O'Donnell.

"Well, it's your word against hers, and I got a team of lawyers ready to handle any misunderstanding."

Mrs. Morgan tilted her head, giving Mr. O'Donnell a pointed look.

He took his cue. "That's all well and good, Mr. Marshall, but . . . your daughter is suspended for the rest of the school year."

Jules shot up to her feet. "What?"

"She can attend graduation after she takes, and passes, her finals from home."

"Daddy!"

Mr. Marshall waved his hands, instructing the room to settle down. "Okay, look. Clearly, this was . . . a mistake. Jules learned her lesson, and she'll never do it again. There's no need to overact 'cause of some teasing. Really, kids need to toughen up these days. How d'you expect them to make it in the real world with all this coddling?"

Mr. O'Donnell glanced at Mrs. Morgan as if checking for approval. "I'm sorry. It's out of my hands."

Mr. Marshall sighed through a tight smile. "Alright. That's fine. I'll see what my buddies on the school board have to say about this."

Jules's phone pinged again. Twice.

Mr. O'Donnell folded his hands on the desk. "It . . . was the school board's decision. Your daughter has brought a lot of unwanted attention to Springville, and they feel the best course of action is to remove the . . . problem."

Jules unraveled. "But . . . this is my last week as cheer captain with my friends. You can't do this to me!"

Mr. Marshall patted Jules's leg. "Steve, she's just a kid. She didn't know what she was doing."

"She knew exactly what she was doing, which is why she did it," Mrs. Morgan snapped. "How do you expect her to make it in the real world if she doesn't know there are consequences to her actions?"

Jules's phone pinged three more times. Annoyed, she ripped it from her bag. Hundreds of notifications and text messages clouded her home screen. Her heart sank to the floor as she slowly began to process it all.

"Daddy," she gasped, eyes flooding with tears. "The picture . . . it's everywhere. And . . . oh God. Texas A&M just posted on Twitter . . . they're revoking my acceptance."

Mr. Marshall whipped around, face contorted in fury. "Steve, this is excessive! Don't you think suspension is enough? You want to jeopardize her future too?"

A stunned Mr. O'Donnell held his hands up. "We made no calls to her university."

"Then who did?" Mr. Marshall demanded, turning to stab a finger toward Mrs. Morgan. "Was it you?"

She shrugged. "No. But they probably caught wind of it from—oh, I don't know—the dozen outlets that have reported the story. Have you seen those cameras outside? That's your daughter's doing."

Jules collapsed in her chair, sobbing. "Daddy, please. Do something!"

Mr. Marshall continued berating the principal. "I want the name of every person involved in this, including the girl she allegedly bullied, and I want them now!"

"Daddy, I'm not going to college? I won't be on the cheer squad?"

Mr. Marshall turned to his daughter. "We'll set up a call with Texas A&M tomorrow," he said firmly. "Get this all straightened out. We're not going to let some dramatic little girl ruin everything you worked hard for."

Mrs. Morgan shot out of her seat. "Did it ever occur to

you how much you hurt Maddy? You're lucky Mr. Washington refuses to press charges or push for resolution. You're pretty much walking out of here scot-free. Because if I were Maddy's mother, I'd be setting fire to rain for treating my little girl like that!"

SEVEN

May 19, 2014

Your bloodline was marinated in rage.

There will be pain in carrying this dark secret. A pain you must endure for others and for yourself.

This sickly power you hold without hands will eventually burn until you no longer can hide it. You must learn to control it. Or it will control you. But be not a doormat. You can ease the pain by leaving all that you know. Become so drunk on life and love that it blinds you to the hate threatening to drown you. Chew on grief for breakfast, devour aches for lunch, inhale life's acid, let it burn the costume he has forced upon you.

MADDY SAT ENRAPTURED by her mother's words, reading them over and over, cutting her fingertips on page edges, leaving breadcrumbs of blood throughout the book. How had she known Maddy would find the journal? Did Papa know she'd written it? Maddy hadn't had much time to sit and decipher her mother's cryptic riddles. She often talked in circles about blood.

Oh God . . . could Mama be a witch?

That would make the most sense, explain Maddy's own capabilities. But Papa said witches were evil. He wouldn't have been with an evil woman. Unless he didn't know. Unless she fooled him. And if her mother's blood flowed through her, did that make Maddy a witch too? She turned in her seat, spotting a free computer in the back of the library.

Despite Papa's decree about modern technology, Maddy knew how to use a computer, a requirement for school assignments and access to the class portal. She pulled up Google and began her search. For what, she still wasn't sure yet. But she knew she couldn't be the only one able to move things with their mind. There had to be others.

She stuffed her mother's journal back in her bag. It wasn't safe to keep it at home, and it was the only piece of her mother she owned. If Papa found it and read the words inside, he'd set it on fire. And there would be a heavy price to pay. She touched the crusted scalp burn along her edges, swallowed hard, and typed in the first search term.

"Black witches"

Maddy's heart raced as she combed through the terms *African spiritualist, voodoo, Santería.* . . . But from what she gathered, they used candles, incense, feathers, even dolls to obtain their desired results. As she closed another article, she stumbled across a picture, a group of Black women dressed in all white gathering by the water. None of them were alone. They had each other. She touched the screen with her index finger.

Mama?

Maddy shook the wish away. Her mama was dead. Died giving Maddy life. There was no bringing her back. But . . . could Maddy have extended family? Were they like her? Moving things with their minds? She closed the window and pulled up a fresh Google page.

"Witches who move things with their minds"

And at the very top, the first term that popped up was *telekinesis.*

She wrote the word down in her notebook and began from there.

MADDY DID IT
EPISODE 5
"Mind over Matter"

Kurt Von Keating: I'll explain it in three easy words: Mind. Over. Matter.

Michael [narration]: This is Kurt Von Keating, author and founder of EmbraceYourPlace.com. I invited him to the studio to give us a baseline and lay the groundwork for understanding Maddy's abilities. According to school records, Maddy checked out four books on telekinesis, eventually returning three but keeping one, Keating's debut handbook on harnessing telekinetic powers. After about a dozen calls to his agent and a few volleys with an appearance agreement, I had to take a personality test before he would agree to meet with me. I'm assuming I passed.

Michael: We were hoping you could explain a bit of what telekinesis is. Your book was one of the texts Maddy studied in her school's library.

Kurt: So I've heard from several forums. It's tremendous what she was able to accomplish, despite the lives lost.

Michael: Uh, okay. Can you maybe explain what telekinesis is? You know, for someone who might not believe.

Kurt: Belief is a source of energy that holds space for consciousness. The laws of science, man!

Michael: But maybe you could—

Kurt: Do you know how much energy she must have used that night? You could siphon it out of the ground, bottle it up, and light up the city of Tokyo. The intersection of quantum physics, neuroscience, and consciousness . . . powerful stuff, man. Powerful stuff.

Michael: Right. So about your book . . .

Kurt: Telekinesis is the ability to move objects, great or small, with the power of the mind. Simple. Like I said, it's all about mind over matter. It tracks. But you can learn more on my YouTube channel, Keating's Way, or in my new book, *Mind Pollution*, available for preorder at EmbraceYourPlace.com.

Michael: Um. Tanya? Do you have any questions?

Tanya: Mr. Keating, I want to read you something. "In the 1970s, Uri Geller became the world's best-known psychic and made millions traveling the world demonstrating his claimed psychokinetic abilities, including starting broken watches and bending spoons. Though he denied using magic tricks, many skeptical researchers observed that all of Geller's amazing feats could be—and have been—duplicated by magicians." Now, when you hear this, do you really expect us to believe that you have telekinesis despite the hundreds of people, over a century, who have disproven it?

Kurt: I stand in my truth with love and kindness.

Michael: What is the connection between telekinesis and fire? There were reports that Maddy seemed to be able to control the flames.

Kurt: Oh, well, that's impossible. Completely fabricated.

Tanya: That's impossible, but you expect us to believe telekinesis is real?

Kurt: There is no connection. There are, however, many people who do have pyrokinesis. I've interviewed them as well on my YouTube channel.

Tanya: Pyrokinesis? A term literally made up by Stephen King. A fiction writer? We're done here.

May 20, 2014

Wendy sat on the plush lavender carpet in Jules's room, leaning against a four-poster bed, knees curled up to her chest as Jules paced in front of her.

"I can't believe they're doing this," Jules spat with a sniff. "All because of a joke? This is such bullshit!"

No matter how many times they hung out at Jules's house, Wendy never ceased to be amazed by her massive bedroom, almost the size of Wendy's entire living room, not to mention the walk-in closet stuffed with clothes. Wendy often joked that if she moved in, it would take weeks for anyone to notice.

Black eye makeup stained Jules's bone-white cheeks, her hair a tangled red mop draping over her shoulders. It looked like she hadn't slept in days. Kayleigh sat cross-legged on the bed, wiping away a tear.

Charlotte, on the love seat by the window, gave Wendy a pointed look. If anyone could soothe Jules, it would be Wendy.

But Wendy didn't know where to begin. Of course, she felt horrible. Jules had been dying to go to Texas A&M since they were freshmen. She already knew all the chants and wore the burgundy T-shirt to bed on most nights.

Any other joke, Wendy would call the school heavy-handed. But she couldn't stop thinking of Kenny's reaction. She'd never seen him so upset before about anything. Jules had clearly crossed a line.

Wendy took a deep breath, falling back into her loyal best friend role. "Jules, just . . . just calm down."

Jules shot her daggers. "Calm down? I'm not going to college, Wen!" She held back another raging sob. "Daddy doesn't think A&M is going to budge. My whole fucking life is ruined!"

"There are other schools," Wendy countered, trying to inject optimism. "You're supersmart and really pretty. Like, dozens of places are going to want you."

Jules wasn't listening. Her red eyes jiggled in their sockets as she burned a hole through the carpet.

"This is so stupid! And to think this started because fucking Maddy Washington has been catfishing us her entire life!"

"More like whitefishing," Charlotte said, chuckling at her own joke, then quickly biting her lips shut.

"We didn't do anything wrong," Jules shouted, defiantly. "Really, she brought it on herself."

"Maybe you can change their mind by apologizing," Wendy offered, musing on a strategy.

Jules whipped around. "What?"

Wendy gulped, her back tensing. "I, well . . . you came to school in blackface. That's just so . . . not cool. But an apology would be some good damage control."

Charlotte's and Kayleigh's eyes widened as Jules stormed up to Wendy, fuming.

"It was a JOKE! A fucking JOKE!"

Wendy shrank back against the bed, stunned by her venom. Did Jules really not see how messed up blackface was? Did she really think she was beyond reproach? She couldn't have been that blind. But Jules would never listen to reason in her current state, so Wendy kept her mouth shut.

"And if she was just honest about being Black, then no one would give a fuck," Jules carried on. "But she's been lying. To all of us! How is lying okay?"

"Yeah! She's basically, like, ruined our entire senior year," Charlotte added.

"How?" Wendy balked, offended. Up until then, senior year had been everything they'd dreamed of. She had made sure of it, down to the very last detail.

Charlotte counted her fingers. "Jules is suspended. The Black kids hate us. Reporters are putting our business on front street. And prom has turned into a shitshow. I mean, all this change, and Maddy's not even going to prom!"

Wendy blinked, the words somehow blindsiding her: *Maddy's not going to prom.*

And though she tried, she couldn't shake Kali's words.

"You wanna help Black people? How about you start by actually helping them instead of just helping yourself?"

If Kali could see through Wendy's weak plotting, could Kenny? What would it take to make it seem like it wasn't about her but more about the greater good for everyone?

And at that exact moment, an idea that would eventually change the entire fate of the town hit Wendy in the gut.

From David Portman's Springville Massacre: The Legend of Maddy Washington (pg. 123)

There were many questions after that night of carnage, but one stood out among the rest: What was Maddy Washington doing at the prom in the first place?

According to testimony, Maddy had been considered

an outcast among her peers, teased, bullied, and tormented relentlessly throughout her years at Springville High School. No one could recall her attending a single after-school event, football game, homecoming dance, or Halloween bazaar. She entered the school seconds before the bell rang, then exited just as quickly.

Thus, the concept of Maddy going to the prom with the most popular boy in school seemed almost unfathomable.

This was where the finger-pointing began. Because if they had never thrown that pencil, if they had never uploaded that video, if they had never decided to combine dances, and if her date had never asked her to the prom, half the town would still be alive.

May 20, 2014

Parked in a clearing facing the power plant with a view of the reservoir, Wendy and Kenny lay in the back of his truck, a fleece blanket covering their half-naked bodies. Kenny kissed her neck, lips trailing down to her collarbone. He ran a hand up her left leg, squeezing her hip. Wendy stared through the sunroof at the night sky. This was usually her favorite part of sex. The part where he lavished her skin, making her feel like the most beautiful creature on the planet. She held him tight, trying to remain present, but her mind kept wandering back to Maddy.

"Maddy's not even going to prom."

Maddy had to go to prom. For optics, it needed to appear

like they were one big happy family and that she, in turn, had forgiven them. But Maddy couldn't go with just anyone, and definitely not alone. The "new" Black girl had to go to the All-Together prom with a Black guy to further drive home the point that all the Black kids were happy at Springville High. Maddy needed a Cinderella-style night.

And there was only one guy Wendy could think of who would be the perfect prince.

Kenny stopped, pushing up on his forearms to stare down at her.

"You okay?" he panted, uncertainty marring his face.

Wendy hesitated before uttering, "Yeah. Of course."

She tried pulling his mouth back on hers, but he tilted his head.

"You seem . . . distracted."

Wendy nibbled on her bottom lip. Kenny nodded and rolled onto his side with the groan of a boy who knew he wasn't about to get laid. Without her human blanket, her skin grew cold and she sat up, pulling her knees in. Her eyes wandered across his body, from his six-pack abs to his cut shoulders—so perfect he took her breath away.

"What's on your mind?" he breathed, a hint of annoyance in his tone. He might as well have said, "What is it this time?"

Wendy plopped her chin on her knee and sighed. This wasn't the place she wanted to have the conversation. She hadn't even thought through all the details. But she needed to start the ball rolling sooner than later.

"It's just . . . I need you to do something for me. Something important."

He chuckled, leaning on his elbows. "Okayyyy. Sure. What's up?"

Wendy took a deep breath. "I need you . . . want you . . . to take Maddy Washington to prom."

Kenny stared at her for several beats before letting out a loud laugh.

"Good one, babe," he said, shaking his head.

Wendy remained very still, eyes focused on the blanket, trying not to lose her nerve, hoping she'd played her hand right.

Kenny measured her face and his smile fell. "Wait, are you serious?"

"Yes," she admitted sheepishly. "It's important."

He shot up. "But . . . but why?"

"Because I want to make things right. It's not like I was planning to go to prom anyway. And what girl wouldn't want to go to prom with Kenny Scott?"

He sighed. "Is this about Jules?"

She shrugged with a wince. "Sort of, yeah."

He shook his head. "Wendy . . . you didn't throw the pencils. And you didn't show up to school in fucking blackface. You're not Jules!"

Wendy's chin trembled. The words were meant to be complimentary, but they didn't land that way. She knew she wasn't Jules, that she could never be Jules, that she'd never live up to such perfection. And yet deep down, behind her spleen, hid the truth: she didn't want to be Jules. She didn't want to be the type of person who tormented people without care.

"But I didn't stop her either," she muttered. "I never stopped Jules from messing with Maddy. None of us did. We all just . . . stood by."

Kenny leaned back against the window, staring as if trying to make sense of her, but remained flabbergasted. "But why me? Why can't someone else take her?"

"Because you're both . . . I mean, you would look good together."

Kenny's eyes widened. "Oh God, Wendyyyy." He pinched the bridge of his nose, breathing in.

She scooted closer to him, holding the blanket over her bare chest. "It'll be good for your image," she insisted, nuzzling his shoulder. "The star quarterback, five-star recruit takes the town's reject to the first All-Together prom. No one will forget it. They'll write about it in the paper. And then people will see that we're . . . nice people."

Kenny's face darkened, and he shrugged her off him. "You trying to prove that by pimping me out to some girl I don't even know?"

Her eyes went wide. "No! It's not like that. It's about—"

"What about what I want?" he snapped. "Have you ever thought of that?"

Wendy pressed her lips together, feeling an argument

lurking in the air, beating at the constructed walls of their avoidance game. "Just think—for one night, you'll make some girl's dream come true. She hasn't had it easy. And a lot of us are to blame. Me included."

Kenny's eyes softened as he stared at his knuckles.

"Please, Kenny? For me."

They sat for a long silent moment, the mood shifting. Wendy questioned her judgment, since Kenny rarely said no to anything. Always easygoing and down for whatever. But as he sat like a frozen statue, she wondered what lived on the other side of his reliability.

Finally, he huffed, yanking a T-shirt over his chiseled chest. "I'll think about it," he mumbled without looking at her, and opened the trunk hatch. She exhaled in relief.

He'll come around, she thought. And really, it wasn't a big deal. It was just one night.

EIGHT

May 21, 2014
SIXTH PERIOD. English.

Mr. Bernstein walked through the rows of seats, handing back the quarterly book analysis assignments. He placed an A-minus paper on Kenny's desk and tapped it twice.

"Need to see you right after class about this," he said.

Heads turned in Kenny's direction, all wearing the same *Uh-oh! Someone's in trouble* expression. Kenny grinned at the gazes as if it was no big deal but felt his organs harden. Had he answered the right question? Added the bibliography? Numbered the footnotes?

He slyly peeked over at Jason's desk, his paper sitting face-up. C-minus, the same as his last two papers. So why hadn't he been asked to stay after class?

The bell rang, and Kenny waited for the class to clear out before he stepped up to his English teacher's desk.

"What's up?" he said, his voice light and airy.

Mr. Bernstein nodded at the report. "Did you get some help with that?"

Kenny handed him back the paper. "No. Why? Did I do something wrong?"

"No, no, it's great! Incredibly insightful."

Kenny frowned at the minus symbol sitting next to his grade. *Then what's the fucking problem?* he thought, yet forced out a "Thanks, Mr. Bernstein."

"But . . . it's the third one like it that you've done. Not saying your work wasn't good before, but this sudden improvement is, or to someone else, could be perceived as, well, a little inconceivable. I know you have a ton on your plate. So maybe . . . did Wendy perhaps help you write it? I'll be okay with it if you're just honest with me, son."

Kenny gripped the strap of his book bag, careful not to react to the burning lump of coal in his throat. He'd stayed up half the night finishing that paper, put in more effort than necessary, only because the book interested him. He studied the lines in his palm, something he tended to do when he needed to regain composure. He rubbed a thumb down the long life line that started near his pointer and ended at the top of his wrist. A reminder that he had a full life ahead of him. A life with football, fame, and money. Why waste his time trying to prove himself to some asshole who couldn't run or throw a ball to save his life?

So he gave his English teacher exactly what he wanted.

"You know, you're right, Mr. Bernstein," Kenny said, the lie burning his lips. "I asked Wendy to read a draft, and she helped me polish it up."

Mr. Bernstein nodded. "That's what I thought. No worries, son. We all could use a little help now and then. I'm sure you won't have any issues in college. They'll have plenty of people to help you with your schoolwork."

There was an undercurrent to his words. He didn't mean *help you*, he meant *do it for you*.

Kenny chuckled, his toothy smile straining. "You right! Thanks, Mr. Bernstein. I appreciate the tip. Later!"

Out in the hallway, he rolled his paper up, strangling it with both hands. It wasn't the first time a teacher had covertly suggested Wendy was the key to his stellar grade point average. A star quarterback with brains? Highly improbable. He so badly wanted to believe teachers treated him different due to his athletic stardom. But when he clocked his fellow teammates, none were faced with the same doubts and insulting allegations.

"Hey, Kenny!" a group of freshman girls sang by the stairs, waving. Kenny bucked up.

"What's up, what's up, what's up," he sang back. Once out of sight, he dropped the smile, took a deep breath, and headed to study hall. The rock-solid wall he'd built around his emotions was starting to chip and crumble, a leak threatening the status he'd worked so hard to achieve.

Study hall felt like the one place in Springville High that

Kenny could have some privacy to breathe. Sitting in the corner nook of the library near the stacks, he could read books in peace without worrying about his dad forcing him to watch game footage, Jason's childish digs, or Wendy guilting him into taking pity on Maddy Washington.

He could read through the lines: it wasn't about *his* image. It was about Wendy's, to clean up her look. Why couldn't she ask someone else? Besides their backgrounds, debatable at best, he had nothing in common with Maddy. Just because they were both Black, they should go together? He doubted Maddy would even want to go. Probably wanted nothing to do with prom.

Just like him.

Kenny's temples throbbed. Deep down, even when he didn't know she was Black, he had always felt sorry for Maddy. Now knowing that even he wasn't absolved from his friends' ignorance, he could only imagine what Maddy had been through the last six years. How would taking her to prom make up for it all?

At that moment, Maddy flew past him, disappearing into the stacks. She always walked around at warp speed, head down, arms stuffed with books, sweating in that itchy brown wool sweater covering some dress straight out of his grandma's closet. He sighed.

She's not your problem. Just let it go.

"What a freak," a voice chuckled.

"Yeah, and not the good kind."

Behind the tall magazine stand that provided Kenny privacy, two boys stifled their snickers.

"I heard Mad Mad Maddy got excused from gym and US history," the other said, not even bothering to whisper. "She just lives in the library now like some squatter."

They sounded young, probably freshmen. Kenny tried to refocus on his book and ignore their heckling. But if he could hear them, couldn't Maddy?

Let it go. It's none of your business, he told himself, straightening in his chair.

"Yo, what do you think her mom looks like?" the first boy asked. "Do you think she's real dark?"

"Then how did Maddy end up looking like that?"

"I don't know, but you saw that video of her hair? Bro, it didn't even seem real."

The boys' laughter grew louder. Kenny gripped his book tighter, grinding his teeth. Who were these little assholes, talking about a girl they'd never even met?

"They said on all her school forms that she put she was white," the little asshole continued.

"Well, she kinda is, right?"

"No way. She's definitely way more Black than white."

Kenny slapped his book closed and pushed himself up. The two kids' eyes widened as he rounded the corner, standing in front of them.

"How?" Kenny barked, crossing his arms, his muscles flexing.

The boys leaned back in their chairs, faces blanched.

"Wh-what?" one mumbled.

"How is she more Black than white? Explain it to me like I'm a five-year-old. If she has one parent that's Black and another that's white, what makes her more one than the other?"

The boys threw each other panicked looks, realizing there was no right answer or easy way out.

The first one gulped. "Well, we didn't mean . . . or what I meant was . . ."

"You don't mean shit. That's what you mean, right?" Kenny snapped.

"No! It's just that . . ."

Kenny shoved their table, and the boys jumped back. "Man, get the fuck gone!"

The boys didn't hesitate. They packed up their belongings and raced for the back exit as Kenny headed for the stacks. He didn't exactly have a plan, more or less operating off emotions, which wasn't like him. But people had always underestimated him, their preconceived notions based on appearance. Now Maddy was experiencing the same thing, only worse. And his friends had everything to do with it.

"It ain't never too late to do the right thing."

It'd just be one night, he thought. What's the worst that could happen?

He turned down the third row and found Maddy on her tiptoes, reaching for a book on the top shelf.

"Hey, Maddy!"

Maddy jumped with a scream. All at once, books on either side of her hurled themselves off the shelves. She ducked, wrapping her arms around her head.

Shit, how the hell did that happen?

"Damn! My bad," Kenny said, rushing over to her. "Didn't mean to . . . here, let me help."

Maddy dropped to her knees, scrambling to collect her stack. "Uh . . . uh no, um, no."

Kenny caught the name of one book—*Psycho-Kinesis: Moving Matter with the Mind.*

Must be for some science project, he thought as he continued to scoop books off the floor, placing them back on the shelves. They worked quickly in silence, stealing glances over their shoulders at one another. When they were done, a disheveled Maddy faced him.

"Uh, hey," he said, offering a smile.

Maddy gulped and glanced over her shoulder at the dead end, then back to Kenny, blocking her one exit. She squeezed the books to her chest.

"Um, hey," she mumbled meekly.

Kenny blew out some nervous air. Why was he nervous? *It's just Maddy.*

"Sooo . . . listen, I wanted to ask you something."

She squirmed. "Huh?"

"You, uh, probably heard about the whole All-Together

prom thing, right? Well, I was wondering, if you didn't have a date if you'd want to go with . . . me. To prom."

Maddy froze, her big owlish eyes widening behind her brown frames. They stood in silence for what seemed like forever.

Kenny let out an uneasy chuckle. "Uh . . . soooo is that a yes?"

A whimper escaped her lips. She spun, frantic eyes searching the stacks as if expecting something to pop out and grab her.

"Uhhh, Maddy?" he said, stepping forward, and she shrank away.

"Please, no. Stop," she begged, choking back a sob.

Stunned, Kenny took another step. "What? Maddy, I'm not going to hurt you!"

"Please!" Another whimper, her eyes jittery glass orbs, her hand up as if to stop him from coming any closer.

Books behind him hurled themselves off the shelf, like a strong gust of wind had knocked them over. Maddy stared at the pile.

"Just . . . please let me go. Please."

It dawned on Kenny that she wasn't acting weird or being a freak. Her movements were more like a petrified cornered animal. This was fear.

Damn, what had they done to her?

Solemnly, he nodded and stepped aside.

Maddy shuffled forward, head down, hugging the shelf,

putting as much space between them as possible as she passed.

Then, she ran full speed out of the library, books in hand.

Maddy held her breath as she sprinted down the empty hallway—the only way to keep the sob climbing her throat bottled up. Clutching her books like a shield, she turned a corner in a frantic dash for Mrs. Morgan's classroom. The room was still off-limits due to the earthquake damage, but she slipped inside. They had swept up all the glass, boarded the windows, and pushed the mangled desks against the wall. She hunched down in the corner, peering out to see if Kendrick had followed her. When the coast seemed clear, Maddy coughed out a loud breath. The room spun. She fanned her face, trying to swallow as much air as she could.

They're trying to get me again.

Her earliest memory of torture had happened during her third day of seventh grade, after social services insisted Maddy start attending school, hoping to acclimate her with the other students, as most of them had been in the same class since pre-K. Maddy spent the week prior excitedly hemming skirts, mending buttons on her sweater, thanking God for the new adventure. But Papa drilled countless warnings in her head: *Don't talk to anyone. Don't get close to anyone. Stay away from the Negroes; they're dangerous. Stay out of the sun. Protect your hair at all costs. No one can know. No one can ever know!*

For the first time, Maddy had wondered why she had to pretend, why Papa had such a distrust of the world. It all felt so irrational and contrary to the Bible he taught. Proverbs 12:22 says, "The Lord detests lying lips, but he delights in people who are trustworthy." Weren't they lying to everyone about what she was? Wasn't that a sin? Torn, Maddy decided that she would make a friend at school, someone she could trust. She'd tell them everything, testing her theory . . . that Papa could be wrong, and find help to save his soul.

That's why she remembered the moment vividly: spring field day, when kids played games—balancing eggs on spoons, three-legged races, and hopping in potato sacks. Maddy sat at a shaded picnic table, away from the brutal sun, watching her classmates, wondering who her first friend would be. On the soccer field, a boy named Kendrick Scott tossed a football with some other boys. Palms dampening, she couldn't help staring. She had never been so close to another Black person before. Could he somehow sense that she was one of them?

SPLASH!

A water balloon cracked open like an egg next to her black-and-white oxfords. Startled, she sprang to her feet, the liquid painting the concrete. She pushed her glasses up her nose and spotted a group of kids holding water balloons in a rainbow of colors like giant M&M's.

"Why are you looking at Kenny like that?" a girl with bright red hair snapped. "Weirdo."

SPLASH!

Maddy gasped, instinctively reached for her hair. Still dry. Water and her hair . . . a lethal combination, but she couldn't tell them why, could she?

"No one can ever know!"

"My brother said your daddy used to sleep with Black hookers," a boy said. "You Black?"

Maddy's lungs twisted into a pretzel. "N-n-no. I'm white," she croaked.

The kids cackled. Did they believe her?

"Well, you stink!" another girl with brown hair shouted, and the group giggled. Maddy, at first so proud of her poodle skirt and sweater, was told within minutes of her arrival that she stank of sweat and old people, her skin greasy with sunblock. She couldn't take many showers; the humidity would've ruined her hair.

"She needs a bath!" the redhead laughed.

"So let's give her one," someone suggested.

"YEAH!"

"Bath time for Mad Mad Maddy!"

Heart leaping into her throat, Maddy glanced at the field. Kendrick stood watching, ball in hand, his face unreadable. She thought of screaming for help, but the words lodged in her throat.

"Stay away from the Negroes!"

She turned in time to see another balloon sailing toward her and took off running.

SPLASH!

"Get her!" someone shouted, and footsteps charged after her.

SPLASH! Another balloon at her heels. Panicking and turned around, she couldn't figure out which door to the school would open. They were all locked.

SPLASH!

She spun, back pressed against the wall as the group surrounded her.

"Please," she whimpered. "Don't. I . . ."

SPLASH!

Maddy let out an agonizing scream, fingernails clawing at the brick, ready to climb up the walls.

"Ha ha! Mad Mad Maddy spazzing out again!"

Maddy screeched, inching into a corner. "No, please, stop. Please . . ."

"Wendy, we need a countdown!"

A blond girl standing next to the redhead giggled before she sang. "Okay, ready? One! Two! Three!"

The balloons rained down in front of her, snapping and popping, soaking her shoes and white stockings. Arms wrapped over her head, Maddy begged and pleaded. The blond girl slowly stopped laughing.

It took an eternity for a gym monitor, who also seemed to be laughing at her, to arrive and break up the crowd.

"Maddy, it's just water." She chuckled. "It'll dry."

An inconsolable Maddy, wheezing panicked, painful breaths,

collapsed into her arms with bloody fingers. That night, she tried to tell Papa about the incident, but he offered no comfort.

"God makes no mistakes. It's not up to you to lean on your own understanding. It's up to you to obey."

Was that God punishing her for even considering disobeying Papa?

The day after, Charlotte, as an apology, invited her to a "secret spot" for lunch; Maddy was locked in a janitor's closet for the entire afternoon. Another girl invited Maddy to teen Bible study; Maddy was trapped in a classroom with a stack of porn printouts. She found a love letter in her locker, and when she thanked Jason for it, he loudly rejected her for ten minutes in front of the entire cackling school.

"Middle school is a cruel place," the nurse had told her. "It'll be better in high school."

But it wasn't.

Freshman year, someone filled her locker full of super-absorption pads. Sophomore year, someone stole her glasses and watched her bump into walls in the hallways. Junior year, someone hung air fresheners around her homeroom desk. But Maddy never reacted the same way she had the day of the water balloons. Because she had remembered another scripture: Proverbs 21:23, "Whoever keeps his mouth and his tongue keeps himself out of trouble." Maybe the Lord gave her to Papa to teach her discernment. Maybe they were not lying but shielding themselves from evil.

Thus, Maddy remained all but mute. If they treated her that way believing she was white, who knew what they'd do if they knew the truth?

Now, curled up in the corner of a dark classroom, Maddy once again fought through violent wheezing, her heart trying to hammer its way out of her chest.

The door squeaked open. Maddy gasped, pulling her knees close, squeezing herself tighter.

They found me!

"Maddy?" Mrs. Morgan stood in the doorway, bag hanging off her shoulder, the hallway light turning her into a dark silhouette. But Maddy recognized her voice. "I saw you running this way. Is everything okay?"

She didn't know what to say. Mrs. Morgan had only been in the school for two years. How could she explain what life had been like for her in Springville?

Mrs. Morgan closed the door and sat on the floor beside her.

"This is cozy," she quipped.

"I'm sorry," Maddy sniffed. "I know I'm not supposed to be in here."

"Don't be sorry. Just tell me what's wrong."

Maddy wrung her fingers.

"Come on, you can talk to me," Mrs. Morgan insisted.

Maddy hesitated, her trust in people broken beyond repair,

despite Mrs. Morgan being the nicest teacher she'd ever had.

"A . . . boy asked me to prom. Kendrick Scott."

"Kenny?" Mrs. Morgan frowned, then nodded as if impressed. "Whoa. That's . . . amazing! Are you excited?"

"No, I can't go. I can't! They're trying to trick me."

Mrs. Morgan blew out some air. "Boy, this whole prom thing has really shown people's true colors around here, hasn't it? If it's this bad for a prom, I can't imagine anyone's wedding." She leaned her head back as if deep in thought. "I know teachers aren't supposed to admit things like this, but I'm going to let you in on a little secret: we pay close attention to you kids. We listen in on your convos, see your text messages. We know all the juicy gossip. And I know this is going to sound crazy coming from me, but Kenny . . . he's different. Real mature for his age. Down-to-earth, thoughtful, focused, and humble—nothing like his friends. Even though he pretends to be. Knowing all that, I just can't see him, of all people, trying to trick you. So it's possible he really is just being nice."

Maddy shook her head hard.

Mrs. Morgan laughed. "I know. Hard to believe. But what if I'm right? Would it be so terrible to go to prom?"

Maddy nibbled on her bottom lip. She had never given prom a single thought. She only heard about it in passing, but she had no intention of going. Papa would never let her.

"You know what I think?" Mrs. Morgan said with a smirk.

"I think going to the All-Together prom would be a major statement to everyone."

"You do?"

"Hell yeah! Do you know, back in 1965, when this school first integrated, they literally canceled prom because they didn't want Black people attending, potentially dancing with one of their own? They didn't even want Black people to have a prom. Like, 'you can integrate, but we'll be damned if we allow you to have joy.'"

Maddy stared. It was the first time someone had spoken to her like she was a real Black girl. She didn't know how to respond.

"The fight for equality can get really ugly," Mrs. Morgan continued, shaking her head. "Segregation ended in 1964, and yet this town is carrying on like it's STILL 1964. Treating Black people like second-class citizens they only want to interact with when it suits their needs."

"But JFK gave them civil rights," Maddy retorted.

Mrs. Morgan cocked her head to the side. "Huh?"

Maddy licked her lips. "Well, I mean . . . Negroes marched peacefully, and in return, our thirty-sixth president, Lyndon B. Johnson, honoring our assassinated thirty-fifth president, John F. Kennedy, signed the 1964 Civil Rights Act."

Mrs. Morgan gaped at her for several beats. Maddy's stomach tightened. Had she messed up the dates?

"I don't know . . . if I've failed you or if someone else has.

But that's *not* what happened at all! It wasn't always peaceful."

"I don't understand."

Mrs. Morgan sighed. "Let me show you something."

Mrs. Morgan pulled out a laptop, booted it up, and opened a browser to YouTube. She pressed play on a black-and-white video—a group of Black people sitting at a lunch counter, as a group of white people swung and violently yanked at their clothes, pulling them off their stools, shoving them to the ground, blood splattering as they kicked them.

"What is this?" Maddy gasped, horrified.

"This is what you're not allowed to see. The school system pulled this out of the curriculum. Parents complained it was 'too disturbing.' Probably worried someone will recognize their grandpa's or mother's face."

"Why are they hitting them like that?"

"These men were called the Greensboro Four. They were doing a 'sit in' to protest the racial segregation policy at a store's lunch counter."

Maddy frowned. "But why were they sitting where they weren't supposed to?"

"Because sometimes you have to, like John Lewis said, 'Get into good trouble, necessary trouble,' for your voice to be heard."

Mrs. Morgan clicked through more videos: two Black teens being pummeled by a surging water hose; a man in his church suit being beaten by a mob; a bleeding girl carried out on a stretcher; German shepherds sinking their sharp teeth into arms and legs; policemen wielding their batons like swords slicing through weaponless marchers . . .

"It wasn't always gospel hymns and peaceful marches. The civil rights movement was a battle in the war against racism. People risked their lives to fight for equality. Let me show you one more thing."

She pulled up a black-and-white photo with a large crowd surrounding a tree near train tracks, a Black man tied to the trunk. Maddy squinted, and it took her a few moments to process the familiar scene. She knew the giant oak well, rooted close to the East Side border, near her home.

It was Springville.

"They say that this man fell in love with a girl from the West Side. No one was charged with his murder."

Maddy read the photo caption, calling it *The Lynching Tree*.

Mrs. Morgan pulled up more pictures of Springville: a *Whites Only* sign in front of the old market. Black people picking cotton up near Mr. Henry's farm. Maddy couldn't pull her eyes away from the screen. All those tapes Papa had, all the hundreds of black-and-white films and history documentaries they'd watched together, the way he boasted about Springville being a wholesome place in the past . . . Why hadn't she ever seen any of this?

Maybe he has seen it, she thought with stunning realization. Did he make her pretend to protect her?

"Don't you see?" Mrs. Morgan continued. "Just the act of you going to the prom, your school's first integrated prom, is a protest in and of itself. Your presence adds to the resistance. It speaks out against the racism happening in this town and others."

She paused to look at Maddy, as if making sure her words were penetrating. No teacher had ever paid much attention to her. Most blew her off as a nuisance or forgot she existed. But around Mrs. Morgan, she wasn't invisible. The tenderness had an unfamiliar motherly quality that made Maddy wary yet hopeful.

"You go to that prom, Maddy. You go to that prom, and you show everyone that you're not some girl who can be pushed around or made fun of. Your actions will speak louder than any words could. They'll say that you are strong, brave, and powerful beyond measure."

Maddy released a breath and studied her hands.

"Powerful," Maddy mumbled.

Yes. That's exactly what she was.

"You want to watch a movie tonight? My parents will be home late, so I can skip curfew."

Wendy gripped Kenny's hand as they strolled down the hall.

He shrugged, giving her a fake smile. "Yeah. Sounds good, babe."

Wendy ignored the panic tugging the back of her brain. She

couldn't catch a good read on his mood. They used to be so in sync, but the closer they sailed toward graduation, the further he seemed to drift.

Maybe he's nervous about us going to different schools, she thought, wondering if she should tell him about her change of plan.

"Hey," she started. "I . . . got something to tell you."

"Yeah, what's up?"

But just as Wendy opened her mouth, Mrs. Morgan flew around the corner, her face lighting up as she spotted them.

"Ah! Just the two dummies I was looking for!"

"Excuse me?" Wendy blanched, realizing she sounded as bitchy as Jules.

Mrs. Morgan ignored her, glaring right at Kenny. "You asked Maddy to prom?"

He stiffened before his shoulders sagged. "Yeah," he mumbled.

Wendy tried to keep the shock off her face. He had asked her and never mentioned it? *How could he keep something like that from me?*

"Why?" Mrs. Morgan spat, crossing her arms.

Kenny opened his mouth but stopped himself, eyes flickering away, full of something close to shame. Wendy ping-ponged between them and went into protective girlfriend mode.

"That's really none of your business," Wendy said, her tone clipped.

Mrs. Morgan scoffed and continued to address Kenny.

"After everything that's happened these last few weeks, you really think this is a good idea?"

"Yes," Wendy snapped, refusing to be ignored. "That's exactly why. After everything that's happened, we owe it to Maddy. Right, Kenny?"

"Yeah," he mumbled, eyes on the floor. "Right."

He didn't sound super convincing. Why did he seem so defeated?

"Maddy is in a very delicate place right now," Mrs. Morgan explained. "After being brutally outed and humiliated by your friends, if you can even call them that, she's now in the middle of a self-discovery journey. So whatever you have up your sleeves—"

"She wasn't outed by anyone! It wasn't our fault she got her hair wet. If anything, she brought this on herself."

Mrs. Morgan chuckled. "Well, aren't you the perfect little Jules Marshall clone?"

Wendy's jaw dropped. Could a teacher even talk to them like this?

"So, you're okay with this, Kenny? The most popular guy in school taking Maddy Washington to the prom?"

He looked up at that comment, his eyes going dark. The same way they did during spirit day.

"What's so wrong with Maddy Washington?" he sneered.

"Absolutely nothing," Mrs. Morgan balked.

"Then why are you asking me like that?" he barked. "Like

there's something wrong with her. Like I should be embarrassed to be seen with her!"

Mrs. Morgan's face fell as she tripped over her words. "That's not what . . . I just mean . . ."

"Yeah, I know what people like you really mean. Always looking for some sob story so you can play savior. You think you helping by pitying her?"

Wendy glanced down at Kenny's hand, balled into a tight fist.

Mrs. Morgan quickly collected herself. "Well, I can say the same with the stunt you two are trying to pull."

Wendy moved to end her ambush. "This isn't a joke. We're not pulling anything, and we don't pity her. Besides, prom has nothing to do with school, so it has nothing to do with you. Right, Kenny?"

He shook his head. "I've gotta get to class," he grumbled, and stormed off, leaving a stunned Wendy behind.

Two periods later, his anger had not cooled. In the past two weeks, she had seen him more worked up than she had during their entire relationship. Even after losing a game, he seemed firmly indifferent and rational about it.

When she later inquired why he didn't tell her about asking Maddy to prom, he shrugged it off and said he forgot.

Wendy stared straight through his lie, trying to detect the reason but finding none.

• • •

Maddy sat cross-legged on her bed, staring at the hurricane lamp sitting on the windowsill, the tall white candle unlit. They had candles all around the house, some collecting years of gray dust. Papa said many of them were from his father's church. She wondered why they never used them.

The four books on telekinesis she'd checked out of the library floated around her, spinning like little planets. She rubbed the invisible threads between her thumb and forefingers. The faster she rubbed, the faster they went. She let go of the threads, and the books came to a halt, hovering arm's length over her head. She breathed in and concentrated on the lamp. The books talked all about focusing one's energy, but practice was key. She called to the lamp.

Move.

The lamp shook and glided across the room, bumping into a hairbrush floating nearby.

Maddy had been practicing with smaller items around the house. Ones she could explain if they happened to fall or break. The bed had a strange creak that hadn't been there before she dropped it, and she'd found a small crack in the vanity mirror.

Maddy held the lamp victoriously, glancing up at the various items orbiting her, wondering if the others sat in their homes, belongings wafting about. She grinned at the thought. There were other people in the world like her. She wasn't alone. She just needed to find them—someday.

As the lamp drifted back to its place, she reached for one of the books and leaned back into her pillows. What else could she learn to do? The lines on the page blurred to a foggy spot. She squinted, taking her glasses off to rub her eyes. But when she opened them, her vision sharpened into perfect focus, the words crystal clear on the page. She froze, examining the glasses still in her hand. She tried them on again, and the words became a cloudy haze. She ripped them off, blinking. The dark room seemed to sparkle, a psychedelic brightness of colors, the silver handle on her brush like a new nickel.

"Oh," she mused. She had needed glasses ever since she could remember. Now no longer.

She glanced at the lamp again. Its gold base shone as if it belonged in a palace with kings.

"Madison," Papa called from downstairs.

A jolt hit Maddy in the spine. In an instant, the candle in the lamp flickered and a flame burst, soaring up to the ceiling. Maddy gasped, and the books fell to the floor. She dove for the lamp, the fire blackening the glass vase.

"Oh God, oh God," she whimpered as the spot on the ceiling formed a circle.

Focus, focus. Focus.

"Stop, stop."

The flame danced in response. She had to put it out before it burned the whole place down. She threw open the window, poked her head out to check the ground clearance below, and reached for the lamp's base. But holding it, her hand . . . her nerves hardened. She took a deep breath, in through the nose, out through the mouth.

Stop.

The fire put itself out as quick as it had started.

"Madison? What are you doing?"

Heart pounding, Maddy sucked in the night air. She straightened up and patted her freshly washed hair.

"Yes, Papa," she croaked. "I'm coming!"

Maddy rushed downstairs, her mind in shambles. The books never mentioned anything about fire. Was it a sign from God?

Papa stood in his apron, behind the kitchen chair set up next to the stove. He had one hand on his hip and the other holding the hot comb.

"You've kept me waiting," he hissed.

She lowered her head, slipping on the smock. "I'm sorry, Papa."

"Hurry up," he snapped, turning on the burner.

Maddy sat with her neck straight, eyes forward. The kitchen walls glowed, the floor pristine. She surveyed the room in awe as Papa angrily sliced parts through her hair.

"Which event triggered the Cuban missile crisis?"

Maddy forced down a groan. She was tired of the questions. Tired of reciting the same facts when there was so much more to learn. And if Papa knew so much about their country, then he must know about the people in the videos Mrs. Morgan showed her. The pain and agony. Why did he never mention how wicked humanity could be?

But she took a deep breath and answered his question. "US planes discovered Soviet nuclear missile sites being built in Cuba. The US had to respond to protect the lives of men, women, and children."

"Who was the vice president when the US entered the war?"

"Lyndon B. Johnson.

Papa smacked the back of her head, and she whiplashed forward, ducking to block another blow.

"You know better!" Papa spat. "It was Henry Wallace!"

"But you didn't say which war, Papa," she cried, petting her own head.

"I know exactly what I said!"

Maddy's eyes snapped to the burner, where the hot comb sat sizzling. She bit her lip and straightened, gripping the sides of the chair to keep from shaking, the heat from the burner roasting her cheek. If she messed up again . . .

"Which Negro radical was found to be a communist spy, threatening the security of our nation?"

Maddy blinked, and in the seconds her lids closed, an image flashed from the video Mrs. Morgan had shown her flashed. The agonizing expression on a woman's face burned in Maddy's mind's eye. "Martin Luther King Junior," Maddy replied, her voice hoarse as she fought back tears.

Papa grunted, gathering a dollop of grease.

It was just a flicker of an idea. Didn't even realize she was already doing it until a hot thread slipped between her fingers and her eyes darted to the burner, into the blue flame.

And just as Papa reached for the hot comb, the flame shot up.

Papa jumped back. "Eh! Lord in Heaven!"

Maddy kept her head straight and perfectly still . . . with the tiniest smirk on her face.

NINE

MADDY DID IT
EPISODE 6
"Mad Mad Maddy"

Tanya: So you knew Maddy well, then?

Nina Floros: Not really. But I did see her from time to time. We were, what, five years apart? So it's not like we were ever in school together or even had a real conversation.

Michael [narration]: This is Nina Floros. She grew up living next door to the Washingtons before leaving for college. We decided to try and find someone who might have seen or known Maddy before she turned twelve to get an idea of what she was like.

Nina: Springville was such a small town. I knew I wanted out of there ASAP. My parents moved away about two years before Prom Night, and thank God they did. I haven't been back since.

Michael: What do you remember about Maddy?

Nina: After everything that happened, the things I do remember
make a lot of sense now. I honestly didn't know she existed
until she was maybe five. There were whispers in the
neighborhood that Mr. Washington had a kid, but no one
ever saw her. He never let her outside. I only got a glimpse
of her once or twice over our back fence. Usually, she
snuck out and would stand in her backyard, just staring up
at the sky. She was . . . quiet. Her hair was always braided
in pigtails. It wasn't until those birds that I finally got a good
look at her. Pale as a ghost.

Michael: Birds?

Nina: Yeah. When the birds, I mean, the crows, attacked their
house. Like, hundreds of them. Maddy ran out the door,
carrying on about the end of days. You didn't hear about
that?

Michael: No!

Nina: But . . . that's the whole reason why she started going to
school in the first place! It's why they called her Mad Mad
Maddy. They say she went crazy that day.

Michael: Do you remember anything from that day with the
birds? Like, how you were feeling?

Nina: Uhhh . . . not really. After the police cleared out, I was
supposed to go on a date with my boyfriend but . . . I
wasn't feeling well.

Michael: What was wrong?

Nina: I had this headache. Actually, yeah, I remember. I had a crazy headache and was super nauseous and dizzy. I was scared that I might've been pregnant or something. I told Ian to pick up a test from the pharmacy and I ended up taking it at a gas station bathroom. Thank God it was negative. I broke up with him right after high school.

Springville Metro, August 2008
Birds Mysteriously Attack Home

A flock of more than a hundred crows crashed into the home of Thomas Washington, a local business owner. The birds broke several windows, covering the roof and nearby trees, before falling to their deaths.

Washington's twelve-year-old daughter was seen running out of the house screaming, bloodstains on her pants. Police were called to the scene, and she was rushed to Springville General. After examination, it appeared that she was not hurt during the incident.

Animal control could not determine the cause of the birds' strange behavior.

May 23, 2014

There's something about a well-meaning white woman telling a Black man what to do that will always rub them the wrong way. Especially when that well-meaning white woman is kind of right.

The ambush with Mrs. Morgan made Kenny more determined

than ever to bring Maddy to prom. He'd camp outside Maddy's home for days if he had to. But first, he decided to strike where she couldn't possibly run.

Parked in front of Sal's, he glanced in the rearview mirror at the Good Old Days, truck engine still running. He hadn't told Wendy about asking Maddy to prom because Maddy's reaction had just been too . . . sad? Pitiful? He didn't have the word for it. But one emotion had eclipsed the entire moment: guilt. His friends were bullies. Racist, asshole bullies, which made him just as much of an asshole.

He didn't want to be an asshole. And it wasn't too late to do the right thing.

A few kids from school were hanging out on Sal's terrace, some inside playing arcade games. Sal wiped the counter for the tenth time, stealing glances out the door, waiting for Kenny to step inside. Everyone would see him.

Am I really about to do this?

"Fuck it," he grumbled, hopped out of his truck, and jogged across the street.

A cowbell clanged as he pushed the front door. He had never stepped foot inside the Good Old Days before. He'd never needed to.

"Oh, hello! Be right there," Maddy called from somewhere in the back.

He glanced around. The place resembled a hoarder's den with an impressive number of artifacts crammed inside.

On a shelf next to a dusty typewriter sat several porcelain dolls. Below them, the sight of a figurine made his back tense. He examined the mammy statue, a big woman with Black skin, thick lips, wearing a red dress with an apron, and a kerchief on her head. He'd read about these images from minstrel shows. What white people thought all Black people looked like, eating watermelon on their porches and dancing a jig. Jules had just about come dressed similarly to school.

"What the fuck?" he mumbled.

"Kendrick?" Maddy stood by the counter in an oil-stained apron, her mouth gaping. Kenny hadn't heard his full name in so long he almost looked around to see who she was talking to.

She rushed over to him, peering out the glass door with frantic eyes. "What are you doing here?"

He gripped the statue like he would a football, ready to chuck it across the room. "This is what you be selling up in here?" he snarled.

Maddy glanced at the statue then back at him. "What's wrong? It's in mint condition."

He gawked, coughing out a laugh. She didn't have a clue how offensive it was. How could she? "Nothing, I guess," he grumbled.

Maddy peered out the door again, wringing her fingers. "My father went to the bank. He'll be back any moment."

Kenny nodded. Something seemed different about her, but he couldn't place it. He switched gears. "We didn't get a chance to finish our talk the other day. About prom."

Maddy balked, her eyes growing wide. "I . . . I can't. Now, please. Can you—"

"You have plans or something?"

She backed away. "Um. No."

"Then what's the problem?"

She checked at the door and huffed, frustrated to the point of tears. "Why . . . can't you all just leave me alone?"

The crack in her voice made him pause, but he still felt determined to change her mind. He took in her wool sweater, and a question popped in his head. "Hey, that stuff about you having lupus. Is it true?"

She blinked, thrown off by the sudden change in subject. "No."

"Then why lie?"

Maddy sighed, her shoulders slumping. "I didn't . . . want to lie," she mumbled, staring at her feet.

He nodded, gripping the mammy statue, and placed it back on the display. Maybe they had something in common after all. "Yeah, my parents make me do a lot of things I don't want to, too."

Maddy stopped shaking, eyes sweeping over his face, and it finally occurred to him what seemed so off—he'd never seen her without glasses before. The afternoon sunlight beaming through the door turned her brown eyes hazel; she almost looked like a completely different person.

"But why me?" she asked. "You're with Wendy Quinn."

So she does notice things, he mused. "Wendy doesn't want to go. And I guess I know how it feels to pretend to be something you're . . . not."

She gulped, wringing her hands. "I . . . I don't know.

"It's just one night."

Maddy sighed in defeat. "If I say yes, will you leave?"

He shrugged. "Maybe."

Her eyes flared and he laughed. "I'm messing with you! Of course! But I . . . want you to say yes because you want to go. Ain't trying to force you or nothing."

Arms wrapped around herself, she glanced outside for a long while, but not checking for her father. Seemed like she was staring right into Sal's. The panic melted from her face.

"Okay. I'll go with you."

TEN

May 24, 2014

JASON'S PARENTS WERE out of town, which meant only one thing: house party. Half the school took up every inch of his massive ranch-style home in the same subdivision Jules lived in. A speaker blasted from the kitchen, next to the kegs, chips, and boxes of Sal's pizza. Bodies in the outdoor pool glowed, the fire pit roaring. In the living room, Jason played bartender, tossing a shaker in the air, mixing various concoctions that Kayleigh happily tried as Chris played beer pong on the dining room table. Wendy snuggled on Kenny's lap, sipping a beer, laughing at Charlotte retelling cheerleading fumbles. A lightness had returned to their group after weeks of tension. But still, all anyone wanted to talk to them about was Maddy.

"I can't believe you two are really going through with this," Kayleigh said from the sofa.

Wendy shrugged. "Well, I wasn't going to prom anyway.

173

And after everything that happened, Kenny just wanted to do the right thing."

That was her carefully crafted answer. In truth, it killed her to give up prom, but she hoped her orchestrated efforts would pay off big further down the road, where it really mattered. And it seemed to be working. Everyone commended her on being a selfless person, giving up prom for the less fortunate. She had received a ton of interview requests and hoped she could parlay the opportunities into possible summer internships where she could forge even more connections to help Kenny when he entered the league. Kenny shrugged off the attention. Their after-prom plans hadn't changed, still heading to Greenville to party with their friends at the Hilton hotel.

"You know. I don't think Maddy got it too bad," Jason mused. "My dad told me some of the stuff him and his buddies used to do back when they were at SHS, and man . . . they pretty much ran people out of town or back to the East Side. All anyone did was laugh at her hair."

Kenny stiffened beneath Wendy. She quickly tried to change subjects.

"OMG, did anyone watch *The Vampire Diaries* last night? It was so good."

"What do you think she's going to wear?" Charlotte chuckled, ignoring her. "OMG! You think she'll come in that dusty sweater?"

Wendy rubbed small circles in Kenny's shoulder, hoping to calm him.

"No clue," she quipped, and changed the subject again. "But! You're still going to help me with decorations, right?"

"You expect me to help decorate *both* proms?"

"Please," Wendy whined. "You promised. We'll do the All-Together prom first. It'll be real quick."

"Uh-oh," Chris said, staring at the front door, holding a pong ball midair.

Jules walked in wearing tight dark jeans, boots, and a midriff top, Brady not far behind her. People cleared the foyer. No one had seen or heard from her in over two days. They had started to wonder if her dad had sent her away. Jules scanned the house until her eyes locked on Wendy. The temperature in the room plummeted.

Jason toggled between Wendy and Jules and chuckled. "Welp. I'm out of here," he quipped, heading for the kitchen, but Kayleigh grabbed his arm.

"Don't you dare," Kayleigh growled, glancing back at Jules. "We may need your help tearing them apart."

Jules strutted across the room, her head held high, stopping a few feet in front of Wendy, a cruel smile on her lips. Wendy tried to keep her red cup from shaking.

"So. I heard a little rumor that Mad Mad Maddy is going to prom. Know anything about that?"

Wendy gulped, the tension palpable, yet made no move to close the distance between them. "I . . . I was going to tell you."

"When, exactly? After you told everyone else?" She swayed, thigh bumping into a sofa arm.

Wendy's mind worked fast to find a problem-solving tactic before a fight could reach epic proportions. It's not like she wanted to make Jules mad, she hated the idea of a blow-up happening in front of the entire school. She decided to try to downplay and smooth it all over with a compliment. "It's just one night," she said, with a forced laugh. "It's totally no big deal. And you're still going to the . . . regular prom. You're going to look so pretty in your dress! You won't even see—"

"That's not the point!" Jules screamed, bringing the house to a standstill.

Wendy bit her lip. This time, Kenny rubbed her back.

Jules grabbed a bottle of vodka off the coffee table. "You know she ruined my life, right?" Her eyes set on Kenny. "And you, her predictable puppy, you're just going along with it?"

"It was my idea," Wendy said, jumping up, her words shaky. "Leave him out of this."

She snorted. "Nice. Practicing for *The Real Housewives of Springville*, I see?" Jules's claws were fully out now.

"Jules, can we go somewhere private and—"

"Why are you helping her?" Jules interrogated. "Don't you realize what she's done?"

"She didn't do anything," Wendy insisted. "We did something to her. I know it was a joke but . . . we really hurt her."

"So what?" Jules slurred, her steps unsteady. "Seriously, why should we give a fuck about Maddy Washington?"

"Because she's a real person!" Kenny shot back. "Try putting yourself in her shoes. That's if you can."

Wendy stuttered to a confused silence. He didn't even yell on the field. Why was he coming to Maddy's defense so aggressively?

Jules snorted in disgust. "Oh yeah? Really? Tell me, have you ever talked to Maddy Washington before all this? Have either of you ever said more than two words to her before now? Ever been by her house or know what college she's going to?"

Kenny froze, his jaw going slack.

"Right. You don't even know her! And just because she's Black now, you're trying to stick up for her when before you were laughing along with us. So don't sit and judge me for not giving a fuck about someone I don't even know, putting her above my REAL friends!"

The room fell silent, all eyes on Wendy. She flushed red, glancing back at Kenny, who gazed down at the floor.

Wendy sighed. "Jules, I'm—"

"Hypocrites! The both of you. That's what y'all are!"

Kenny pushed himself out of the chair and turned to Wendy. "Come on. We're leaving."

"Are you really going to let *this* guy tell you what to do?" Jules balked before sneering at Kenny. "Don't think for a second you're better than any of us because you can throw a freaking ball. People have been blowing your head up for years, and I'm sick of it."

"Yo, Jules," Kenny said, a smirk on his lips. "How about you stop worrying about Maddy and me and start thinking about what gas station you're gonna work at? Considering no school is gonna touch you now."

Wendy gasped as Jules stood motionless, eyes flooding with tears.

He set his beer down and walked off, the crowd parting to make way.

"Fucking dick. You know he's not even that good, right? Probably some affirmative action recruitment bullshit."

Wendy gaped at Jules in horror. She turned toward the door and followed. "Kenny, wait!"

"Hey! We're not finished!" Jules shouted.

Kenny was already down the front walkway as Wendy shivered in the chilly night air, avoiding the stares. How could Jules say something so disgusting? Didn't she know how hard he had worked?

"Wendy!" Jules grabbed her arm, digging her hot-red nails into Wendy's flesh. "You're supposed to be my best friend," she shouted, hurt in her eyes.

"I *am* your best friend," Wendy cried. "But . . . what you did, we did, it was really shitty."

"But she ruined my life!"

"I know. And I'm . . . I'm just trying to make everything right."

"God, Wendy, no one's falling for this con you got going on! Everyone knows you're doing this to look all innocent for

Kenny, trying to secure your bankroll 'cause your parents are broke, and it's fucking pathetic!"

The words knocked Wendy's teeth in. She was used to hearing Jules spit her vitriol. But not at her, never at her. It was the last straw.

"You know what, Jules?" she started with a shaky voice. "Maddy didn't ruin anything. She didn't do anything to you. You did this all on your own. YOU threw the pencil. YOU came to the rally in blackface. There's no one to blame here but YOU."

Jules lost her composure for a fraction of a second before her eyes narrowed. She shook her head with a scoff. "Oh, we're so done. No more sleepovers, no more shopping in my closet, no more rides to school, and no more being my best friend!"

Wendy crossed her arms and straightened her neck. "If that's what you want, then fine."

Jules chuckled and clapped. "Ha! Nice. Way to stand by your man. You know you're going to be real sorry you picked him over me."

Wendy spun around, speed walking to Kenny's truck, desperately trying to hold in an earth-shattering sob.

From the May 2014 New York Times article "A Siren with a Double Meaning"

For more than forty years, the Springville Power Plant siren sounded twice daily: once, at four p.m. for their routine testing, then again at six forty-five p.m., letting non-white residents know it was time to return home. Herman Merriweather Sr., a mechanic, had lived in Springville his entire life before his children moved him to Greenville.

"Springville wasn't a bad place. We all got along fine enough. But once that bell rang, Black folk knew that they better get theyselves back over them train tracks by dusk if they wanted to see another day."

Mr. Merriweather grew up on the East Side, a descendant from a long line of sharecroppers and railroad workers. He remembers vividly when Springville High School (which has been in the media frequently due to recent incidents causing growing racial tension in the small town) first integrated.

"I was seventeen at the time, and if I'm honest, we were all fine keeping things the way they were. Because we knew, just knew, that if them white folk had to do something they didn't want to do, they'd make all our lives a living hell."

The siren ordinance made it impossible for him to play sports or participate in certain after-school activities. Mr. Merriweather remembers running from a car of white kids close to sundown.

"They chased me all the way back to the East Side, then was sitting next to me in English the very next day like nothing happened."

Springville's history and politics are a closely guarded

secret, with most records sealed, unavailable, or lost in an alleged basement flood. When asked about the siren ordinance, officials placed responsibility on the power plant.

"That's just an old rumor," Mayor Helen Arnold said. "The power plant tests the system daily to keep us safe. Nothing more."

Despite numerous emails, the power plant could not be reached to confirm its testing protocols, but Merriweather remembers an alarm prior to the plant being built.

"Before that power plant went up, it was a train bell letting us know it was time to head on home."

According to reports, in the fall of 2000, the town turned off the second alarm. But the alarm returned after the town voted to restore it for "nostalgia's sake."

"Same people on that town council were on the school board and had kids in the school too. If they wanted their kid to star in the school play, she gonna star in it. Wanted they son to be the valedictorian, that's what he'll be. You make a fuss, you might find yourself out of a job or worse."

Although no one follows the sundown rules anymore, the alarm still blares like a readying threat.

ELEVEN

May 26, 2014

THE LAST BELL rang, and for a change, Maddy wasn't running out the door. She didn't want to go home just yet. She wanted to watch more YouTube videos in the library. Once she found one, she'd fallen down a rabbit hole. She reviewed dozens of speeches and mini-documentaries on the civil rights era. The images of riots imprinted on her brain replayed over and over each time she blinked. But like a drug, she couldn't stop herself from watching, and when she felt herself sinking, she'd think of Kenny . . . and his proposal.

The muscles in her face twitched. She was really going to prom. Every time she remembered, her chest tingled, lips curling into a sugary smile. She hadn't decided to go to prom because of Kenny or for all the reasons Mrs. Morgan spoke about. She had chosen for herself, for the possibility of having just one day as a normal girl. The gift, her powers—it had to be a sign from God to start truly living in the light. No more hiding. Nothing could make up for the years she'd lost, spent pretending to be something she wasn't. But one normal day could be a new beginning.

If she could only find a way to ask Papa.

"Hey, Maddy."

Maddy yelped, spinning in her chair. "Kendrick?"

Kenny stood behind her. His smile gleamed in the afternoon sun. "Did I scare you again?"

She quickly closed her browser and stood up. "Um, no," she squeaked, her head lowering as her stomach sank. *He's changed his mind*, she thought. She knew it was too good to be true. How stupid to have let her heart swell even a centimeter with hope.

"You busy? Feel like grabbing a milkshake?"

She blinked up at him. "W-w-what?"

"Milkshake? You want one? It's a nice day out. And, figured, since we're going to prom, we should at least get to know each other a little."

Maddy took a cautious step backward, glancing around. Was this all some joke? Another trick? "Um, I don't know if I . . . well . . . I think I shouldn't . . . I—I . . . can't." She couldn't drive alone in a car with a boy. Papa would murder him *and* her.

Kenny nodded, but his expression remained. "I'll have you home in an hour. You can ghost for an hour, can't you?"

No, she wanted to cry out. But then again . . . so much was different now. The power made her different, stronger, braver.

Maybe just this once.

"Um, okay."

• • •

Maddy sat at a round picnic table under a bloodred umbrella at the Dairy Queen, sweat building on her neck and between her legs. Every time she tried to stay in the shade, the sun seemed to inch closer to her. She gripped her sweater, jerking at every car passing by, petrified one of them would be Papa coming to collect her.

You're here. You're doing this. Everything will be fine.

She watched Kenny place their order at the counter, admiring his sharp chin and dimpled smile, the way he crossed his arms, making his shoulder blades push at his T-shirt like angel wings. God makes such wondrous creatures.

The Dairy Queen was just at the town's edge, near the power plant and one of those gas stations truckers stopped at to take showers and refuel. Maddy couldn't remember the last time she had been so far from home. Far enough where no one would see them.

Because he doesn't want to be seen with me.

The dark thought slipped in quick. Maddy nibbled on her thumb.

A group of girls skipped out of the Dairy Queen, giggling in their midriff tops and hip-hugging jeans, blond hair blowing free. Maddy gripped her itchy sweater, staring down at her own outfit. She yanked the sweater off, opened the top button of her shirt, freed her hair from its bun, and combed down the thick strands with her fingers. A small step in the right direction of something ordinary. Something less embarrassing. The heat and humidity would surely make her hair swell. But she no longer had a secret to protect, and the world had not ended like Papa had made her believe. Instead, a weight had been lifted. But the freedom still tasted bitter, like medicine she had always needed, a cure for something unseen.

"Here we go," Kenny sang as he approached. "Vanilla for you. Strawberry for me."

"Thank you," she muttered, gripping the icy cup to cool her clammy hands.

Kenny sat across the table, noticing her wardrobe change with an appreciative nod. Maddy couldn't help staring at his bulging biceps. How smooth they must feel to the touch . . .

She snatched her straw and sucked the lustful thought away, silently promising God fifteen more minutes of prayer before bed.

"How is it?"

It wasn't until he asked that she took a moment to take in the flavor. "It's . . . good," she admitted, surprised. "I've never had a milkshake before."

He laughed. "What? Really?"

She sighed. "Never."

There were so many nevers. Never been to a dance, never been to the movies or a football game or bowling, never been to a city, never driven a car, and never been kissed. A terrible sadness filled her stomach, the aching hunger for well-lived life.

"Wow. That's crazy."

Maddy had dreamed of this—going to a soda bar with a boy, sharing a milkshake, everything she saw in *Happy Days*. Papa loved that show but still thought it was a little too advanced for his Madison.

They sat at the table, slurping their frosty drinks, avoiding each other's eyes. The whirl of the afternoon power plant siren filled their ears. Growing up with it, most didn't even notice the noise. But Kenny craned his neck toward the sound, then turned back.

"My dad works at the plant," he admitted, as if embarrassed.

Her arms softened. "Are you close with your papa?"

His eyes went blank. "No."

"Oh."

Kenny drummed his fingers then snapped. "Ah! Almost forgot to tell you, I got tickets. They tried to tell me it was past the deadline and all the tables were full, but I told them they better rethink that since I was taking you."

She gulped. "Tickets?"

"Yeah. Prom tickets."

Prom tickets? She hadn't even considered it. She knew so little about . . . everything. "Oh. Um, how much do I owe you?"

He shook his head. "Naw, don't worry about it."

He was being nice. Too nice. The nicer he seemed, the more pitiful she felt.

"You don't have to do that," she insisted, trying to sound strong.

"Well, what if I just want to?" He laughed.

She sucked in a breath. *Be normal*, she reminded herself. *It's normal for boys to give gifts.* "Then . . . thank you."

They stared at one another, the wind kicking up Maddy's freed hair. Kenny's eyes widened, and he cleared his throat. "Soooo . . . what color is your dress?"

"Dress?"

"For prom. I have to make sure my vest and stuff match. Probably aren't many suits left, and I ain't trying to look like a waiter."

Maddy's heart sped up. "Um. I don't know yet. Haven't had a chance to go shopping."

"Oh. Right."

Maddy glanced down at her hands, hoping her lie was believable. Another thing that had never crossed her mind: she needed a dress. She also needed shoes, a bag, maybe makeup. He probably would look so handsome in a tux, she thought. Like Gene Kelly in *Singin' in the Rain*. But then her heart thumped hard against her rib cage.

How will I do my hair?

Most days she wore her hair down or tied in a low ponytail. But for something like the prom, she would need to style it, maybe with curls, like Ginger Rogers or Shirley Temple. Would Papa help her? Would he finally buy the curling iron she'd been dreaming of or bring her to a real salon?

They sat in awkward silence. Kenny, staring at his palm,

shook his head with a chuckle. "You don't talk much, do you?"

So distracted with worry over all the prom preparations, an answer slipped out without her knowing. "Or maybe you talk too much."

Kenny cocked his head to the side and let out a barking laugh.

Mortified, she gasped, hands flying up to cover her face. "Oh! Oh no, oh no, oh no. I'm so sorry!" What was that? The voice was almost unrecognizable.

"Naw, it's cool," he said, waving it away, laughter quieting. "I just didn't know you had it in you. Come on, you don't have to hide."

She peered at him through her fingers at his dazzling white smile. Papa always said women should be seen and not heard, but Kendrick didn't seem to mind. In fact, he liked it. She righted herself with a deep breath.

"There you go," he chuckled. "Much better."

Maddy's shoulders inched up to her ears. She wasn't used to talking. She remained mute at school. Even at home, Papa spoke at her, not with her. But she should at least try. That's what normal kids did.

"Uh, do you know where you're going to college?"

Kenny frowned. "Are you . . . kidding?"

Maddy replayed the question in her head. Had she said something wrong?

He coughed out a laugh. "Did you miss the whole press

conference in the gym, where I picked up the hat?"

"The . . . hat?"

Kenny rubbed his face, holding back a smirk. "Okay. Yeah, I'm going to the University of Alabama."

She nibbled on her straw. "Is that a good school?"

"Is that a good—oh, now I know you're shitting me!" He laughed. "Yes. It's a very good school. The top school. Well, at least for football."

She gripped her cup. "Um, what will you major in?"

"Does it matter?" he scoffed.

Her eyebrows pinched. "But you're more than just football, right?"

Kenny looked at her as if seeing her for the first time, and a certain serenity melted into him. "English," he said, with a small smile. "What about you? Where you going to school?"

Maddy stiffened. "Papa won't . . . I mean, I don't want to go to college."

Kenny started to say something, then quickly changed his mind. Just the mention of her father made her hands tremble. She glimpsed over both shoulders, her neck growing hot.

"You okay?"

"I'm fine," she chirped, pasting on a smile.

He set down his cup and folded his hands. "I got so many questions. About what you did. Or why you did what you did. But . . . I also think I know the answers already. And it really wouldn't help me get to know you better. Sounds weird, right?"

189

She shrugged. "A little."

He cocked his head to the side, amused by something. "Give me your hand."

Maddy gulped, trying to remain brave, and extended her arm on the table.

"Damn, you're freezing," he laughed. He turned her hand palm-side up, pressing two fingers to her wrist. "And your pulse is racing. You're either lying, or you're nervous."

"Or scared."

Kenny's mouth dropped, releasing her. "Why are you scared of me?" he asked, seeming wounded.

"Um, not of you, this is just . . . all so wonderful but a bit out of my lane." She touched her own wrist where his fingers once sat. "That was an interesting trick."

"My mom's a nurse. When I was little, she had me convinced she was a psychic palm reader. She knew everything I was thinking. Then . . . my dad told me the truth." He sighed with a smile that didn't quite touch his eyes.

Maddy yearned for such memories with her mother. Her mother would have wanted her to go to the prom with a boy like Kenny, she told herself. She'd even help pick out a dress and do her hair. If she was still alive.

"Okay, how about a quick game of twenty questions?" he said, drumming the table. "I'll start. What's your favorite book?"

He asked her so quick she said the first thing that came to mind. "The Bible."

He barked a laugh. "What?"

Maddy gulped then let out a small giggle. "There's so many characters, heroes, and villains all in one book. God inspired a lot of stories."

"Well, at least I got a laugh out of you. Don't think I've ever heard you laugh before." He nodded. "Okay, now you ask me a question."

"Anything?"

"Yup?"

She placed her cup down. "Uh, what are some of your hobbies when you're not at school?"

"Hm," he mused, staring at the table. "I was going to say training and running, but that all has to do with the game. I guess I don't really have any. Other than maybe reading, which I don't tell people."

"Why are you embarrassed that you read?"

Kenny started. "I . . . I'm not. And it's my turn anyway."

She nodded.

"Favorite song that gets you hyped?"

She assumed he meant excited and could only think of one that Papa liked to listen to when he worked on his car. "Elvis Presley's 'Blue Suede Shoes.'"

"What the fuck?" he cackled, slapping a hand over his face.

Maddy winced. "Um, can you, please, not curse at me? Please?" Cursing had a violence to it that seemed too familiar to home.

"Oh! My bad. I wasn't cursing at you, though . . . but, sorry."

She took a breath. "My turn? Where's the farthest you've ever been?"

"Easy. USC in California. My dad wanted to check out their stadium, even though I knew I wasn't going to play there."

"Is that near Hollywood?" she asked, leaning in. "What was it like? Did you see any movie stars?"

"No movie stars," he mused. "It was nice, though. The palm trees and beaches. But no place like home."

Maddy smiled, thinking of how glamorous all the mansions must be, just like in the movies.

"Okay, my turn," Kenny said, resetting himself. "When you have kids, what is one thing you'd do different than your parents?"

Maddy knew the answer right away. "I'd love them for who they are. Not who I want them to be."

Kenny blinked as if struck in the face. Had she said the wrong thing or maybe said too much?

"Um, my turn?" she mumbled, wringing her hands. "What's your favorite movie?"

"Oh, I love action movies! Like *Wolverine*, *300*, *The Avengers*, but I like the classics too, like *The Matrix*. What about you?"

Maddy bit her lip, trying to remember all the titles so she could look them up later.

"Well, I love so many, but *Sabrina*, staring Aubrey Hepburn, is one of my favorites."

"Hm. Never heard of it. Is it on Netflix?"

What's Netflix? She wondered, but decided to play it off. "I think it's my go, right?"

He laughed. "You getting good at this."

Maddy smiled proudly. "How did you know you were in love with Wendy?"

"I didn't . . . well, I didn't really know. Just sometimes you grow into it."

She nodded. "Like buying clothes too big for you."

"Damn, well, when you put it like that." He laughed. "Alright, when you graduate, where do you want to live? Maybe Hollywood?"

Her heart sank. "I don't know if I'll ever leave Springville."

"Naw, you can't think like that." He shook his head. "You will. You'll meet some guy, run off, and get married. Happens all the time around here. And when you do, where are you gonna call home? Sounds like you wanna check out the West Coast."

Maddy thought back to all the great love stories she'd watched with women running off to be with the men they loved and smiled. "Well, I guess, wherever he is, that's home. That's how love is supposed to be, right? You just feel at home."

Kenny sat motionless and Maddy feared she had said the wrong thing again until he smiled.

"Yeah, it is."

Maddy tensed, a sudden wave of heat hitting her chest. She could feel Kenny without touching him. Every emotion, like a shaken Coke bottle ready to pop, hummed off his skin as threads snaked off her fingertips.

Kenny's eyes widened with a gasp. Did he feel her too?

Maddy shot up out of her seat and the threads retreated. She couldn't lose control, not here, in front of him. She needed to be normal, or she'd never go to prom. "I—I'm sorry. I . . . I need to get home."

"Oh, r-right," Kenny stuttered with a frown. "I guess when you know what color dress you gonna get, you can just text me."

"I, uh, don't have a cell phone," she admitted, face flushing red.

"What? Why?"

She gave him a trepid shrug. "I don't go anywhere to need one."

Conscious of her shortcomings, she began to panic. *He's going to change his mind about prom. I know it. He won't want to be seen with me!*

"Uh, alright. How about this." He ripped a piece of paper out of his bag and scratched down his details. "Just call or email me."

A smile wiggled its way onto her lips. "Thank you."

MADDY DID IT
EPISODE 7
"A Mind of Its Own"

Michael: In a 2020 episode of *Unsolved Mysteries: Springville Massacre*, producers interviewed Kendrick Scott's sister and president of Springville High's Black Student Union,

Kali Scott. I'm going to play a clip for you that didn't make the episode but really gives us a broader scope of the racial tension happening around prom:

"Was Springville High racist? Not loudly, but silently. That's how microaggression works. A year before prom, one of the history teachers had an assignment, asking students if they believed slavery should still exist. Almost fifty percent of the students debated yes, because of course cotton wasn't going to pick itself. Black students were angry and tried to get parents involved, but most of them waved it off. 'That's just Springville for you.' Ridiculous.

"We were tired of the blatant disrespect, so we started the Black Student Union. We needed a collective, unified front to battle some of the issues we were facing. We respectfully presented several actionable items, along with context, to the school board. Even had representatives from BLBP endorse the plan. They said they would take it into consideration. Next day, I found a banana in my locker.

"After the hair and blackface incident, we went AGAIN to the school board with our plan. Even parents came. Once again, they blew us off. Then out of nowhere, one white girl suggests having a joint prom, and the school board suddenly talking about, 'See? We don't need to implement any changes; prom will solve all our problems.' They really thought we'd all come together, hug it out, and erase all the damage that had been done. It was a slap in the face to all our efforts."

At her insistence, Kenny dropped Maddy off on the corner two blocks away from her home. He watched her speed walk down the road, clutching a stack of books. She hadn't needed to give him directions; everyone in town knew where Maddy lived, right on the border of the East and West Sides. The infamous house sat far back from the street on a hill of half-dead grass. An old colonial-style white home with black shutters, the paint and wood chipped where the birds had rammed into it all those years ago, leaving its face marred as if by acne scars.

Kenny shook his head, catching her lingering scent, sweet and fruity, like candy apples. A strangely comforting smell. He placed a hand where she had just sat, the seat still warm, and took a deep breath.

Stop being weird, he thought, just as his phone buzzed.

"Hey, Mom," he answered, making a U-turn.

"Son. Where are you?" Her voice sounded serious.

"I'm . . . um, dropping a friend at home. Why?"

She sighed. "Did you forget something?"

"Uh . . . did I?"

"Does the word 'donuts' ring a bell?"

"Donuts? Mom, what are you . . . oh! Damn!"

Kenny whipped around and spotted his jersey hanging in the back seat.

"Yup, sounds like you did," Mrs. Scott said with a chuckle.

He'd completely forgotten about the appearance his dad had scheduled at the new donut shop that had opened downtown. His mother had even pressed his jersey for him to wear for pictures. His face on their ads would've been great for business.

Kenny rubbed his forehead. "How mad is he?"

She laughed. "Very."

"And you?"

"I'm . . . surprised, to be honest. You're usually good about this type of stuff. Everything okay?"

He glanced in the rearview, watching Maddy's hair blow in the wind, and cleared his throat.

"Guess I'm just a little . . . off."

"Well, Mercury is in retrograde, so the whole world is a little off. But you'll be doing a lot more of this in the future, you know?"

He held back a groan. "Yeah, I know."

Kenny didn't bother heading home. He went straight to the gym to put in three extra miles and a lonely boy workout.

It's what his father would make him do anyway.

"So you're really okay with Kenny taking Maddy fucking Washington to prom?"

Wendy lay back on her bed with the phone to her ear, laughing.

"Char, for the thousandth time, yes! I really do feel shitty about what happened to her."

"I get it, but I don't see why you have to be the sacrificial lamb here. And breaking up with Jules on top of it? Wendy, Jules is hurting real bad."

Just the sound of her name made Wendy's jaw clench. "Well, so am I. Are you going to stop being my friend too?"

"What, are we in middle school? Of course not!"

Wendy exhaled, relieved; lunch period was already awkward enough. Thankfully, school was almost done, then summer, then college. She could last that long without Jules—they probably would've drifted apart anyway. It's what she told herself when the pain of losing a best friend kept her up at night. She missed their late-night chats, their dance-offs, and terrible off-key sing-alongs in her car.

"But as your friend," Charlotte started, "are you seriously telling me you're okay with your boyfriend taking another woman out on a date?"

Wendy rolled her eyes. "It's just one dance. Don't be so dramatic."

"No, it was a *date* date."

Wendy chuckled. "What are you talking about?"

"Ali Kruger saw Kenny and Maddy at the Dairy Queen today."

Wendy gripped her phone and sat up. Dating the most popular boy in school (hell, in their whole town), she was used to receiving unsolicited reports of Kenny's whereabouts. Nine times out of ten, she already knew. It's not like there were many places to be, and she had his moves down to a science. In her four years of high school, she'd studied Kenny Scott the way one would study for the SATs.

But this new piece of information caught her off guard. And she hated being caught off guard.

Why were they at Dairy Queen? And for how long? And why didn't he tell me?

She realized she had been silent for seconds too long and cleared her throat. Her response had to be strategic. Couldn't seem too shocked or too apathetic, sparking rumors that there was trouble in paradise. They were fine. They'd always been fine.

So the best course of action was to lie.

"Ha! It wasn't a date," she scoffed, playing it off like she already knew.

But Charlotte giggled as if she'd read right through her act. "Kenny and Maddy has a nice ring to it, doesn't it?" she teased. Charlotte reveled in mess.

Wendy sat up straighter, gripping the phone. "Really, Char?" she said, her voice ice cold, anger leaking through. Charlotte probably enjoyed that part most.

"Well, you better put the reins on that boy if you want to keep him in check when he goes to Alabama. There will be way more dangerous girls there than Maddy Washington."

Wendy's jaw clenched. "I . . . gotta finish this paper."

They said their goodbyes and Wendy immediately checked her texts. No new messages from Kenny.

Since when did he start doing things without telling me?

She threw her phone across the bed, wishing she had never picked up.

Five minutes later, it dawned on her what Charlotte was alluding to. That Kenny needed to be broken in like a horse, like he was a farm animal, merely livestock. She cursed at herself for not setting Charlotte straight just as a betraying thought crept in, moving her pen.

On top of her English notes, she wrote *Kenny + Maddy* and drew a heart around their names.

They did look good together, she thought, before proceeding to rip the page out of the binder. She crumpled it into a ball and chucked it into the trash can, which wasn't hard considering her room was the size of a closet.

Wendy's family didn't have a solid footing in middle class, like the rest of her friends. Her parents tightroped over their status in a heavily coordinated dance and were too busy keeping a roof over their family's heads to be bothered with cheerleading dinners, high school games, or fretting over their only child dating a Black boy, despite the scandalous whispers.

Wendy had been acutely aware of their precarious situation from a very early age, but she never complained. Instead, she swore to herself that she wouldn't wind up in her parents' shoes come hell or high water and did what she did best: strategized, playing a long game with an offensive strategy. Anticipating people's needs, always willing to volunteer and hand out compliments. She would finish reading entire textbooks ahead of class and offer to do homework for anyone who felt they were falling behind. She practiced her jumps and splits long before cheerleading tryouts were possible, baked cookies (premade dough, never from scratch) every Monday, and had a specific calendar just to keep track of birthdays so she could bring cupcakes to the caf or classroom. And in the ninth grade, when Kenny's future of going pro started to become clear, she brought his favorite candy to lunch every day so he'd have no excuse not to talk to her. She told herself that Kenny wasn't a part of her master plan—just a bonus, not the goal. But his rise to small-town fame did make her sparkle a touch brighter to others, which pleased her.

Staying a step ahead of everyone's expectations and aligning herself with the right popular friends made it easy to hide the slight cracks in her facade.

But her senior year was threatening to bring everything down.

TWELVE

May 26, 2014

PAPA SAT IN his recliner, watching *The Beverly Hillbillies*, chuckling at their antics while Maddy finished dinner. She made something extra special, hoping to soften him, make him more malleable to the conversation that she intended to have. Pork chops in a cranberry glaze, Brussels sprouts, mashed potatoes, and a key lime pie for dessert.

I am powerful, she thought. *I have power now. He can't take it away from me.*

But her mouth went dry at just the thought.

"Dinner's ready," Maddy announced, lighting the stick candles on the center candelabra. Papa sauntered into the dining room, inspecting the setting. When satisfied, he nodded and sat at the head of the table. Maddy took her seat beside him. Papa prayed over their food for almost five minutes before ending with an amen. Maddy dutifully fixed his plate.

"So. Madison," he said, cutting into his chop. "What did

you think of *North by Northwest*?"

Papa always asked her about movies as if she had never seen them before, as if they hadn't watched them too many times to not remember.

"It was wonderful, Papa."

"Ah yes. Cary Grant. Wasn't he terrific? He had done four movies with Alfred Hitchcock. And Hitchcock was very selective about his cast. Pushed them all to impossible limits. They say there were all these problems on set. But what I think was . . ."

Maddy poked at her sprouts, her appetite nonexistent. Heart racing, she pretended to be enthralled with Papa's meandering thoughts, agreeing at the appropriate times. When he broke to take a bite of his pork, she took a deep, steadying breath.

"Papa, I was invited to a dance."

Papa's fork hovered in the air, right at his mouth. He stared at the empty seat on the other side of the table. Maddy could feel the air tense. She pressed on with a gulp.

"It's the prom. His name is Kendrick Scott. He plays football and is going to college. A really good college, on a full sports scholarship. He's going to study English and likes to read."

Papa gently set his fork down, wiping the corner of his mouth with his cloth napkin. Her heart plunged into her stomach with a shudder.

"He's from a nice family, and I—"

It happened so fast she didn't have a chance to shriek. Papa backhanded her across the face, his rough knuckles connecting with her cheekbone. Maddy's chair tipped, dumping her out on the floor. She rolled onto her side with a whimper, tasting the blood on her lip.

Papa stood over her, fist rolled into a ball. "You are having lustful thoughts for some Negro."

Maddy scuttled away from him, one-handed. How did he know Kendrick was Black?

"No, Papa, I—"

"I'll be damned if you go anywhere with some Negro!"

How did he know? she thought through her panic as she tried to regain control.

"Papa . . . can we please talk about this? Please!"

"Go to your closet."

Trembling, Maddy shook her head. "No, Papa."

He slapped her again and she screamed.

"Go to your closet now!"

Her eyeballs twitched. *No, not yet. No. No. No.*

Dark thoughts swirled around her, and the inside of her palm itched to strike back, but she resisted.

"No closet, Papa. Please. Just let me finish telling you about him. We can—"

He hit her again. "You dare defy me, child! 'Children, obey your parents in the Lord, for this is right.' Ephesians 6:1." He pulled back to hit her again.

But an unrecognizable voice bellowed deep from her belly. "I said NO!"

Her hand shot out, stopping his raised arm midswing. The lights flared, radio hissing to a pitch. The candles on the table blazed toward the ceiling.

"Oohff," Papa grunted, staring at his own arm, frozen stiff in the air like a tree limb. Papa's wide eyes roamed as he yanked, and it remained unmoved. His mouth hung open. "Heavenly Father! Lord in heaven!"

Maddy stood, backing away, her hand still raised, each breath intentional, the threads wrapped around her fingers so tight they cut off circulation.

Papa panted, sweat building above his eyebrows as realization dawned on him. He turned to Maddy. The tall flames made the room a hot oven, their skin glowing orange. They stared at each other, unblinking.

"Witch," he hissed.

"I'm not a witch, Papa," she said calmly. "I can move things with my mind. Lots of people can. I've been reading about it. It's a gift."

It was the first time Maddy had spoken the truth aloud. With the weight of her secret off her chest, she finally felt free. She had been dying to tell someone, dying for someone to see her in all her glory.

"Witch," he repeated, and attempted to yank his arm free, but it remained stuck in its L shape.

She swallowed. "I've had it for a while, Papa, and I just didn't know how to control it. But I think I can now."

But as she spoke, she glanced at the candles, the flames dangerously close to the ceiling, wax raining onto the white lace tablecloth, and realized she still had some work to do.

"Witch. Worshipper of Satan!" Papa spat, his face going red.

"No, Papa. I can show you. Then you'll—"

"What evil have you cast upon my house?" he demanded, his voice full of pain.

"I'm not evil, Papa, please."

"You pray! You get into your closet and you pray for forgiveness this instant!"

Maddy couldn't understand how even in such a miraculous moment, even with his arm frozen in the air, how he could act as if he was still in charge. Then, the sad fact sank in: Nothing would cure him of his paranoia and hysteria. Because it had never been about protecting her, never about love. It was about control.

"Papa, please," she begged, fighting tears. "I just want to talk to you."

He lunged, his other arm swinging at her, but she remained too far out of reach.

"GET IN YOUR CLOSET!"

"NO! I'm not going in that fucking closet again! I'm going to that dance, and you're not going to stop me. Try it and you'll never have a left arm again!"

Her voice sounded foreign, like it didn't belong to her, coming from someplace deep and dark, the most savage part of a soul. Her mother's words rose to the forefront and shook her back to center.

This sickly power you hold without hands will eventually burn until you no longer can hide it.

Stunned, Papa stomped his foot, shaking in indignation. "Madison. I am your father!" He said it as if it was supposed to mean more than it did. The fact remained, no matter how amazing she could potentially be, he would always see her as less than nothing. The glimmer of hope was nothing more than a mirage on the horizon. He would never change.

But he was still her father, the only person loyal to her, even if that loyalty was soaked in poison. She slumped with numbing despair and lowered her hand. Papa gasped as his arm came down, hugging it tight to his chest, panting.

The candles eased back to a tiny flame. Black smoke swirled around the room.

Maddy nodded. "I won't go in the closet, Papa. But I'll go to bed without supper."

She turned on her heels and went upstairs.

In the parking lot of the Marshall's Hardware flagship store, Jules and Brady sat in the back seat of his Audi A4, sharing a bottle of vodka stolen from her parents' bar. Not that they would notice. They were too busy canceling her graduation party to avoid explaining to all their friends why Jules wasn't going to Texas A&M, spinning the story in a more positive direction—Jules was taking a gap year to travel through Europe, so she could be a more cultured, well-rounded student. Gap years were all the rage in more sophisticated cities like New York and Los Angeles.

"What are we doing here?" Brady asked with a smirk, shifting closer, walking his fingers up her neck. "Trying to relive some old memories?"

Jules flipped down the sun visor, admiring the new red lippy she'd treated herself to. She shrugged her cropped leather jacket off her shoulders, revealing her new white lace bustier. The type of top she knew Brady would drool over. She caught him staring at her tits, painted with body glitter, and winked. "Maybe."

The wink was the green light Brady needed. He grabbed her chin and kissed her hard, hands roping around her waist.

Jules had met Brady at the store during summer break right before his sophomore year at Georgia State. He worked in the paint department, mixing and matching color swatches, which he thought would be excellent experience for his architecture degree. Brady had a tall swimmer's body with perfect white teeth, honey-tanned skin, and dusty-blond hair that he tied back in an adorable man bun. He was neither scared nor impressed by Jules's status or money. His indifference had intrigued her enough to allow him to take her on a first date.

Of course, her parents had disapproved of their only daughter dating an employee, but they also knew that Jules got bored with toys quickly. While growing up, Jules would often ask for two of every toy she required. One for her, and one for her best friend, whose asshole parents neglected.

Ex-best friend, she thought bitterly. After everything she'd done for her.

Brady had lasted longer than the others, making the two-hour drive to visit Jules whenever he had a spare moment, sacrificing his carefree college life. Although he had the pedigree and an impressive college major, he was as smart as a bag of used nails, and a future together was completely off the table. Jules would hold out for some oil-tycoon trust-fund baby, venture capitalist, or maybe even a football player.

Kenny would've been perfect, if Wendy hadn't gotten to him first.

Couldn't Wendy tell he wasn't in love with her? That his interest waffled with the wind? That he would probably dump her before freshman orientation? Wendy deserved to be worshipped, not tolerated. Another reason why Jules knew they were dead wrong about her. Jules was a good person and cared about her friends. But as they say, actions speak louder than words. And she had a plan that would let everyone know she wasn't one to be fucked over.

Jules pulled away from Brady's kiss, her lipstick now smudged.

"What? What is it?" Brady asked breathlessly, still holding her tight.

"I feel like painting," Jules said, staring at the darkened store sign.

"Painting?"

"Yeah. I want to paint a big-ass message to every single one of those assholes. And you're going to help me."

His eyes shifted to the store, down to her tits, then back again.

"What do you need me to do?" he asked, ready and eager.

She dug into her leather jacket and procured her father's master keys. "You remember how to turn off the alarm, right?"

Jules had grown up in the hardware store, the first of ten that her father opened, following her daddy around the aisles, watching him deal with customers and direct his staff. She paid close attention. One day it would all be hers, and she wanted to know how everything functioned so she could teach someone else to do the job for her. Work smarter, not harder.

So it was easy for her to slip into the office and turn off the security monitors. Easy knowing which section of the parking lot didn't have cameras. Easy to delete any record of her being there at all.

Brady and Jules skipped through the aisles with flashlights, their drunken stupor making everything three times funnier than usual. They made a hard left down aisle seven—the paint department.

Brady lifted Jules up on the counter next to the mixer, unbuttoning her shirt, their slobbery kisses and moans filling the air. They'd had sex in the store several times, playing to her every fantasy while she stared at the seemingly endless shelves of Benjamin Moore and Sherwin-Williams paint cans. But that night, she didn't want sex. She craved revenge.

"Come on, Brady, focus," she said with a giggle, running her fingers through his hair.

"I can't help it, you just look so hot, and you're so damn brilliant," he mumbled into her breasts.

Jules had divulged her plan in the car, and his eyes sparkled. He wanted revenge just as bad. No one had seen the way she'd broken down crying after Jason's party. But Brady had, and said he felt helpless. She'd known he would do anything for her.

Brady helped her off the counter, then turned on the mixer to warm it and took off his jacket. Jules stood in front of a rainbow display of paint strips, shining a light on all the choices.

"What color do you want?" he asked, standing behind her, nibbling on her ear. "We got glass sapphire blue, construction orange, buttercup yellow, park picnic green . . ."

Overwhelmed by the variety, Jules pondered which color would say the most, scream the loudest.

And just as she started to settle on one, she looked down and a smile crept on her face.

"I want that one."

Brady frowned and stooped to take a better look. "This one? You sure?"

Jules licked her lips. "Yes. It's perfect!"

Brady scratched his head. "Um, okay, babe."

She patted his chest. "We'll need two cans."

Then she turned, walked down the aisle, and grabbed the biggest plastic bucket she could find.

THIRTEEN

May 27, 2014

WENDY STOOD BY Kenny's locker, protein shake in one sweaty hand, binder stuffed with their homework in the other. She had on his favorite red dress of hers, the one that stopped right at the school-appropriate knee length (another Jules hand-me-down), and she'd spent thirty minutes straightening her hair. For a split second, she'd considered adding clip-in extensions to make it fuller.

Full like Maddy's, she'd thought, but shoved the ridiculous comparison away.

Between prom, the blow-up with Jules, and school coming to an end, Wendy was on edge, her nerves frayed. She tried to keep this in mind before deciding to confront her boyfriend of three years.

Kenny turned down the senior hallway and spotted her by his locker. She couldn't say for sure, but she swore she saw a brief look of annoyance in his eyes. Just her imagination, she told herself. She hadn't slept well the night before. Too wound up on caffeine with a mouth full of questions.

"Hey. What's up," he sighed, pecking her cheek. She smiled, leaning into his lips, and waited for an explanation. He had to have been anxious about the lack of texts and goodnight call. She wasn't mad, but watching him empty his book bag like he didn't have a care in the world made her squint, mouth forming a terse line.

Unable to hold it in any longer, she blurted it out. "You went on a date with Maddy?"

Kenny froze, cocking his head to the side with a raised eyebrow as if to ask if she was serious.

"I wouldn't call it a date," he laughed. An uncomfortable laugh. One full of guilt. "Just got some milkshakes after school."

Wendy remained mute. She did this whenever something bothered her but she didn't want to express it, and rather wait for him to figure it out. It annoyed Kenny. Not that he'd ever say it, but she always caught the faces he made and eyes he rolled.

Kenny registered her silence and pursed his lips.

"What?" he snapped. "You don't expect me to take some girl I don't even know to prom without at least having a conversation with her. Do you?"

But they all knew Maddy. They'd known her since the day she walked into seventh grade wearing those thick glasses, frilly ankle socks, poodle skirt, and a brown sweater she still wore to this day.

Something untamed threatened to bubble up. Wendy swallowed and painted on a smile. She had to remain in control. She couldn't let the past few weeks spin all she had worked for sideways.

"No. Of course not," she said, her voice pitched high. "Made you a protein shake."

"Oh, cool." He beamed. "Thanks, babe!"

Wendy laughed at herself. She couldn't believe that she'd even entertained the delirious thought. Of course he wasn't interested in Maddy! He loved *her*. He would do anything she asked, including taking some random girl to prom. Besides, they had plans—a future. And she wasn't about to lose him to Maddy fucking Washington.

MADDY DID IT
EPISODE 7, CONT.

Tanya: So once the power went out, was the plant in any danger
of a meltdown?

Dr. Ron Englert: Well, under normal circumstances, no.

Michael [narration]: This is Dr. Ron Englert, a physicist in the
nuclear power industry. He was a part of the Springville
Commission, investigating issues that occurred at the
power plant during Prom Night, but was terminated before
the investigation concluded.

Dr. Englert: The loss of power wasn't necessarily a problem,
since there are procedures in place in which the reactors

will shut down automatically. But here's where the problem truly lies—modern nuclear reactors cannot power themselves. They need grid power. Thus, all nuclear plants have diesel backup generators. In the event of an outage, they keep the fuel cool and the spent fuel covered with water for a specified number of hours until power can be restored. For some unexplainable reason, in this situation, the backup generators became faulty, and the system refused to recognize the auto-shutdown command.

So with a load rejection, plus lack of shutdown, and insufficient backup generators, the cooling system began to dissolve, and the reactor started to have a mind of its own. Once that happened, supervisors were alerted, and it was all hands on deck.

Tanya: That sounds intense. Why didn't they evacuate the town?

Dr. Englert: The nuclear power industry defines emergencies according to four levels of increasing significance: unusual event, alert, site area emergency, and general emergency. They alerted local authorities, who were, at that point, under siege at the prom. They sounded the emergency siren and directed everyone to shelter in place via radio broadcast and social media channels to reduce any possible radiation exposure. But by that time, most of the citizens in Springville were outside watching the fires, waiting for their children to return, or in the commotion of the crash.

Tanya: So how does this relate to Maddy?

Dr. Englert: I want to speak in layman's terms here because, well, I don't know how else to describe what happened. But based on my findings, it appears the reactors were drawn to something . . . like by a magnet of some sort, causing the core to overheat, resulting in dangerously increasing levels. When we later had a timeline of all the events that transpired through the evening, the increasing levels directly coincided with Maddy's location. The closer Maddy got to the plant, the more the plant wanted to get to Maddy. I checked records, and the only other times that happened in the plant's history, on a much smaller scale, of course, were June 23, 1996, and August 7, 2008.

Michael [narration]: Those dates happen to align with the day Maddy was born and "the birds incident."

Dr. Englert: The commission refused to acknowledge these findings, as it went against the picture they were trying to paint. Look, I'm a man of science, and I've been in this industry for over thirty years. So, much like you, Tanya, I went in skeptical about talk of flying cars and glowing girls. But I say that all to say, I believe that if Maddy had lived and made it within a mile of that plant . . . there wouldn't be a soul alive within fifty miles to tell the story.

May 27, 2014

Kenny came home covered in sweat with bone-deep exhaustion. His father had left drills for him to do at the gym with a personal trainer—in preparation for his first season at Alabama and the rest of his life. Wendy had sat in the corner of the weight room, cheering him on. Her clinginess felt suffocating at times, but he also felt like a total asshole for thinking that. Guys would kill to have a girlfriend like her.

So why couldn't he stop thinking about Maddy?

Ever since their trip to Dairy Queen, he had been replaying their conversation on a loop. He liked knowing how sharp her tongue could be, the way she checked him about his cursing, and how she wasn't giving him the answers that she thought he wanted to hear. On the surface, she seemed rather jittery, insecure, and criminally out of touch. But he also recognized something buried deep—a spark, a longing. She didn't need saving or changing, she could handle the world on her own. He felt in on her little secret. And in a town like theirs, he usually didn't have the luxury of secrets. Not with everyone watching his every move.

A career in football meant resigning himself to interacting with an endless number of yes-men, fake people, and leeches. But what he didn't realize, until those milkshakes, was how much he craved connection with someone who he could be his entire self around without his guard up. Someone who knew nothing about him before they'd even met. Someone just like him, estranged from their own race, forced to pretend. Someone like Maddy.

Why hasn't she called yet?

Every time his cell rang, he'd jump, answering unknown numbers, expecting to hear her voice on the other line. He checked his email multiple times and considered changing his class route to pass her locker. But that would have been too much.

Kenny walked into his room and spotted the copy of *The Autobiography of Malcolm X* peeking out from under his pillow. The sight of it made his nostrils flare.

He stomped across the hall and rapped on Kali's door.

"Come in!"

Kali sat on her bed, homework textbooks spread out. Their rooms differed drastically: a colorful, art-filled sanctuary with soft music, incense, and candles vs. a plain beige shrine to football.

"Here," Kenny said, throwing the book on the bed. "I see you folded the pages with Malcolm dating a white girl. Nice. Real subtle."

She shrugged. "Just giving you historical examples of what to watch out for."

"Wendy's not like that. Aye, why you gotta be so mean to her? She takes care of me. Supports me! What she ever do to you?"

Kali palmed the book, staring up at him with amused curiosity.

"Do you love her more than football?"

His head drew back as if he had been kicked in the throat.

Flustered, he hesitated before leaning against the door. His little sister always knew how to ask questions that made him reconsider all his life choices. Which was why he never lied to her.

"I don't know how to answer that," he admitted. Not because he didn't love Wendy, but football felt just as important, if not his whole world. If he was honest with himself, Kenny could also admit that deep below the surface, rotting beneath the floorboards, lay resentment over the responsibility of loving them both more than he loved himself.

But what scared him most? When he stopped to picture what his life would look like in a few years, he never saw Wendy in the frame.

Kali pursed her lips. "Whatever. Looks like you've moved on already anyway."

"With who?" He paused. "Wait, are you talking about Maddy?"

Kali rolled her eyes and went back to her book, flipping to the next page without sparing him another glance.

"Ha!" Kenny huffed, turning to walk away, but reconsidered.

"Fine, I'll bite," he said, closing the door. "What's wrong with Maddy?"

"Pshh. Everything."

"Everything like what?"

"You know what," she snapped.

Kenny rolled his eyes, annoyed with her game. "I'm a dumb jock. School me."

Kali slapped her book closed. "So, we're just going to ignore the fact that all this time she been pretending to be white because being Black is clearly a problem."

"Come on, she ain't like that."

"Sure," she laughed. "'Cause you know her sooo well."

Kenny crossed his arms. "Kali, be honest: If you had known she was Black, would you have given her a second thought? Would you have accepted her, tried to be her friend, or even talked to her?"

She raised an eyebrow. "I would've accepted her if she acknowledged her light-skin privilege."

"Privilege? They threw pencils in her hair! How's that a win?"

"You don't get it," she snapped. "Maddy wasn't born with the stacks up against her. She'll get things that I'll never get, let into rooms I couldn't even dream of, all because of the way she looks. Already she's deemed softer, more delicate and sensitive. Peep how you're caping for her now! She acted like being Black was the worst thing that ever happened to her, and she don't even realize how good she got it."

"So she should be left defenseless? You're the one always saying we need to support one another. Unity and shit. I'm not the one treating her different because she's light-skinned. You are!"

"When have you ever looked out for anyone who looked like you? It's not like I've ever seen you at one Black Student Union meeting."

"Oh, so you mad I haven't shown up to your little Black club?"

"It's more than that! And it's a good thing we exist, or the school would be treating us any old way."

"But how does that help Maddy?"

"Who cares about Maddy? She'll be straight."

Kenny shook his head. "Just admit it, Kali—you would've ignored Maddy Washington from the jump. 'Cause even though she's Black, she's not Black enough for you the way I'm not Black enough for you, and that's bullshit!"

Kali gaped at him, then scoffed. "That's not true."

"It is. So don't pretend you value everyone's Blackness equally."

She jumped to her feet. "So maybe I do! Would that make me much different than anyone else in the world? Kenny, you don't think I've had things thrown in my hair? Or been the butt of jokes? Or was told how I'm very articulate or very pretty for a dark-skinned girl? Or accused of being too aggressive for simply stating an opinion? Do you know how many times I've been sent to the main office since kindergarten, just for asking a question? I've had a thousand microaggressions to Maddy's one, and yet everyone has jumped to coddle her. She gets to be upset and cry, but ME? I gotta be in control and strong but not too strong or I'll—how did you put it?—'make people uncomfortable.' Must be nice to just exist. So yeah, I ain't worrying about Maddy cause Maddy ain't ever been worried about *us*. Bottom line—when she had to choose, she chose to be white. When asked if she was Black, she straight up denied it because she knew damn well how Black people were treated and wanted no part of that. And she had the privilege to do so while the rest of us don't. We can't take our skin off at night like it's a costume or straighten our hair to blend in. If we could, thousands of us would still be alive today!"

Kali's chest heaved, her eyes full of rage. Kenny's mouth hung open. He couldn't believe it. Why hadn't she told him? People were making fun of her and he didn't know? Or had he known and chosen to turn a blind eye, ignoring all the little comments, not necessarily at his sister, that made his pulse beat three times faster. What kind of brother wouldn't protect his little sister? He thought he'd never have to worry about Kali. She always seemed so strong, cutthroat even. But that's where he had failed, assuming she needed no one.

Everyone needs someone.

He sat on the edge of her bed, palming the book, thinking of Maddy and her father. The way Maddy tensed at just the mention of his name. He understood, more than he cared to admit, Maddy's true motivations.

"You're right," he muttered. "But . . . I don't think she had a choice in any of that."

"We all have a choice," Kali spat.

He eyed her. "Really? You think I've had a choice about anything in this house?"

Kali's scowl softened. She opened her mouth but came up short as a knowing exchange passed between siblings commiserating under the same roof.

"Maddy chose to survive," Kenny said. "We all do things to survive, to just get through it. We shut up and do what we're told, because it's better than any other option. You always talking about wanting to be a change. How about accepting difference within our own people?"

Kali shook her head. "Kenny, she . . . betrayed us with her denial. You expect me to just let that go?"

"Naw. But instead of ignoring her, how about help her, teach her better? Just like you try to teach me. I know that ain't your job and you shouldn't have to, but you're good at . . . leading. I mean, you've made me want to be better."

Kali rolled her eyes as he stood to face her, pulling her into a hug. She resisted at first but relented. They stood there for a long while until Kali began to softly cry into his shoulder. A cry that seemed to have been stuck somewhere deep, buried under a mountain.

"I'm sorry, K," he said in her ear, squeezing her tighter. "I am so sorry."

Maddy sat on her knees in her closet, her hands clasped in prayer. She thought praying, in a familiar setting, would help her battle the bitterness leaking through, the darkness roiling inside her chest, and the unfamiliar voices shouting in her head.

But the more she prayed, the more her prayers felt hollow and empty. What comfort had God ever brought her? When had He ever saved her from Papa's wrath, from the hell at school? Why hadn't He saved all those people protesting or being hanged on trees, kidnapped on slave ships? Where was the salvation He promised? Where was He?

He was never here, a voice hissed inside her, vibrating like a struck church bell. The tendrils of her dark thoughts wrapped every corner of the house as the cross hanging above her clattered to the floor. Her eyes flew open with a whimper. She stared at the pasted pictures of women Papa wanted her to be, their edges frayed. She stood and peeled back the corner of a photo, exposing the dark wood underneath with a strange burnt marking. She kept peeling, exposing the full scope of the burns, and stood back. Carved in the wall were symbols—circles with five-point stars, a goat's head, letters drawn backward, lines and forked crosses.

It took several seconds for it all to register.

Mama believed in Satan?

"No," Maddy gasped, slapping the pictures back, trying to iron them with the heel of her hand and erase them from her memory. She stumbled out of the closet, slamming the door behind her.

She couldn't believe it. She wouldn't believe it. Her power

was a gift, not something evil. Her mama was beautiful and pure and loved her. It said so in the book she left. Well, in so many words. She grabbed the journal once more and sat on the bed.

The darkness inside your blood will wring you dry. But lessons are built in struggle.

Reading through her mother's thoughts felt like swimming through molasses toward memories deeply implanted. Maddy wondered if her mother had cooed these words while Maddy floated inside her belly.

You were born on a cusp, the smirk of the stars. This gives you great power. You are more than just a Cancer, more than just a Gemini. You are a combined force, made with the type of magic no one could steal even if they tried. You, my moon child, shine brightest in the darkness. Laugh at their feeble attempts to put out your light. Let your moon draw the oceans close so that they may bow to you.

But what did all this mean? Cancer? Gemini? Moons? Oceans? Her thoughts exploded, collided, and intertwined as she turned each page, trying to understand the riddles. Were these the words of a madwoman? A Satan worshipper? Had Maddy inherited her mother's madness? Was that same madness making her fall for a boy she could never have? It didn't feel like madness; it felt holy and inescapable. But what would Kenny think if he knew about her gift? She couldn't bear to imagine it.

As she neared the end of the journal, she felt no closer to her mother, only more confused. Had her mother known about all those violent protests? Had she participated in any?

Why didn't she kill them all? the voice hissed. *She should've killed them all!*

"Don't say that," Maddy whimpered to the air, and turned a page.

> *The stars within you will guide, sustain, and nourish you. There is power in knowing oneself. 7:38 a.m. 6/23.*

Maddy sat up bone straight. June twenty-third . . . her birthday.

> *When you feel the need to run without ceasing, I will be where the low country meets the sea. Until then, I will fly to you, whenever I can.*

How could her mother write Maddy's birthday in a book tied to the bottom of her bed if she'd died giving birth to her?

Unless her mother hadn't really died. If not, then what happened to her? Where was she?

Maddy closed the book. She thumped down the stairs in a daze, staring at Papa's locked office door.

Everything she'd thought she knew no longer made sense, yet she had unwavering certainty that her mother would never have abandoned her, would have fought for her. If her mother was alive and still around . . . Maddy's life would have been so different. She would've been protected from Papa, from the kids at school, she wouldn't have been so alone, she would've known real love. The thought of the potential existence she'd missed out on, a dream deferred . . . took her breath away. Something must have happened to her mother. But what?

She found Papa on his knees in the living room, among the tapes, movie posters, and candles, praying. For days, Papa hadn't spoken to Maddy. Hadn't even looked at her. The lunch she'd prepared, egg salad on Wonder bread with a thermos of Campbell's tomato soup—his favorite—sat untouched.

She didn't want to tell him about the journal. Not yet. But she had questions only he had the answers for.

"Papa, you need to talk to me."

Papa mumbled his prayers at the ceiling, a picture of Jesus looking down on him.

"I'm not evil. And I'm not trying to hurt you by going to prom. I want to obey. But . . . I also want to start living a normal life now."

He hummed, rocking back and forth.

"It's just that, Papa, everyone knows about me now. So we

don't have to hide anymore. We can be like regular people. I want to be a regular person. We have to start trying to be like everybody else."

Papa stopped his muttering to glare up at her.

"Why would I want to be like everyone else?" he spat.

For a change, she could almost appreciate his stance. Almost.

"Get out of my house, witch," he hissed, seething.

"Papa," she gasped.

He grunted, rising to his feet, his knees cracking, and it occurred to her how old he seemed. As if the last few days had aged him.

"You are no daughter of mine!" he shouted, spit flying out of his mouth. "Mine was good and pure, and you don't belong here! If you don't get out, I will drag you out!"

Maddy stared up at him, heartbroken. Where would she go if Papa threw her out? Where could she go? She had no family she knew of, or friends. Home was the only world she'd ever known. She hadn't changed all that much and was still very much his daughter.

But then she thought of her mother's journal and realized . . . Papa had lied to her. About everything. He'd said she died in childbirth, that Maddy had killed her coming out of her womb. The guilt ate at her self-preservation, made her eager to please him, begging for his love. And she hated him for it.

Nails biting into her palms, she sighed. "That's not going

to happen," she said, her voice sharp and calm. "I'm your child. There's a lot I could say about you if you kick me out. Is that what you want?"

Papa only stared, unblinking.

"Say something."

His eyes narrowed as if weighing her threat.

"Papa, say something!" she shrieked, tears streaming down her face.

Nothing.

She tilted her chin up, glaring at him, blood boiling. The clock stopped ticking. She lifted her hand and snapped her fingers. Every single candle in the house lit up, flames shooting high. Papa's eyes bulged at the scene, a fist to his mouth. His father's church candles melted onto the green carpet. He took a staggering step back, shaking his head, mumbling prayers.

Maddy snapped her fingers again and the flames snuffed out.

Smoke swirled around the room. Breathing heavy, Papa struggled to find his tongue.

Maddy nodded, pleased with herself, and walked into the kitchen. She set the hot comb, grease, and clips on the table and turned the burner on without touching the stove.

It was time to do her hair.

FOURTEEN

CHRIS LEAPED IN the air and caught the ball with both hands.

"Whew! That boy good," Kenny shouted, clapping.

Chris laughed, jogging back to the middle of the field.

The guys had wanted to have a friendly game of touch after school, but Kenny had strict orders not to engage in anything that could cause an injury before training camp. So they'd settled on tossing the ball around instead, recruiting a couple of their teammates to join them. Kenny took a moment to appreciate that it would be the last time they shared a field, and to be honest, he missed the simplicity of just throwing the rock around with his brothers. They'd been through it all the last four seasons.

Chris threw the ball across to a sulking Jason.

"Still don't see why we can't play touch," Jason said, his voice hard.

Kenny shrugged with a smile. "Coach said I can't. You know how it is."

Jason paused, his eyes narrowing. He didn't know. He'd probably sit out his entire first season. "Whatever," Jason mumbled, tossing the ball to Kenny.

Kenny gripped the ball, squinting at Jason. *What was his problem?*

Ever the peacekeeper, Chris toggled his eyes between them. "Uhhh . . . so you guys get your tuxes yet?"

Kenny tore his eyes from Jason and flicked the ball over to Chris. "Uh . . . naw. I was waiting for Maddy to tell me what color her dress was, but I guess I should just put an all-black on hold."

"You get her a corsage? My mom flipped when I told her I hadn't. I mean, how am I supposed to know all these stupid rules?"

"Yeah," Kenny chuckled. "My mom is gonna order the corsage and one of those flower things you pin on your jacket."

"Isn't the girl supposed to buy that?" Chris asked.

"Yeah, but Mom said she probably wouldn't know about that 'cause of her dad, and well . . . guess I really didn't want her spending money on me."

Maddy *still* hadn't emailed or called. Wasn't she interested in getting to know him too? Some girls would kill for the chance to be alone with him. *But Maddy isn't like other girls*, he reminded himself. She was different.

He liked different.

232

"Oh, that's real cool, bro," Chris said. "Yo, you about to give her the best night of her life!"

Kenny grinned. Why did the thought of making her happy make him feel so . . . good?

"Yo, bro, don't you think you're laying it on kinda thick?"

The boys turned to Jason.

"What?" Kenny barked.

Jason tossed the ball. "We get it, okay? You're the town's freaking golden boy. Now you're taking the class reject to prom. It's a little over the top, don't you think?"

Kenny rolled his eyes. "Whatever, man. Just worry about your game and stop worrying about mine." He chucked the ball back to Jason using his full force, knowing it would hurt his hands when he caught it.

Jason glared at him then chuckled, tossing it back. "Oh, I get it now," Jason said, grinning. "It's like those guys who take mercy dates like the fucking mental rejects to prom, so they look like the hero and stuff. Chicks love that shit! Guaranteed pussy."

Kenny let the ball slip out of his hand, stepped over it, and marched across the field toward Jason. "What the fuck did you just say?"

"Oh boy," Chris quipped, racing in between them. "Uh, guys? Hold on, wait!"

Jason laughed. "Relax, bro. I'm only kidding."

Kenny stormed up to him, standing nose to nose. "Don't call her that."

Jason leaned back with an incredulous stare. "Are you serious? It was just a joke!"

"Doesn't matter. Don't fucking call her that," he said, his tone deadly.

Chris shook his head. "Yeah, dude, that's so not cool."

Jason narrowed his eyes and flung his hand up. "You know what? I'm sick of this shit," he spat, pointing at Kenny. "Ever since you got into Alabama, you've been up on your high horse, looking down at the rest of us. Now you're using Maddy to show off. It's bullshit. She doesn't even deserve to go to prom."

Kenny scoffed. "Yo, what did Maddy ever do to you?"

"What did she do? She got Jules kicked out of school and college!"

"Jules got herself kicked out of school," Kenny retorted.

"And she completely fucked up prom."

"Jules fucked up prom with that pencil! Maddy had nothing to do with any of that shit!"

Flabbergasted, Jason gazed up at the sky with a groan. "Bro, why are you all of a sudden sticking up for her?" Then, a thought dawned on him, and he grinned. "Oh, I get it. Now that we know Maddy's Black, you're trying to . . ."

Kenny's eyes flared. He took another menacing step forward. "Trying to what? Huh? Say it!"

Jason stood tight-lipped, but his eyes were laughing. Laughing at him.

"Guys, cool it!" Chris shouted, pushing between them.

"Jason's only joking. Right, Jason?"

Kenny clenched his jaw, his pulse pounding. They stood motionless, glaring at each other.

"Right, Jason?" Chris urged him again.

Jason tilted his head to the side and grinned. "Yeah. Right."

Chris turned to him. "See? It's all good."

Kenny backed up several feet, taking stock of his friends. The ones he thought he knew, thought were his brothers. And now, he wanted nothing to do with them.

Kenny shook his head and waved them off. "Whatever, man."

Jason rolled his eyes as Chris reached for Kenny. "Bro! Kenny, wait!"

But he was already gone, sprinting back into the school, through the near-empty halls, everyone cleared out for the day. He stopped near the freshman lockers, panting. Not out of breath, but out of anger. Chest heaving, he paced back and forth, cracking his knuckles, ready to hit anything moving.

Maddy.

Kenny jerked straight. The name popped in his head and hit a nerve. Questions dripped in—is she okay? Where is she? Are they bothering her again? He swallowed and stalked down the hallway.

Maddy.

He squeezed his eyes shut, trying to shake his thoughts free of her. But maybe . . . he could stop by the store or her house just to make sure she was okay. No harm in that. He walked faster, determined to jump in his car in search of her.

Maddy.

The air thickened. He could almost smell her, feel her cold hand in his palm. He turned a corner, by the far end of the library, moving with a sense of urgency.

And inside, there sat Maddy at one of the computers, her back to the door. His legs stiffened. The sight of her dunked him into a pool of freezing water. She wasn't in danger. She was fine, watching some videos on YouTube, black-and-white footage from the civil rights movement, water hoses being turned on protesters.

What is she doing?

Maddy jolted straight in her chair and spun around, looking directly at Kenny. He jumped, shoving away from the door.

"Shit," he mumbled.

Maddy stepped into the hall. "Kendrick?"

"Uh, hey," he said, trying to sound smooth and nonchalant like he hadn't just been spying on her like some creep.

She took him in with a furrowed brow.

"What's wrong?" she asked, wrapping her arms around herself.

"What makes you think something's wrong?" he asked, faking a laugh.

She squirmed. "Just a . . . feeling."

And here he thought he had a solid poker face. With a great exhale, he slumped against a locker.

"You know, no one calls me Kendrick except you," he admitted with a small smile.

"Oh," she mumbled. "Sorry."

"Naw, it's nice! I like my name. Always have."

"Then why Kenny?"

He shrugged. "Guess it was just easier to say."

"Easier for who?" she asked, but something about her expression made it clear she already knew the answer, and he liked that they were already reading each other's minds.

Maddy looked different. Still in a long navy skirt but no sweater, her thin arms exposed in a men's white undershirt, baggy on her bony frame. He couldn't remember her ever dressing so . . . casual.

He glanced back down the hall, relieved no one had followed him, and that they were alone. He didn't want to be anywhere near his friends or even in the school that revered him. He turned back to Maddy.

"Hey, you wanna get out of here?"

Kenny sped down Old Millings Road, a single-track lane, miles away from town. His copilot gazed out the window, taking in the scenic route—the lush tree-covered mountains, thick green underbrush, cable bridges, and narrow gorges they passed. He turned up the music and rolled down the windows. The air rushing in smelled rich with spring, honeysuckle, and newness. Maddy's hair flowed wildly around her, but she did nothing to tame it. Just sat back and snuggled into the seat with a satisfying sigh. Kenny watched her strands dance in the wind like they were moving in slow motion and found it hard to focus on the road. She turned, met his gaze with intense eyes, and gave him a smile that felt like the warmth of a thousand suns. The tension eased out of his shoulders as he grinned back, fascinated by how just being near her both calmed and excited him.

Behind them, an old blue pickup truck flew around the bend, gaining speed. Kenny stiffened as a truck passed them on the left, its massive Confederate flag flapping in the wind, a wide-eyed deer in the bed, mouth gaping in horror. It wasn't hunting season. The three passengers in matching sunglasses nodded at him. Kenny sat up straighter, placed both hands on the wheel, and nodded back. Any other day, he wouldn't pay them any mind. He'd seen plenty of those Klan banners before, even on his friends' parents' cars. But for some unexplainable reason, his chest tightened. It wasn't just him in the car. He had Maddy. And he needed . . . no, wanted to keep her safe. He slowed down, putting as much distance between them as possible. Maddy didn't seem to notice. She was just enjoying the ride.

After another two miles, Kenny made a sharp right turn into the woods. He drove up an unpaved road and stopped at a clearing meant for parking.

"We're here," he said, jumping out of the truck, and ran around to open her door.

"Hiking?" Maddy asked, with a curious expression, nodding at the signage.

"It's a pretty flat trail," he said, noting her black ballet shoes, and grabbed an orange vest from the back seat. "Come on. I wanna show you something. Trust me, it'll be worth it. But, here, put this on first."

Maddy stared at the vest, her eyebrows pinched.

"Why? It says no hunting."

He thought of the passing truck, its Confederate flag, and its victim in the truck bed. "Just . . . you never know."

What he really wanted to say was, we're Black, and they'd use any excuse. But he wasn't sure how it would land or what unsaid rules she knew.

She raised an eyebrow, considering, then slowly unlocked her arms and took the vest, slipping into it. Kenny grabbed his book bag and locked up the car.

This wasn't cheating, he told himself as he led her to the trail. He was just getting to know his prom date. The one everyone accused him of taking advantage of, somehow. This was just another way of becoming acquainted without everyone watching. Nothing wrong with that.

Maddy clumsily tripped up the trail, squeaking a "sorry" every time he caught her arm. He only chuckled. Not that he was laughing at her. He found it pretty adorable.

They walked in silence, the quiet familiar somehow. Shouldn't he say something? Ask her more questions? But he honestly didn't feel the need. In fact, he felt at ease.

The soundtrack of the woods replaced his music. Birds chirped and bugs croaked around them, the trail shaded by tall evergreens, their feet crunching over leaves and fallen branches. Maddy's head moved from the right to the left, gazing upward and down. She seemed fascinated by every aspect of nature. He wondered if she'd ever been hiking before or even in the woods at all. *Impossible*, he thought. But he couldn't remember her at a single class trip or in summer camp.

The sound of water grew louder. Maddy glanced back at him, uncertain.

He gave her a reassuring smile. "It's up ahead."

They came to a clearing in the trail, where the path led down toward a narrow cable bridge hanging over a babbling brook, surrounded by a scattering of moss-covered rocks, reeds, lush bushes, and wildflowers.

Maddy stopped in awe. "Wow."

Kenny grinned and walked ahead. "Jason's dad took us on a camping trip here when we were in middle school. I always remembered passing this spot."

He took one step on the bridge and it shook, the cables creaking. Maddy jumped back, her sharp intake of breath startling.

"Naw, it's safe," he said, reaching for her.

Wide-eyed, she nibbled on her thumb, shaking her head.

"Trust me," he said, offering his hand. "The view is better over here."

Maddy scanned the cable, tucked her hair behind her ear, and glanced back the way they'd come.

Please don't be scared of me, he thought, his heart twisting.

She met his gaze and took a cautious step forward before gripping his hand. He grinned inwardly as he threaded their fingers, a tingle in his palm, and led her onto the bridge, the metal rattling. They walked single file down the center to the very middle, where he stopped and placed her hand on the rail.

"See?"

Water trickled over the rocks, pooling beneath the bridge, the surface dark and smooth. Maddy took a deep breath, her body easing, as a pair of butterflies fluttered by.

"Reminds me of a Norman Rockwell painting," she whispered. "Do people fish here? Like Huckleberry Finn did?"

"Uh, probably. It's freshwater, comes down from the mountains."

"Hm. Water can be so beautiful."

Kenny stood beside her, itching to touch her hand again.

"I come here when I want to think. Clear my head. Get in the game." He stole a glance of her. "Pray."

Maddy focused on the water, her lips parting. He immediately felt ridiculous for dropping the prayer comment. Didn't even know why he'd said it. Maybe to impress her but why was he so worried about impressing her?

"My father made me a prayer closet," she said, her tone a bit removed. "Guess I think in there."

"That sounds nice."

She sighed. "This . . . is nicer."

He measured her mood and threaded his fingers through hers. "Come on."

He led her across the bridge to a group of flat rocks by the water's edge. They sat side by side in silence. If she noticed him staring at her, she didn't show it. She seemed more mesmerized by the tranquil sound of flowing water and the breeze rustling through the trees. It felt as if they were the only two beings left on an entirely different planet. The enormity of being so alone with her suddenly hit him. Self-conscious and unnerved, he started to question himself.

What the hell am I doing? This is crazy. I've never even brought Wendy here!

"I . . . uh, read about football," she mumbled, staring at her fingers. "It's a very complicated game. A violent game."

He chuckled. "Yeah. It can be."

"Aren't you afraid of getting hurt?"

"All the time."

"Then . . . why play?"

"'Cause I love it! The rush, the complication, the violence, my team. Just hate all the other stuff that comes with it."

Her head tipped to the side. "Like what?"

"Well, like not having a life of my own. Not being my own person. Every conversation always about football or someone sucking up to me about football. Can't even have a slice of pizza without it having something to do with the game. I miss when it was just me and the guys kicking it, having a good time. I love the game, I wanna play for the rest of my life, but I didn't ask for all the other shit!"

He shuddered a breath, realizing he'd said too much, and was afraid to look at her. But Maddy met his gaze, staring back with a strange tenderness. No further request to elaborate nor chastising him for being ungrateful. He could be fully honest with her without debate. It made the worry melt out of his shoulders.

"Hey, you hungry? I got a sandwich."

"Yes. Thank you," she said with an appreciative smile.

He pulled out the sandwich Wendy had made for his training session, which he planned to miss, and hoped she hadn't added those weird hot peppers like last time. He didn't know if Maddy liked spicy food. Other than milkshakes, he didn't know what kind of food she liked. But he could learn. He wanted to learn.

Maddy took a cautious nibble like a bunny.

"Ham and cheese," she noted. "Is this your favorite?"

"No," he laughed. "It's actually PB&J. I can smash, like, five of those with no problem."

She blushed, unable to meet his eye. "That's my favorite too."

"Really? Okay, grape or strawberry jelly?"

"We only have grape."

"What? Nah, you gotta upgrade to strawberry preserves! It'll change your life."

"Life-changing sandwiches? Guess I have to try that." She laughed and it sounded like bells chiming, chipping away at the awkwardness.

"Hey, can I ask you something?" he said, grabbing a blade of tall grass beside him.

"I don't know, can you?"

Kenny leaned back, whistling through his teeth. "Whoa! Maddy Washington with the jokes!"

Maddy covered her face, her neck beet red. "I'm sorry! That was something silly I heard on a show once."

Kenny reached forward, gently pushing her arm aside so he could see her eyes. She had real beautiful eyes. She gazed up at him, searching, their laughter dying to silence.

"Um, you were going to ask me something," she prodded.

He blinked and cleared his throat. "Oh yeah. Uh, were you ever going to tell anyone you were Black?"

Maddy's smile faded. "No."

"Why not? I mean, folks straight up asked you and you lied."

"It wouldn't have changed anything. Still hasn't."

He shrugged. "So what's it like? Pretending to be something different?"

She raised an eyebrow. "You tell me."

In a matter of minutes, Kenny had seen several sides of Maddy he didn't think were possible.

And like a late reaction to her own words, Maddy gasped, her mouth forming an O. "I'm sorry. Oh! That was . . . I mean, I didn't mean to . . . oh, I . . ."

"Naw. Say what you mean." He tried to keep his tone light, but there was a sharpness behind every syllable.

Maddy curled inward, biting her lip.

"I want you to say it," he insisted. "Don't hold back. Please. Too many people hold back with me as it is."

She hesitated, twisting the hem of her skirt. "Well, you just don't seem like the others. And it just . . . must be so exhausting being so many people for so many people."

Kenny's mouth went slack. How could she know that?

"I'm sorry." She winced. "I guess I'm bad at being normal."

He scoffed. "Normal's boring."

"That is very easy for you to say."

He noticed an edge to her voice, the defensiveness and lack of humor startling.

"I think, what I mean is . . . everyone you think of as normal ain't normal. Never know what's going on behind closed doors." He laughed. "Don't seem like it, but I know what it's like to feel like you don't belong. Walking a tightrope day in and day out gets pretty old . . . don't it? But like my aunt used to say, 'Wherever you go, there you are.'"

A shock of recognition passed across her face.

"The truth is . . . you're right," he admitted, staring at the water. "It is exhausting. 'Cause no matter what you do, you can't outgrow, out-lie, out-perform, out-play, out-run, or out-joke being different. And, after a while, it starts hurting, like in your chest, being something you not. The older you get and the more you learn just how different you really are, you get tired of trying to blend in. You get lonely, even when you surrounded by people and you end up wanting to chill with someone who's just like . . . you."

Kenny exhaled, and turned to Maddy, her eyes taking up her whole face.

Shit, what I say?

She wrapped the last of the sandwich. "I . . . um, I have to get home soon. Gotta start dinner."

He smiled. "Wait, you cook?"

"Yes," she said sheepishly.

"Really? What's your favorite thing to make?"

And so, as they walked back to the car, Maddy told him about all the dishes she loved to cook. He listened, enraptured by the sound of her voice, his hand gently guiding her elbow as their conversation slipped through the space between his ribs, filling him.

Wendy stood on a ladder near the Barn's front entrance, putting finishing touches on the printed backdrop. She jumped down and tested the lighting, pleased with the final results.

When the prom guests arrived, they'd walk down a red carpet under a ceiling of twinkling white lights to a photo booth, then take an official picture before entering the banquet hall, where they'd be offered sparkling cider and pick up their table number. She wanted people to feel like movie stars when they first arrived.

It was what she would want.

"Perfect," she muttered as she walked into the hall, clipboard in hand. So far, she had everything checked off on the master to-do, just waiting for a few more orders to arrive. The Barn's audience chairs, which usually faced the stage, were stacked in the corner, leaving room for dozens of tables surrounding a white marble dance floor ordered from a local wedding company.

The same one Wendy wanted to use for her own wedding. Someday.

Volunteers worked to hang the various decorations designed by the art club and set up centerpieces. Across the room, Kayleigh painted letters over the DJ booth, and Charlotte wrapped navy-and-silver tulle bows around the back of faux bamboo chairs.

"Thanks again for helping with the decorations," Wendy said, for maybe the tenth time.

Charlotte rolled her eyes. "I promised I would, so here I am!"

The lights dimmed and the walls glowed blue, a scattering of lights twinkling on the dance floor. They'd been working on creating the perfect ambiance that would accentuate the prom's dynamic theme, voted on by both prom committees.

"I think it's going to look beautiful." Wendy sighed.

Charlotte paused to watch her friend standing in awe.

"This is probably the best it's ever looked," Wendy said, straightening a place setting. "You know, since more people bought tickets and we had a bigger budget. The Black prom never even had a dance floor before. Can you believe that?"

"What would they do without you?" Charlotte quipped. "And to show you my full support, Chris and I will be attending this prom . . . first."

Wendy beamed, throwing her arms around her. "Really? Oh, Char, that's so great! You can keep an eye on things since I can't be here. Thank you, thank you, thank you!"

"Yeah, yeah, yeah," Charlotte muttered, shrugging her off.

Wendy gave her a knowing smile before her mind drifted. "Have you talked to Jules lately?"

Charlotte hesitated, pretending to be focused on her task. "Uh, yeah. Yeah, I have."

"How is she?" she asked, trying not to sound too eager for any intel on her former best friend. Especially since Jules had blocked her on all her social media accounts.

Charlotte didn't meet her gaze across the table. "She's Jules, you know. But . . . she's really excited about prom."

"Do you . . . think it's going to be weird . . . with all of us at the after-prom together?"

Charlotte barked a laugh. "Of course it's going to be weird! For a whole slew of reasons. You picked a hell of a time to get all noble on us."

Wendy closed the gap between them. "You think I shouldn't go, don't you?"

She sighed. "Wendy . . . let's just see how the night plays out. Besides, Jules may be so drunk she'll forget about everything."

"Hey, Wendy," Kayleigh called from across the room, holding a large silver box. "Where do you want the ballot box?"

"Just put it over by the refreshment table!"

Kayleigh nodded. Even though she wasn't attending the All-Together prom, as Jason had made it clear that wasn't an option, Kayleigh had still offered to help set up. It amazed Wendy how sweet and thoughtful her friends were being.

See, we're not monsters, she thought, and took a picture for Instagram, so that everyone could witness their kind efforts.

"Oh, shoot. Almost forgot," Charlotte said, dropping the tulle. She dug into her tote bag and waved the stack of light blue papers, cut into quarters. "King and queen ballots and tiny pencils, as promised."

"Oooo . . . let me see," Wendy chirped, and grabbed the stack.

Vote for Your Prom King & Queen
Regina Ray and Vernon Spencer Jr.
Rose Harris and Tom Taylor
Madison Washington and Kendrick Scott
Emily Grey and Pete Smith
Jada Lewis and Will Alexander

Wendy had almost skipped over the name, so used to calling him Kenny that "Kendrick" didn't immediately ring any bells.

But when it did, the chimes were deafening.

"Um . . . Maddy's on here," she said, as if there had been some error.

Charlotte frowned. "Well, yeah. Because of Kenny."

Wendy blinked, utterly confounded. She gripped the stack tighter, the names loud and hot against her fingertips.

Kenny + Maddy.

She looked up and realized Charlotte was staring at her, waiting.

"Oh. I . . . right. Yeah, of course," she mumbled, handing the stack back over, annoyed that the sight of a name had elicited such deep feelings. After all, this was her plan, and Maddy being nominated would add fuel to the feel-good story. It didn't really mean anything. Besides, no one would ever vote for Maddy.

Charlotte smirked. "So, where do you want them?"

Wendy pivoted, busying herself with another table setting as she tried to gain control of her face.

"Um . . . I guess, just put them on each table."

"Hey, Wendy!"

The girls turned to the door.

Rashad pointed a thumb at the exit. "The king and queen chairs are here."

"You ordered thrones?" Charlotte balked.

Wendy ignored her. "Just put them on the stage. I've marked the spots."

FIFTEEN

MADDY DID IT
EPISODE 8
"Another Theory"

Caleb Adler: I heard you guys talked to Keating.

Michael: *laughs* Yeah. He was something.

Caleb: Did you know his real name's Bob Smith?

Michael: Are you serious? That's hilarious!

Michael [narration]: That's Mr. Caleb Adler, accompanied by Mr. Kit Bernaski, both top specialists and leading experts in telekinesis. Because let's face it, our last expert didn't give us much to go by, and I couldn't move forward without some fact-based intel.

Caleb: We pretty much all know the gist of what telekinesis is. I mean, who wouldn't want to call a remote over from across the room? But telekinesis is actually quite spiritual. We're all born with the ability, but various factors, such as nature or nurture, can hinder it. To make any object move, you have to have faith in your abilities to actualize those powers.

Tanya: So are you suggesting that Christianity is the key to telekinesis? To believe in the unseen?

Caleb: Jesus said you could move a mountain with the faith of a mustard seed.

Tanya: I find it highly doubtful that God, if she does exist, would give superpowers to every human being ever created.

Kit: Ah! A skeptic! Well, let me break it down scientifically. All objects are made up of atoms. Thus, moving objects involves manipulating those atoms through the four forces of nature: the strong nuclear, the weak nuclear, the electromagnetic, and the gravitational force, which are all powered through the mind.

Tanya: So, if this is something that everyone has, why can't it be proven? The lack of repeatability prevents further research.

Kit: TK is a human capability, and we, at our core, are ever-changing flawed creatures. The same blood in my fingers today could be in my toes twenty minutes from now.

Michael: So how was Maddy able to do it?

Kit: Given what you've told us, other than her father's religious influence, her mind was a proverbial blank slate. She had no interaction with other people or media until she was twelve, thus wasn't subjected to skepticism or acculturation forcing her to adhere to societal norms. All the perfect conditions to hone in on one's power. Other qualities would help, like muscle coordination, proper

nutrition, and having enough iron present in your body, as

it assists with the ability to call on atoms.

Michael: Wait, iron? Maddy had anemia! Her doctor prescribed

her iron pills three months before prom.

Kit: That would explain the sudden discovery, which would make

her first period the original catalyst of her powers.

Michael: Wow!

Caleb: But . . . I'd like to offer an alternative theory.

Michael: Please. I'm all ears!

Caleb: I'm not sure we're dealing with just a normal girl

embracing her powers. See, we in the TK community

understand that our abilities can be limited. I mean, we are

human after all. But we also know it's nearly impossible for

a human to have every macro and micro psychokinesis

trait known to man. So one would think to maybe question

whether she was human at all.

Tanya: Great, now she's an alien?

Caleb: No. But that type of power wouldn't live in a regular girl.

More a . . . supernatural one.

Michael: Supernatural?

Kit: What we're saying is . . . given everything we know and

heard, Maddy Washington seems to have all the markings

of a witch.

Tanya: Oh, come off it!

Kit: Think about it—the ability to call her powers on demand, controlling fire, metal bending, the birds . . . it all starts to add up.

Michael: I'm . . . I'm . . . I don't know what I am. Do you think she knew?

Kit: I think she had a feeling there was "something." Hence, her studying TK. But if she was a witch, the intensity of her powers might have only manifested when she was under extreme duress and needed to protect herself.

Michael: Like prom. Holy shit!

Caleb: Consider this—a girl with that much untapped, untamed raw power, believed she was just innocently learning about TK. But that was the equivalent of studying a math textbook for a French exam. The wrong concentration consequently opened a Pandora's box she wasn't prepared for.

Kit: Then there's the high-frequency sound that only kids heard when she used her powers. One described it as mic feedback? She could've inadvertently been communicating via telepathy. But without guidance, she was a mic standing too close to the speaker. That could also explain the birds. Back in 2011, one thousand blackbirds were found dead in Arkansas due to a silent sonic wave that skewed their senses.

Michael: Wow. Just wow. Tanya, say something!

Tanya: I don't know where to begin. How do you even prove something like this?

Caleb: Power like that is something you're born with. Definitely
     an inherited trait. I'd suggest tracing her lineage.
Michael: Well, no way could it be the father's side. They were
     devout Protestants.
Kit: What about her mother?
Michael: DNA samples from medical records trace her roots
     back to Haiti and Ghana. So, maybe we start there?

May 29, 2014

Maddy had waited until the last possible moment to shop for a dress, afraid that Kenny would change his mind and she would've wasted her meager savings on something she'd never wear. But now, prom was in two days, and nonstop thoughts of Kenny pulsed through her bloodstream. She stood in front of Able's Consignment Shop, next to the pharmacy. There used to be a drinking fountain beside this building, with a *Whites Only* sign hanging above it. She remembered the picture well.

Maddy had never been clothes shopping before. Everything she wore Papa bought for her, or she altered from her grandmother's old wardrobe. Including her sweater.

I'm wearing his dead mother's clothes, she thought bitterly.

Maddy considered making a dress out of curtains like Scarlett O'Hara did in *Gone with the Wind*. But she wasn't an expert seamstress. Her skills were in the kitchen. So she took her pitiful savings of fifteen dollars she'd squirreled away over the years to Able's, hoping to find something worthy of prom. Something nice. Something that Kenny would like and be proud to be seen with her in. The thought of going to the dance with him made a smile bloom on her face. She imagined them spinning around the dance floor like Ginger Rogers and Fred Astaire in *The Gay Divorcee*.

She gazed at the mannequin in the front window, wearing a pink satin slip dress with spaghetti straps. It was beautiful. But would Kenny like it?

"Maddy?"

To her left, a Black girl stood outside the pharmacy, blank poster boards in her hands. Maddy didn't know her, but she recognized her from school.

"Kali. I'm Kenny's sister."

"Oh," she mouthed, and flushed red.

"You okay?" she asked, glancing at the mannequin.

"Yes," she said.

They stood awkwardly, Maddy stealing glances at the window display. Something about Kali felt off. Maddy couldn't pinpoint it but didn't want to feel it either. She wanted to continue savoring the way Kenny felt flowing through her.

"Heard he's taking you to prom."

"Yes," she said with a growing grin. She was actually happy. Giddy. Excited. Emotions so foreign they gave her goose bumps. She turned to his sister. "Do you know your brother's favorite color?"

Kali frowned. "Red. Why?"

"I have to buy a dress," she admitted. "For prom."

"Oh. Ohhhh. Well, you should get a dress that you like! The dance ain't all about him and his big head, you know? You should buy the dress of your dreams."

Maddy bit her lip. She'd never dreamed of herself in a prom dress. What if Kenny didn't like what she liked?

Kali read her mind. "Seems like your whole life you've been doing what other people want you to do. But what do you want? You're going to the prom because you want to, so buy the dress you want to wear. Girl, be your own person for a change."

She swallowed. "I . . . don't know who that person is yet."

Kali nodded, then blew out some air. "Come on. I'll help you pick one out."

Is this some sort of trick? Why would she help me?

Maddy hesitated, feeling guilty for thinking the worst of every person she came in contact with.

"Um. Okay."

A bell chimed as they walked inside the shop. The older white woman sitting behind the counter put down her paper and smiled. Able's smelled like her father's store, except music vibrated out of wireless speakers, the place full of light, the walls painted candy pink.

Maddy walked around as Kali dug into the nearest dress rack.

"Hm . . . okay, how about this one? Oh naw, this green is nasty. What about this one?"

A hum of energy flooded the small, stale space, threads tugging at her fingers. Maddy stopped her browsing and faced Kali.

"I'm sorry," Maddy said.

Kali whipped around, frowning. "For what?"

Her smile wavered. "For not knowing . . . how to be Black."

Kali chuckled nervously, glancing at the saleswoman. "Yeah. And? A bunch of people don't. You expect me to teach you or something?"

"No. I just don't want you to think I don't understand because I don't want to understand."

Kali paused, her face expressionless. "You gotta crawl before you walk, I guess. But you better start crawling quick. No more excuses."

Maddy nodded.

Kali pulled three dresses off the rack. "I'm doing this for Kenny."

In a way, so was Maddy.

Maddy followed Kali to the back fitting room, and just as she reached the counter, she spotted a dress hanging off the register.

"Is that one . . . for sale?" she asked.

The saleswomen came around the counter. "Oh yeah. That just came in yesterday. Haven't even had a chance to price it yet.

It has a small rip, so I can cut you a deal."

Maddy took it off the rack, palming the fabric, and dragged a finger along the neckline with a smile. The dress of her dreams was also the dress from one of her favorite movies.

TWITTER @TEXASAM

On Wednesday, following a racist video and photo surfacing on social media, the athletics department at Texas A&M has decided not to allow the prospective student to join their spirit program. She will also not be attending the university this coming fall.

As she walked in the house, rereading the Twitter statement on her phone, Kali smiled at her handiwork. She was the one who'd sent the photo to media outlets. She was also the one who'd posted the photos of Jules from a burner account on Twitter, alerting Texas A&M and BLBP. She'd singlehandedly started the snowball that would eventually ruin Jules's life.

Payback is sweeter than honey.

She'd never told Kenny how Jules and her friends had treated her. They never did anything egregious or made school a living hell. They did much worse. They made her feel small and insignificant. Like she didn't matter. Like the Black Student Union was meaningless because their parents had the school board wrapped around their pinkies.

Jules had released a statement through the media in response to Texas A&M's decision. "For the record, my ill-informed decision to paint my face black had nothing whatsoever to do with racism or discrimination."

"Heh. Yeah, right," Kali mumbled, taking the stairs.

Heading to her room, she noticed Kenny lying on his bed, hands behind his head, staring at the ceiling, a dreamy look on his face as if he was thinking of something pleasant.

Or someone.

She stood in the doorway and cleared her throat. "Hey."

Kenny sat up on his elbows. "Hey. What's up?"

"You okay?"

"Yeah." He smiled. "Guess I don't just chill that often. Kind of nice."

As different as their childhoods had been, Kali could see how their father's pressure had pushed Kenny to be the very best. How the pressure forced his hand and every move he made. Their father's expectations were a weight he silently carried. A weight that made him choose survival over culture. And still, she loved him, through all his blind, ignorant transgressions. Could she make that same peace with a girl pretending to be white?

Kali took a deep breath. "Black."

He frowned. "Huh?"

"Her dress. Maddy. She's wearing black."

And with that, Kali closed the door.

• • •

Pacing in a circle, Wendy dialed Kenny for a third time. *He probably fell asleep*, she reasoned to herself. So why couldn't she shake off the feeling she was being ignored? She put down her phone and opened a document in her drive called *Plan D*. In it was a list of scholarships she'd been collecting since the seventh grade. She'd given up her full ride to Brown but had secured enough scholarship money to last her at least two years at Alabama. Kenny would help her with the rest. But if he didn't, she'd have to resort to plan D.

Wendy walked into the kitchen, opened the fridge, and grabbed a bottle of water. She gulped it down, trying her best to ignore her surroundings.

In the middle of the living room, her parents sat on green plastic lawn chairs, eating microwave popcorn, watching another episode of *Grey's Anatomy* on Netflix. They had turned off the cable over six months ago, leaving just the internet, at Wendy's insistence. Most of their furniture had been sold to neighboring towns, her father transporting it in the dead of night. They kept the curtains and blinds closed, leaving the house in perpetual darkness.

Money and status mattered in a town like Springville, and they no longer could afford to keep up appearances. They planned to put the house on the market the day after Wendy graduated, hoping for a quick sell, and had already placed a security deposit on a one-bedroom apartment down in Florida. A brand-new start, her father had called it. He'd been looking forward to one since he'd been laid off from the power plant. Once the house sold, Wendy would be on her own. She wasn't too surprised. They weren't all that concerned about her future. They'd never once asked where she planned to attend in the fall. But . . . something about giving up the house, her one piece of concrete safety, the ground she juggled on and planned from, made anxiety grip her by the throat, strangling her daily.

She could've visited and stayed with Jules; she practically lived there on the weekends anyway. But they might never be friends again.

So if everything didn't go to plan with Kenny, she would never come back to Springville. She'd never see what friends she had left again, and she would have no place to truly call home.

The idea had come to Jules in a dream. An idea so wickedly perfect, she couldn't stop giggling about it. Every time she remembered that the plans for her future had been squashed like a lightning bug, she'd think of her dream and it'd give her a high.

"Can you see it from the floor?" Brady whispered from the stage rafters.

"No," Jules whispered, shining her flashlight up. "The stars and banner block it."

Sneaking into the Barn was easier than either of them had imagined. The back doors were unlocked, and there were no security cameras to worry about. They moved their supplies in quick and got to work.

Since Jules couldn't go to school and hated being stuck in the house, she occasionally accompanied her father on the golf course, practicing her swing. One day, Jason's father had joined them, and the men spent eighteen holes reminiscing about all the pranks they'd played on the East Side kids. It kept them in line, reinforcing unspoken rules that went back generations. She brushed off their childish old-school antics, but that very night, the dream came to her.

A few drops of paint trickled out of the bucket onto the stage.

"Careful," Jules warned, wiping it clean.

"Relax, babe. I know what I'm doing."

Jules doubted that.

Brady fastened the bucket around the piping on the stage lights with thick black rope to blend in with the curtains, making sure the string held the bucket in place, right on the edge of the beam. He then finished filling the bucket with the paint color of Jules's choosing. Two cans' worth: she wanted maximum carnage.

Jules swept her flashlight across the room, the silver decor glimmering back at her. The tables surrounded the dance floor in a U shape, trees of starburst lights arranged in each corner. Even in the dark, the decorations were exquisite. It didn't even look like the Barn.

"Wow," Jules muttered, touching one of the place settings, the napkin folded into a fan—something Jules had seen Wendy practice doing with McDonald's tissues. Her ex-best friend had a magic touch for these sorts of affairs. Leave it to Little Miss Perfectionist to turn shit to gold.

Her jaw clenched as she fought back angry tears. How could Wendy abandon her during her time of need? Jules had been there for her since the second grade; didn't their friendship mean more to her than helping some stupid girl or impressing her lousy boyfriend? Jules had done more for Wendy over the years than he had. He wasn't even that great of a boyfriend.

"Babe, I need some more light over here."

Jules sniffed, unraveling the napkin with a yank, and turned back to the stage. "Are you almost done?"

"Almost," he mumbled with one final tug of the rope, then shined his flashlight directly down on the stage. "Mark that spot."

Jules snapped two pieces of white tape where the light hit and made an X.

Brady climbed down and joined Jules on the dance floor, staring up at the stage.

"When it's time, I want to be there, Brady. I want to see it all."

"That's fine, babe. But . . . how do you know she'll be up there?"

Jules couldn't tear her eyes away from the thrones. She licked her lips, imagining the scene, how the chaos would all play out. A giggle escaped her. Brady frowned, as if worried she had become unhinged.

"Don't worry," she muttered. "I got friends in high places."

PART

THREE

SIXTEEN

MADDY DID IT

EPISODE 9

"Wendy: Part 1"

Michael: Thank you so much for agreeing to talk to us.

Wendy Quinn: You said something about having new, never-
before-seen evidence or something like that?

Michael [narration]: Aside from Maddy and her father, another
key character in the events leading up to Prom Night was
Wendy Quinn. Over the years, I've reached out to her
on multiple occasions, but she frequently changes her
address, phone number, and email, citing death threats.
Currently, Wendy lives in an undisclosed location out of the
country, under a different name. It took a lot of convincing,
begging more on my part, for her to join the show.

Michael: Yes! But first, I have a few questions, if you don't mind.

Wendy: What d'you wanna know?

Michael: Well, we'd love it if you could tell us what you were doing on Prom Night. Several witnesses stated that you were there, at the Barn, but that you weren't supposed to be.

Wendy: For the fifty thousandth time, I went there to meet my boyfriend, Kenny Scott. We were supposed to go to the after-prom party, and I got there a little early to pick him up. Not a crime. Next question.

Michael: Guess I'll just cut to the chase. Do you know where Maddy Washington is?

Wendy: Are you kidding? We all know she died in the fires.

Michael: But we don't know. They never found her body.

Wendy: They didn't find a lot of bodies. You're not much of a journalist, are you?

Michael: Okay. What did you do after everything happened?

Wendy: You mean after the explosion? I went home.

Michael: Home?

Wendy: That's what I said.

Michael: Wendy. The reason why we were so insistent upon interviewing you . . . Well. Okay, so we recently tracked down some CCTV footage of you at a gas pump within a mile of Greenville. Do you remember what you were doing there?

Wendy: Oh. Yeah. I was giving a friend a ride to the Hilton in Greenville. That's where the after-prom party was supposed to be. Folks wanted to get out of Dodge.

Michael: Was it Maddy?

Wendy: Ha! No. Around that time, Maddy was busy burning
        down the town.

May 30, 2014

Wendy's legs were like clamshells, pinching Kenny's waist as
he lay between them. Her lips were thin. Chapped. Her mouth
never opened wide enough for him to hungrily kiss her the way
he wanted. He felt himself pretending to be satisfied . . . just
like at school.

Had it always been like this?

Wendy insisted they spend some time alone, which seemed
excessive. Didn't he already see her at school enough? Weren't
they going to the after-prom together? Kenny wasn't really in
the mood but appeased her. What else could he do? He didn't
want to be *that* guy.

As he listened to her forced moans and overacting, his
thoughts continued to churn—

Were her lips always this dry? Were her hips always this stiff? Were—
Maddy, Maddy, Maddy.

Kenny jumped out of his skin, hitting his head on the truck
ceiling with an "Ow!"

"What's wrong?" Wendy gasped, quickly covering herself.

Kenny caught his breath. "I . . . I thought I saw something."

Wendy looked around the dark woods and chuckled. "It's
nothing," she cooed, trying to pull him back to her. But he
resisted, his body unresponsive to her touch. He wasn't in the

mood for sex. The flight response overpowered him.

"Guess I'm just tired. Overdid it at the gym today."

"You went to the gym? You didn't tell me that."

Kenny rolled his eyes, trying to smother his growing impatience with her constant tracking. Truth was, he'd gone home, read a book, and eaten a sandwich. He'd wanted to be alone and just think, for a change. The same thing he wanted at that very moment.

"It's . . . getting late," he said. "Come on. Let me take you home."

A crushed expression washed over Wendy's face, but she quickly wiped it clean. "Um. Okay," she mumbled, reaching for her bra.

Outside Wendy's house, she kissed him hard, caressing his face, but to him, it felt stale and meaningless.

"Good luck tomorrow," she said with a smile, hopping out of his truck. She placed a hand on the window frame, searching his face for a faint glimpse of reassurance.

He could barely muster a smile in return but nodded and sped off, not even waiting until she made it inside. Instead of making a right down the block toward home, he turned left, toward Mills Road. He needed some air. He needed a long drive and a cool breeze to clear his head. He opened the sunroof and turned his music on high.

He'd been having second thoughts about Wendy for a while, but the events of the last few weeks seemed to be compacting them. Could he be with her forever? The way she always talked about? He wasn't so sure anymore. Was there more out there for him? Would he be settling for what he knew without giving the world a try?

Break up with her, a voice inside him said. *If you feel this way, break up with her, don't hurt her.* It would be a cathartic release.

The endless dark roads were merciful to the growing pressure on his temples. He drove in circles, letting the road take him wherever it wanted.

Maddy. Maddy. Maddy.

Maddy's name kept beating against the walls of his skull. Two weeks ago, he'd hardly uttered her name. Now she was all that he could think of. All he wanted. He turned down a residential street, then another, snaking all through town.

Maddy. Maddy. Maddy.

The name drowned his thoughts and slowed his reflexes, as if he'd had one too many beers. His vision blurred and the truck swerved. He gasped and slowed down, pulling over to catch his breath, his heart racing. He looked to his left and found himself in front of Maddy's house, parked across from her driveway.

"Shit," he mumbled, and turned off the engine.

Maddy stepped back from the kitchen counter to admire her work of art. The freshly baked pound cake sat on a kelly-green stand, rich and golden brown. She pulled another pan out of the oven without a mitt. Nothing burned her anymore.

The house was quiet. Papa had locked himself in his office, keeping his distance, mumbling prayers. He came home from work and took his dinner upstairs rather than sitting at the table with Maddy. She didn't mind, as long as he ate. He was starting to look thin, wasting away. Even through all his lies, she still cared for him.

Kendrick is outside.

The thought fluttered in and perched on her frontal lobe. She stiffened, glancing over her shoulder. She knew he was there without anyone having to tell her, without even looking outside. The realization of how incredible she had become over just a few weeks sank in. Her lips curved into a small smile.

Then she grabbed a red-checkered cloth napkin from the cupboard and laid it out on the table.

Kenny leaned against his car door, staring out of the window at the Washingtons' house as if casing the place, wondering which window belonged to Maddy. The house looked as if it could collapse at any moment, and he hated the thought of her being inside. He had no clue how he'd gotten there, and it wasn't his intention to be some type of stalker. Yet he didn't want to leave. There were thousands of places he could be, but sitting outside her home seemed to beat them all.

Five more minutes, he promised himself, then he'd go home. Suddenly, the world grew quiet, as if the bugs and owls had all gone mute. An unsettling silence.

Then her front door creaked open.

"Shit," he muttered, bolting upright. Fumbling, he turned on the engine, clicked buttons, and was prepared to speed off when he spotted Maddy walking down the driveway, holding something in her hands.

The moment she climbed into his truck, he was immediately enveloped in her scent, causing the restlessness to dissipate. An incomprehensible relief. Was she all he needed?

"Hi," she said in an impossibly small voice.

"Hey," he breathed.

Hair tied in a low ponytail, she wore a men's white under-shirt with a plaid skirt, shorter than her other ones, allowing him to catch a quick glimpse of her bare knees. He gripped the steering wheel. It was fucked up, he knew it was fucked up, but at that moment, he didn't care. He was just so happy to be alone with her again that nothing else mattered.

"What are you doing here?" she asked.

Kenny hesitated, unable to cook up a solid reason. "I don't know. I just . . . found myself in front of your house."

Maddy raised an eyebrow, mouth forming an O.

Kenny jumped to explain. "I know, it sounds crazy. But I was just taking a drive and, well, here I am."

"Do you do that a lot? Take drives?"

He shrugged. "Sometimes. Guess I have a lot on my mind."

She cocked her head to the side. "Like what?"

He sighed. "School. Life. Prom."

Maddy's eyes fluttered down at her lap. "You don't have to take me if you don't want to. You can still go with Wendy."

"No!" he blurted out, and quickly adjusted his volume. "No, I want to go with you. It'll be fun."

She chuckled. "I'm not that much fun."

"I have fun when I'm with you."

She stared at him, or through him; he wasn't certain.

And it was true. He could see them laughing, smiling, not just at prom but at the movies, on camping trips, in the back of his truck, or at Sal's. Was she the type of girl who'd come to his games? he wondered. Would she help him work out? He'd never seen her in the weight room or on the track. But then his thoughts shifted. He didn't want a gym buddy. He wanted someone he could just exist with on nights like these.

"Something wrong?" she asked.

"No. Why?"

She bit her lip, glancing from the corner of her eyes. "Um, you're . . . staring at me."

Bro, stop being a creep!

"Oh shi—shoot, my bad," he said with a strained laugh. "Hey, how'd you know I was out here?"

"I, uh, just . . . knew." Her eyes grew big. "And! I can see your car from my window."

He grimaced. "Oh. Yeah, right."

She smiled. "Here, I brought you something."

She placed a red-checkered napkin in his large hands.

"What's this?" he asked, opening it up. "Oh cool, cake!"

"I just made it."

"Really?" He broke off a piece and took a bite. "Whoa."

The buttery loaf melted on his tongue. Warm, moist, flavorful, and sweet . . . the best cake he'd had in his entire life.

"Whoa," he said again. "Aye, this is really good. You weren't playing when you said you knew how to cook."

She beamed with pride. "Do you want some milk? I can get you some."

Her hand inched toward the door and he shot out to stop her. "No! Don't leave. I mean, can't you stay just a little longer?"

She glanced at the house then nodded and let go of the handle. Kenny finished the cake, resisting the urge to lick his fingers. She'd probably make him an amazing cake for his birthday or Christmas or any time he wanted. He rested his head back, daydreaming of the idea.

"You're really quiet," she quipped with a smirk.

He laughed. "I'm just . . . actually, can I tell you something? Or wait, I'm *going* to tell you something."

She giggled. "Okay."

"I like being quiet. Everyone always wants me to talk, expecting jokes and burns, and I'm just like . . . it's cool not to say nothing. Sometimes I just want to chill. Like this."

He had her full attention. "Oh."

She leaned back, her eyes fluttering up to the ceiling, out

the sunroof, staring up at a fat moon in a black velvet sky. They sat there for a long while, the silence not loaded with alienation but comfort while the crickets came alive, competing with the radio.

"See that?" she said, pointing up, drawing a shape in the air. "That's Aries."

"Oh, so you know your signs?"

She shrugged. "A little. Read about it the other day."

"My mom's really into that stuff. She's always reading my horoscope. You believe in it?"

She thought for a beat. "It seems . . . strange that God would put people on this earth who can read stars and they mean nothing. God doesn't make mistakes. So maybe that's their purpose. To tell people about the stories written above us."

He chuckled. "Well, we do live on a floating rock in the middle of the universe with like a billion stars and other rocks floating nearby. Kind of makes sense for that stuff to be real and God be the puppet master."

Maddy giggled, an adorably sweet sound. "What's your sign?"

"I'm a Leo. You?"

"I'm a Cancer," she said proudly.

"Ah, right. The sensitive type."

"I was born on the cusp," she said, wringing her fingers. "I'm made of magic."

He smirked. "Who told you that?"

She lifted her chin, gazing at the sky with a deep exhale. "My mother."

Kenny noted the longing in her voice and wished for nothing more than to take her pain away. But then he tipped his head and squinted.

"Hey, what happened here?" he asked, brushing a cool finger against a patch of burnt skin on the back of her neck that he'd never noticed before.

Maddy slapped a hand over the scar, her eyes wide. She ripped out her rubber band and combed her hair down.

"I, um, it was an accident."

"Oh," he said. "Yeah, my sister used to burn herself with a curling iron all the time. Back when she used to straighten her hair."

Maddy squeezed herself into a tight ball with a shudder. His hand hadn't left her shoulder. It felt good there. It looked good there.

"Hey," Kenny said, shifting closer. "It's cool. Accidents happen. You don't need to hide that stuff from me."

They stared at one another, and though he was attempting to comfort her, he also realized he didn't need to hide from her either. At that moment, something unsaid passed between them. Something that had been hovering in the air since the day they got milkshakes. His heart thumped hard against his ribs, eyes shifting to her lips—how plump and delicate they seemed—as a surge of feverish longing pulsed through his veins, the need for her taking over reason. The whites of her eyes shimmered as he moved in closer . . . and closer. And right before their lips could touch, the engine roared, the radio squealing, windshield wipers coming to life. Maddy reeled back with a yelp, her head slamming against the passenger-side window.

"I . . . I'm sorry," she babbled, fumbling with the door. She jumped out of the car and ran up her driveway.

Kenny gripped his chest, coughing up a gasp.

Holy shit. I almost kissed Maddy Washington!

David Portman's Springville Massacre: The Legend of Maddy Washington (pg. 220)

In the desert of northern Mexico, there is an area called la Zona del Silencio, or the Zone of Silence. It's considered to be the country's very own Bermuda Triangle, where radio signals fail and compasses spin out of control, leading locals to believe that it was the site of a UFO crash. Researchers hypothesized that hundreds of years ago, a massive meteor with an exceptionally high iron content landed in the area, causing strange magnetic anomalies.

After Prom Night, the people of Springville wondered why their cell phones continued to malfunction, radio contact was near impossible, and GPS devices were unable to locate a satellite signal. Researchers argued there could have been a natural magnetic variation, similar to the

Zone of Silence, that might have been overlooked, but testing disproved the theory. Further, no agency would build a power plant within miles of such a potential electromagnetic void.

During my various research trips to Springville, I visited the location where the country club once stood and placed a compass on the rock memorial. It spun in both directions. To this day, there is no official explanation for the phenomenon.

May 30, 2014

Kenny couldn't wipe the grin from his face as he stepped inside his house close to midnight. It took him thirty minutes to drive away from Maddy's.

He'd almost kissed Maddy Washington. He wanted to kiss her, more than he'd ever wanted to kiss anyone. It was a feeling he didn't know he'd been missing, a rush of something more. The giddiness cut through his blood like a drug. High on hope, he floated up to his room.

Maybe he could convince her to come to Alabama with him. He'd talk to his coaches—they could probably find her a scholarship. After all, he was their top recruit, future starting quarterback. They would want to make him happy. He'd drive back to Springville to pick her up after training, help her move into her dorm, buy her everything she needed, make sure she had the warmest sweaters so she would never be cold. He'd teach her about football, music, and Black history.

She'll probably want to get married before we do it, he thought. And he wouldn't mind. He would wait for her. They'd have a small wedding, just them and close family, right before the draft. Then, she would really be all his. A virgin Maddy. He'd be her first everything—kiss, boyfriend, sex. He'd buy a house with the biggest kitchen he could find. Or maybe have one built, right next to the water. He'd make a lake if he had to.

He had a plan. And as it firmed in his mind like a brick, he walked into his room to find his father leaning over his desk.

"What's this?" Mr. Scott said, books in hand.

"Yo, what are you doing in my room?" Kenny shouted.

"This is my got damn house!" he barked. "Now answer me."

Kenny clenched his jaw, remaining mute.

Mr. Scott shook a book in his face. "Boy, your sister can waste her time reading all this Afro-centric junk, but you . . . I expected more from you. You should be studying game footage, not studying this crap. Where's your head, son? You should be in the game! After all we did to get you here."

"We?" Kenny scoffed, infuriated.

"Yes, we! Who put in extra hours at the plant to pay for private coaching, clinics, and dietitians? Who shuttled you to every game, sacrificed every waking hour, and put even their only daughter's wishes second to yours? This isn't just your win. It's a family win. A family's sacrifice for your dream."

Kenny's eyes flared. "My dream? This was never my dream.

I just wanted to play football. I didn't want football to be my entire life. I wanted to have a life!"

"You have a life!" he shot back. "A good one. Better than most. You know how many boys would kill to be in your shoes?"

Kenny opened his mouth but shut it. What good would it do? His father only heard what he wanted.

Mr. Scott narrowed his eyes. "Boy, what's gotten into you? Is this about prom? Is that Washington girl distracting you?"

Kenny crossed the room in three quick strides, charging up to his father. They'd been the same height for the last few years, but Kenny had a solid thirty pounds of muscle on him.

"Leave her out of this," he growled, his hands flexing. He'd never once thought of hitting his father but knew one punch would land him in the hospital.

Mr. Scott cocked his head to the side and chuckled. "Oh. So it is about her. Well, like they say, once you go Black, you never go back."

"What's that supposed to mean?" he spat, furious he didn't understand the joke.

Mr. Scott shook his head. "That Wendy . . . she'll look better on your arm, take you further than that Washington girl ever will. No matter how white she may look. No one will care. You best remember that."

Then he tucked the books under his armpit and strolled out of the room.

Transcript from ESPN College Football LIVE,
June 3, 2014

Host: Breaking news out of Georgia today. Top college recruit Kendrick Scott is alleged to be one of the multiple victims in a May thirty-first explosion near a high school senior prom that took the lives of over a hundred people. The family reported him missing and his remains have yet to be identified. A Gatorade National Player of the Year and three-time all-state selection, Scott led his school to three state championships and would have likely been the first true freshman to start at quarterback for the Crimson Tide since 1984.

Alabama released a statement today: "We are devastated by the loss of such a phenomenal athlete and send condolences to his family . . ."

SEVENTEEN

May 31, 2014

THE BLACK SATIN off-the-shoulder dress had a sweet-heart neckline, cinched waist, and mesh short sleeves. Maddy had hemmed it tea length, adding layers of itchy tulle beneath to make it fuller. The diamond brooch pinned on her side was from the store, kept in the glass display case that was rarely looked at. It sparkled in the dim light of her bedroom as her trembling hands tried to apply a second coat of mascara. The YouTube video she'd watched at school said three coats would draw out her eyes, but she couldn't hold still. She took a deep breath.

Nerves. Everything would be fine.

Her hair hung long in classic Hollywood waves, fluffed with several brush strokes, and kept in place with dollar-store hair spray. With her lips stained a deep red, she looked like Bette Davis in *All About Eve*.

"Fasten your seat belts. It's going to be a bumpy night."

"No," she whispered. It wasn't going to be a bumpy night. It was going to be perfect. And Kendrick would be there soon to pick her up. She slipped into her black kitten heels with cutouts at the sides and velvet bows on top. She had made a thin shawl with leftover fabric from a white dress to cover her bare shoulders and hide the burns on her neck. Would Kendrick notice? He'd seen one but not all of them. Would he be worried?

"Black. Of course," Papa bellowed behind her. "Only jezebels would wear such a color. A harlot. The color of the darkness from which you came."

Her stomach tensed, but she chose not to respond.

Papa stood in the doorway, seething. "How dare you dress like some whore in my house?"

Maddy couldn't fathom what he saw. The dress looked straight out of every movie they'd ever watched together— modest, classic, and sophisticated. How could he find fault in it?

He stepped closer. "Madison, I am ashamed of you."

She sighed. "I know, Papa. I've always known that."

Papa's brows knitted before he slumped, the anger seeming to leak out of him. His face softened, bottom lip trembling.

"Madison," he started in a meek voice. "Daughter. Please, I'm begging you. Don't do this. Stay here. Stay with me."

The crack in his voice made her wobble. But Maddy lifted her chin and stuffed a lipstick inside her clutch.

"Papa, please. I need to finish getting ready. He'll be here any moment."

Papa took a step closer with a trembling smile, his eyes glassy.

"I've bought some ice cream. Your favorite, vanilla. We could watch *Grease*. You always said you wanted to see that, right? Wouldn't that be nice? Madison?"

Maddy smoothed down her roots in the mirror.

"Maybe tomorrow, Papa. Tonight, I'm going to the prom."

Even saying the words felt surreal and dreamlike. She, of all people, was headed to a dance. Not just any dance, the prom! She almost burst with laughter, body flooding with joy.

But then Papa lunged across the room, gripping her shoulders.

"Papa, let go of me, please!"

"Take off this filthy dress," he said, shaking her. "We can pray together for redemption. Cast away your sins while there's still time."

"I haven't sinned, Papa! I'm just going to a dance. Everyone goes to dances, even in the movies, and they turn out just fine. It's not a sin!"

"You don't understand, child. You don't understand what those people are like."

Maddy stared into his petrified eyes and tried to pull away. "Stop it, Papa."

"Don't you see? All this time, I've only tried to protect

you!" he cried with a raspy voice. "Because I know . . . I know ·they're going to hurt you." Papa's mixture of anger and pain frightened her, but she couldn't escape his grip. "Dear child, these aren't good people. Don't you see? They are not nice to your kind."

"My kind?" Maddy balked.

"Yes! Yes, child. Your kind. Negroes and whites were never supposed to fornicate, but I succumbed to that woman's powers—"

"Papa, no, stop it," Maddy whimpered.

"They don't know what to do with someone like you. I knew this. I knew they would only see you as an abomination. That you didn't belong . . . anywhere."

Her neck strained. She couldn't stay in the house another minute. Air. She needed air.

Maddy shoved him off and grabbed her purse, rushing down the stairs. Papa followed.

"It's why I kept you so close," he said, stumbling behind her. "It's why I didn't want them to know about you. They would punish you, not me. For what I did . . . with that woman. I didn't want to see you get hurt, child."

Maddy's eye twitched. Fanning her face and neck with her hand, she tried to steady her breathing.

"Papa, please. You're going to make me sweat, and my hair—"

"They'll hurt you. They always hurt your kind!"

"I am just going to a dance," she said in a deliberately calm voice. "Kendrick is taking me. I was trying to tell you he's a really smart young man, and I—"

"From the beginning of time, they've always hurt your kind!"

"Papa, STOP IT!"

The radio shrieked. Papa flew up, banged into the ceiling, and landed on his stomach with a loud smack. The room shook, candles crashing onto the floor around them.

Papa moaned and spit out a broken tooth, his cheek filling with blood. Panicking, he reached for Maddy's shoe just within a foot from his face, but his arm froze. Maddy had him pinned. His stomach turned, acid boiling in his gut, cooking his insides on high, his mouth glued shut to keep him from screaming.

She took a deep breath and swallowed back tears, torn between wanting to help him and wanting to kill him.

"Papa, I made your favorite," she said in a small, shaky voice. "Meat loaf, mashed potatoes, and string beans. There's cake in the fridge."

Papa's eyeballs moved frantically in their sockets, the only piece of his body that still belonged to him. The rest was under Maddy's control. She gripped the invisible threads tighter, and he moaned.

"I know you're . . . scared. I'm scared too. But there are some really nice people in the world, Papa, and we need to start believing that. I'll be home by eleven. And then after tonight, you'll see that everything is gonna be okay. We don't have to be scared of folks finding out about me anymore. We can start living like everybody else."

Papa jerked, willing himself free.

"No one is gonna hurt me. I promise."

Papa moaned, trying to shake his head. Maddy sighed and stepped over him. No sense in trying to change his mind. She walked out onto the front porch just as Kenny made his way up the steps. Her mouth dropped, and she quickly slammed the door shut behind her, hoping he hadn't seen Papa lying on the floor. She blinked, turning on the TV inside to mask Papa's moans.

Kenny stopped short, backing up with a whistle. "Wow," he mumbled, stunned.

Kenny wore a crisp black tux with shiny black shoes, the satin bow tie matching his lapels. The scent of his cologne made her heart skip. He looked straight out of a Cary Grant movie. Out of her dreams, dropped right onto her doorstep.

They drank each other in with sweet relief, chasing the desperate need to be together again. As her blood eased, she noticed a plastic box in his hand.

Kenny followed her eyes. "Oh! Um, this is for you."

With buttery fingers, he took out a corsage of white roses and baby's breath with a gold stretch band.

"Thank you," she said, a blooming smile taking over her face. Kenny slipped it on her wrist, stealing a touch of her palm. He stepped back to admire her again, grinning.

"Um, should I say hello to your dad or . . . ?"

"No," Maddy blurted, rushing toward him. "We can just go."

Kenny frowned, glancing over her shoulder at the closed door as if debating his next move. Her jaw clenched, gripping the threads tying Papa to the floor tighter, praying Kenny wouldn't ask to come inside.

He clicked his tongue. "Well. Okay then."

Maddy smiled and loosened her grip. She could hear Papa cough out a wheezing gasp.

Kenny offered his hand to help her down the porch steps, held it all the way to his truck, and opened her door.

"I should've gotten us a limo," he said as he started the engine, stealing another look at her.

Maddy rubbed a velvety rose petal between her fingers.

"I think your car is really nice," she said, with a coy smile.

"Yeah, but you deserve . . . more."

Maddy blushed, squirming at his gawking, then glanced back at the house.

Everything is going to be okay, she thought. She'd prove to Papa that the world was safe for a girl like her. That they didn't have to hide and lie anymore. That he could let her go off to college and make a life for herself. All would be well. The night would be perfect and then he'd see for himself that he was so very wrong about everyone.

From David Portman's Springville Massacre:
The Legend of Maddy Washington (pg. 220)

It was tradition that the outgoing seniors of Springville High converged into a caravan downtown on the way to their respective dances. The townspeople would line the Main Street parade route in lawn chairs to catch glimpses of the partygoers in their fine gowns and tuxedos. Students would blast music, waving from cars and limo rentals, pausing to take dozens of pictures that flooded social media feeds.

No one knew it would be the last time that most of them would be seen alive, and the students had no clue they were participating in their own funeral procession as they headed to prom.

EIGHTEEN

MADDY DID IT
EPISODE 10
"The Prom"

Michael: It's Prom Night, so let me set the scene for you here:

You have two proms—the white prom and the All-Together prom—happening simultaneously within yards of each other, separated by the railroad tracks.

The Black Student Union is lined up in front of the country club, protesting its racist practices. Mrs. Morgan, their advisor, is standing by, supporting the students' constitutional rights. She was the only teacher present at prom, as the dances typically had no adult supervision.

Four police units were on the scene, blocking the front gates of the club to "maintain peace," leaving one officer at the station, located on Main Street.

Two camera crews parked near the country club.

Two volunteer firefighters slept in their bunks.

There were approximately forty students at the white prom, mostly seniors. Their dance was held inside the ballroom toward the back of the country club.

At the Barn, there were approximately eighty students, seniors and their dates.

The overflow from the Barn parking lot took up most of the front lawn, stretching almost to the train tracks, fifty yards from the door.

The surrounding area consisted of thick woods and marshlands. Days prior, heavy rains had left the ground muddy.

A half mile south of the proms was the Springville transformer station. Five miles north was Springville Power Plant. You could see the lights of the reactors from the parking lot.

As students arrived at prom, no one in the town had any idea what was about to go down that night.

May 31, 2014

Kenny pulled into the last free space in the crowded parking lot of the Barn, the building lit up with spotlights. He turned off the engine, dropping them into silence. His stomach twisted, that familiar achy dread he felt almost every morning before walking into school.

Maddy sat quiet and pensive. He took one final sip of free air, bracing himself for another performance, and grabbed the door handle.

"Kendrick," Maddy said, touching his arm. "Can we wait a minute? Please."

Her eyes glimmered in the moonlight. He'd give her just about anything she wanted if she'd only look at him that way for the rest of their lives.

"Yeah, sure." He exhaled, relaxing into his seat with a small smile. "We can stay as long as you want."

She nodded and stared out the window. They watched kids decked out in their formal wear amble down the red carpet to the Barn's front entrance. While the door had Maddy's attention, she had his. He hesitated before reaching out, tucking a strand of hair blocking her face behind her ear, pinky grazing the scar on the nape of her neck.

"You look beautiful," he whispered, aware he sounded like a lovesick puppy, but couldn't help himself.

"Thank you," she mumbled, never taking her eyes off the Barn. She fidgeted with her purse, unsnapping and resnapping the clasp over and over, before nibbling on her thumb.

She does this when she's nervous, he thought, and he liked knowing that about her, liked being attuned to her emotions. He hated seeing her so skittish and timid, regressing to old Maddy when she was finally starting to warm up to him.

What if I just drove away? Went somewhere so we could just be alone. Who cared about some stupid dance anyway? He sure didn't. He only cared about Maddy. Glancing at the Barn door, he gripped the steering wheel, a finger hovering over the push-to-start button.

"Have you ever seen *Madame Bovary*, with Jennifer Jones?" she asked. Maddy stared out the window with the strangest longing in her eyes. The soft light from the Barn bounced off her pale skin, as if she glowed in the dark.

"No," he admitted. "Is that on Netflix?"

She sighed, leaning her head against the window. "It's a real old movie. Jones plays this girl named Emma, who lives with her father on a country farm, longing for the perfect life with a man who adores her. She marries a local doctor but isn't satisfied with his modest salary. She wants to live a life of luxury, desperate to be in high society. There's this scene where the doctor is finally invited to a ball, and Emma is wearing this gorgeous white tulle gown with sparkles in her hair. All the men fight for her attention. The waltz comes on and a dashing aristocrat takes her hand, leading her onto the dance floor. He spins her round and round, and she grows dizzy, but she doesn't care because she's having the time of her life. It's all she ever dreamed of. Ever since I saw that . . . I've always wanted to go to a ball."

Kenny glanced back at the door for several heartbeats, still debating before releasing the wheel with a nod. "Then let's go to one."

She gripped her dress with both hands. "I'm . . . scared," she whimpered.

Her voice snatched the beating heart out of his chest. Kenny leaned across the console, resisting the urge to scoop her up into his arms, searching for the right words to comfort her.

"Um, hey. Can you look at me for a second?"

Maddy tore her eyes away from the busy entrance and met his, their faces so close he'd only have to move a mere inch to kiss her lips. And damn, how badly he wanted to. The need sucked all the air out of him.

She stared back at him, waiting with unnerving stillness.

"Look, I know it probably took a lot to come here tonight," he started. "So no matter what happens, just know that you did it. Stepped out even when you really didn't want to. Even after I begged."

She smirked. "I wouldn't call it begging."

"Man, I practically had to stalk you," he laughed. "But for real, you're brave. Not a lot of them so-called normal kids would be brave like you are right now."

She nodded, tears welling.

"I'm not going to let anything happen to you. Just trust me. Okay?"

She nodded again, and in that moment his mission became clear: protect her at all costs. The resolve made all the restless pieces, the questions that ached inside him, settle in his soul.

"Cool. Let's do this!"

With her hand in the crook of his arm, they climbed the Barn's steps, following the red carpet to a hall of floor-length mirrors.

Inside, white birch trees trimmed with lights arched over them, the ceiling glowed a deep blue. *Wendy did a good-ass job,* Kenny thought, the guilt eating him, and glanced down at Maddy. She gazed up at the sparkling lights and glowing stars in awe, a wisp of a smile on her lips. As they made their way through the entry, she caught a glimpse of herself in the mirror and froze, seeming stunned by the unfamiliar reflection. Her eyes roamed over every detail—the tinted lips, the loose curls spiraling down her shoulder, the satin shoes with bows, and the unique dress that no other girl at school would have. She looked like one of those old Hollywood movie stars. A heightened version of the Maddy he had always known. He patted her chilly hand and gave her a reassuring smile.

"Told you. Beautiful," he said. "So, about how many dances you think we can get in tonight?"

She blushed pink, pushing a strand of hair behind her ears. "Um, I don't really dance."

"Naw, you will tonight. Can't leave me solo dolo on the dance floor!"

She beamed as he pulled her forward. They took their entry photo, Maddy wincing through the blinding flashes, and were handed sparkling champagne flutes as they entered the hall. The entire room came to a screeching halt at the sight of them. Her smile dropped, eyes taking up most of her face. Kenny frowned, for once seeing the world from her point of view. The gawking and glares, as if she was some freak show, a damn circus act. His hand balled up into a fist.

Maddy took a shaky step back with a slight whimper only he could hear. He held her arm, pulling her closer beside him. He wouldn't deny her the one moment she had dreamed of, even if that meant walking into the lion's den.

Protect her at all costs.

"It's okay," he whispered, rubbing a finger along her knuckles. "No one's gonna mess with you."

They wouldn't fucking dare.

"Everyone's staring," she whispered, voice filled with terror.

"Well, that's 'cause you look amazing," he said, grinning as they slowly made their way in.

She peeled her eyes away from the crowd to look up at him and took a deep breath, her steps more relaxed. The compliment seemed to ease her panic.

"And you look . . . the same."

"The same?" He chuckled. "Damn, girl, I brushed my teeth and everything."

She giggled then stopped short, gazing up at the moon spinning in the middle of the room like a giant disco ball.

Stars and planets hung from the ceiling, a galaxy of constellations surrounding the prom banner announcing the theme: *Under the Starry Night.*

They glanced at one another for a silent beat, then burst with laughter. At their table near the edge of the dance floor, Kenny pulled out her chair, something he'd seen in movies, and they spent the next twenty minutes pointing out the different astrology signs twinkling above them. Somehow, it all felt completely normal, like they'd been together for years and it was just another night. During a simple dinner of chicken and rice, he kept stealing glances of her while she rattled off movies he'd never heard of. She looked happy, relaxed, and gorgeous. After dinner, the lights dimmed and a slow song came on. Couples drifted to the floor. Kenny hopped to his feet and extended his hand.

Maddy gulped. "I . . . um, we don't have to."

"Come on, you," he chuckled.

"No," she protested, but he managed to pull her out of her seat. He held her hand, wading through the other couples on the floor, stopping right under the moon.

He placed one of her hands on his shoulder, outstretched the other and began to sway.

"You're a good dancer," he mused, surprised how at ease she seemed with the music.

"I've, um, watched a lot of movies with dancing," she mumbled, seeming distracted. "In *The King and I*, Deborah Kerr taught the king how to dance on the three counts."

"I'd like to see some of these movies you always talking about."

Maddy winced a smile, head whipping from left to right.

"Sooo, this ain't so bad, then, right?" he asked.

"It's . . . um," she mumbled, noting the random couples

staring at them, her body locking stiff.

He threw everyone a murderous glare then grabbed her chin. "Hey, hey. Look at me."

The light glimmered in her gaze, the eyes of his future.

How'd I not notice these eyes before? It's like she's been hiding in plain sight all this time.

"Just me," he breathed, cupping her cheek. "There's no one else here but us."

She swallowed and nodded in agreement.

He slid her hands up to his shoulders, freeing himself to grip her waist, pulling them closer. She shivered under his touch, skin goose fleshed.

"Oh, uh. Is this cool?" he asked, realizing he might have overdone it.

"Mm-hmm," she squeaked. "That was in the movie too."

"You're shaking."

"I'm nervous."

"Me too," he admitted.

"Really?" She frowned, raising an eyebrow. "Give me your hand."

Kenny smirked, extending his arm. She wrapped her icy fingers around his wrist and blinked up in shock.

"Your pulse is racing."

"Told you."

"What are you nervous about?"

He shrugged innocently. "You."

"Me?"

"Yes. I just . . . want to make sure you have a good time."

"But why?" she asked, her question desperate and pleading.

He hesitated, not wanting to lie, afraid the truth would scare her. But under another starry sky, he wanted no secrets between them and knew it might be his last chance to come clean.

"I really want you to have a good time because I've been an ass—I mean, an a-hole all these years. You didn't deserve to be treated the way you been by everyone."

"Oh," she coughed. "Well, it wasn't your fault."

He shook his head. "Yeah, but I just kinda stood by."

Her lip trembled, eyes shooting down to the floor. "I . . . I understand why people think I'm weird. If I could've helped it . . . then maybe . . . things would've been different for me."

"I think everything happened the way it was supposed to. I mean, if you weren't 'weird,' I don't know if we'd be here . . . like this."

Her eyes softened. "Like this?"

He pulled her closer, resting his forehead against hers, and closed his eyes.

"Like this," he repeated, words affirming everything they both knew to be true, that they couldn't be without each other after the night was over.

Her breath hitched, but she didn't pull away. Instead, she leaned against his chest and sighed. Her hair smelled of apples, and he placed his chin on top of her head, breathing in, relaxing, savoring the scent. She felt right in his hands. He knew they were being watched, knew everyone would tell Wendy, but he didn't know he could feel the way he did, and he wasn't willing to give it up. Not for anyone.

The music switched to an up-tempo song, and kids swarmed the dance floor. Maddy's eyes widened.

"Guess you don't like Pitbull, huh?" Kenny laughed, leading her away.

"Yo, Kenny!"

Kenny whipped around, positioning himself in front of Maddy, never letting go of her hand.

Chris and Charlotte emerged through the crowd and strolled up to them, grinning.

"Man, I've been looking for you all night," Chris said. "Dude, looking fresh!"

"What's up," Kenny replied, his tone deadly, pulling Maddy closer to his back. He didn't trust them. And he wouldn't let anyone hurt her again.

Charlotte noted their interlaced fingers and grinned. "Hi, Kenny," she said in that nasally teasing tone. "You look great! And Maddy, I love that dress." Insincerity oozed off her tongue.

"Um, thanks," Maddy mumbled, her voice tinged with fear. He hated it. Hated that she felt the need to shrink herself around his friends.

They terrorized her. They've been terrorizing her for years.

"Thought y'all were going to the white prom," Kenny said, scanning the room. Who else was with them?

Charlotte gave him a rueful smile. "We are. But I *was* on the prom committee and I promised Wendy the night would go off without a hitch. You know, Wendy? Your girlfriend."

Kenny could feel Maddy's rapid heartbeat against his back like a second heart in his chest. He needed to get her away from them.

Chris swatted his shoulder. "Hey, man, loosen up!"

"What?" Kenny snapped.

"You got your game face on," Chris laughed. "I've only seen that look on the field. What's up? Something wrong?"

Kenny took stock—the adrenaline rushing through his veins, his balled-up fists, the tension in his legs. He *was* in the zone. But no one would dare mess with Maddy, not with him standing right there. And besides, Chris wasn't like the others.

Kenny cleared his throat and tried to smile. "Naw, just . . . too much punch."

Charlotte raised an eyebrow at Chris and smirked. "Soooo, we're all thinking about stopping by Sal's before heading to the Hilton. Wanna come? You could bring Maddy."

"Umm . . ." Kenny glanced over his shoulder at Maddy, her wide eyes staring up at him, resembling a fragile doll, and he thought of what Kali had said. How people saw her as more delicate because of her complexion. He didn't want to make that same mistake. No one had seen the fire behind her gentle demeanor like he had. She could hold her own if given the chance. But in that moment, he wanted nothing more than to just be alone . . . with her. He turned back to his friends.

"Naw," he said bluntly. "We're gonna head out early. But hey, catch up with y'all later."

Kenny pulled Maddy back onto the dance floor, leaving his friends speechless.

On the opposite end, with the coast clear, he spun her around and eased into the music.

"Sorry about that," he sighed. "Are you okay?"

"I thought you said you had a party to go to?"

He shrugged it off. "It's a nice night out. We can go for a drive, see some real stars. Then I'll get you home before curfew. Don't want your dad hating me without getting to know me first."

Maddy glanced at the floor. "Oh."

"What's wrong?" he asked, his back tightening. Damn, he really *was* nervous. He couldn't believe it and almost laughed out loud at the exhilarating, cathartic feeling.

"You don't have . . . I mean, you can go and—"

"No! No, I'd rather be with you. I mean, I *want* to be with you."

She frowned. "What about all your friends?"

"Fu—I mean, screw them."

"And . . . Wendy?"

He held his breath for a beat. "We'll . . . face her, together. She'll understand."

Maddy nodded, her eyes glassy. He pulled her close, and she melted in his arms. He didn't care who saw them. In fact, he wanted someone to see. He wanted someone to ask, "Do you love her more than football?"

And the answer would be yes. I love Maddy more than football.

What the hell was happening to him?

Wendy had just finished microwaving dinner when her phone buzzed with a text from Charlotte. A picture of Kenny and Maddy . . .

Your boyfriend and his date look mighty cozy.

Wendy zoomed in on the photo, examining the placement of his hands, his gleaming smile, and the gaze in Maddy's bright eyes.

A thought wiggled, jerked, and wormed its way up to the surface, its teeth bearing down on her dream. But she was doing the right thing. Wasn't she?

Your boyfriend and his date look mighty cozy.

Her chest tightened and she slammed the phone down on the counter.

"Mom! I need to borrow your car!"

I'll just . . . stop by prom, make sure everything's running like it's supposed to, she reasoned to herself as she jumped into the shower.

Then, she and Kenny would take Maddy home together before heading to Greenville. They could go early, order room service in the suite she'd reserved . . . a snapshot of what their life would be like on the road when the season started. Maddy probably wanted to be home anyway. Not like prom was her scene.

NINETEEN

May 31, 2014

"HEY, HEY! HO, ho! Racist students have got to go!"

Sheriff West sat in his truck, parked facing the country club with the windows rolled down, sipping a cold cup of coffee to take the edge off his hunger.

Missed dinner again.

But he had to check on his boys' formation for the evening.

It wasn't much of a protest. A mere ten or more students with painted signs marched in a circle at the country club entrance. And there weren't as many cameras as they had estimated. Just two from local affiliates, not even a live feed. But that was one too many, and he had strict orders from the mayor to keep a cool, level head while they were nearby.

"Hey, hey! Ho, ho! Racist clubs have got to go!"

His youngest son, Deputy West, had insisted they should wear riot gear, citing safety concerns, but Sheriff West had shot down the ludicrous idea.

"They're carrying goddamn posters, not AK-47s," he'd barked during the team huddle earlier that evening.

The boys had been watching footage of riots from all over the country . . . buildings set on fire, rocks lobbed at cop cars, stores looted, and monuments vandalized. He also saw how his brothers in blue manhandled protestors, throwing tear gas like they were in the middle of a war. West didn't care what other cities did to their citizens, but he wasn't about to let his own men treat their fellow neighbors as anything less than human. Springville had been a peaceful town until all the gossip from the high school spread into the streets. Blacks and whites always got along just fine—everyone knew their place. Now, he couldn't even grab a cup of coffee without tasting the tension in it. It stank up the air, and he had had just about enough.

But as the mayor had warned, he had one goal—get through the night without incident. Then, when all the attention died down and the seniors headed off to college, the town would go back to the way things were, including separate proms.

West stepped out of his truck and slogged over to the caution tape.

Aside from Officer Jessup Brooks, who'd stayed behind at the station, almost his entire force stood in front of the country club, their squad cars parked like a wall. They'd been tipped off about the protest and spent days deciding their best course of action.

Deputy Chip West led as commanding officer, along with Officer Eric Sawyer, Officer Avery Channing, Officer Heath Marder, and newcomer Officer Jacob Ross, a transfer from Athens.

"I said back up!" Officer Ross barked, his hand on his belt.

"Sheriff," Mrs. Morgan huffed, utterly exasperated. "The students have been in the same spot for the last hour, yet this man seems to have a problem with his eyesight and thinks the students are somehow moving closer to him."

Ross narrowed his eyes. "And you must be hard of hearing because I said to BACK UP! Another ten feet!"

"We're not on private property," a young Black girl snapped. "We can stand where we want!"

The group slowed to a halt, all eyes falling on West.

He sighed. "Ma'am. A word?"

Mrs. Morgan gave him a curt nod and they stepped aside.

"Say, is this all really necessary?" he asked, waving his hand at the crowd.

She shrugged. "The kids are just exercising their constitutional right to free speech."

"By making a bunch of noise about water under the bridge?"

She raised an eyebrow, crossing her arms. "Guess we have a difference of opinion there. Real question is if your boys are gonna behave themselves tonight, which is why I'm here, to act as an adult witness. I'm sure your department doesn't want any messy press."

West's upper lip stiffened. "You right. We don't want no trouble."

"Neither do they."

"Then we in agreement. As long as everyone stays behind the line."

Mrs. Morgan regarded the invisible border. "Sounds reasonable."

West ground his teeth. He hated feeling like he was answering to some woman. "Alright. I'm heading on back."

"Hey, Pa." Deputy West ran over to the sheriff's car. "Um, what's up with the new guy?"

"Ross?"

"Yeah? You don't think he got a couple of screws loose?"

West paused. "I don't get your meaning, son."

"He's a little . . . hot-tempered. This might not, well, just thinking maybe this ain't the best place for him tonight."

The men glanced over their shoulders at Officer Ross, openly glaring at the crowd. During his interview, Ross had admitted he had been released from his previous position due to a "misunderstanding." But West hadn't pushed any further. He had spectacular references and they really needed the manpower.

Still, a little reminder could go a long way. It'd make them look like they had some good sense.

West charged back toward his men. "This is a peaceful protest and y'all gonna keep it peaceful! Whatever you do, do not lay one hand on these kids. Absolutely no weapons!" He looked pointedly at Ross. "And I don't even want to hear about your thumb being near your holster. Got it?"

"Yes, sir," the men mumbled.

West tipped his hat at Mrs. Morgan and got in his truck, heading for home. The wife had promised to leave a plate out for him, and he could almost taste the crisp cold beer waiting in the fridge. He didn't plan to leave the house again all evening. The boys could handle whatever came up.

And with the prom behind them, tomorrow would be another beautiful day in Springville.

Kenny's hand didn't leave the dip in Maddy's spine all night. Even when they sat down, he seized any opportunity to touch her in some small proprietary way. His clammy palms felt like raw chicken cutlets as he held hers under the table. He was nervous, and she liked that he was nervous. It made her feel less alone. But he didn't need to be. She was having the best night of her life. And that's when it truly sank in, that their differences brought them together and made them whole. They didn't need to be on edge; they could just be themselves.

"Well, what do you feel like doing next?" Kenny asked. "Dessert? Photo booth? More dancing?"

She looked around the room and pointed at the refreshment table. "We can have some punch?"

Kenny glanced over at the crystal bowl and grimaced.

"Yeah, let's get you some water instead," he said, drawing her closer. "Don't trust it."

Maddy frowned. *What's not to trust about punch?*

"What's up, Kenny!"

Kenny stiffened at the voice, whipping around and throwing himself in front of Maddy. "Oh. Uh, hey," he said, seeming surprised.

Jada's satin burnt-orange dress looked beautiful against her chocolate skin. Her long locs were curled and pinned up with crystals.

"Didn't think you'd show," she said, as if impressed. "But glad you did."

"Uh, yeah."

Maddy sensed a strange hesitancy, a different type of nervousness in him. She brushed a finger over his knuckles—something she'd felt him do before—hoping to put him at ease.

Jada nodded at her. "You look real pretty, Maddy."

"Thank you," she said, becoming more comfortable with compliments and attention. "You look really pretty too."

Kenny smiled at Maddy proudly, giving her side a light squeeze.

"Well, I'm having a little party tomorrow. Sort of an after-the-after-prom. Y'all wanna come?"

He blinked, mouth popping open. "Yeah! I mean, that'd be cool. We'll come. Thanks."

Maddy liked the way he answered for them and leaned into his chest, holding in a giggle.

"Cool. I'll holla at y'all later then. Good luck tonight!"

"Thank you," they said in unison.

Good luck?

"Alright, y'all," the DJ's voice came over the speaker. "Don't forget to vote for the king and queen. We're tallying up them ballots in about ten minutes."

They took their seats, the king-and-queen voting slips placed in front of them. Maddy gazed around the quieted room, drinking it all in—the decorations, the music, the sparkling dance floor, the twinkling lights. She committed to memorizing each detail of the night, so she could recall it whenever needed. Her eyes fell on Kenny, catching him staring again, and her pulse quickened, cheeks blushing scarlet.

At their table, kids hunched over their papers like an end-of-the-year final.

Oh!

She pulled the blue slip closer. "Um, so, who should we vote for? You know everyone better than I do."

Kenny chuckled. "Who do we vote for? We vote for ourselves!"

"Huh?"

He tipped his head at the paper. "We're on here."

Maddy glanced down at the slip, catching sight of herself, third from the top.

Madison Washington and Kendrick Scott

She couldn't help thinking how nice their names looked together on a piece of paper as the pencil slipped out of her fingers and the panic melted in.

"Did you do this?" she gasped.

"Ha! I don't got that much power now."

She whipped around to the stage, set for the royal court, glittery crowns twinkling on red plush pillows in the bright spotlight. Her lips dried, tongue sticking to the roof of her mouth like a glue trap.

He wants to be on stage, in front of all these people?

"No," she gasped. "No, tell them . . . tell them we can't . . . I . . ."

"Hey, hey, hey." He cupped her face in his hands. "Hey, look at me. Look at me."

She swallowed, trying to reel herself in and focus on Kendrick's soft, kind eyes. He rubbed a thumb against her cheek with a small smile.

"There ain't no one in this room more worthy or deserving than you to be up there."

Maddy's heart expanded, stretching against her skin, and she finally exhaled. Had she been holding her breath all this time?

"So we're voting for us," he said, offering her a pencil. "Cool?"

Maddy stared at the pencil, the corners of her lips creeping upward. How funny that a simple sharp object had changed the entire course of her life.

"Cool," she said with a nod, the new word tasting sweet on her lips.

"There you go." He grinned and filled out his own slip.

Another slow song came on, and Kenny headed for the floor, Maddy following more willingly than before.

"Two dances in one night," he said, with an impressed nod as he spun her around. "Man, you're a party animal."

Maddy giggled, biting her lip.

"Uh-oh. And was that another smile? See, told you, you're fun."

"Yes. You did."

He nestled her against his chest as they swayed, the proximity overwhelming. Was Kenny serious? Did he really want to be with her? But he would be leaving for college soon, and she would be still in her father's store. And what about Wendy? What would everyone say about him? What would they do to her for taking him away from Wendy?

"Stop it," Kenny said.

She tipped her head up, frightened. "Huh?"

"Stop all that overthinking," he scolded. "This is what I want. Don't you?"

She nodded. There was nothing in the world she wanted more.

"Alright then," he said. "Everything's gonna be fine. We're going to be fine."

She gazed at him, studying the features in his perfect face, then chuckled. "Are you sure you're not a psychic like your mama?"

He shook his head with a chuckle. "I'm sorry. Just don't

want you to worry. About anything. You're safe with me."

Something unsaid passed between them, a palpable mental intimacy, the connection sizzling in her ear.

Maddy swallowed. "Kendrick?"

"Yeah."

"Before we go, um, go look at stars . . . can we get some pizza?"

He grinned. "Hell yeah! We'll get a whole pie and some sodas too."

Maddy could have burst into a million pieces of light.

But something sharp gnawed at the bottom tip of her spine. At first, she ignored it, but it became louder, wet teeth smacking on bone, demanding to be acknowledged, intuition screaming for attention. It didn't make sense. How could anything be wrong when Kenny looked at her like she was made of pure gold?

I'm safe with him, she told herself, trying to remain in the moment. *You're just being paranoid. Papa's not here. No one's trying to trick you. You're safe with Kendrick. You're safe.*

She repeated the words over and over. But her skin felt too hot. She needed air. Space. A chance to collect herself.

"I . . . need the ladies' room."

"I'll go with you!" he yelled, then squeezed his eyes shut. "I mean, I'll stand outside and wait."

He didn't want her out of his sight even for a moment. The thought brought a smile to her lips. She was safe. Safe with Kendrick.

Nothing's going to happen, she thought. *Just being silly.*

The mic on stage squealed. "Hey, everybody! It's almost time to crown the king and queen!"

He stole a quick kiss of her temple. "Come on. Let's sit."

From the corner of the room, Charlotte eyed the placement of Kenny's hand on Maddy's back, the look in his eyes bordering on infatuation.

He's never looked at Wendy like that.

It wasn't a bitter thought, more of an observation. Served Wendy right after parading him around, acting like she was better than everybody by letting him take Maddy to prom. She loved her friend but also found her self-deprecation annoying and hated the way the last few weeks had torn their once-tight clique apart. She missed what they used to be. How could Wendy turn her back on Jules? Yes, she shouldn't have done what she did. But Jules didn't kill anyone, and based on all the true-crime shows she watched with her sisters, even mothers still loved their murdering sons.

Charlotte took another picture. She needed more evidence for Wendy.

"Hi!" Kayleigh bumped Charlotte with her hip.

"OMG! What are you doing here?" she shrieked happily.

They hugged as if they hadn't seen each other in forever.

Kayleigh wore an iridescent plum spaghetti-strap dress with bubble-gum-pink shoes, her brown hair in soft waves.

"Prom's kinda lame without you guys," she said with a

shrug. "Jason's already pissy drunk, and Jules is hooking up with Brady in the limo. Figured I'd walk on over and help out for a bit. They're about to announce the king and queen soon, right?"

"Yeah. Was just about to grab the ballot box and start counting."

"Oh, I'll do it!"

Charlotte froze, frowning. "Really?"

Kayleigh grinned. "You know I love this type of stuff! Go dance with Chris."

"You sure?"

She waved her off. "I totally got this!"

"Um, alright."

Kayleigh smirked and took off. She snatched the box from the table and made her way backstage.

What Charlotte didn't see, as Chris led her onto the dance floor, was that Kayleigh's dress—much like most of her dresses—had pockets. And inside one of those pockets was a small stack of blue paper.

The day they'd been decorating, neither Wendy nor Charlotte had seen her unlock the backstage door or steal a single ballot from one of the tables.

It made photocopying that much easier. And all it took was one episode of her favorite reality show to mark each ballot for the ill-fated winners of that night.

TWENTY

May 31, 2014

JULES AND BRADY parked Kayleigh's truck in the shadows of the overflow lot. Jules's car would've been too noticeable, sending immediate red flags to the All-Together prom. She stepped out of the truck, her glittery heels sinking into the muddy grass, and glanced around, making sure the coast was clear.

Brady rounded the car and roped her into a hug, pressing his whiskey-drenched lips to hers.

"Ow! Brady! Watch it," Jules shrieked, leaning away. "My makeup."

"Shhh, babe. Keep your voice down."

Jules had on an icy-blue A-line floor-length dress with a halter neckline. The moment she'd tried it on in the store, she'd known it was the one. It pushed her cleavage up to just the right height to not look purposeful and gaudy. Her red hair was curled and pinned into an updo with a rhinestone tiara. She could imagine wearing it that way on her wedding day.

They had just served dessert at the country club, so no one had thought twice about her and Brady stepping out for some air. She absolutely planned to dance the rest of the night away with her friends. She'd been dreaming of the perfect prom for years.

But there was just one matter she had to tend to first.

"You sure this is gonna work?" Jules asked as Brady popped the trunk, pulling out a small black duffel.

"Relax, babe. I got it covered."

How could she relax when Brady was dumb as rocks and the whole night was riding on him not fucking up?

"Okay, let's go, then. And remember, we have to hide behind the curtains. We cannot be seen."

"Right," he agreed. "But that means the moment it goes, we have to get out of there fast. You won't get to see your work of art."

"Oh, I will," she grinned. "Everyone will be posting pictures. They'll be laughing so hard, folks downtown will hear them. Now, hurry it up, will ya? They're starting!"

They crept toward the Barn, staying out of sight, and slipped in the back door.

"Hey, y'all!" Jackie Torrence's voice blaring through the speaker brought the room to attention. Everyone clapped and cheered.

Brady and Jules tiptoed into position, the thick black stage curtains keeping them hidden.

"Thank you all so much for coming tonight. This is the start of a new tradition in Springville. Something that should've happened a long, *long* time ago. So let's toast to us! The game-changers!"

Jules peeked from behind the curtain, Jackie's back to her with the mic, the crowd swarming the dance floor with bright happy faces. It brought her immense pleasure knowing that they wouldn't be smiling for long. Their night was about to end.

Right of the stage, she spotted Charlotte standing with Chris, clapping along with everyone else. *Traitors!*

On top of a stage prop, Brady unzipped his bag, the crowd's cheers masking the sound.

"Special thanks to the prom committee and all who volunteered to make this amazing night happen!"

Wendy made this night happen, Jules thought, seething. Their picture-perfect prom was all her doing. As Jackie prattled on, Brady pulled out his mini drone and remote control. With one click, it powered up and whirled to life. He nodded at Jules. They were ready.

"Okay, let's get down to business! The moment you've all been waiting for. I got the king and queen names right here."

Jules double-checked her phone for the thumbs-up from Kayleigh. Up above, the bucket sat in place on the steel beam.

"Are you ready?"

Everyone clapped and whistled. Jules licked her lips, eagerly searching the crowd for Maddy. She wanted to see the look on

her face during the fleeting moment of happiness before it was
ripped away.

"And the winners are . . . oh my God. Maddy Washington
and Kenny Scott!"

The place erupted, the crowd roaring. Music blasted out of
speakers, and sparklers popped a silver blizzard in the air.

A spotlight sliced through the room, landing on Maddy and
Kenny, their white teeth gleaming. Jules gripped the curtain, a
thrill pulsing through her as she nodded at Brady.

He let the drone fly. It buzzed up to the ceiling, then hovered
directly behind the bucket, like a hummingbird to a petunia.

"Maddy Washington and Kenny Scott!"

Maddy heard her name and froze, the cheers stunning her to
silence. Above them, the moon spun faster. Her breath hitched.

"Yooo! We won!" Kenny screamed, holding her face between
both of his hands.

"What?" she coughed, cold air wheezing in.

He searched her face, and then, without hesitation, crashed
his lips on hers. Body jolted by the sensation, her pulse spiked.
The passionate kiss she'd seen in so many movies was finally
happening to her. Instincts took over. She closed her eyes and
leaned in, deepening their kiss. A moan escaped him, and he
gripped her tighter, hands fisting into her hair. Currents bounced
off him like waves of heat.

He loved her. He loved her. He loved her . . .

The room shook with applause. Cheers growing louder, deafening.

Kenny pulled away, letting their foreheads touch. He laughed, and it was the happiest sound she'd ever heard. Tears sprang into the corners of her eyes.

Silver confetti rained down around them, the sudden spotlight stinging her retinas. She winced away. The colors were too bright, the sounds too loud. Should she feel everything so intensely?

Kenny stood up and turned to her.

"Wait," she mumbled. But he already had her by the hand and out of her seat. She struggled to regain her equilibrium, torn between running away and running toward.

Heart racing, Maddy kept her head down, focusing on Kenny's shiny shoes.

"Look at me. Just me."

They walked through the crowd, her name shouted from every direction, people patting her shoulders and back. She could feel their happiness pulsing through her, catching snatches of conversation as they passed.

"Congrats, Maddy!"

"Kenny and Maddy!"

"I can't believe they won!"

"Go, Maddy! You deserve it!"

She raised her eyes just as they reached the stage and stared at the gilded thrones, mouth hanging open, stunned by the opulence.

Kenny helped her up the stairs, the spotlights bouncing off her diamond brooch.

He raised his arms, victorious, and the crowd cheered louder. Her legs felt as if they might falter. He wrapped an arm around her waist, squeezing her close.

"Congrats, Maddy," Jackie said, holding the crown, sparkling in the bright light. In awe, Maddy bowed slightly. Jackie pinned it in her hair, as another person fitted a white *Prom Queen* sash over her shoulders and another person placed a bouquet of red roses in her arms, the fragrance potent and intoxicating.

Maddy tried to catch her breath and steady her nerves, finally allowing herself to look up at the crowd, into a sea of smiling faces.

They were actually happy for her, of all people.

"Places! I need to take the photo!" someone shouted.

"Smile, Maddy," someone said. "You look like a deer in headlights."

"What? Huh?" she mumbled, lead-footed, turning every way possible. Flashes blinded her, and she reeled backward.

Kenny was there again, gently taking her arm, and he looked so lovely in his crown, like a prince. No, more like a king. He led her to the thrones, pointing to a marking on the floor. As they stood side by side, their eyes never left each other's. An overwhelming need, an indescribable hunger to kiss him again boiled up. So she stood up on her tiptoes, grabbed his satin lapels and pulled him down to her lips. Cheers erupted and a joyous thunder shook the room.

Kenny laughed into their kiss, his face beaming, and in that moment, she wanted to be alone, staring at the stars, just the two of them.

Kenny waved at the crowd. She watched and mimicked his movements, waving like a real princess, like Grace Kelly in *The Swan*, her heart swelling, a smile settling into place.

But then her ears perked, the tips burning. Something buzzed nearby. She felt it more than heard it. The furious fluttering of wings as the flock crept closer. A splinter of panic ripped through her.

The birds!

Kenny continued to wave, grinning at her, love in his eyes. *Does he not hear it?* It eclipsed the roaring applause in Maddy's ears, the room going all but mute. She glanced over both shoulders, searching.

What is that?

Her pulse slowed, lungs hardening. A thread, thick as a rope, tugged at her wrist, trying to pull her off stage, pull her away.

If only she'd listened to that gnawing at her spine, she would have known to look up.

Before a tidal wave came crashing down.

TWENTY-ONE

May 31, 2014

JULES'S EYES SPARKLED as she watched the carnage unfold. Her grin nearly split her face in two as a collective gasp took over the room. She slapped a hand over her mouth to hold back a giggling yelp.

Brady's drone landed by her heels. He snatched it up, along with the bag.

"Come on," he whispered. "Baby, come on."

He grabbed her arm, pulling her toward the door. She couldn't take her eyes off the back of Maddy's hair.

Outside, Brady eased the door closed and headed for the car.

"No," she gasped with a dizzy smile, yanking her arm away. "Wait! I wanna see."

"I thought you said—"

"She must look fucking ridiculous," she giggled. "Did you see everyone's faces? Fucking priceless!"

"Shhh. Babe, we gotta go before someone comes back here looking."

"Hold on! Just listen. We can probably hear them from here."

Jules stood still, holding her breath, the night air filled with shrieking cicadas, until they suddenly stopped their song. She stepped closer to the door, tipping her head, then frowned.

"I don't hear anything. No one's laughing." She spun to Brady. "Why aren't they laughing?"

"I don't know, but we need to get out of here. Now come on!" He grabbed her hand and took off running.

Wendy stopped at the entrance of the Barn's packed parking lot, cursing under her breath. She would have to drive around both lots to park behind the building. Her shoes would be covered with mud. Not exactly how she wanted to make an entrance. She had already put more makeup on than necessary for her little surprise inspection.

Not because of Maddy, she told herself. She just felt like dolling up.

She rolled down her window to examine the mud. To her right, protestors' chants mixed with music pumping out of the country club across the tracks. But the Barn was silent. Where was the DJ? They'd paid him enough.

Suddenly, Jules and Brady flew through her headlights like passing deer, her dress shimmering.

"Jules?" she muttered, and hopped out of the car. "Jules!"

Jules spun around in shock, a ghostly apparition. But then

she recognized Wendy, and her face morphed into a devilish smirk.

"Now Maddy's the white girl she always wanted to be!" she shouted.

"What? What are you talking about?"

Brady tugged at her arm. Jules strutted backward, grinning. Then they jumped in the car and sped off.

Wendy turned to the Barn with sickening dread.

Oh God, what did she do?

She hopped back into the car and threw it in reverse, driving through the grass to the side of the Barn. Headlights connected with a large rock hidden by tall weeds. Wendy screamed as she swerved, rolling into the thick mud. The back wheel sank into a deep hole and sputtered.

The car was stuck.

From the Buzzfeed article "What I Remember" by Nicole Rhinebeck

The paint came down like a giant splash, splattering everywhere. We all jumped back from the stage, trying to get out of the line of fire. But poor Maddy was just covered in it.

She stood there, her arms held out away from herself, trying to wipe the paint out of her eyes. She looked like one of those mute mimes.

Kayleigh started laughing. You knew it was her. She had

a very distinct laugh. But no one else was laughing. It was too f*cked up.

Kenny started yelling at everybody. I told my boyfriend to go up there and help her, but his suit was rented. He couldn't get it dirty, or he'd lose his deposit. Same went for everybody else.

The white kids started to leave, some of them at least. I tried to take pictures, but my phone wouldn't turn on. That's when we noticed none of our phones were working. I should have known right then and there, something was up.

May 31, 2014

Charlotte gaped at the stage in sheer horror. The royal chairs were covered in paint, and for an insane moment, she thought about Wendy freaking out over the security deposit. The music hissed to an abrupt stop, like a plug had been yanked. Above them, a light flickered, popped, and kids dodged the raining glass. Then . . . silence, everyone just staring at Maddy. Until behind them, Kayleigh's cackling echoed and bounced off the walls. Charlotte had almost forgotten she was there. A door slammed shut, the hall quieted once more.

"My phone ain't working," a girl mumbled behind her. A hush of confused mumbling peppered the air. How could anyone worry about their phone at a time like this?

"Yo, what the fuck!" Kenny barked and the crowed cringed.

The whites of Maddy's wide eyes blended with the paint. Who would do something so heinous? It wasn't even funny. Just sickeningly sadistic.

Charlotte felt the slight tug of her hand and turned.

Chris. "Come on," he whispered, not taking his eyes off the stage. "Let's go."

"What?"

"We have to get out of here."

"What?" she gasped, trying to yank herself free. "We can't just leave."

Chris, conscious of those surrounding them, leaned in close. "There's nothing we can do. We gotta go before they start blaming us for this shit."

His rationale sank in quick. *They* meaning the Black kids. The dangerous, explosive ones. Of course, they would blame any white person within twenty feet for ruining their prom. The thought of all those protests on TV made her stomach drop.

They were outnumbered five to one. They had to leave.

Voice gone, she nodded, allowing Chris to lead her out the hall, avoiding death stares before fleeing into the night.

"Hey, hey! Ho, ho! Racist students have got to go!"

Mrs. Morgan stuffed her hands in her jeans pockets, watching Officer Ross sneer at her students. She couldn't decide whether the other officers were dangerous or not. Most of them were roughly her age, with at a least a decade on the force. But there was an edgy uncertainty in their eyes, like any loud noise would frighten them.

All except Ross. He looked like the kind waiting for action.

Regardless, she stood proudly by her students' side. It wasn't time to voice her trepidation. They weren't scared, and neither would she be. *Don't talk about it, be about it*, she thought. She intended to stay until the very end.

"Racist club! Racist club!"

Ross chuckled, shaking his head. "Dumb little assholes," he grumbled to Officer Channing.

She crossed her arms in front of Officers Sawyer and Ross. "Don't you think this is a bit too much?" she asked, nodding at their makeshift barricade. She'd seen smaller ones in front of the White House.

Ross smirked, jutting his chin at the group. "How about you call off your dogs, then we wouldn't have to be here, babysitting your little gang of Malcolms and Martins."

Deputy West blanched, looking to Officer Marder for backup. But they were the youngest on the force and weren't used to real conflict. Especially in their own town.

"Hey!" Mrs. Morgan shouted. "These are children! Not animals! They have every right to be here."

Before Ross could respond, a heckling voice cut through the air. The crowd whipped around.

Kayleigh came running out of the darkness, face red from

laughing so hard. She leaped over the train tracks, heels in hand, but abruptly stopped once she caught sight of the protestors, straightening with mock civility.

"Excuuuuse me," she sang, passing through the protestors with a grin, waving at a cameraman.

"Hey, what's so funny?" someone asked.

"Maddy Washington, that's what," she giggled over her shoulder. Kayleigh gave the officers a salute and then ran through the gates into the country club, squealing with delight.

The students stirred with uncertainty.

"What's so funny about Maddy?" Kali snapped.

Another set of footsteps. Charlotte and Chris running hand in hand in their direction, a look of panic stretched across their faces.

They crossed the train tracks, passing through the crowd, their eyes low. Charlotte spotted Mrs. Morgan. She opened her mouth but shut it as Chris dragged her through the gates.

Mrs. Morgan's heart lurched as she slowly turned toward the Barn.

"Oh no."

TWENTY-TWO

May 31, 2014

THE ROOM WAS dead silent.

Maddy glanced up at the yellow plastic bucket dangling above her head, the stage lights twinkling off its metal handle, as paint dripped down her arms, shoulders, and back.

The white paint was thick, gooey, the smell so strong it burned her eyes. Every single bone shifted under her skin. Her muscles liquefied, turned solid, then liquefied again. She slowly glanced down at her black dress, now soaked and sticking to her skin, a bizarre work of art. By her foot, her crown lay in a white puddle.

But all she could focus on was the fact that her hair was wet.

She touched her roots with trembling fingers, feeling nothing but paint. Within moments, her hair would swell to a beastly size.

Papa is going to be so mad, she thought reflexively as flashes of flames, water hoses, and hot combs blurred her vision. Her left eye twitched, and a stage light above her head popped.

The room buzzed, a screech in her ear, her heartbeat a slow gong.

She didn't realize right away that someone was talking to her. Screaming at her.

Kendrick.

She tried to respond, but her throat closed up, tongue covered in baking powder.

Then his hand was wrapped around her wrist, yanking her behind him, off the stage and onto the dance floor. There were other voices, trying to talk to him, trying to stop him, reason with him. As her stiff legs followed, she felt something inside her chest break and crumble like a burnt cookie.

She had no idea her body was morphing to accommodate an erupting savage madness.

The night air brought her back to reality. Shouting came from the Barn behind them. But she couldn't turn around. Kendrick was walking too fast. She had to take two steps to match his one, heels sticking in the mud. The sash fell off her shoulder, drifting to the ground, and she read the sparkling gold letters one last time.

Prom Queen.

Kendrick picked her up over the tracks, a white paint pattern now silk-screened on his suit.

Voices gasped ahead of them. A crowd of silhouettes. Someone said her name again.

"Maddy?" Mrs. Morgan. "Oh God, Maddy, what happened?"

Kendrick was still pulling her, somewhere. The crowd parted like the Red Sea. He was supposed to be her Moses, leading her to the promised land. Did hope ever exist for a girl like her?

Her eye twitched. No one noticed the police cruiser's windshield splinter.

"Kenny! What happened?" Kali said, aghast. "Oh shit, Maddy . . ."

Kendrick stopped short, a numb Maddy running into his back.

"Whoa, whoa. Where do you think you're going?" another voice said. Maddy looked up. A police officer stood eye to eye with Kendrick.

"Excuse me, I need to get through," he snapped.

"Why?"

"What you mean why? Look what they did!"

Maddy eyed the ground as the world seemed to swim around her, keenly aware of what she might look like and the pity that would follow.

"Who's they?" the officer countered.

"Them white kids," he shouted, pointing ahead. Kendrick still had his fingers wrapped tight around her wrist.

Mrs. Morgan gently turned Maddy toward her, her face stricken. She pulled tissues out of her bag to wipe Maddy's eyes clean.

"Oh, Maddy," she whispered, a sob in her throat. "I'm so, so sorry."

Maddy swayed, staring back at her. "You said . . . I was powerful," she mumbled groggily.

Mrs. Morgan stood gaping like she wasn't sure what to say. Then she swallowed, gripping Maddy's shoulders. "You are. They're cowards. And what they did . . . they'll pay for."

At that moment, the voice Maddy had tuned out all night piped up. *She lied! Everyone is always lying to you.*

"Let them pass," Kali shouted. "Them assholes need to know what they did wasn't right!"

"How do you know that 'they' did anything?" The officer laughed.

"Yo, are you serious?" Kendrick spat.

"We saw them running back here! Laughing!" someone in the crowd shouted.

"It wasn't just them," Kenny said. "They were all in on it. I know them. And they need to see what they've done for themselves!"

Behind her, dozens of footsteps stomped through the gravel as a thick cloud of voices surrounded them.

"Yo, we need to get in there," Jackie barked. "They ruined our fucking prom!"

Maddy could feel her hair frizzing, a slow-moving monster. And her dress . . . it was ruined. How deftly she had worked on the fabric, repaired the zipper, pulled up the straps so her breasts wouldn't be exposed. Now, it looked as if she had been dunked into a bowl of pancake batter. Her eye twitched.

A cameraman shifted his pack off his shoulder, tapping the side. "What the hell? It went black! I don't know, I can't turn it back on."

"Let them in!" the crowd chanted. "Let. Them. In!"

"Call for backup," an officer barked. "Now!"

When Wendy finally freed her trapped wheel and parked the car in the back of the Barn, she ran through the mud and swung open the side stage door, fighting her way through the black curtains. The room sat half empty, house lights on, decorations torn down, chairs knocked over . . . But what hit her first was the stench of paint, as if the room was drenched in it. White footprints tracked across the dance floor. She whipped around and yelped, hands flying to her face. The stage was a monochromatic crime scene.

"Oh God . . ."

"You!"

Across the floor, Regina stormed toward her in a royal-navy dress. Her date held her back as she clawed the air, reaching for Wendy's neck.

"You fucking bitch!"

"I—I . . ." Wendy stuttered. "Wh-what happened?"

"Don't play stupid! You set Maddy up! You set us all up!"

"Maddy? What? No! I didn't!"

"You were in on all this shit from the beginning! Working with the rest of them, just to ruin our whole fucking prom!"

"Them? No! I had no idea—"

"Then what are you doing here, huh? What were you doing sneaking around backstage, dressed in jeans?"

Wendy's lips flapped open and closed. She couldn't think of a single answer that didn't sound crazy.

"Yeah, that's what I thought," Regina spat. "You insisted on being prom chair, got your little friends to come help, all so you can do this? Don't you people got anything better to do? Haven't you done enough to Maddy?"

Wendy stood speechless just as Rashad ran over. "Guys! Come on. Something's going down outside!"

But Regina wasn't done. She stabbed Wendy with one final stare. "I'll deal with your ass later," she snapped, and followed everyone out the door, the entire hall clearing out.

Wendy stayed rooted to the dance floor. A wretched sob threatened to explode as she took in the wreckage. All her hard work, her meticulous planning and attention to detail erased with Wite-Out. She had thought of everything . . . everything but this. There was nothing to fix; the night could not be salvaged. She had failed. She'd never failed at anything before.

On the stage, the crown twinkled in a puddle of white water. She climbed up the steps, tiptoeing around the paint, and glanced at the bucket hanging above, an orange Marshall's Hardware logo printed on the side.

Jules.

There were so many practical jokes Jules had played in their

339

lifetime, but never anything this monstrous. Had Wendy not realized just how cruel Jules could be? If she was honest with herself, she'd known all along and she'd chosen not to do anything about it. Because being Jules's friend meant protection from everything she feared not being.

Wendy sank onto the edge of a throne, its red velvet seat riddled with paint. No one would ever believe Wendy had nothing to do with the joke. Not Regina, not Kali, not even Kenny. In a way, she deserved it after years of looking the other way.

Outside, a bloodcurdling scream made her head snap up. She jumped off the stage and raced for the door.

Across the tracks, the crowd stood in front of the country club, the whole prom shouting.

"Kenny! Kenny!" someone screamed.

"Oh God," she gasped, sprinting toward them.

"No! Stop!" someone screamed, followed by a girl's guttural sobs. "Kenny!"

Wendy pumped her arms hard, trying to run faster.

Please, please, please.

Suddenly, her face spasmed and it felt as if a nail had hammered itself straight into her ear. She gripped the sides of her head, the sound so loud, her whole body shook. She fell, gravel cutting into her knees. The crowd's choked screams pierced the air.

Straining through the pressure, she glanced up, eyeballs jiggling in their sockets . . . just as the first police car floated up into the sky, dangling in midair as if from a puppet string.

TWENTY-THREE

May 31, 2014

THE BALMY AIR crackled with tension. Maddy tried to lean away, find different air to breathe. But Kendrick was holding her hand tight, blood pounding through his veins. They stood sandwiched between the entire prom shouting behind them, protesters yelling on the sides of them, and police lined in front of them, blocking access to the country club. She shivered, the paint drying sticky on her lashes. Her scalp tingled and burned like a chemical relaxer left on too long.

"Look what they did!" Kenny barked, pointing to Maddy. "They set her up! Ain't that assault or something?"

A tall, redheaded officer looked at his colleagues. Maddy read his badge: *Ross.*

"Son, you need to go on home," he said in a smug voice. "Take your girlfriend, get her cleaned up, and out of here."

"Naw, I ain't leaving. I need to talk to them!"

Ross's eyes narrowed as he stepped closer. Kendrick stood in front of Maddy, never letting go of her hand.

"Boy, I said go home!" Ross yelled, pointing in the direction they'd come from.

"Who you calling 'boy'? I ain't your boy!"

Panic filled every square inch of Maddy's body. She squeezed Kenny's hand.

"Please, Kendrick," Maddy whimpered. She didn't care what happened to her. It didn't matter; nothing would change. He knew this. But her words were drowned out in a sea of anger.

Ross's hand sat on his belt, inching toward his gun.

The crowd pushed, shoved, and shouted, the thickness of the line becoming thinner, smothering. Maddy lost her balance, fumbling into Kenny. He caught her up against himself, winning his full attention. Anger melted from his eyes, his jaw softening, and for the briefest moment, the world around them disappeared.

"Hey," he whispered with a half smile, cupping her face. She leaned into his palm, calluses scratching her cheek.

And before she could open her mouth to beg him to leave, behind them, Rose tripped on her long lavender lace dress, landing on Kendrick's shoulder blades. He tipped forward like a domino, falling into Officer Ross.

"What the fuck!" Ross barked, shoving Kendrick off him. He righted himself and, in one swift motion, reached for his baton.

As he stumbled back, Kenny's eyes widened, his body flooding with terror, leaving Maddy gasping for air.

"Wait!" Kenny stuttered, his hand held up, turning to push Maddy out of the way.

The baton hovered in the air before cracking down on Kenny's skull. Something sprayed in her face and she flinched.

"NO!" Kali screamed, and the crowd fell silent. "KENNY!"

Blood dripped down the middle of Kenny's face, swerving around his nose. He swayed, his eyes rolling back, as Ross's arm arced to strike him again. And again.

Rooted to the ground, Maddy jerked with every blow, the blood misting on her, her muscles steeped in ice. Kenny never let go of her hand, not even when he fell and Ross stood over him, the cords in his neck straining as he delivered another blow. And when Kenny finally let go, he gripped her bare ankle before going limp.

"Stop," Maddy quaked with a bleated cry, her hand raised, but fear ate her powers. The air smelled of pennies. She could taste it on her tongue.

An officer jumped in, yoking Ross away. "Hey, man! What are you doing? Are you crazy? Do you know who that is?"

Ross stood, sweat on his brow, pointing his bloody baton at the crowd. "You saw him! He assaulted an officer!"

The crowd backed up, afraid of being Ross's next victim. It took three people to hold Kali back, her tortured cries blaring into the night.

"Kenny! Kenny!"

Kenny lay unconscious at Maddy's feet, his face almost

unrecognizable. His blood felt heavy on her skin. It dripped down into her armpits, mixing pink with the white paint. She could feel every ounce weighing down her muscles, seeping into the fabric of her dress. Her heart shuddered.

No . . .

She fell to Kenny's side and held his hand, aching for the safety of his warmth.

"Kenny?" she whispered. He didn't move. Trembling, she hovered over him, unsure of what to do. Her threads unspooled and tangled around them. She cupped his cheek, his skin wet with blood. Eyes full of tears, she pressed two rattling fingers to the inside of his wrist.

She could not find a pulse.

A nerve twitched behind Maddy's eyes, sharp and stinging. Her scalp prickled. Raw power pooled in her palms, heavy like an iron. She stopped hearing at that point. Something else took over, and the world went quiet.

"Call 911," Mrs. Morgan shouted, trying to break through the crowd. "Someone call 911!"

Two students held her back. "Don't! Or they'll shoot us!"

The officers looked at one another, flummoxed and speechless.

"For Christ's sake, do something!" Mrs. Morgan cried, measuring their collective confusion.

"You saw him. He attacked an officer," Ross spat back.

"He didn't hit you. He just tripped," someone sobbed. "You didn't have to beat him like that!"

"We all saw you! We saw you!"

"He . . . he was resisting," Ross insisted, then turned to his team. "We need a medic."

A panicked Deputy Chip West scowled at Ross then raced over to his cruiser. He attempted to radio for help but received nothing but static.

"Hang on, I got a first aid kit," another officer said, rushing to his vehicle.

"Hey, is your walkie working? I can't reach base."

A few feet away, Debbie Locke's hearing aid squealed. She yanked it out with a whimper, then slowly realized she could still hear the piercing noise without it.

She searched for the source, only to see the faces of her classmates, just as confused. The noise rang, like an elongated sound of TV zapping off.

"Do you hear that?" someone mumbled.

"Yeah, what is that?"

The sound sharpened, pressing down. Every student jerked with a yelp. They covered their ears, falling to their knees, screaming in agony. Mrs. Morgan glanced around, baffled.

The police officers stood, hands readied on their weapons, uneasy and on high alert.

"What are they doing?"

The kids lay on the ground, writhing and wriggling on their backs and bellies, a screaming heap of worms.

"What the hell are they doing?"

"I don't know," Sawyer muttered, confused.

"Is this some kind of joke?"

The noise pressed down harder. Rashad vomited. Debbie fainted. Kali tried desperately to push through, crawling toward her unconscious brother.

Officer Heath Marder, the youngest on the force, leaned to the side, palming his ear. "Ahhh. What's that noise?"

Deputy West glanced at Sawyer, dumbfounded. "You hear anything?"

Sawyer shook his head. "No."

Ross huffed, rolling his eyes. "Are you shitting me? They're making all this up! We didn't lay a hand on these assholes."

But something was killing them. Or someone.

Maddy shakily rose to her feet, her vision blurring. A kaleidoscope of images blinded her—firehoses, spitting, beatings, marches, swinging bodies, *Whites Only* signs, blood on the concrete . . .

"What the . . ." Officer Channing gasped. "Holy shit!"

Mrs. Morgan shrieked, pointing up.

Behind them, the police cruisers lifted off the ground, slowly hovering, floating higher and higher in the air.

Deputy West spun around to see if anyone was seeing this. But the crowd remained bellowing on the ground—all except Maddy.

She stood beside Kenny, fingers splayed, his blood dripping from her palms. Maddy raised her hands higher, and the cars rose higher. In the Barn parking lot, more cars rose, the sky a traffic jam.

The officers' faces tilted upward, watching the cars levitate above them, too stunned to reach for their weapons.

Time stood still. And in one quick movement, Maddy swung her hands down and the cars dropped, crushing all those below. Blood sprayed like exploding soda cans. A car burst upon impact, pieces flying in all directions, knocking Mrs. Morgan and a few others over. Kids screamed and scrambled. Maddy turned her gaze to the country club gates, the music inside thumping through her veins. She glanced down at Kenny one last time.

Heat and flames ballooned as kids attempted to crawl to safety. Officer Sawyer stumbled to his feet, tripping over Officer Ross's severed head. The crowd was so shocked by what they were witnessing, so distracted by their will to live, that by the time anyone looked up, Maddy had opened the gates and walked inside.

As the nightstick cracked down upon his son's skull, Kendrick Scott Senior was preparing for bed. He had a consistent nighttime routine—shower, teeth, pajamas, iron work clothes, then thirty minutes of reading before lights out. Routines gave him a sense of control. Purpose. Belonging. He had just plugged his work phone into the charger when it buzzed on the counter. He held back his annoyance with a deep, steady breath. Even when he was by himself, he never wanted to seem ungrateful for his position of authority. Without his well-earned salary, his family wouldn't be able to afford the life they'd become accustomed to.

"Yes," he answered, clipped and no nonsense. Whatever his crew was bothering him about past ten o'clock, it had better be good.

"Ken, you gotta get down here. Now!" Alvin Lewis shouted, seeming out of breath. "The meters . . . they're all going crazy!"

"Slow down," Mr. Scott snapped, but kept his voice measured. He wasn't interested in entertaining exaggerations. "Tell me exactly what's going on."

"There . . . couldn't get . . . you have to help!"

"What are you talking about?"

Snowy static filled the line. "It . . . meter . . . no . . . twelve thousand!"

"Hello? Alvin. Alvin?"

"Holy shit!"

"Alvin?"

The line went dead.

Mr. Scott was known for his pragmatism and ability to perform under pressure without breaking a sweat. He'd attempted to instill these qualities in his children to better prepare them for the world. It's important to stop, think, assess the situation, and proceed accordingly.

He stared at the phone for a moment, collecting his

thoughts. Twelve thousand? Alvin couldn't have been talking about a meter reading. That would have been a two hundred percent increase. He tried to dial Alvin again. No service.

"Ken? Ken! Where are you?" Feet padded down the stairs.

"Meryl?" he shouted back. Her voice seemed alarmed. "What's wrong? What happened?"

Mrs. Scott rushed into the kitchen in her house robe. "Ken, I think I just heard something. An explosion somewhere."

Mr. Scott scowled at his wife. "What are you talking about?"

Mrs. Scott opened her mouth to explain as they were dipped into darkness.

"What the devil?" he muttered, clicking the light switch.

Mr. Scott grabbed a flashlight out of the bottom cabinet, and pointed it toward his wife. She gripped her robe, her eyes holding a strange panic.

"Ken? Ken, what's happening?"

He tried another light switch, turning to face her. They held each other's gaze. Mr. Scott tried to process the last few minutes—the static call, the explosion, the blackout.

"Ken?"

He nodded with resolve. "I need to go to the plant."

Mrs. Scott gasped, face crumbling.

He left her in the kitchen, running up to their bedroom to change. As he made his way back down, he passed his daughter's empty room with a jolt.

"Where's Kali?" he asked, entering the kitchen.

Mrs. Scott's frown deepened. "She was with her friends. She should've been home by now."

"Call her and Kenny. Tell them to come straight home."

Mrs. Scott nodded, rushing over to the kitchen landline. She clicked twice.

"The phone's dead."

"That's impossible." How could both the landline and cell service be down?

In the distance, the plant alarm went off, the sound disorienting in the late evening. It wasn't a drill. It was the real thing. Mrs. Scott blanched, holding a hand on her cheek. They stared at one another for a long moment—a silent understanding passing between them. Mr. Scott took a deep breath to steady himself. Then he stormed down the hall, snatched his jacket and keys, and ran out the door.

He had to get to the plant before it was too late.

Wendy pushed against the stampede of bewildered kids, her vision skewed, stomach threatening to purge itself on the gravel. A girl hunched over, projectile vomiting in front of Wendy, keeling over. Some kids couldn't manage to stand up from where they had withered.

"Kenny?" Wendy called, weak and drained. "Kenny!"

A uniformed man pinned under a car let out a wet scream, blood sputtering from his mouth in a hoarse cough, his body nearly severed in half. He reached for her as another officer tried helplessly to lift the car off him, his face covered in sweat and soot. Leaking gas pooled around the broken cars, the smell nauseating. Smoke puffed from their engines. She tried to run, but the ground tilted, and she leaned sideways, ramming right into one of the burning police cars. She tripped over another kid, falling headfirst. And there was Kenny, lying on the ground, forgotten in the chaos.

"Kenny!" she screamed, diving for him, his face a bloody mess. "No, no, no. Please, Kenny. Wake up?"

He didn't move. She whipped around, searching for the police, but they were all trapped under their own vehicles, crushed like lightning bugs. She screamed for help, hot tears streaming down her face, her head throbbing at the sound of her own voice. Frazzled and panicked, she almost gave up hope.

Hectic footsteps stopped behind her. Kali's skin looked green, her eyes drooping. She swayed and flung herself over her brother.

"Kenny," she moaned, shoving his chest. "Kenny, wake up!" She moved closer, ear to his mouth, and felt for a pulse. Wendy held her breath, her heart sinking.

"He's still breathing," Kali whimpered. "Come on, help me."

A symphony of screams echoed out of the country club. Wendy stared at the open gates.

"Oh God," she gasped. Maddy was in there, with her friends, the people she'd known all her life. She had to help them.

But Kali shook her shoulder.

"Wendy! We have to get him to the hospital! You have to help me."

Wendy looked into Kali's teary eyes, down at Kenny, then back at the country club.

"But I . . . I . . ."

"Please!" Kali begged, rising to her feet, one of Kenny's arms in her hands. "I can't carry him alone."

Wendy didn't know what to do. She couldn't think, with all the sounds and smells bombarding her senses.

"Wendy, he could die! Please."

Kenny? Dead? Oh no . . .

She took one last look at the country club. She couldn't save them. Even if she walked in there, how could she stop it all from happening? Tears in her eyes, she nodded and pushed herself up.

"Okay. Okay."

They scooped him up, one under each arm, and struggled to carry him back to the Barn.

TWENTY-FOUR

MADDY DID IT
EPISODE 10, CONT.

Michael: I'm so happy you were willing to talk to us, Cole. Thank you for stopping by.

Cole Lecter: My mama heard about what you all were doing. I listened to an episode or two.

Michael [narration]: This is Cole Lecter. You heard testimony from his mother, Amy Lecter, at the beginning of this series. She mentioned Cole came home with the blood of other children on his clothes.

Cole: So y'all really think she was a witch?

Michael: We're not all the way sure. How does that make you feel?

Cole: Well, you know that movie *Unbreakable*? The one where Bruce Willis is the only person that survives some big train accident that killed everybody? That's how I feel. Or that's what my friends call me now. What's left of them. I guess if

353

she's a witch, then I must be some sorta superhero too.

Michael: I'm so sorry. It must have been really hard for you.

Cole: *sigh* Eleven minutes. That's how long it took. I didn't
know that at the time. It felt like hours. But I read that
somewhere. She was inside the country club for only
eleven minutes.

Michael: Can you recall what happened that night? We'd love for
you to tell us whatever you remember.

Cole: I don't remember everything. Some things are real fuzzy
on account of my drinking. We had pregamed at Jason's
house, and I had a bottle of Jack all to myself. Felt like I
had to take a piss every fifteen minutes. Bethany, my, uh,
girlfriend, was super freaking mad at me all night. She, uh,
didn't make it.

Michael: Hey, man. Do you need a break?

Cole: No. No. I'm fine. I need to do this. Uh, right, so, I
remember I was headed to the bathroom when out of
nowhere, the doors just came flying, opening toward me.
Both of them at the same time. The same way we used to
rush the doors before we ran out on the field. One door
sorta scooped me up and slammed me right into the wall
behind it. I blacked out for a minute, maybe longer. When
I opened my eyes, I tried to push the door, but it wouldn't
budge, and the bar was digging into my stomach.

Michael: So you were stuck behind the door?

Cole: Yeah. At first, I thought it was a joke, you know. 'Cause, it

354

felt like it was glued to the wall or something. The guys, we were always pranking each other. But when I was looking through the little square window, I could see that everyone had stopped dancing and was staring into the hallway. I tried to see what everybody was looking at.

Michael: What happened next?

Cole: I saw Charlotte. I thought she said she was going to the Black prom. I mean, the everybody prom. She said she was. But she was there with Chris, whispering in folks' ears. Kayleigh was with them. She turned around and started laughing. Everybody was laughing then. I was wondering what was so funny. Then Maddy walked into view, covered head to toe in that paint. Her back was to me, but she was just standing there, watching them all laugh. I remember suddenly feeling real, real sick. Like I was about to throw up. That's when a chair flew across the room and smashed into Kayleigh's face. The leg . . . it went right into her eye. The room went quiet. And then Maddy raised her arms, like she was asking for a hug, turned her palms upward, balled her hands into fists, and snatched the air back real quick. The floorboards yanked under everyone's feet, sending folks tumbling, like she snatched the rug up. And then . . . and then . . . Christ, she looked so small, like she was one of those guys directing an orchestra. A conductor, right? That's what she was doing, waving her hands around, making stuff move. Everybody

was screaming, trying to run out the back, but the doors
were locked. Folks tried running past her kept getting
knocked out. Chris tried taking a chair to her head; she
looked at him and he froze like a statue, blood coming out
his eyes and ears and mouth. Behind him, I saw Bethany
running with Charlotte. I was calling her, telling her to
hide, but she tripped on her dress and went sliding into
the DJ table. Them wires got all tangled around her and
Charlotte's throats, started choking them, stringing them
up like a noose. Jules and her boyfriend, Brady, something
fell from the ceiling, came down on them, split his head
in half. The chandelier shattered and all that glass . . .
it just hovered in the air for a few seconds. Then, them
shards came raining down, slicing necks . . . I could see
everything, hear everything. Jason . . . he was screaming
at her, "You stupid bitch. You stupid nigger bitch!" He
stopped, and it sounded like a pile of twigs snapping
before he fell to the floor. That was the last sound I heard
before it all went quiet.

Michael: My God.

Cole: When she was just about to walk out, she stopped and
looked dead at me. Her eyes were so black. I started
begging and crying. Christ, I was so scared. But . . . she
just walked by. The doors slammed behind her. I couldn't
move for a long while until I heard this voice in my head
telling me to go home.

Michael: Was it Maddy?

Cole: I don't know, maybe. I don't recall ever hearing her voice
   before. She didn't really do much talking at school.

Michael: How did you get out?

Cole: Last thing I remember was slipping and falling in a puddle
   of water . . . or I thought it was water. It wasn't. It was
   blood. They found several types of blood on me. I must
   have walked out back, into the trees, and just kept walking.
   Didn't remember hearing an explosion, ambulances,
   alarms, or nothing. The next thing I knew, I was in the
   hospital. When I told my folks what I saw, they told me to
   keep quiet. Said that door knocked me into that wall real
   good and I was seeing things. Had a knot on the back of
   my head to prove it. But I know what I saw. That's why I
   think you're right. I think she's still alive.

Michael: Why do you think that?

Cole: 'Cause I can still hear her. In my head. All the time.

May 31, 2014

"—Oh God! Here she comes—"

Maddy walked out of the country club, the building on fire
behind her. No one noticed. Not right away. They were still
dealing with the shock of flying cars, bleeding ears, and dead
bodies. She ambled in a trance, her steps stiff, eyelids frozen
open, vaguely aware of the screaming around her. The busted
police cruiser radios, full of static, roared as she neared. A girl

screamed at the sight of her, others ran in every direction. Some tried to scramble back to their own vehicles that wouldn't start.

"—*Shoot her! Someone shoot her!*—"

She could hear everyone's mean thoughts about her, echoing through her skull.

The red-and-white arm of the train-crossing bar came down, a bell dinging, caution lights flashing. In the distance, a train whistle blew.

Maddy stumbled toward the tracks, her feet heavy as a voice screamed her name.

Mrs. Morgan.

"Maddy! Wait! Maddy!"

Maddy stepped around the gate arm, headed for the road toward town. The ground rumbled as the train made its way around the bend. She stepped over a metal rail, her shoes catching on the wooden track.

"Maddy! MADDY!"

"—*Fuck her*—"

Maddy swayed, the voices making her head hurt.

"—*Someone throw her into the train*—"

The train headlights beamed off her skin, the white paint glowing, streaks of blood running down her face and hands.

"Maddy!" Mrs. Morgan screamed while others watched, waiting with bated breath.

"—*Kill her. Please let it kill her! Please*—"

"No," Maddy mumbled sleepily, turning toward the headlights. And she did nothing but flick her wrist before the train jerked, hitting an invisible wall. Train cars smashed into one another like crushed soda cans, shrieking, bending metal mixing with screams. The train cars rolled into the Barn parking lot, mowing over scrambling students. The last car derailed, flying into the air and crashing onto its side, skating fifty feet into the trees, ripping power lines that sparked like fireworks before exploding into a firebomb of heat and smoke, blinding everyone left alive. Within seconds, the lights went out in all of Springville. Mrs. Morgan stumbled to her feet through the growing black plume, coughing, lungs full of soot as a piece of flying metal whipped through the air like a frisbee, slicing off the top of her head. She stopped, fell to her knees, and flopped over, her brain leaking onto the gravel.

Maddy didn't notice any of it. She was already walking home, the raging fire lighting her way through the dark.

As soon as Mr. Washington heard the alarm in the distance and the power went out seconds later, he knew his daughter had something to do with it. The moment had been inevitable since the day she was born.

Over the years, he'd considered all the ways he would kill her. So many times he had left her in the crib to starve, or in a fast-filling bathtub. But his weakness was an affliction. His mother had reminded him of that often. "Nothing but a weak, useless boy in a man's skin."

He'd thought he could control his child's destiny. That feeding her God's word and wholesome values would cast the devil out of her. But he knew then, as the alarm blared, that she was beyond salvation. She was no longer his daughter.

Resolve hardened in his stomach, a heavy aching knot. He knelt at his altar, praying for strength. The Lord would not give him more than he could bear. If the Lord could sacrifice his only son . . . he could sacrifice his only daughter.

Thomas rose to his feet, the alarm blaring in the distance. He procured his father's revolver from a tin lunch box in his office, loaded four bullets, sat in his chair, and waited for his Madison to come home.

TWENTY-FIVE

MADDY DID IT
EPISODE 10, CONT.

Michael [narration]: Rebecca Longhorn, or Becky, was at Sal's
Pizzeria during Prom Night.

Becky Longhorn: Some juniors stayed out past curfew to catch
the seniors on their way to the after-parties. Kinda like a
sneak peek of what life would be like for us the following
year. It was the one night a year that Sal's stayed open
past closing time. My sister, Kat, was at the All-Together
prom. We were really close. We had made plans to meet at
Sal's, so my mom dropped me off. Then, probably around
nine p.m., Kat sent me a picture of Maddy.

Michael [narration]: Kat's photo is known for being one of the
last and only photos taken of Maddy Washington at prom.

Michael: Tanya, can you describe what's in the photo for us?

Tanya: So in the photo, you have, I think, Kenny Scott, who was
her date, on stage in a crown. Then you have Maddy. It
looks like the bucket was just dumped. She's completely

covered in white paint, head to toe—hair, face, arms,
shoulders. The spotlight is in her eyes.

Becky: Everyone at Sal's saw the picture. People were laughing.
Some even left to go up to prom to see for themselves.

Tanya: Were you laughing?

Becky: No. I think I was shocked someone would do something
so . . . messed up. Kat had texted me earlier that night,
saying that she thought it was weird that Charlotte and
Chris were at the All-Together prom. Later, when everyone
put the story together, it made sense that they were in on it.

Tanya: What happened next?

Becky: I don't know, maybe twenty minutes later we heard the
explosion, and then the power went out. The whole town
went dark. Everyone started to panic and filed out onto the
street. Some kids headed over to the country club to see
what was going on, while the rest of us waited. I kept trying
to call Kat, but it was like my phone just stopped working.
That's when the siren from the plant went off. I'd never ever
heard it at night before. I started freaking out, but I also felt
really . . . sick. Just nauseous and dizzy—my head was
killing me.

The cars parked on Main Street started going berserk,
alarms and lights blinking, windshield wipers clicking all on
their own . . . That's when I saw Maddy. She was walking
in the middle of the road, looking just like the picture Kat
sent me. And she was kinda . . . glowing. Don't know how

else to describe it. She looked like a faded glow-in-the-dark sticker. Her eyes were real wide, not even blinking. She stopped in front of her dad's store and just stared at it. Some power cords came down, and poof! The building caught on fire. Then the next building. No one moved, all so stunned, I guess. When she was closer, I could see she wasn't just covered in paint but also in blood. It was all mixed together. And her hair, it was . . . huge.

Sal ran out in the street with a bat trying to, I guess, stop her. But Maddy . . . all she did was flick her wrist and he flew into the air, landing on a truck windshield. Everyone started screaming and running. Some people got in their cars, but it was like they had no control of them, and they were running over the other kids before slamming into storefronts or straight into brick walls. The fire hydrants all came loose and were spraying people. I tried to run, but something blew and I hit my head on a mailbox. When I came to, the smoke was so thick I couldn't see what was in front of me. All of Main Street was on fire, bodies everywhere. The only reason I'm alive is because Officer Sawyer was driving by, looking white as a ghost. He stopped long enough for me to crawl into the passenger seat then booked it straight outta town, babbling about everyone being dead. I was having trouble staying awake and was so out of it that I didn't even realize someone was in the back seat. Honestly, I thought I imagined it all,

or it was just some crazy nightmare until I woke up in the
hospital.

Michael: And your sister?

Becky: She died. In the accident. They say Maddy didn't kill
her, like she killed everyone else. Just wrong place at the
wrong time. But it's hard . . . really hard to keep that in
mind. She was my best friend.

FROM THE SWORN TESTIMONY OF
OFFICER ERIC SAWYER

You believe Jesus walked on water, but you
can't believe Maddy Washington made cars fly
with her hands? You bunch of hypocrites! I
was there, okay? I know what I saw!

When Maddy walked out of the country club,
I ran in there quick as I could and . . .
Jesus, it was a bloodbath. It was as if she
had taken a shoe to some blood-filled mos-
quitoes. Limbs cast aside like doll parts,
the floor . . . just a carpet of hair, guts,
and satin. I couldn't tell who from who or
what from what. The ceiling started caving
in, and I tried to do a quick search for any
survivors. Only found one, right before the
train ran off the tracks and the whole city
went dark.

I didn't even see the Lecter boy walk out.

    The fact that he survived . . . well, God
    bless him.

May 31, 2014

Inside the Barn, the few remaining students who survived the chaos huddled in the dark, tending to each other's wounds. Outside, the world seemed quiet—no more screaming. Which meant anyone who wasn't with them was more than likely dead. The fires spread around them, crawling closer to the Barn. They needed to move, but where could they go?

On the stage, Wendy filled the crystal punch bowl with warm water, using a torn tablecloth to gently clean Kenny's face. Kali propped a red pillow, the one meant to hold a crown, under his neck, applying pressure to the gash on his forehead. She sobbed, trying for the tenth time to dial 911, then home, in that order.

"Shit," she muttered, throwing the phone aside.

Breath rushed out Kenny's nose as he startled awake with a cough, arm flinging.

"Kenny! Kenny," Kali sobbed, trying to keep him still. "You're okay."

"Kenny," Wendy said, wiping his face, her own tears surfacing. "Thank God you're alright."

"Wh-where are we?" he moaned, then stiffened. "Where's Maddy?"

Wendy's stomach hardened. "Maddy?"

"Yeah. Did something happen to her?" he asked, trying to sit up, taking in the room with the one eye that wasn't swollen shut.

"No," she spat. "She happened to us!"

He didn't seem to process the sobs and flames surrounding them. All he cared about was Maddy.

"No, no . . . you gotta help her," he quavered.

"What?"

"We did this," he insisted. "We did this to her. This is all on us. I promised her everything would be alright."

Outraged, Wendy scoffed. "Kenny . . . all our friends are dead! All of this is because of her!"

"Naw. All of this is because of what happened to her."

She shook her head. "I don't know where she is," she snapped.

"You can find her."

Wendy ignored him, wringing her makeshift towel dry.

Kali reached over and grabbed her wrist. "Can you for once in your life do something for someone else that isn't motivated by your own gain? That isn't completely self-serving?"

Wendy balked just as the room stirred. Rashad ran back into the hall, standing in the middle of the dance floor, cradling a broken arm. "Maddy ain't outside," he announced. "She's gone to town. The coast is clear, and cars are working now. They're telling everyone to drive to Greenville, where it's safe."

"But . . . my mom and dad," someone cried.

"They called for backup. State troopers. They'll be here soon. They'll get her. But we gotta move. This place about to burn up."

Kenny grabbed Wendy's hand, pulling her closer. "Please, Wendy," Kenny begged. "Please, help her before it's too late. I'll do whatever you want. Just help her."

Wendy's heart sank as she stared into his mangled face. He'd risk anything for Maddy. Meaning he'd never love Wendy the way he loved Maddy. Tears stabbed her eyes. "I can't," she blubbered. "She hates us. I can't . . ."

He gripped her hand, his voice hoarse but insistent. "You're. Not. Jules."

Wendy stilled, glancing at the white paint splatters on the stage, and finally realized what Kenny had been saying all along—he didn't mean she would never live up to Jules's beauty and intoxicating allure. He meant that she was nothing like Jules.

She was better than Jules.

Wendy met Kali's eyes. "But . . . I don't know where she is or how to find her."

Kali shrugged. "Where would you want to go if you were her?"

The muscles around her neck tightened as the answer popped in her head. Even if Maddy killed her, what did she have left to lose? She'd lost everything that mattered already.

Wendy didn't say another word. She got up, walked to her car, and drove away from the Barn in search of the girl who had stolen her future.

TWENTY-SIX

FROM THE SWORN TESTIMONY OF JUDE FRIEDLANDER

I didn't hear the alarm right away. Don't
even think it was the alarm that woke me
up. It was . . . something else. Like . . .
intuition.

Anyway, I heard the alarm and tried to turn
on my bedside light and everything else in
the house. No dice. Tried calling my neighbor Candace to see if she had power, but
the phones were out. I left my cell in my
truck since I don't really need it once I'm
inside. As soon as I opened the front door,
the first thing I smelled was smoke. Knew
something was wrong right away. I thought,
if that plant's about to blow, then it was
about time I get the hell on out of Dodge. I

jumped into my truck and that's when I saw her. Maddy. Could barely recognize her under all that paint and hair, but I knew her well enough. Bought a few things from her daddy's store.

She was walking kind of funny, feet dragging, her heels scraping against the road. I'll always remember the sound they made. So dang loud.

Looking around, I realized I wasn't the only one out there seeing what I was seeing. The whole neighborhood was standing in their jammies and robes, just watching. No one said a word. None of us even asked her if she was alright. Think we were all so stunned. At one point, she just stopped dead in the road. And I swear to you, everyone gasped at the same time. She stood there for a couple of seconds, then turned around, looked at each one of us, saying nothing.

Then, she raised her hand, snapped her fingers, and there was some type of sizzling from the power line before every single tree on our block burst into flames. It happened so fast. Folks started screaming and scrambling. Branches were falling on houses and cars. I was already in my truck, so I hightailed it out of there. Got downtown and saw the whole place was up in smoke. Nothing left to do but head for the highway. I was about ten miles out when I finally saw the cavalry from Greenville on its way. A state trooper stopped me, asked if I was coming from Springville. I couldn't even get a word out. I was shaking like a leaf so bad.

My house is gone. Most of my neighbors are gone too, all burned up. They say I was one of the lucky ones. I say, ha! Tell that to my nightmares.

Transcript of the Local FOX 5 Breaking News
June 1, 2014

There have been reports of riots in the town of Springville tonight. Witnesses say a group of protestors threw bottles at police officers, which led to a series of fires in the area.

Wait. We have just received word of a freight train on its regular route that has derailed into the town's power grid.

No word on any casualties.

Emergency Alert System
ATTENTION SPRINGVILLE RESIDENTS
PLEASE SHELTER INDOORS IMMEDIATELY
AND CLOSE ALL WINDOWS
PLEASE STAND BY

June 1, 2014

Squirrels fell out of trees like large gray rocks, smacking the pavement, their guts spilling out on the sizzling road. Maddy stepped around them, the familiar threads pulling her around the corner, down the blackened street, her heels worn to nubs. Behind her fully dilated pupils, a nerve twitched. The fire hydrant in front of Mrs. Mobley's home blew, water gushing up like a volcano, raining wet lava. Somewhere nearby, a little boy screamed. All night, so much screaming. Did any other noise exist?

Despite the heat and thick smoke, goose bumps riddled her arms. The paint and blood had mixed into a sort of muddy paste.

All she wanted was one night to be normal.

Now, all she wanted was to go home.

Kendrick was dead. They'd killed the one good thing that had come into her world. He loved her. He loved her. He loved her. She could remember every detail of his lips, the grip of his hand on her waist, the way he coveted her like a precious jewel. No one had ever made her feel so safe. Acid burned her esophagus. He was gone.

Maddy's legs stopped, and she turned to her left. In the windows, flickering gold flames invited her inside. She stumbled up the familiar wooden steps and through the door, collapsing against it to shove it closed, muting the world outside.

She took a deep, choppy breath, gripping the white lace door curtain with both hands, the scent of home a salve, before peering over her shoulder. Church candles lit up the dining room, living room, and kitchen, but the shadows still seemed to swallow her whole.

"Papa?" she whispered, her voice raspy. It was the first time she had spoken in over an hour.

She took off her shoes, her feet bloody, and tiptoed through the house.

"Papa?" she called softly. The house moaned, the wood creaking like an open-mouthed yawn.

Maddy stood at the bottom of the stairs, a light flickering above. She took the steps, painfully aware of her own heaviness. She shuffled through the pitch-black halls toward her bedroom, the disquiet rippling through her. The hurricane candle haloed in the darkness, the spot on the ceiling a reminder of how far she had come. She blinked, turning to her vanity mirror. Even in the low light, she could see the paint dried on her face, her hair sticking out in every direction, a thick black jungle, her soggy dress frayed. Fingers rattling, she touched a spot of blood on her cheek. It wasn't Kenny's blood. It was someone else's. She gasped as the fog lifted, eyes flaring.

God . . . what have I done?

You made them PAY!

A long creak in the floorboards made her spin. Papa emerged from the shadows near her prayer closet, a ghostly figure. In the hours since she'd been gone, he had aged a hundred years.

"Papa," she whimpered.

He stood motionless, seeming to be looking through her, and she almost questioned her own existence. Something about his gaze made her stomach tense, but she was desperate for any sort of comfort he could provide.

"Papa . . . I think I've done something bad."

He stared at her, his expression giving away nothing.

The power plant alarm blared in the distance, her neck craned toward the sound. Was this the first time it had gone off? She couldn't remember anything after they killed Kendrick. What did it mean? What should they do? She was lost without her lone parent. Maddened by his silence, she fisted her own hair, clotted with blood, the paint drying it to matted thick clumps.

"I need help, Papa! Please." She hiccupped a sob. "Please! Say something. What do I do?"

After several ticks of the cuckoo clock, Papa blinked, then sat on the corner of her bed, staring at a spot on the floor.

"I thought . . . things would be different," he mumbled. "I thought, if I kept you close, raised you right, with good wholesome Christian values, taught you to have pride in your true history, gave you inspiration to live up to, like all these classy women . . . that you wouldn't end up like her. But I was wrong."

Maddy swallowed. The gnawing at her spine returned.

"Mama got the cancer, and I hired your mother to take care of her. No one else wanted the job, and she had nowhere to go." He stopped to look around. "Your mother stayed in this very room."

Maddy thought of her mother's journal, tucked under the pillow behind him.

"But Mama was so cruel to her. Spat at her, slapped food out of her hands, struck her with a cane, poured her bedpan over her head. When Mama passed, I thought it was finally over. But then your mother . . . I gave in to temptation. I prayed you wouldn't have it, prayed you'd have more of your mama's blood in you than mine, that it'd skip you like it skipped me. But I knew the day you were born that you had it. Because we fornicated before marriage, and God was punishing me."

Blood rushed to Maddy's feet, her face going numb.

"My mama . . . wanted so badly for me to be just like her. I favored her most of all. But it was clear . . . pretty soon, I didn't have what she had. What you have."

He rubbed his thigh with one hand, softly rocking back and forth.

"Papa had promised Mama a different kind of life. One with a nice house, clothes, and money. But we were barely scraping by. So when Papa wanted to invite this new Negro family to the church . . . well, Mama wasn't going to be a poor reverend's wife sitting next to some Negroes. She grew tired of pretending to be something she wasn't. One day, she took one look at Papa and . . . he just fell dead. She stopped his heart with her eyes.

"I tried to pray it out of her: the sickness, the evil. Mama just laughed at me. She was always laughing at me. But I couldn't leave her. I was all she had. She saw . . . saw all the unclean thoughts I was having about your mother. Said 'no son of mine is gonna be with some nigger.'"

Maddy leaned back into the vanity, trying to put as much distance between them as possible. Her fingers, searching for a talisman, wrapped around the silver paddle brush handle, nails biting little half-moons into her palm.

"Your mother wanted to love it out of you. But love wasn't going to cure you. Didn't cure Mama. You would grow to become her, taunting me until the end of my days. And if Negroes knew what kind of evil you wield . . . they would've used you. Your mother tried to leave with you, and I said I'd kill you first before I let you out of my sight. Couldn't let you out in the world to be a sickness to everything you touched. So she left, in the dead of night. She left me. Left you."

Maddy didn't like this story. Nor the emptiness in his voice. She didn't want to hear how her mother had abandoned her. It was too much to bear.

"Mama . . . she always called me stupid. Lazy. Weak. And

I was weak." He looked right into Maddy's eyes. "I should've killed you the day you were born. I should have stopped the evil from spreading long ago."

Maddy's stomach sank. Tears pooling, she lowered her eyes. Her power wasn't from her mama. It was from Papa. He'd given it to her. He also hated her. Just like everyone else.

Except Kendrick. Kendrick doesn't hate you.

But Kendrick is gone!

The shot was so loud, so sudden, Maddy thought she'd imagined it. The entire night felt like a fever dream. But she looked down at her shoulder and saw blood blooming out of a burning, gaping hole. She floundered, tripping over the vanity bench, and flopped down on the ground with a shriek.

Papa stood over her, lips in a hard line, gun in his hand.

Papa has a gun!

She scooted backward, whimpering, her wound throbbing, blood leaking down her arm. "No, please, Papa."

He muttered a prayer and aimed for her head.

"No," Maddy whispered, and the bullet meant to end her life stopped inches from her eye, the thread vibrating like a plucked violin string.

They stared at the brass slug hovering between them before it dropped to the floor, rolling under her bed.

Maddy raised her hand and squeezed it into a fist.

Papa's face spasmed. He dropped down to his knees, hands at his temples, emitting a gurgling scream. After five seconds of his open-mouthed horror, she let go. Papa gasped and dropped flat on his face, panting.

"Please stop. I don't want to hurt you, Papa."

She touched her wound with a whimper. The bullet had passed right through, inches from her heart, drilling itself into the wall of white faces surrounding the vanity.

Papa arched his head up to look at her, a face of warring emotions. He had failed. He kept failing. He glanced at the gun beside him. The air charged. Maddy straightened.

"No . . . Papa, don't!"

He snatched the gun, turned it, and fired.

Wet concrete churned through Kenny's veins, his head a thousand-pound rock on his shoulders, weighing him down.

He was going to pass out again.

He fought against the indescribable pain as he leaned on his sister, taking staggering steps away from the Barn, smoke and flames edging closer.

"Damn," Kali groaned, trying to hold her balance under his armpit. "You heavy as hell."

Some students had run toward town, ripped dresses flying in the wind, desperately trying to reach their parents. Others limped into the woods to hide, worried Maddy would be back to finish what she had started. But what had she started? Everyone cried about flying cars and trains running off the track, all while Kenny had lain unconscious. His fuzzy thoughts couldn't comprehend their wild imagination and yet, deep down, he felt a sense of calm, like he'd known all along of her secret.

Blood dripped down his face, his eye swollen shut as he dragged a tongue along his broken teeth. The pressure of his swelling brain pulsed behind his eyes and temples. Despite the agony, all he could think of was the terrified look in Maddy's eyes as the baton came down on him. He recognized the look. The same expression she'd had in middle school, the day of the water balloon fight. He replayed the moment on repeat, recounting the way he'd watched his friends torment the new girl while he did nothing. If he had only stopped them that day, if he had only befriended her . . . would it have all ended differently?

"Mind your own business, and be so good they can't ignore you."

His father's words were tattooed on his skull, now cracked by an officer's baton. It didn't matter how many times he minded his business or how good he was; at the end of the day, it hadn't saved or protected him. Just like how Maddy pretending to be something she was not hadn't protected her. Dread mingled with angst as he thought of his future. The future so many had constructed for him. He couldn't go back to a life of pretending not to see what was right in front of him, to minding his business. Maddy was his business.

"I can't go back," he moaned.

Kali huffed. "We're not. We're gonna get to town and get you to a hospital."

"No, K. I can't go back home."

At first Kali seemed to ignore him, then stopped short. "What?"

Jules let out a gasping scream, wincing at the light piercing her eyes.

"Sweetheart, can you hear me? Do you know where you are?"

The unfamiliar voice made her flinch. She slumped over, her head throbbing, trying to make sense of the searing pain in her right shoulder.

"Uhh, uhh," she moaned. "Brady?"

"It's going to be okay, sweetheart."

Jules tried to sit up and the room spun, the white hospital lights blinding. She was lying on something hard. The floor? No, a board. The room bumped, her right shoulder flaring, cutting through her foggy brain.

"Brady?" she croaked, her throat raw from screaming.

"Hon, can you tell us what happened?"

Maddy!

The sight of Maddy standing in the ballroom doorway, drenched in white paint, flooded her vision. Then, the blood. There was so much blood. The support beam had split Brady's head open. Brains on her dress . . . her arm hurt. The pain, the pain . . . tears hiccupped.

They'll blame it all on me. They'll say I did it and they'll hate me.

Unless . . .

Something thick and bitter slid down her throat. She

swallowed and cooked up some extra-fat tears.

"Maddy did it," she cried. "Maddy . . . she attacked us. She attacked my friends and me for no reason. My boyfriend. . . . Oh God, Brady."

The exhaustion melted into her, too hard to stay awake. But she had to say one last word.

"Why do they . . . she hate us so much?"

Her body shook hard, her skin arctic cold. She wrapped her arms around herself but didn't feel the relief, only hot pain. She reached to touch the sore spot and came up empty.

Her right arm was gone.

TWENTY-SEVEN

June 1, 2014

WENDY PARKED THE car in front of Maddy's house, staring up at the tranquil candlelight flickering in the windows; a complete opposite of the chaos surrounding them as screams echoed into the night. Neighboring streets were flooded with smoke and flames. Wendy could taste burning rubber and copper on the back of her tongue. Or was it blood? The knot in her belly tightened. She switched off the engine and walked up the cracked driveway. The front door opened with one turn of the knob.

"Hello?"

A wooden cuckoo clock ticked on the wall. Wendy took in the home—the mahogany dining table with lace tablecloth, the dark green carpet, shelves of endless videotapes, a TV she'd only seen in old movies, a ruffled apron draped over a chair. Shadows danced on the walls, the candles burned to near stubs. On the floor near the kitchen sat a pair of black kitten heels covered in mud and white paint.

She's here.

"Maddy?" she called out, her voice peaking.

Wendy cautiously made her way through the dark house, unsure of what to do when she finally found Maddy. Talk to her? Would she listen to reason?

Her ears perked at the tiny cry above.

"Maddy?" she whispered.

Wendy crept up the stairs, anxiety multiplying in the silence. She approached the attic door, a faint glow around its jagged frame. It creaked as she pushed it open.

Maddy sat on the floor cross-legged, a ball of white hair rocking and sobbing over the body of Mr. Washington. She held his head in her lap, petting his face, his eyes open and vacant, mouth frozen. Maddy sniffed and glanced up, tears streaming down her painted face.

"You," she hissed, and the room seemed to darken.

Blood dripped out the side of Mr. Washington's head.

Wendy stood speechless. "Maddy, I . . ."

Maddy's hand shot out, gripping the air, and an invisible rope looped around Wendy's throat, hauling her up. Wendy gasped, feet frantically kicking the air.

"Maddy, please," she choked, clawing at her neck.

"You tricked me. You all tricked me."

Wendy shook her head. "No. No. It was Jules—"

"My papa's dead because of you!"

"Maddy," she wheezed. "Please . . . I . . . I was trying to help you."

Her eyes narrowed. "Did I ever *ask* for your help?"

Wendy coughed, tears springing, her vision fraying at the edges. "Maddy, please," Wendy begged.

"I suppose I should thank you," she hissed. "It's because of you that I'm this strong. If it wasn't for you and your friends, I wouldn't know what I could do."

Legs dangling, Wendy struggled to pry the invisible fingers digging into her esophagus. "Please Maddy. Please don't kill me."

"Oh, so now *you're* begging me?" Maddy seethed. "I begged, too, once. Begged for you all to leave me alone. You didn't listen to me, so why should I listen to you?"

Wendy couldn't think of an answer. She could only cough out a "Please."

Maddy stared for five long seconds before she closed her eyes and lowered her arm. Wendy dropped to the floor, gasping and coughing.

"He's dead," Maddy sobbed, patting her father's face. "And it's all my fault. He was only trying to protect me."

The muscles around Wendy's neck ached as she scooted away from the blood pooling on the floor.

"Maddy . . . I'm sorry. I . . ." Wendy's hand brushed against something metal behind her. A gun sat inches from her fingertips.

"Why couldn't you leave me alone?" Maddy wailed, petting her father's waxy face. "He was all I had."

Wendy glanced at the gun, replaying memories of Jules's dad teaching them how to shoot on camping trips. Would she remember what to do when it counted?

"Kendrick's dead. Now Papa," she sniffed, squeezing her father tighter. "I have no one now. No one cares about me."

Wendy straightened at the mention of Kenny, the tips of her fingers touching the cold steel. Maddy had killed so many people. She would be doing everyone a favor, could easily claim self-defense. Someone had to stop Maddy. Someone had to end it all. The town's hero—she could write op-eds, appear on morning talk shows, maybe even land herself a book deal. Kenny would eventually forget all about Maddy once the checks started rolling in. They could still have the future she'd dreamed of.

All her problems . . . solved.

"They should have killed me," Maddy sniffled, arms shaking. "Papa was right; you're not nice to my kind. I thought it was going to be different. You all made me think it would be different . . ."

The sight of Maddy so broken and despondent made Wendy's heart sink into a pool of shame.

"I . . . I didn't do it," Wendy mumbled.

Maddy cuddled her father's head to her chest, sobbing into his hair. "Please. Just go."

Wendy opened her mouth and shut it, guilt stunning her to silence. She hadn't set up the bucket of paint, but she'd assisted in every other way. If it hadn't been for Wendy, Maddy would never have gone to prom.

"Can you for once in your life do something for someone else that isn't motivated by your own gain?"

Wendy's eyes roamed around the room, seeing Mr. Washington baked into every nook of it. In his own warped, obsessive way, he'd loved Maddy. Wendy had no clue what that was like, having a parent who cared, who hovered, but she did know how it felt to have hope in a future, to pray that it would all be different on the other side of a dream. She blinked back tears, hand sliding away from the pistol.

"Kenny's alive," Wendy mumbled, her shoulders sagging.

Maddy stopped rocking, her neck snapping up. "What?"

"He's alive. He's with his sister. He asked me to come find you."

Maddy considered this, her face forming a deep V. "He's alive? Is he okay?"

Wendy leaned forward, noticing the blood leaking out of Maddy's shoulder, and sat up on her knees.

"Jesus, Maddy, you're bleeding!"

She looked down at her wound and sniffed. "Oh."

Sirens blared in the distance. Wendy absorbed the scene—a bloody Maddy, a dead Mr. Washington, a gun—and rose to her feet, wiping her face clean.

"Come on, Maddy. We gotta get you out of here."

Maddy gaped at her, baffled. "And go where?"

"I don't know. But you know if they catch you, they'll likely kill you for what you did."

Maddy shivered, gazing down at her father, stroking his face. "The lynching tree . . ."

"You got anywhere to go?" Wendy asked. "Any family you can hide out with?"

Maddy sat with the thought for a few moments.

"Papa . . . said my mama left me."

"Why?"

"Because of him. But . . . I don't know where she is. Or who she is."

Wendy paused to stare at the body of Mr. Washington, her stomach turning. A man like him, who loved old junk and kept Maddy such a secret . . . no way he wouldn't keep anything on the woman who made her.

"Where does your dad keep his papers and stuff? Like birth certificates."

She froze. "I think . . . maybe . . . in his office."

Wendy grabbed the hurricane lamp and headed for the door. "Come on!"

Maddy limped down the stairs after her and pointed to a door. Wendy burst into the office and scrutinized the old desk, boxes, papers, and books stacked almost to the ceiling.

"Shit," she mumbled, and snatched a folder off the desk,

flipped through it, then tossed it aside.

Maddy watched from the threshold, threading her fingers, seeming too nervous to step inside.

"Wh-what are you doing?"

Wendy dug through a bin on the shelf. "There has to be something in here. Something that has her name on it. Help me!"

Wendy shuffled through papers, knocking over boxes, ripping books off the shelf. She yanked open each drawer, dumping the contents on the floor. Maddy flinched at the sound. Searching on the top of the bookcase, Wendy knocked over a tin lunch box. It crashed, pennies scattering, and a stack of letters, written in delicate blue script, fanned across the desk.

Wendy grabbed one of the letters, studying it close.

"Maddy," she breathed.

Maddy hesitated before taking a tentative step inside, papers scattering away from her feet as if by a strong breeze. She took the narrow, thin sheet and read the opening line—*My dearest moon child . . .*

Maddy's breath hitched as she stared at the letter in awe before mumbling, "'I will fly to you, whenever I can.'"

Wendy frowned. "What?"

"It's her," she choked. "Mama. She said she'd write to me. Letters . . . they fly."

Maddy wasn't making any sense. Wendy grabbed another

letter from the stack, flipping over the envelope.

"Mireille Germain. There's an address here. Saint Helena Island, South Carolina."

Maddy blinked. "'I will be where the low country meets the sea.'"

Maddy flipped through the stack. The letters were all from the same place. She wrapped a rubber band around them. Then she placed a hand over her gaping wound and closed her eyes. The wound began sewing itself shut with an invisible thread. Wendy lost all feeling in her legs and fell against the desk.

Maddy let out a staggering breath, staring at the letters in childlike wonderment.

"I'm gonna go find my mama. She's been waiting for me."

Wendy heard the rock-solid resolve in her voice, but the plan lacked believable execution. That's where Wendy always came in handy.

"Does your dad keep any money in the house?"

"In the coffee can, above the stove," Maddy answered, still enraptured.

Wendy snatched the letters out of her hands. "Hurry up. Take off that dress and wash up."

Maddy nodded and did what she was told.

Wendy ran up to Maddy's room, stopping short at the sight of Mr. Washington's lifeless body. In the candlelight, she could see the various photos wallpapered around the vanity, a collage of laughing white faces . . . and felt nauseous.

I have to get out of here!

She snatched open what she thought was a closet door but found more faces glaring back.

"Oh my God," Wendy mumbled, a lump in her throat, slamming the door shut. She grabbed a few pieces of clothing out of a drawer and stuffed them into a book bag.

Maddy emerged in a towel, her hair dripping wet, a large thick gauze taped to her shoulder. Without the paint and blood, she looked like herself again . . . small and mousy.

Wendy spotted Maddy's sweater on the chair. She threw down the bag and yanked the T-shirt over her head.

"What are you doing?" Maddy asked.

Wendy shimmied out of her jeans and kicked off her sneakers.

"Here. Put these on."

"Why?"

"You'll be spotted a mile away in anything else."

Maddy nodded, slipping into the jeans that hung on her hips, touching the fabric in wonder. Wendy grabbed a moldy-smelling dress out of the drawer. As she jerked it on, Maddy walked over to her bed, pulled a worn-down book out from under the pillow, and stuffed it into the book bag.

Wendy didn't bother asking any more questions. "Let's go."

Her sneakers were a half size too big on Maddy's feet, but she flip-flopped in them down the stairs. They rushed into the kitchen and found the coffee can exactly where Maddy said it would be. Wendy counted out the cash. Less than two hundred dollars. Maddy stood in the doorway watching, her hair already drying and frizzing around her face. She thought of the day Jules threw the pencil, the day that changed everything. Maddy's hair had started it all.

"Where are your scissors?"

"Scissors?"

"We have to cut your hair."

Maddy froze, and Wendy wondered if she'd have to convince her. But she marched across the room, pulled open a drawer, set the scissors on the table, dragged over a chair, and sat.

Wendy started chopping off huge hunks, cutting into the thickness, thinning it from the root. There wasn't time to make it pretty. It just needed to get done.

A hysterical giggle escaped Maddy's lips, tears streaming down her face. Wendy stopped, baffled by the reaction, taking a hesitant step back. Was she losing it?

Maddy gazed up at her and shrugged. "I've always wanted short hair."

Wendy nodded wordlessly and finished the job, leaving Maddy with a short pixie cut.

In the distance, the power plant alarm went off. The second time that evening. Wendy had a gut feeling Maddy had something to do with it.

"Come on. We gotta go."

Maddy stepped out the front door but stopped on the porch steps.

"Wait," she gasped.

"What are you doing?" Wendy whispered. "We don't have time."

Maddy stared inside the home, taking in every detail. She raised her hand, paused one last time, and snapped her fingers. Every candle burst into tall flames, climbing to the ceiling, the curtains catching, the wallpaper crisping.

Wendy took a staggering step back, the air sucked out of her lungs.

Maddy closed the door on her old life and looked at her expectantly. Wendy gulped hard, trying to regain her composure as they walked to the car.

She opened her trunk, shoving the contents aside. "Get in."

Maddy eyeballed the trunk, nibbling on her thumb. She scanned the street uneasily.

"Why . . . why are you helping me?"

Wendy shook her head. "I didn't help you the right way before. Let me do it now."

Behind them, flames began swallowing up the house. Maddy watched it burn, the fire sizzling in her eyes. She turned to Wendy.

"God doesn't make mistakes," she breathed, and climbed in.

Wendy absorbed her words for a moment before slamming the trunk closed. She jumped into the driver's seat, checked the gas gauge, and sped off for the highway, flooring it all the way to Greenville.

FROM THE SWORN TESTIMONY OF
LAURA COATES

By the time Ken Scott Senior arrived at the command center, all hell had broken loose. We were doing everything we could to bring the backup generators on. We had enough power for another thirty minutes before we'd have to evacuate. Phil Dung came in. Said the town was on fire. That there had been an accident by the prom and kids might've been trapped. Poor Ken, both of his kids were out there. We all told him to go on, but he insisted on staying. Said he had to save his family.

The meter shot up another ten K. We couldn't make heads or tails of it. There was more than enough water to keep the system cool for at least another two hours. But the temperature kept rising every fifteen minutes or less. It peaked, and Ken was just about to hit the evacuation command when the meters started declining and stabilized, quicker than quick. I remember looking at the time, 1:12 a.m.

I kept thinking about what Phil had said about the town burning, and so we ran up to

the roof deck. You could see fires everywhere—
a ball of them in the distance. Didn't even
hear Ken behind me, but he took one look and
broke down crying.

Other than the power going out, I don't
know what that Maddy girl would've had to
do with the system failure. But that genera-
tor had multiple system checks that month.
I supervised two of them myself. All passed
with flying colors. So I can't say for certain what went wrong.

But I did see something else kind of
strange that night—when I was standing on
that roof, I remember looking up and seeing
the sky full of crows; just a blanket of
them, circling, as if looking for the right
place to land.

•

TWENTY-EIGHT

MADDY DID IT
EPISODE 11
"Wendy: Part 2"

Michael: There's a lot of conflicting reports about who was really responsible for the paint. Do you have any idea?

Wendy: Don't think it matters at this point. Some could say we all poured that paint on Maddy.

Michael: Okay. So . . . where is Kendrick Scott?

Wendy: Ha! Your guess is as good as mine.

Michael: There was record of him being in the hospital the night after prom, but then he went missing. You were his last known visitor.

Wendy: I'm aware. And like I told everyone before, they got it wrong, 'cause I went looking for him and couldn't find him.

Michael: So you really have no idea what happened to him?

Wendy: If I did, it would make my life a hell of a lot easier. Look, you haven't asked me a unique question yet, and I've told you everything that I know.

Michael: Alright. Who is Mireille Germain?

Wendy: I . . . got no clue.

Michael: You don't know the name?

Wendy: Am I supposed to?

Michael: Mireille Germain was a live-in nurse who worked for a family on the East Side of Springville. That family referred her to Thomas Washington. Her last known address was in Beaufort, South Carolina, about a year before prom. Then, she seemed to disappear. Wendy, there are cell phone tower records pinging you near a Greyhound station in Greenville. On Prom Night, a Boston-bound bus left the Greenville Greyhound station at four a.m. It made stops near Beaufort.

Wendy: Hm. Did you ask the driver if he saw Maddy? Or if anyone saw Maddy that night?

Michael: Well . . . no.

Wendy: So you're making assumptions that any bus that just happened to stop in the state of South Carolina had Maddy on it?

Michael: Well, not exactly. These are theories, of course.

Wendy: Doesn't seem like you can prove any of these "theories" to me.

Michael: But the cell phone records put you in the area.

Tanya: Wendy . . . I have to agree with Michael here. Given the updates in forensic data analysis, they can track your phone via pings off cell phone towers within a mile radius.

Wendy: No one's cell was working right that night. You even mentioned that on this little show.

Tanya: But it looks like yours was once you were away from Springville.

Wendy: Why are you looking at my cell? Isn't that an invasion of privacy or something?

Michael: It was a part of the commission's investigation. They didn't have evidence, outside of the cell phone records, of you being in Greenville. But that CCTV video proves you were indeed there. Once we linked the times with the bus schedules and tower pings . . . it's very clear you were in Greenville only mere hours after you were last seen at the Barn.

Wendy: Look, I don't know what to tell you. Yes, I was in the Barn. Yes, I went to Greenville. But I didn't carry Maddy to some bus stop. I'm sure you've heard by now how she basically threw herself at my boyfriend and he fell for it. She also killed just about all of my friends worth knowing. So no, I didn't help Maddy escape. Why the hell would I help her? Maddy never left Springville. As far as I know, she burned along with the rest of the town.

Michael: So you don't think Maddy's alive?

Wendy: It honestly doesn't matter what I think. Dead or alive, everyone thinks what happened is my fault. Whatever way I thought I was helping her did more harm than good. Hell, if I could go back in time and take it all back, I would. But

I can't. No one can. Maddy is where she needs to be and we're all safer for it. Let's just leave it at that.

FROM THE SWORN TESTIMONY OF SHERIFF PETER WEST

In my fifty-something years, I ain't never heard that alarm at night. Woke me right up. Radios weren't working, lights were out . . . I just knew there was trouble.

We're a small town. Small town, small police force. When we call for backup, we're calling the state troopers, a good thirty to forty minutes away. With the power out and phones down, I had to floor it to the nearest rest stop to ring them. That was more than enough time for Maddy to burn us all up.

The country club ain't that far from Main Street. The old train station was built that way on purpose, to attract new settlers. It took Maddy a little over an hour to walk them three-plus miles home.

By the time I brought the cavalry, my station had burned down, along with half the town. Most of the hydrants were bone dry—it's why the fires ate us up so quick. Maddy's house was the last to go. Weren't sure if she was inside or not. Alive or not. And God help me, I was praying for the latter. Lost almost my entire squad that night . . . my youngest boy . . . gone.

It wasn't some race riot or uprising. Don't know where them rumors came from, but they need to stop. It was Maddy and Maddy alone that made that train run off the tracks and lick us up good. No one helped her. And ain't no looting either. No one even had time to run in and grab a loaf of bread, much less steal some flat-screens and fancy purses.

We blocked the street the Washington home was on so them dumb tourists and eager beavers would stop passing through. We're a town, not a freak show! I ain't got the manpower to babysit and entertain these yahoos. And we've had all kinds of people come sniffing. Witches, ghost and UFO hunters. Matter fact, about a year after it happened, two men came to the station, claiming to be Maddy's uncles, asking if we'd seen her 'cause they "knew" she was still alive. I told them to get lost!

I regret a lot of things from that night,

but my biggest regret was not staying. Maybe things would've turned out different. Maybe my boy would still be alive.

FROM THE SWORN TESTIMONY OF JULES MARSHALL

We've been doing active shooter drills since the second grade. We'd all seen those PSAs warning us to look out for students who'd been bullied. But Maddy wasn't bullied. She came into the seventh grade acting strange. Brought all that attention on herself, wearing those weird poodle skirts and that smelly sweater every day. No one did anything to her. She just hated white people. Everyone knew that. Hated us 'cause she wasn't us, even though she was pretending to be.

Growing up, I learned how to play dead with my brothers. That's the only reason why I'm still alive. She would've killed me. Folks say Black people can't be racist, but she hated us. You could see it in her eyes.

I don't know anything about some paint. Yeah, it came from my daddy's store, but lots of stuff came from my daddy's store. That doesn't matter. A little paint doesn't mean you go killing everybody. Just like when someone gets killed for resisting arrest, you don't go burning down other people's businesses. It's selfish.

Just look at me! Lost my friends, my boyfriend, my arm . . . all thanks to her. I hope she burns in hell. In fact, hell would probably be too good for her.

TWENTY-NINE

MADDY DID IT
EPISODE 12
"There Are No Winners Here"

Michael: So, Tanya. It's our last episode. For now, at least. And I
don't know if I'm more anxious or curious to hear your final
thoughts.

Tanya: It's hard to form any sort of rational conclusion. What
we're missing here is forensic evidence. Statistical and
analogical analysis. The type of data we're working with
is anecdotal at best. Observations from witnesses during
a traumatic encounter, strong opinions without supported
facts or even logic . . .

Michael: But you can't boil this down to hearsay and mass
delusion?

Tanya: Alright. Let's say I do believe that Prom Night happened
the way everyone says it did and that Maddy is, in fact,
very much still alive. The fact remains that she was an

innocent bystander in a long overdue comeuppance for a town holding on to outdated ideologies. And instead of holding the community at large accountable for their actions, everyone has continued to place blame on the greatest victim, creating a monster out of a young girl and using her legacy as a scapegoat to avoid self-reflection. The very title of this podcast, *Maddy Did It*, shows a lack of understanding of the consequences of one's actions. To me, Maddy didn't do anything. So whether she was a witch or not, alive or not, is inconsequential to the larger issue at hand.

Michael: Which is?

Tanya: Mike, when we first met and I had never heard of the massacre, you pitched it as more of a paranormal phenomenon. That Maddy had superhero-esque capabilities. But what you unconsciously left out is how societal racism played a large role in the incident. Which, as a white man, would be rather typical. Even if we took race off the table, identity would still be at play. Because if she had been who she was meant to be from the start, if she'd been allowed to just *be* herself, in fact if everyone involved was allowed to be their true authentic selves without fear of recourse or ridicule, none of this would have ever happened.

Michael: Wow. I guess I never really thought of it like that.

Tanya: So how about it? What did you actually learn from all this?

Michael: Me? I . . . I'm not sure.

Tanya: Mike, you've spent years obsessing about this one girl. In a perfect world, what outcome did you expect?

Michael: Well, I guess I expected or wanted . . . confirmation. I wanted to show the world that she was real. That her power existed.

Tanya: Ah! So you wanted proof there really is a Santa Claus, so to speak.

Michael: It just seems so unfair that she didn't get her just dues. People deny it ever happened, continue to tarnish her name and underestimate her capabilities.

Tanya: Couldn't her living a life on her own terms, without any interference, be considered adequate restitution? Isn't she owed peace?

Michael: But after everything, I thought she would've popped out of hiding and stuck it to everyone who lied about her. Who blamed her.

Tanya: Sometimes . . . the best response is no response at all.

Michael: I guess. But—wait. If she really was still alive, wouldn't you want to talk to her? Collect the proof you keep referring to?

Tanya: Nope.

Michael: Why not?

Tanya: It's hard for me to answer that, ethically. Because if she was still alive, aside from the extensive rigorous testing she would have to undergo, she'd more than likely stand trial for mass murder, terrorism, maybe even a hate crime. So yes, from an anthropological lens, there's so much we could learn. But . . . she's honestly been through enough. What good would it do, for her or anyone? Like Wendy said, we can shout the truth about what really happened until we're blue in the face. It still wouldn't change anything. Maddy will always be the villain. People need to want to see the truth. Comprehension is key, and that hasn't exactly been mastered by the citizens of this country.

Michael: It just seems like there are no winners here. No justice.

Tanya: So, what? You want her to return and kill even more people just to prove herself again?

Michael: Did I want all those people to die? No! But I mean, you got to admit that the way she snapped seems almost . . . understandable. That bucket of paint was the straw that broke the camel's back. But admittedly, it also begs the question, did Maddy's punishment truly fit the crime? Was it fair that other victims, both Black and white, were caught in the crossfire?

Tanya: And I would counter if racism is ever truly fair? There are always consequences, both seen and unseen. In fact, I gather it's one of the reasons the state worked so hard to brush this under the rug. Because if people knew revenge of this magnitude was even a remote possibility, there would be far less incidents of racial injustice in the world.

Michael: I guess after everything she's been through, I just want
her to be okay.

Tanya: And if she was still alive, what would you want to say to
her? In fact, talk to her as if she's listening to you right now.

Michael: Well, Maddy . . . wherever you are, I hope you find what
you're looking for. And that you're happy. You deserve to
be happy.

From David Portman's Springville Massacre: The Legend of Maddy Washington (pg. 350)

Prom Night claimed nearly 90 percent of the graduating seniors and over a hundred other Springville residents. Main Street and the country club were never rebuilt, the Barn torn down. Of all things, the high school was spared.

Upon the release of the commission's final report, the Springville Power Plant permanently closed its facility. No official reason was given to the press, but people suspected it had everything to do with the events that transpired on Bloody Prom Night. Without the plant, unemployment increased by nearly two hundred percent. Many residents relocated to distant cities and states, banks foreclosing on the few homes that weren't burned down.

After the recovery of Thomas Washington's body, the ruins of the Washington home were fenced off, the entire block eventually abandoned. No one wanted to live near the strange reminder. Five years later, the city set aside a budget to clear the property and put it on the market, hoping to encourage buyers to consider Springville as their new potential home. During the excavation of the Washington home's remains, only a few items were left intact.

One of which was a hot comb.

ACKNOWLEDGMENTS

These last five years have been nothing short of amazing. If you saw my dedication, you know I still stand in awe at the fact that I'm an actual author with several books. A HUGE thank you to my awesome devoted readers. Bookstagrammers, Tik Tokers, students, educators, bloggers, boozy book clubs, and Grandmamas. I really appreciate how much you have all loved on me. Hope you've enjoyed this homage to Stephen King, as he has been one of my idols for as long as I've been a reader and lover of horror.

Speaking of which . . . to Mr. King, you are one of my greatest inspirations. Thank you for giving me the books and movies that have kept me company most of my life.

Specifically want to thank Marlene Ginader for helping me with the telekinesis research, Justin Reynolds for the crash course in football, Donald Short for the power plant info, and Linda Jackson (aka MOMMY) for the list of classic movies and TV shows. All these years of watching TCM has really paid off.

Thank you to the copy editors. Despite me wanting to fight you half the time, you are the absolute unsung heroes of our industry. My books would be a hot mess without you.

To my editor, Benjamin Rosenthal, thank you for always standing by my side and having my back. To the entire team at HarperCollins, it takes a village to raise a book and I'm glad to be a part of yours. To my agent, Jenny Bent, I am immensely grateful for your brilliant brain.

To my beta readers Natasha Diaz, Bethany Morrow, and Ashley Woodfolk, your notes on Black Girls took this book exactly where it needed to be. Big shout-out to my twin, Lamar Giles, who while welcoming his baby girl into the world, still took the time to field my anxiety. To Shanelle and Jessica, thank you for holding me down during the height of COVID-19. I loved our bubble and weekly zoom updates. To my family, thank you for being constant supporters and never pulling me away from the TV when I was little, especially when my favorite horror movie came on.

And to God, I thank you.